11/01.

# Murder Among
# The Personal Ads

*To Paul Saagpak
esteemed lexicographer and friend*

# Murder Among The Personal Ads

*C.K. Cambray*

PIATKUS
CRIME

Copyright © 1990 by Dimitri Gat

This edition first published in
Great Britain in 1991 by
Judy Piatkus (Publishers) Ltd of
5 Windmill Street, London W1

**British Library Cataloguing in Publication Data**
Cambray, C. K.
  Murder among the personal ads
  I. Title
  813.54 [F]

  ISBN 0-7499-0065-2

Printed and bound in Great Britain by
Bookcraft, Midsomer Norton

# CHAPTER

 1

Amanda should have gone to Stephan to have her hair trimmed and shampooed, but she didn't have the money to spare. So she washed the bright copper mop herself and brushed it out until every last strand shined. Shorter hair would require less time. Of course then she couldn't wear it gathered and pinned up, her choice for the special upcoming rendezvous. What she had always liked about being a real redhead was belonging to an exclusive minority. Blondes and "blackheads," as she liked to call them, were everywhere. But hair like hers, along with green eyes and very fair skin, were unusual. Added to those pluses were nicely angled facial bones and what she thought was a good nose.

Oh, there was a gray strand! She reset the hairpin to hide it, knowing how silly that was. Thirty-four wasn't too early for the gray to start, considering her divorce, raising Justin alone, and scrambling for every dollar. Managing a Muncher's restaurant franchise certainly wasn't the path to fame and fortune. It was a decent job—especially for a woman with only two years of college. And of course working for Gordie Locker was no Mardi Gras festival, either.

She checked her outfit: skirt, blouse, and light sweater, in its pattern some red. That *was* the theme for the encounter all right. She contemplated make-up. No, *au naturel* this evening.

1

# PERSONAL

She thought of Pamela Peterson who had started it all. She had known Pam from their first days in Hartford. They had met at the Connecticut Bureau of Motor Vehicles in Plainville in the line for registering out-of-state cars. Falling into laughing conversation, they decided their vehicles should get waivers because they were junkyard bound. That had been better than three years ago—and Amanda was still driving her VW beetle, the rust holes in the floor panels quite a bit larger now and the speedometer cable still broken.

Pam was also a single parent. She had just taken a position as a librarian at Hartford's Central Community College. In the following months they met occasionally over coffee, modest at-home dinners, or for a movie at the Newington, where every night was dollar night. The talk was of children, men, and careers, in that order. With Justin and Pam's Kate it was a case of battling for discipline and hoping for the best. They kept fingers crossed for the public schools to hold together. As for men, Pam said, "I think the Marines have got the few good ones."

They had played the how to meet men game, trading ideas with one another. You met men—at the laundromat. Study their clothes whirling in dryer windows for clean character insights. You met men at church. But neither of them were worshipers. You met men at pro football games. But tickets were too expensive. You met men at health clubs. But who had the time?

In moments of shared depression they admitted meeting new men could be a dismal exercise. They gave names to the worst to salve the sting of time wasted and months passing: Mucous Mike, Jug of Whine, Ahab the A-rab. Deep down they wondered if they had become simply too picky. Divorces could do that.

Amanda was able to bury some of her loneliness with her job. She had started at Muncher's as a counter girl, dishing out grease and starch with a smile. Looking back she saw, had she been more patient and less frightened, she could have found better work. At minimum wage, she had slaved long hours to make any money at all. Even at that, without her father—dear

Pop-Up!—she could never have made ends meet. Now he was going back and forth to the hospital, the Crab crawling deep into him. She remembered the day she had heard the diagnosis. He had called her at work, voice dry as fallen leaves in July, telling her the cancer was "inside where they really can't get at it." She remembered pressing the black receiver harder to her ear against the shout of orders and kitchen crew chatter, hoping she had misheard.

That afternoon, Mendoza, the night manager, didn't show— as usual. The day manager, Florian Shrube, couldn't get a substitute. He was supposed to stay on to cover the night shift. Amanda said she'd take it; she knew the routines, even if she didn't have the rank. Florian squinted and pulled at a prune-shaped ear. "You won't get the pay," he said. "Muncher central says that's a no-no."

"I need the experience, Shrube."

"You got it, Mandy. But don't screw up."

"Why, *shouldn't* I be like you?"

When she closed the doors at 2:00 A.M., instead of going home she sat behind the service counter and stared at the condiment station, the plastic wood booths, the window boxes of plastic flowers, and the Muncher's decor, featuring blood-bath red and white. Before her stood the man-sized menu cutouts offering the Maxi-muncher, the daddy, the Midi- and Mini-rounding out his family. All had feet shod with turned-up-at-the-toes harem slippers, like those she wore. Muncher's Magic Mixture dripped from between square buns and square patties. Missy Morgan, who manually made the Mixture, chiefly shredded lettuce, mayo, and dried spices plundered from the cuisines of a dozen cultures, said nothing beat it for cleaning under your fingernails.

Weariness hung like sash weights from her neck and shoulders. Beyond the front glass wall the parking lot was deserted except for a discarded Muncher's-logo wrapper and Styrofoam containers stirring like ghosts in the night breeze. News of her father's illness served as the latest milestone on what seemed the long descending road of her fortunes.

Sixteen years ago she had entered the University of Pittsburgh with a grand hunger for reading, learning, and understanding something of the vast mechanisms of this world. She plunged eagerly into her courses, pleased with them and her life. At the end of her sophomore year she met Ned Stanton. Seeing him in his snap-brim thirties hat shading those bright brown eyes, coming to know his confidence and daring, how could 19-year-old Amanda have been immune? She dropped out of school to follow him. Oh, what a Pied Piper he was, playing tunes of travel and adventure! She followed him straight into the mountain of disaster.

After the divorce and her mother's unexpected death, she rejoined her father who had moved to Hartford. Confidence crushed by her failure with Ned and virtually penniless, she needed stability for Justin's sake. She had no choice but to turn to the loving man whose misfortunes in recent years had paralleled her own. Now the one solid support in her life at that time was being threatened by disease.

She wasn't the kind to feel sorry for herself. But that night it had been so late and she had been so tired. . . . She had leaned forward slowly, rested folded arms on the stainless steel counter, and wept.

In a way that night was the nadir of her life. Since then, she had struggled and fought her way up the ladder. She was now day manager for that Muncher's franchise and had an apartment big enough for Justin and herself. Her father had surprised the doctors by living longer than they had expected, though it was clear he was now finally failing. She kept to a modest budget, had a small circle of Hartford friends, and was on the lookout for a significant other. Maybe she would find him tonight.

Two months ago Pam had arrived for dinner waving a copy of the Hartford *Reformer,* the onetime counterculture tabloid. By now its sixties anger had been replaced by eighties Scandinavian furniture ads. Its personal ads, she said, had undergone similar changes. "The kinky stuff is all gone, Mandy. Now it's real people, like yuppies and all. And an ad only costs a couple bucks. People just pick up copies of this thing free everywhere. *Thousands* of guys read the ads." Some of her friends had tried the personals and met nice men. She, Pamela,

4

was going to try them. "It's the latest and greatest how to meet men game."

Amanda had her doubts as Pam answered a half dozen ads from two weekly issues. For several weeks the two women didn't communicate. Then her friend reported she was "thinning them out." Three weeks ago she invited Amanda to meet "the cream of the crop." She added, only half joking, "And you sign this paper promising hands *off*. Get it?"

Bud was balding and wore a beard within which flourished his "good grin." He owned an auto body shop that covered half a block. Because business demands kept him out of circulation, he had placed his ad as a hopeful shortcut. "It must have been a good idea," he said. "I met Pam."

Amanda knew he meant it, understood he was a nice guy and a good match for her friend. She felt the tiniest prick of envy. Bud was a winner. And so Pam was made one, too. The two of them meeting obviously didn't guarantee a lifetime together. But it was a start.

That was what she wanted: just a start.

The day after she met Bud, Amanda picked up a copy of the *Reformer* from the pile at the local CVS. Standing there by the Cadbury's chocolate bar display, she paged through to the personal ads. There were two pages of small type. Mostly men wanting to meet women. A few gays and bis, as expected. There *were* some promising ones . . .

She hesitated, though. To reply seemed a confession of desperation, an exercise in if-all-else-fails. It wasn't her style to broadcast the condition of her heart or to consciously put herself in a one-woman lineup for a strange man's scrutiny. Yet she had been in Hartford for almost four years, and while she had met some men she liked, nothing had come of the relationships. As always, the months kept passing. She was headed for thirty-five, a milestone that, considering how her life was going, looked to be painted black. Possibly the time had come to take a bit of a risk. She remembered Ned on his way to the dog or horse racetrack or to the jai alai fronton answering her pleas for restraint with the same words: "God hates a coward."

That evening after Justin was asleep, she pored over the two personal pages, circling possibles and sipping hot chocolate. She wasn't as outrageous as Pam. She decided to answer only one this first time, like a swimmer toe-testing the water. One by one, she crossed out those not quite to her liking. So much was guesswork! She might well pass up the "right" one. In the end she made a choice. She dragged out her old portable typewriter and banged out a brief, chatty note signed with her first name and including her telephone number. She then read the directions for replying. She was to address responses to Box A126, care of the *Reformer*'s business office.

Less than a week later her phone rang in the evening. Someone named Floyd had received her reply. His voice was faint, as though he was calling from a great distance. Or maybe it was a bad line. They talked for about fifteen minutes about their lives. Amanda had prepared her mental script. Now she used it to suggest they meet Friday night for coffee at Brothers II, a trendy pub where she went occasionally when the budget allowed it. She knew two of the bartenders. She felt comfortable there and could easily get up and leave if things didn't go well with Floyd. He sounded normal, but she wasn't going to take any chances.

At last Friday night had come. She took a last look at her hair, face, and clothes. You still look good, Walker, she thought. Floyd is going to be knocked out! In about—she glanced at her watch—fifteen minutes. The tap on the door would be Jilly from the first floor. She traded the girl babysitting for alto recorder lessons. Jilly was good with Justin. He had reached the age where the two of them could trade friendly insults. She gave the girl her instructions, issued Justin her customary decree for good behavior, and kissed him good night. "*Gahk*, Mom!" She put on her jacket and grabbed her purse.

Halfway down the second flight of stairs she took the ad out of her purse and studied it, as though to remind herself why she was going out. She read it for probably the thirtieth time. One line.

*Redheads wanted for coffee and conversation.*

# CHAPTER

## ❦ 2 ❦

Right-thinking public officials and the abstemious had been unsuccessful in stamping out the happy hour. No matter possible DWI embarrassment and fines, working stiffs sought liquid consolation and companionship late Friday afternoon. By 7:30, when Amanda arrived at Brothers II, revelry around the large square bar had reached the low shout level. As she had expected. For that reason she had told Floyd she would be sitting off in one of the side areas among counterfeit 1930s Coca-Cola roadside advertising panels and fossilized musical instruments nailed to the beams.

She glanced at her watch. She was on time, 7:30 almost to the second. She scanned the mob at the bar looking for Floyd, self-described as "thirty-five and quasi-sexy." She liked that phrase. It gave her hope that he might be fun. Which of the men was he? There were all sizes and shapes. Some handsome ones, too. Big deal. Ned had taught her the hard way that handsome didn't go that far.

She was getting nervous just being there, waiting. Her pulse pushed determinedly in her neck, and she felt a bit warm. Floyd, where are you? She studied men's faces in search of a questioning glance aimed her way. Glances she got, but none with expectation. She looked at her watch again. Only five minutes had passed.

PERSONAL

A waitress came and took her order. She hesitated a moment
. . . *coffee and conversation*. She ordered a cup of coffee. I
play my part, Floyd. After another five minutes her order arrived. Without staring, she saw a figure detach itself from the
bar mob and move her way. When he was too close to be
ignored, she looked up. His neck was thick enough for Samson
in the temple. Above it, no real chin and slablike, Slavic features, narrow eyes, and curly hair. "You look alone, Red. Buy
you a drink?"

"You're not . . . Floyd." Nerves made her voice a whisper.

"Not *what?*"

"Your name isn't Floyd."

"No, it isn't. Thank God." He moved to sit down. "How
about the drink?"

"I'm sorry. I'm waiting for someone."

"Named Floyd?"

"Yes. I think it's better if I wait alone."

"I could get my name changed."

Amanda smiled politely. "Please . . ."

He shrugged and moved off. "The no's don't count," he
said over his shoulder.

She began to suspect that Floyd wasn't going to show. Maybe
he answered *Reformer* ads, arranged rendezvous, and never
appeared.

She kept her eyes on the bar area, so when someone spoke
behind her she was startled. Her head spun back. The first thing
she saw was a leather wallet and the golden gleam of some
kind of law enforcement badge. The wallet was closed and
whisked out of sight. Its owner was a thin man with a large
Adam's apple, a gaunt jaw, and brown eyes remarkable for
the shortness of their brown lashes. The eyes were serious.
"Chet Greenly. Hartford Vice Squad," he said. The words
lacked inflection, seemed mass-produced, like the sheets from
a high-speed computer printer. "Your name, please?"

"I—Amanda Walker. Why are you talking to me?"

Chet's thin grin disclosed white, uneven teeth. "Could I see
some identification, please?"

8

PERSONAL

Amanda was flustered. She rooted in her purse as though it were a stranger's possession. She found her driver's license. "What's this all about?"

He studied her face, matched it to the license photo. "Woman sitting alone in a place like this. If I had to guess, I'd say you're soliciting."

"I am not! I am—"

"Why don't you get your stuff together and come along with me? We'll go down to headquarters, check the computer, see just how flat your heels are." He lowered, then raised his shoulder to hurry her along.

"I am—not going," she said. "I'm not doing anything wrong. I'm just sitting here waiting to meet someone—"

"Named Floyd."

She felt her eyes widen. "You know him?"

"I am him!" He sank down in the chair opposite and uttered a burst of laughter—a dry, chattering sound that grated in her ears. "Nice to meet you, Amanda! Floyd Hooper Philman's the full name. Hope you don't mind a little joke. The badge is a kid's toy. I just wanted to see how you handle yourself under stress."

Amanda saw no reason to mask her irritation. "That's strike one," she said.

"Huh?"

"You know baseball? Strikes one-two-three, and you're *out*, Floyd Hooper Philman."

He studied her face. His eyes lit with dim watch fires of annoyance. "You don't have much of a sense of humor, do you?"

"The possibility of being arrested as a prostitute doesn't go right to my funny bone, no." She smiled and drew a deep breath. "Let's start over—and try to avoid strike two. How's that?"

"OK."

"Why don't you tell me something about yourself, Floyd?"

Floyd was in pharmaceutical sales and traveled a lot out of state. Not having regular routines around Hartford led him to use the personals. He had never been married. His late father

9

ran a grocery store, was a shot-and-a-beer man who played the accordion semi-professionally. Floyd described him in an even voice. When he came to discuss his mother, a former exotic dancer, his tones grew harsh. Under the name Flamingo Red, she danced around a peel wheel covering a dozen cities in three states. Her gimmick was her long red hair used in place of fans, feathers, or balloons. "She wasn't a . . . nice woman, Amanda," he said too loudly. "She took lovers, rich men who gave her gifts. When one left her, she only laughed and went on to the next. She introduced me to every one of them. I hated them. I think . . . I still hate her. When I got older, we argued. Then we fought." His short-lashed eyes seemed to bulge with the sudden intensity of his emotions. "Sometimes she hit me. She was a slender woman, but she packed a wallop!" He barked brief laughter. "And sometimes . . . I hit her back. Well I mean I had to. Self-defense."

Amanda felt uneasy. "I hope things got straightened out between you in the end."

"They did. She died." He laughed. "Seriously, Dr. Moodleman—he's my psychiatrist—has been a help with all that. A big help."

"I see," she said.

They sat in awkward silence until the waitress came. Amanda tried to rally her thoughts, start up the conversation. When they busied themselves with cream and sugar, he said, "Amanda, did you ever think about doing it?"

"What?"

"Being a whore. Selling yourself. With that lovely head of hair and that face—"

Color rose in her cheeks. "Strike two, Floyd! I mean, come on!" Behind her words loomed real, growing disappointment. "Let's change the subject, please."

"Does talking about your body make you nervous, Amanda?" The short-lashed eyes studied her across the coffee cup rim. "Does dealing with your sexuality lead to uneasiness?"

"No and no. Neither seems the right topic for our first conversation, Floyd."

"Seems perfectly normal to me." He leaned closer. "I really would like to know what it feels like to a woman to make love."

Her smile was too deliberate. "Then maybe you can speculate about my body and my sexuality—on your way home." She met his eyes in a steady deliberate glance. "In the ballgame of my life, Floyd, I'm afraid you've just struck out." She picked her purse up from the floor, began to grope for her wallet. She touched the check. "We'll split this, all right?" She threw two dollars down and got up.

"Hey, don't leave!" He held her forearm.

She jerked free and headed for the door. "Good night, Floyd. I'm sorry it didn't work out between us." He rose and followed her, staying on her heels.

"You're not even willing to give us a chance, are you?" he whispered loudly.

"There's no 'us,' Floyd. Just you. And me. That's it." She shoved by a knot of drinkers, eyes on the doorway.

"You're stuck-up, aren't you?"

Amanda kept moving. "Leave me alone," she said. "I'm asking you nicely."

"Asking you nicely," he mimicked, an edge in his voice. "The snooty broad is asking me nicely. I should feel privileged?"

Amanda found the door blocked by a cluster of young women made up for Friday night hunting. "Pardon me," she said.

"Pardon *us*." Floyd wasn't to be shaken.

On the sidewalk he tried to hold her sleeve. She pulled away, glowering at him. "Hands off!"

"Can't you stop and talk it over?" he said.

She hurried toward her VW, half a block away. "Just leave me alone, OK, Floyd?"

"I got to tell you something, snooty bitch."

Car in sight, Amanda got out her keys.

"Don't you want to know what it is, sn—"

"No! I don't. I want you to shut up and go away." She stepped off the curb to the driver's side of the VW. She put the key in the door lock, swung the door open.

"Listen!"

The harsh volume of Floyd's voice made her look up at him across the car roof, despite herself.

In the cruel illumination of the street lights his face took on a deadly paleness. His humorless grin yawned morbidly. "Things can happen to stuck-up redheads."

"Things— Are you threatening me, buddy?"

"Really bad things. To redheads."

She slid into the car, jammed the key into the ignition and spun it hastily. The engine caught at once. Floyd's groin and lower torso filled the passenger-side window. He squatted suddenly. He shoved his nose against the glass till his flesh bent slightly. He mouthed two words.

*Bad things!*

She popped the clutch and sped away. She couldn't fool herself. She was shaken. During the short drive home she used the rearview mirror a half-dozen times, sure she was being followed. She saw no trailing cars. She needed deep breaths to still her pounding heart.

Back in the apartment, she chatted fitfully with Jilly, then after arranging the next recorder lesson sent her downstairs, urging her to practice. Justin slept open-mouthed, his breathing soft in her ear. She adjusted the covers, studied his smooth, guileless face. She bent over and kissed his cheek. "Mom . . ." he muttered in feigned disgust, but didn't fully waken.

Then she went to the window and looked down the three floors to the street. She wasn't sure what she expected to see— maybe Floyd watching the apartment building. If he was, she didn't see him. She looked at her hands. They were trembling. She didn't like being threatened. "Pam Peterson, if I could get my hands on you . . ."

She phoned Pam and told her she had met her personal column date.

Excited, her friend said, "How'd it go?"

"About as well as open-heart surgery in an African hut without an anesthetic."

"Oh, I'm so sorry!"

Amanda gave her the details.

"He sounds sort of creepy-weird, Mandy. A little scary."

"Amen."

"You're not going to . . . give up on the ads, are you? Like you said: 'The no's don't count.' "

"The jury is still out on that, Pam." She remembered Floyd's hand squeezing her forearm.

"You deserve better, Mandy. Really."

Amanda agreed, then changed the subject.

After chatting with Pam she went to the fridge and pulled out a jug of Cribari Vino Rosso—Amanda Walker's sleeping draft, warmer-upper, counsel and colleague. Small wonder man had made wine since time began. He *needed* it. She poured a few fingers into a Muncher's Merry Mug made of easy-scratch plastic, one of a leftover case from a year-old giveaway program.

She slumped onto mom's throne, as her son called the garage sale lounger covered by a paisley-patterned throw. She spun the radio dial, leftward only, where public and college radio stations clustered. She searched for something soft and calming. Her fingers on the Sony dial were still trembling. She tuned into a jazz trio exploring the rich possibilities of "I Can't Get Started." They were playing her song. So it hadn't worked out. Pam had been lucky. She hadn't. No harm done. As the wise guy had said, "The no's don't count." Floyd had flopped. There was a new *Reformer* every week, each with scores of ads.

It would be easier to shrug him off if he had just been a nerd, pens in shirt pocket, horsy laugh, lover of "Jeopardy!" and Whoopee Cushions. His quick tack to sex had been bad enough. But it was his "bad things" farewell that had really done it. That's what had sent her to the wine. She sipped it and made a face. Bitter. The jug had been open too long.

The door buzzer sounded. She started. Nerves . . . She went to the speaker. "Who is it?" Her voice was tight.

"Gordie Locker."

Not Floyd, anyway. But her employer was not that much of an improvement. "You know I don't like you coming here,

Gordon. You should see me at work. I don't want people—
especially you—getting ideas.''

"This visit's business and social, Mandy.''

"Only for a few minutes. Hear?''

"OK, OK. Let me in.''

"This is the last time.''

"Christ, you'd think I work for *you*.''

As he made his way up the stairs, she reminded herself yet
again why they were cast in their roles. She had no spirit of
enterprise. Instead, she had some education and culture. Gordie, on the other hand, had no education past high school. His
culture was money. The guy with the most dollars was the
biggest and best. So as a young man he had gone straight for
the bucks. He wasn't so young anymore, but he was still going
for it. "I'll get class after I get rich," was his motto.

He had started out as a grill man in a mom and pop drugstore
years ago. When their business failed, he intuitively grasped
why, and like weathermen everywhere, saw which way the
wind was blowing: franchise. From friends, family, and the
gullible he raised enough money to buy a Muncher's franchise
because he could afford nothing more expensive. In that restaurant he worked from dawn to dusk, seven days a week, to
make a go of square burgers with square buns. He begged his
first wife Phyllis to tailor the three-sizes-only headquarters-
issued red and white uniforms to fit his staff. Every penny he
made he put back in the franchise. Then later, every dollar
went into savings to buy a second one, much to Phyllis's distress. She thought he was bagging it away for her. Franchises
three to five came more quickly, as did wife number two,
Darlene. She had lasted until he bought two more. Then she
was disposed of like a used Muncher's Mat Menu. He was
fond of quoting his ex-wives, though Amanda suspected most
of their words originated in his imagination. "They both told
me they finally found work they liked," he said. "Collecting
alimony.''

Opening the door for him, she was dismayed to see he carried
a wrapped wine bottle. He was breaking their agreement. She
had made it very plain she wasn't interested in him socially.

But here he was again, standing in front of her, his lust at full charge like the best Delco. His stare stripped her down to body powder. He was barrel-chested and big boned, piled with flesh like a *fresser*'s deli platter. A tulip-bulb nose emerged from an earth of thick face below a receding hairline. Around his reddish neck hung a gold chain thick enough to keep a galley slave on his bench.

She had learned that you didn't pussyfoot with Gordie Locker. He could be very heavy-handed, if one left an opening. Subtleties and hints were lost on the man. "What's with the paper and ribbon? This is *not* a date. You weren't invited," she said.

He shoved the bottle at her anyway. "Doesn't hurt to try, Mandy."

Reluctantly, she took the bottle.

"Hey, I thought maybe you had a change of mind, that maybe I look a little better to you."

"It's not how you look. We went over all this before—more than once. There's no chemistry between us, you know? You're the boss. I manage one of your franchises. That's it. Soft music doesn't play when I see you. Birds don't sing. They fly for cover."

"You do tell it like you think it is, don't you?"

She saw again the brief, mysterious flash amid the golden flecks in his brown eyes. In earlier encounters, always over the nature of their relationship, she had beheld that flash. She wondered what it meant—past mere annoyance with her. Whatever, it frightened her. So she had learned to walk the line with him. She wouldn't do as he wished just because the flash might mean danger. She wasn't that kind of woman. However, she tried not to provoke that chilling reaction. It wasn't easy. Conversation went best when it dealt only with business. "I was out earlier, Gordon. I didn't have such a great evening. I'm a little strung out."

"I'll give you a back rub."

"You will *not*." She pointed at a chair. "You'll tell me what you want, then you'll be a good guy and leave."

"Open the package."

"Gordon . . ."

"It's champagne. It's to celebrate. That's why I brought it."

"Celebrate what?"

"Your maybe getting promoted."

She frowned, at once suspicious. She knew Gordie too well . . . "You're going to promote me? To what?"

He busied himself with the wrapping. He must have checked with his local wine merchant: Perrier-Jouët Fleur de Champagne. Flower bottle. The good stuff. Damn him! She went into the kitchen for glasses. When she got back, he had moved onto mom's throne, leaving some room for her. She chose the chair, to his poorly masked disappointment. She held out two multi-purpose Czech wineglasses, nine bucks for six at the local Bradlees. He popped the cork. Sunny French summer glugged into her life. The bubbles twisted up like angels ascending. Amanda Walker: the classic case of champagne taste—and beer pocketbook. Champagne, the stuff of seduction all right. But not by Gordon Locker. "You can't promote me, Gordon. You don't have anything to promote me to." She raised a finger. "And don't say 'to Mrs. Locker,' or I'll waste this good champagne on your face."

He raised his glass before a cunning grin. "Let's drink to regional manager. Who could be you, Mandy."

"Oh . . ." They clinked glasses. She sipped and sighed. Gordie explained he had held several meetings with his business advisors. They told him his span of management control had grown too broad. He needed to introduce another level, increase the hierarchy. In short, he needed someone to handle the administrative details that were beginning to fall into the cracks. The answer was a regional manager who reported to him, but worked with the managers of the seven restaurants. "So I'm going to do it," he said. "And I need somebody who knows the whole show. Like you."

Her heart pounded. "I see."

He tossed his champagne down as though it were a glass of beer. He poured more for himself. She sipped, knowing him well enough to wait to hear his terms. "Those dudes at McCormack and Lystradt say I should pick someone with an

M.A.B., A.B.M., M.B.A., one of them. Some business type. I told them, 'Hey, I don't have none of these degrees and I make more money than any of you!' " He laughed, a sound that had always struck Amanda as strangely high-pitched issuing from such a solid man. "I told them I'd find my own regional manager. Somebody with more brains than me. Somebody better looking!" She wondered if his laughter would wake Justin. She hoped not, as this didn't seem the moment to shut him up.

He refilled her glass. "I thought of you first, Mandy."

"Why me?"

His brows rose. "Fishing for compliments, huh?"

"Not really, I—"

"You know how desperate I was to get the West Park restaurant out of the red? How about that time my whole Muncher's deal hung on the seesaw? All the franchises could have gone down for the count. I took a big chance making you manager there. I did it on gut instinct. You came through and pulled me back from the edge. Now you run the place tight as a Marine blanket. You make me money. Maybe I need you again." He leaned forward and touched her lightly on the knee. "If you haven't noticed, the business and you need each other."

"I'm flattered—so long as you don't try to use extortion on me again."

"Hey—"

"Like you did with the Ms. Muncher deal."

"Let's forget that, OK?"

"I don't even want you to *think* about doing something like that again." She swallowed more champagne. "If this is real, if there's a chance you'll make me regional manager, I want to know what you want from me."

"McCormack and Lystradt thought maybe whoever got the job should have had some business courses. You know, accounting and that."

"I'm willing to go to school at night. It won't be easy, but I can arrange it." She met his eyes. "What else?"

"There'd be a lot of travel between the restaurants. Like,

to press the flesh, check on how clean, no rats, no bugs, you know.''

"I'm not afraid of driving around Connecticut. Anything else?''

"You'd have to spend some time in my office. I'll give you some space of your own.''

She shrugged. "Great. Anything else?''

He couldn't quite meet her eyes. "Be nice to me.''

She got up quickly, some of the champagne sloshing over the glass edge. "What does that *mean*, Gordon? Is it like before when—''

"Jesus! You're so touchy.''

"Your behavior has given me reason to be. I told you once: no fleshy deals. No sexual favors, as the newspapers like to say. If that's what brought you up here—hope—then you can leave. Because the answer's no. No!''

"Take it easy. Yeah, I got a real job for somebody to do. You're a definite maybe, all right?''

She waved him toward the door. "Right now, I don't want any misunderstandings like we had over the Ms. Muncher thing. I'll be straight out so you don't get confused, Gordon. I want the job. I'll do what it takes professionally to get it. And if I get it—well, you appreciate how hard I work.''

In the narrow hall before the door, she was aware of his bulk. It made her uneasy. He looked down at her. His fingers found her chin. He tipped her resisting head back with a trivial exercise of his thick wrist. "Someday you'll come down off that high horse, Mandy Walker. You'll see you aren't doing so great, that you'd do better if you went more to your strengths—''

"Please, Gordon. I'm just not up to another of your critiques on how I ought to live my life.'' She pulled away from him.

He unlocked the door and opened it. His *I'm lecturing* scowl was gone, grin back in place. "Hey, I almost forgot. You're invited to a party. My house. Next Saturday night at seven. Full catered buffet, open bar, maybe a hundred and fifty people.''

"I don't think—''

"Hold it! Before you say no, you should understand I'll be talking to candidates for the regional manager job. Informal interviews, you could say. If you're smart, you'll come."

"I find it hard to trust you."

"Hey, I have a date, you know? You're not the only woman in the world. You bring a date, too." He chuckled. "If you know even one guy who'll put up with you."

"Gordon . . ."

"I'm serious." He snapped his fingers. "If you don't show, I know it's no go, Mandy." He winked. "See you next Saturday."

She put the champagne in the fridge while she got ready for bed—but not sleep. Her nerves needed quieting down. She checked Justin, kissed him again. In her nightgown she retrieved the champagne and her glass. She sat in bed propped with pillows. She took deep breaths and sipped.

A chance for a promotion had to be taken seriously. Gordie would have to be dealt with carefully. She wasn't a stranger at sparring with his badly concealed lust. "Report sexual harassment," said the TV public service announcements. Ha! How about sneaky innuendos, unwanted gifts, suggestive behavior, and promises as seductive as the devil's conversations with tempted saints? The guy who practiced them all also signed her paycheck. No doubt, their business relationship was unique. That was the whole reason she might well get the promotion. That was the way the world worked.

She turned on her clock radio. A Schubert trio serenaded the night hours. She sipped the champagne and soon was a bit high. She weighed the quality of highs from cheap wine versus those from fine champagne. She liked to think there was a difference. Those thoughts intruded happily on her anxieties and opened the way to slumber.

She fell asleep realizing she was already beginning to forget about both Floyd and Gordie.

# CHAPTER
## ❦ 3 ❧

On Saturdays Amanda visited her father. To help out, Cooper Sargin's mother always invited Justin to spend the day with her son. The boys were best friends. Peggy was a good, caring woman who wanted Amanda's close friendship. Amanda wished the Sargins weren't so well off, with their big house, bullet-sleek foreign cars, meadows of lawn, and handful of TVs. Spending time there would eventually make it clear to Justin how much he didn't have. Showing all the naivete of his ten years, he had once asked her why she didn't get a job like Mr. Sargin's. Bill Sargin had gone to Yale and to the Wharton School. He spent his days high in a downtown Hartford insurance company tower and "made decisions." Replying to her son, she stroked his light brown hair and said, "Sure he knows insurance. But the real money's in burgers. And Magic Mixture." The boy had learned that when one of his questions couldn't easily be answered, his mother tried to joke.

She knew it wouldn't last between the two boys. Social class would tell. Cooper was already taking piano and gymnastics lessons. Two weeks of the summer would be his first at soccer camp. The Sargins always rented a cottage on the Maine coast for two weeks. None of these indulgences could Amanda begin to afford. Cooper would drift toward those who shared common experiences and interests. Justin would be left out. Enjoy it while you can, kiddo, she thought, pulling away from the Sargin twelve-room. Bill was washing both new cars. In the rearview mirror she saw him wave goodbye with his hose hand, the water silvery showers in the late May morning light.

Her father was tough. An ordinary man would have given in to the cancer two years ago. He hadn't. He had fought and bought worthwhile months of life. During most of them he had been able to go out. He spent days down at the mall. Spring and fall he sat with the other retirees outside on the cement benches in the sun. At midsummer, they clung to the shadows like antebellum ladies. In winter, the gray squadrons, as he called his crowd of cronies, went inside to sit on the faux Gay Nineties ice cream shop chairs by the plastic stone fountain and nurse coffees through half a morning and afternoon. He rode the senior surrey, cadged meals at retirement homes and charitable tables, and watched his pennies closely. "I'm saving them for you," he said, when she urged him to live a little better.

His final battle he fought for her as well: convincing the day nurse not to suggest he be put in some kind of hospice or home. Somehow, during her visits, he put up a hale and almost hearty front. "Got to do it, Mandy," he said. "I go in a home, they take all I have. You get nothing."

On Saturdays the nurse didn't come. Amanda saw Pop-Up as he really was: in pain, weary, stubbornly alone. Her repeated offers to have him leave his small apartment and move in with her and Justin were dismissed with a wave of his knobby hand. "You've got enough of a row to hoe without an old man hanging around your neck." So she did what she could three times a week: cleaned, cooked him a pot meal that he could dip into a few times, and played her alto recorder for his pleasure.

Of course she listened to his familiar tales of Pittsburgh where he had made his living as a steelworker. How many times had she heard the story of the huge ladle bottom melting through and the hot metal pouring down on the mill floor, flaming and exploding like fireworks? The men caught below were seared instantly. Another story: the unlucky falling into the blast furnace. It always ended with the words: "They poured three ingots, one for each guy, and buried them." On and on he went, spinning tales of those long under sod, rich again in memory with the juices of youth. Great loves, great losses, incredible drunks, anatomies of successes and failures, marriages, divorces, meshed somehow with geography, politics, ethnic peculiarities, and sports—all played out on the hills and valleys of what the map called "The Greater Pittsburgh Area."

They had their Saturday rituals: the lunch of BLT's and beer, a half-hour recital. He was partial to Telemann, though she couldn't imagine why or how that taste had developed. She gathered his laundry and they argued cheerfully about why this sock or that T-shirt ought not be discarded. Her most valued ritual: listening to his monologues. Toward late afternoon he went to his chair at the window. When he was in his grave, she knew that was one memory she would cherish: Pop-Up looking down at the street, wearing the usual furry slippers and shiny trousers. He needed both moth-eaten sweaters held together with safety pins where the buttons had fallen off like seed pods too long drying. From that vantage point, he kept track of the comings and goings of fellow tenants.

With her help, he made his way to the kitchen where he could watch her prepare the dinner he insisted he eat alone— "so you can go out and raise hell on a Saturday night!" It did no good to tell him she often sat at home, unless she and Justin went to a second-run movie. This was one of his final acts of generosity on top of all he had given her, and so much more he would have liked to have given. Tonight, those expected words about Saturday night made her bite her lip to hold back threatening tears. Abruptly, all lives seemed so short, so small. All humanity swept along the short sunlit road between the two dark lands. All together in the mayfly dance of life . . . one, two, three . . .

When the table was set for one and the TV tuned to the Red Sox station, she recognized her visit was over. She put on her jacket and bent over to give him a kiss. To her surprise he grabbed her sleeve and held on. "Next time you come, bring Justin."

"Sure . . ."

"You probably don't know it, but I'm doing poorly now."

"Oh, come on—"

He jerked the sleeve like an ill-tempered terrier. "You listen. You bring the boy to see his Pop-Up. OK?"

"Sure."

He nodded, satisfied. Blinking his old man's eyes made squishy sounds. "That's one thing. There's another one."

"Tell."

He angled his face to look into her eyes. She saw their greenness, exactly like her own. The yellow of a worn liver marred his whites, but not the sudden intensity of his gaze. "We're getting down to the end now, Mandy. You're not to leave me."

"I won't. I can't!" She battled back the tears. "I'll be here until—as long as you want me."

"For some reason I needed to hear you say it." He released her jacket sleeve. "God damn! I'm getting to be an old fool."

Outside finally, she had to walk around the block twice, dabbing angrily at eyes that leaked and leaked. She couldn't see to drive . . .

Sunday was always a busy day for her. Weekly shopping at the Food Mart was an exercise in self-control. No, you can't *afford* that! She carted her two bags loaded with generic brands up the three flights. Was somebody adding extra risers, she wondered as she panted up to her door.

Laundry awaited. She had to stand in line for one of the apartment's basement machines. Whitewashed walls hung with cobwebs were the backdrop for a painful chat with Mrs. Clendenon, her next-door neighbor. She carried a hatpin in her purse and a chip on her shoulder. Men were her nemesis. Not her husband Harold, whom she had browbeaten into such a low state that he could only aspire to being henpecked—rather the "rapers" and abusers whose crimes against her sex she carefully chronicled with album clippings from three local newspapers and yards of videotapes culled from nightly news shows.

# PERSONAL

Amanda was well organized enough to have Justin put aside his homework problems until Sunday afternoon. On the throne they sat together, exploring the mysteries of long division and the week's list of spelling words. *"I after E except after C is handy to know, kiddo. Now let's look at some of the little monsters . . ."* The weather held. They went out for a bike ride, she on an ancient three-speed she had bought at a garage sale, he on a ten-speed—only seven of which functioned. She had spotted the sleazy look in the eyes of the kid who had sold it cheap secondhand. Twelve years old he had been. Give him ten more and he'd own his own gouging company—health foods probably. After an hour of pedal-and-coast she and Justin were both ready for medium slushes—her treat. A dollar and fifty-eight cents well spent.

A light supper, a game of Yahtzee, and Justin was ready for his bath. Sunday nights he read in bed before lights out. She dragged out her pseudo-leather briefcase and removed her Muncher's computer-printed accounts. She needed to look at receipts, reconcile some columns. She always found it hard to concentrate on numbers amid the tumult of duty. On a Sunday evening, though, they were the perfect sleeping potion.

At 9:30 the phone rang. She picked it up. "Good evening. This is Amanda Walker."

The voice was airy, distant, sexually undefinable. Its words, though, she heard clearly: "I'm going to kill you."

"Who is this?"

Pause. "I'm going to kill you."

Amanda held the receiver away from her ear and looked at it. Her free hand opened the drawer and found the police whistle she had bought—and used—for just such crank calls. She drew a deep breath and blasted a long piercing tone into the phone—then hung up.

Justin's voice from the bedroom. "Another heavy breather, mom?"

"Something like that," she said. "He won't bother me again."

Despite her fatigue, Amanda imagined she'd have trouble falling asleep. Her burdens were weighing a bit. The demands of nurturing poor Pop-Up through his last months or weeks could only grow. Trying to be both a parent and chum to Justin wouldn't be easier until she managed to find a father figure with whom to share the responsibility. The disappointment of her Friday night quest for romance emphasized that that important person had yet to appear—the last thing she recalled before sleep.

The following morning she held a brief staff muster before she opened the restaurant to the breakfast crowd. My ten-strong platoon, she thought, some of whose uniforms fit. She didn't need a degree in socio-economics to see who worked these days for the minimum wage: minority youngsters and retirees with no financial pillows on which to lay their graying heads. The prosperous social security collectors did volunteer work. The less so made fries at Muncher's.

"I got a directive from central, people," she said. "It was about the standard uniform—sticking to it. No personalization, got that? That means no buttons, Raphael." She looked at the sixteen-year-old boy.

He touched the plate-sized Jesus Is It! item covering a quarter of his narrow chest. "I'm praising our Lord, Jesus Christ, ma'am, who died for our sins."

"I'll die for your sins, Raphael, if you wear that button on company time."

"But we gotta wear those dumb Muncher Mania buttons when this place on that trip," he said.

Amanda pointed in opposite directions. "Jesus is over here. Muncher's is over there. Keep them separate. Everything's easier that way."

Raphael muttered, but the button came off.

"Where's your beanie, Madge?"

"I'm sixty-seven years old, Mandy, too old to wear a silly little cap that's supposed to make me look like a pixie. Whoever heard of a pixie with dentures? Bad enough I gotta wear these slippers with turned-up toes. They're bad for my arches, the doctor says."

"I'm wearing my hat and slippers." Amanda touched the

25

red and white segmented cap, felt its burger-shaped top button. "I like to think I'd look better wearing something else, too."

"It looks good on you. That's why they picked you to—"

"Madge, it's in the contract you signed to work here. It's covered under 'approved working attire,' paragraph six."

"All right! I'll wear the damned beanie. But when my grand-children come in here—"

"They'll be delighted!" Amanda's little crew wanted to disband. "One more thing." She held up a sheet of paper. They recognized the Muncher's headquarters letterhead. "An-other memo on rudeness from the man. Customers have written in complaints. He quotes again . . ."

Groans from the staff.

"Some of those working at other Muncher's sites lost their cool and called customers nasty names. I quote: 'pond scum sucker,' 'dog lips,' 'little rat-faced creep—' ''

"Right on, sister!" said Eddie Green, the wise one.

"Anything like that out of one of you and you're gone. My promise. I know it's hard sometimes. But Mr. Locker's built this business on politeness and courtesy—"

"He your man." An audible mutter from one of the girls. No telling which.

Amanda's face flamed. "He is not my man. Nothing like it." Titters and chuckles came from the staff. "Let's stay away from the personal stuff. And have a good day of work. It *is* possible, you know."

"Look!" Jerry Mecka pointed toward the front doors. "The enemy is at the gates!" Jerry was college bound. He even read books. Amanda turned to see a half dozen breakfast hounds pressing their noses up against the glass. Without looking at her watch, she knew it was 6:59. *This* Muncher's never opened late. "Stations!" she called to her staff. Key in hand, she advanced to the door, beanie and smile both in place. She opened the door. "Good morning and welcome to Muncher's!"

"The friggin' coffee better be ready!" cried the first cus-tomer of the bright new day.

For the first hour she stood watching and giving occasional orders to make sure the weekly and daily routines started smartly. Managing a Muncher's was about Maxi-munchers, Muncher's Malteds, and Muncher's Mud Pies, of course. More, it was about handling the staff, getting work out of them, assigning responsibilities, coming down hard when appropriate, kid gloves on the right cue. It was people—and a vexing, inconstant lot this crew was.

She spent the rest of the morning in the tiny office she shared with plastic trays of extra square buns and odds and ends of equipment that somehow never found a home. She sat at her computer entering orders for next month—so many thousand pounds of patties, paper, and plastic. Monday meant the payroll figures were due. She gathered the time cards from the clock rack and entered that data as well. Checks were mailed from Muncher central.

Just before noon, Raphael hung on the doorway. "Dude to see you, Miz Walker."

She went out to the counter. There she found Hunt Grayson. He wore a light linen suit tailored for his six-foot-plus frame and a Panama straw hat. Eddie Green looked at his clothes with wide-eyed envy. His lips formed a silent Whooo-eee! She had never seen Hunt dressed sloppily. He always seemed to have just been to the barber. His graying hair was carefully trimmed. His well-lined face carried no beard shadow. As usual, though, seeing him brought on mixed feelings. "What can I do for you, Hunt?" she said.

His brows rose. "Not even a hello from you, Amanda? We haven't talked in six weeks."

"Lunch is the busiest time of the day." She looked aside at the four growing lines. The shout of orders nearly drowned out their conversation.

"I'd like to talk to you for about ten minutes."

"What about?"

"A new opportunity for you."

"Hunt—"

"Hear me out. Don't be so negative."

She led him into her office where she could keep an eye on her responsibilities. "I hope we can make this quick," she said.

"I suppose you understand you can be annoying, Amanda. Particularly to someone who's trying to help you."

"I just have a feeling this is another pitch from you on my-life-as-a-model."

Hunt swung his body toward her. "The Ms. Muncher campaign was a big success."

"For everybody but me, Hunt."

"Because you wouldn't let it be. And still won't."

Creating a Ms. Muncher to represent the franchises had been Gordie Locker's idea. He had gone with it to Hunt who headed one of Hartford's largest modeling and talent agencies. She guessed choosing the woman from among the staff had been Hunt's suggestion.

Amanda couldn't imagine two people less likely to be able to cooperate than Hunt and Gordie. Her boss was brash and outspoken, Hunt reserved and thoughtful. Hunt dealt carefully with people, while Gordie tended to trample them down like a herd of stampeded dinosaurs. The competition was announced to Amanda's great indifference. She wouldn't even consider being a part of it. Gordie, who had already made his personal interest in her quite plain, submitted a candid photograph of her that he had taken without her knowledge.

He was clever. He stepped back then, and let Hunt deal with her. Thinking back always made her feel so used. With only the vaguest introductions and an understanding that Muncher's business was involved, she had allowed Hunt to *whooosh* her in his Volvo to one of Apricot's private dining rooms. There, among mesquite-grilled chicken and blackened fish, salads dressed with extra-virgin olive oil, one bottle each of Bordeaux and Riesling—damn her expensive tastes!—the entire campaign was laid out for her. Her role? Well, she would be the centerpiece of it all.

She liked Hunt. Beneath all his business bluff she caught flashes of humor and education. He was rather handsome in his steely executive way, even if he was pushing fifty. He once let it slip that he hadn't ever married. A distant early warning sounded there in any case, she thought. Leaving Apricot's she

28

told him, almost apologetically, that she didn't want to be Ms. Muncher. She thought that would be the end of it.

Gordie waited till her shift was over, then called her to Muncher central, a suite of offices in an executive park finished in orange fabric with Keanelike paintings of wide-eyed tykes on the walls. That day she saw a side of him that filled in the outlines of his character like a child working on a coloring book. Did she like her job? Did she want to keep it? If she did, she would be the first Ms. Muncher. She would get down off her high horse and help her employer and fellow workers. He told her how many hundreds of thousands the campaign was going to cost. She would be paid *something* for being Ms. Muncher. He urged her to weigh all that against the day-in-day-out dull routines of her West Park Muncher's responsibilities.

She asked for time to think. He gave her one day. She thought about going to an attorney, putting forth her case. She wasn't sure just what it was, except being pushed to take an assignment she really didn't want. She was cautious. She didn't believe all she heard and read about women's lib and women's rights. Her personal observation was that despite all the noise, things hadn't changed much. Confrontation wasn't often a woman's wisest course. It led to hardening of hearts. Instead of seeking legal counsel, she went to her father. Pop-Up said, "Do it!"

And so she had. Dripping with make-up, she made two TV commercials, followed them up with a handful of radio spots. "Hello, Hartford, this is Ms. Muncher with good news! You can still get a square meal . . ." From these were spun off a few billboard ads that shared central Connecticut roadside space with those of discount butchers and health spas. Life-sized cardboard cutouts of a creature more than vaguely like her stood by every Muncher's front doors. She held up a Maximuncher and a Muncher's Malted on either side of a grin too grand. She made personal appearances in each restaurant, signed autographs, and gave away cheap mugs bearing her uniformed likeness.

In the long run she got little out of it—small recognition from friends and associates, some kidding, a few passes from the married-looking. Compensation had been a disappointment as well. Gordie showed her an unexpected paragraph in her contract that included public appearances on behalf of the corporation for no extra money. He was having no trouble trying to go back on his word. Hunt Grayson's embarrassed intervention led to a Muncher's check made out to her for three hundred dollars.

Then came the incident at the Look Hill Inn. Gordie had told her she'd be out late making a personal appearance for some of his restaurant owner colleagues contemplating similar campaigns; overnight arrangements should be made for Justin. With some difficulty and more guilt she arranged for him to spend the night with the Sargins. Gordie drove her far into western Connecticut to the Look Hill Inn, a sprawling old relic remodeled with such care and precision that the outrageous prices on the menu were to be expected. His colleagues were meeting upstairs, he said. After dinner she'd put on her Muncher's uniform and meet them. He gave her the long wine list with a disarming grin. "In the meantime, we can enjoy ourselves," he said. She overdid it on the wine. That made it easier to get through the meal with him.

Once past the topic of Muncher's they had nothing in common. She put away nearly a whole bottle of wine. Later in the ladies' room she had a bit of trouble fastening her uniform's buttons and hooks. She had to sit down to put on the harem slippers.

The restaurant owners were meeting in the inn's third-floor suite. She made her way up there, weaving a bit over wide hand-hewn boards and braided throw rugs. She walked in wearing her wide public smile. Gordie stood waiting with arms out—alone. She looked past him, all around.

"What's going on?" she said. "Where are the other guys?"

"No other guys, Mandy. Just me."

She thought distantly that she should be more upset. The wine . . . What a dummy she was! She had actually believed him, thought this visit part of the responsibilities required of Ms. Muncher. Now, with the turned-down bed visible through the not-quite-plumb olde doorway, what was going on was too plain. She turned back toward the door. He was on her in an instant. Hands on her waist, he picked her up and set her back on the floor, like a windup toy, facing the bedroom. "Gordon!"

"I got some things to say." He raised a thick-wristed hand and pointed at her face. "The first thing is: you owe me."

She blinked, a bit bewildered. "For what?"

"For being Ms. Muncher. For getting all the attention. Getting on TV. Signing autographs. Everything!"

"Including the princely three hundred dollars you gave me?"

He looked confused. Sarcasm often went over his head. "Talk straight."

"All right. Your memory isn't so great, Gordon. I didn't want the job. I didn't want to be Ms. Muncher. It wasn't my style. You practically forced me to do it. Now that it's about over, I don't think I'd do it again. To be brief: I don't have anything to thank you for." She waved toward the bedroom. "Never mind sleeping with you."

She had reached him. She saw the color rising in his neck. "You are one difficult lady, aren't you?"

She closed her eyes and drew a deep breath. "We're just on different wavelengths. We don't communicate well." She walked back toward the door. "Ii we just go back to Hartford now, everything'll be fine."

"No, it won't." He blocked her way. He rested his hands on her hips.

She saw desire painted on the brown landscape of his eyes. She inwardly cursed the stupidity that allowed her to get into this situation, and tried to control her growing fear. She wasn't far from the piercing scream that would end their evening and her employment. "Just . . . let me go and we'll talk it over some other time."

Now he was frowning with bewilderment. "Mandy—"

*"Please . . ."*

"You think you're so much smarter than I am. But you don't understand at all. Ms. Muncher, the TV, the radio, being a celebrity. It was all set up for you from the start. I did it for you." He slid his spread hands down the curves of her buttocks.

"I don't understand. Please let me go!"

"I thought having a Ms. Muncher might help sales. But from the start it was to do something for you."

She made a wordless, puzzled noise. "Why?"

"Because . . ." He raised his hand and cupped her face. "You're a good-looking woman. And you do good things to your uniform." His other hand went to her breast. "Everything about you drives me crazy!"

"Gordon . . ." She shoved at his hand. It might as well have been anchored in concrete.

"Grayson wanted to pick a professional model. He didn't know there wasn't going to be any real competition for Ms. Muncher. From the start I knew it wouldn't be anybody but you."

"I'm flattered. But you have to let me go!"

"No!" He grabbed the front of her uniform and tore it open. A button flew across the room as if fired from a slingshot. Her beanie was knocked off.

Panic welled up, and anger with it. She let go of his hand and clawed at his face. "I'm not kidding!" she shouted. "Let me go!" He winced, turned his head away, and grabbed her arms.

When he looked back at her she saw the flash at the bottom of his gaze like the silvery dart of scales seen amid reef coral. Its illusive meaning was colored with threat.

He tore at her bra, exposing a breast. She opened her mouth to scream.

Someone knocked at the door. With adrenalin-sparked reflexes, she shouted, "Come in!" before Gordie could open his mouth.

As the door opened she pulled roughly away from him and covered herself with the dangling panel of her uniform. A smiling gray-haired lady in a maid's uniform entered. "Turndown service," she said sweetly. In her hand she held a box of Godiva chocolates, two of which would adorn the nighty-night pillows of the happy couple before her.

Amanda snatched up her overnight case and fled. At the lobby desk she asked for a pin and a cab—though she had no idea how to pay for the latter. A call was made. She went to the ladies' room and changed. When she emerged, she saw Gordon standing by the desk. He told her she didn't need a cab; he'd take her back to Hartford.

"How in the world can I trust you?" she whispered.

"Hey, I've cooled off. Nothing to worry about." She thought she saw sincerity in his eyes in place of the flash. "One move, Gordon Locker. One move, and I'll go to the police. Swear to God."

"I got it. All right?"

They drove through the night in silence. Her thoughts boiled with resentment, anger, fear, and turmoil.

About ten minutes from her apartment he said, "I did it for you."

"How can you say that? You wouldn't even have paid me if Hunt hadn't shamed you into it."

"What's a few bucks? I wanted to make you somebody."

"You did it to get customers through the door, Gordon. You did it for Maxi and all the little Munchers."

"It just worked out that way. You got to believe it was for you." There was no mistaking the tenderness in his pleading tone.

"Gordon, listen to me. I will never spend an evening alone with you again."

"You don't get it, even with your brains, Mandy. You got to go with what I gave you."

What he had given her, Hunt explained a few days later, was a chance at a modeling career. And he thought she ought to take it. He might be able to get her another assignment. She had to understand that glamour girls made up only a small percentage of the clan. He had arranged contracts for young and old of both sexes. Women Amanda's age could always find work at trade shows as product representatives or portraying TV housewives promoting floor wax or home delivery pizzas. He had some contacts in the shampoo business. Maybe they needed her to wash her hair for the camera.

She told him she wasn't interested. It wasn't her style. She didn't feel right being the center of attention, under any conditions.

"Mandy, you're a *natural*," he said that day six months ago.

Today he said it again—exact same words. And hurried on: "I have a perfect assignment for you. Want to hear about it?" His pleasant square face set itself into an earnest expression. He was anxious for her assent.

"Oh, Hunt . . . I just don't know."

"There's a franchise china and silver store opening this week. It's a classy place. They need someone for four hours every afternoon, one to five. A thousand dollars. I'll waive my 10 percent. All you have to do is smile and help people find what they want. The clerks will handle the rest. Come on, Mandy."

"You know where I am every afternoon."

"Call in sick."

She took a deep breath. "I can't do that. It's against my principles."

"It's possible to be too honest, you know. And that can only hurt you." He rested a hand lightly on her forearm. "You ought to do it."

"And if I do? What would my next assignment be?"

"Well . . ."

"I know Muncher's isn't much, Hunt. But it's steady. And I need steady."

He held her lightly by the shoulders. "You have to take risks in life, Mandy."

"I've never been very good at that." She remembered her Friday evening with Floyd. "When I take risks, things don't work out. I've worked hard to get what little I have out of Gordon. I don't want to throw it all away on . . . just a chance. And I have a son to support."

"You still have a lot of Ms. Muncher recognition left. I'm sure I can—"

She pressed her fingertips lightly against his mouth. "You're nice to try to help me change careers. I'm just not brave enough right now."

He shrugged. "You're just too damned conservative to take good advice, Amanda Walker."

She smiled and reached for the doorknob. "Runs in the sex."

"Hang on a second." He held up two tickets. "For the University of Hartford Jazz Fest tonight. We could have a light dinner and get over there in plenty of time . . ."

"I . . . don't think so." Even as she spoke, she felt a distant depression. Its exact source escaped identification. His being interested in her added to her melancholy. Possibly, it was because she felt he was too old for her. Fifteen years was a big gap. Or maybe his being a determined bachelor put her off.

To some he might be a good catch. He was stable, settled, and prosperous. He had told her his agency provided only part of his income. He owned business rental properties and had invested successfully in stock and bond mutual funds. He hadn't gone into detail about his past business or personal life. She had the feeling he had tried quite a few ventures before finding some that worked. She guessed he had known dozens of women. He showed none of Gordon's wildness and barely controlled desperation when in her company. He was always warm and patient. Behind his relaxed pace and timing she sensed he knew that if she wasn't interested, there were a lot of other women in the world. And in his position he pretty much had his pick.

So why hadn't he picked someone?

Walking back into the restaurant, she wondered if she weren't making a mistake refusing him again. He had invited her to share time with him five times since they met through the Ms. Muncher campaign. Each time his suggestions had been right on target: two classical music concerts, a weekend sightseeing in Boston (Justin included), a one-day Vermont bicycle tour, and a visit to one of Connecticut's wineries. Clearly, they shared some of the same interests. Pressing the question of her resistance even harder, the best answer she could find was a feeble one—there was something about him . . .

Nonetheless, she tuned into the WWUH live broadcast of the jazz concert while she put away the dishes and supervised Justin's homework. She tapped her foot and hummed along when she could understand where the players were going. When Justin was in bed, she sat on her throne, eyes closed, and just listened. Horns and altos built imaginative bridges across keys. Rhythm sections laid foundations upon which chords rose like ephemeral structures, razed and rebuilt under the rules of musical time. Solos rolled on and she understood how gifted these groups were. She wished she was there, dammit!

The phone rang. Smiling, she moved to answer it. She guessed it would be Hunt calling to rub in her refusal. He was undoubtedly listening, too. She lifted the receiver and said, "I'm sorry I said no, Hunt."

"I'm reminding you that you're going to die." That voice again! Airy, sexless, distant.

"Who *is* this?"

She opened the drawer. Her fingertips sought her whistle's cool metal.

"This is someone who likes to kill redheads."

*"What?"* Where was that damned whistle?

"There've been others, Amanda. Before you. There will be more."

She tore at the papers and junk in the drawer. Where was the—

"You're looking for your neat little whistle, aren't you?" The voice crawled like a snake from the wire. "The one in the little yellow chest the phone sits on."

She gasped.

"I visited your apartment today."

The whistle's shrill scream drove like an awl into her brain. She tore the instrument from her suffering ear. When she dared try to listen again, the line was dead. With wide eyes she surveyed the familiar room. A cloud of menace passed across the safe sun of her routine life. What in heaven's name was going on?

# CHAPTER

## ❧ 4 ❧

The next morning she casually asked Justin if he had taken the whistle out of the yellow chest. His no sent her into speculation that lasted well into her workday. The unacceptable seemed to have happened. The unknown caller—Floyd?—had somehow got into her home. Several times she shuddered at that thought. Her personal living space violated, polluted . . .

Past that came the murder threat. She didn't believe that Floyd would call her or mean what was said. She had merely annoyed him. She could be annoying with her sarcasm and refusal to be walked on, but had never provoked anyone to a fatal grudge. No, she had no enemies. Still more disturbing was that neither call was a random event. The caller had used her name! He—if it was a he—knew her phone number and address. Was it Floyd? Why was he trying to frighten her?

She called the apartment superintendent and insisted her locks be changed. She wouldn't listen to his arguments. Someone had gotten in with a key or a pick. If he got in again and harmed her or her son, there would be a lawsuit. She guaranteed it.

At work she settled a squabble between Raphael and Jerry and entered yesterday's statistics into the computer. She conducted one of her dreaded Walker walks for your sins, as religion-minded Raphael called her thorough cleanliness inspections. She issued the expected reprimands, along with the dates and times by which certain areas *would* be spotless. At noon she made her customary lunch from the salad bar. No way would she stuff down standard Muncher's food. Too much cholesterol. Not to mention high blood pressure and odds and ends of cancers. One of the inducements to the teenagers who made up the greater part of the staff was Gordie's personal wish that employment meant you could eat as much as you wanted, so long as food wasn't wasted. Watching string-thin boys and bulimic-looking girls gorge on three or four Maxi-munchers, Maxi-Fries, and a Muncher's Malted carried a fascination equal to one that Amanda felt for fire eaters and sword swallowers. Even after years in the business, lunch time usually brought small wonders. But not today. . . .

Her own appetite was definitely slipping. She sat in her tiny office and stared down at her salad as though it was an enemy. Thoughts of Floyd possibly calling were bothering her. Her musings took a new route, one that focused on that last sexless sighing sentence: *This is someone who likes to kill redheads.* She absently held a strand of her hair, wound it around her finger and pulled it forward. She studied the deep red color as though she had never seen it before. Its thickness and luster had come from her mother. A lifetime of determined brushing and careful shampooing had brought her to some nut's attention. Maybe Floyd's attention.

Floyd liked redheads.

She tried to remember if she had read or heard about any redheaded women being murdered in the Hartford area. Hard as she pondered, none came to mind. But the city was large, and murder scarcely an unknown phenomenon. Real red-haired women weren't that common. Should some have been killed, the police would surely notice the pattern and act on it. Or would they? She picked up the telephone book and looked up Hartford police headquarters. She knew nothing about police operations. When a sergeant answered the phone, she said, "I want to know who I'd talk to to find out if somebody's killing redheads in Hartford."

She had to repeat that, then was transferred to homicide.

Several minutes passed before someone took the call. She repeated her question. Another sergeant asked for her name.

"What does my name matter? I just want some information."

"Ma'am, we keep records."

"I just want—"

"I'm going to have to turn on the tape recorder. I have to advise you that this conversation is being taped as required by law. Now if I could have your—"

She hung up.

What had she expected? Police were part of government. She had no real facts to share with them. Just a threat. She thought of calling back to report that her apartment had been broken into. They would ask her what was taken. A little whistle. She shook her head and turned away from the phone. An idea was niggling. She let it niggle through the rest of the afternoon, gave her memory every chance to recall the details about . . .

Felicity Foster.

She clearly recalled where and how they had met. It had been more than two years ago. Summer on Cape Cod. Pop-Up had taken Justin for a week to free her for her first vacation in years. She had shared a run-down cottage rental with five other women and played being single and irresponsible again. An easy thing to do with plenty of sun, sand, and like-minded crowds filling every restaurant and club from Hyannis to Provincetown. She and her friends were all like eggs: fried during the day and pickled at night.

She tried to show a little restraint. But when you moved in a crowd that never ate, only grazed, and washed summer down with Miller Lite and wine coolers, good judgment fled like mosquitoes before the breeze. That memorable day she had started with a few beers late in the afternoon. Someone mentioned a happy hour spot where all drinks were a dollar. They had to check that out. After that they went to two other pubs where she had at least one drink. Even so, she was in decent shape when their crowd descended on The Catamaran. After a hearty meal of two fried potato skins, she played some part in the emptying of several pitchers of beer. Having had a lot of help, she was only a bit high when her friends started talking about the wet T-shirt contest to begin in about an hour. Prize: One hundred dollars.

The men among them—and a few of the women, too—decided she should "represent the class of our group." She declined, but persuasion and beer somehow had their way. With two couples providing moral support, she added her name to the already lengthy list in the DJ's hairy hand. She wondered dimly what she was doing. There was something too daring about competing with younger women; she, the mother of one, over thirty, a bit of a subversive amid the twenty-three year olds. She still had her figure. She was curious to see how she'd do.

The contestants were already gathering. Each wore her gift Catamaran T-shirt bearing the name in bright blue below which that vessel flew across cotton waters before perfect winds. She went to the ladies' room, took off her bra, slipped into her shirt, and got in line. Making small talk, she noticed there was one other redhead in the group, a taller woman wearing short-shorts carrying in mid-buttock a brand reading Prime.

Her friends kept her supplied with what now was indeed liquid courage. Her propriety wasn't dead yet, and she considered changing her mind several times. When things officially got underway there were a dozen women in line. Beyond the lights she saw leering men and wide-eyed women, faces glistening with the heat of the August summer night, closeness, and alcohol. She was aware of the warmth of her own skin. Her heart pounded as the DJ led them all out in a line.

They each gave their name and hometown and were greeted with whistles, screams, and applause. The bolder women waved their hands and did a few impromptu dance steps, further inciting the crowd. Amanda was glad to see the stage guarded by a half-dozen thick-backed young men sweating in ties and slacks. When her turn came, she managed a brave wave and a clenched fist. Her face reddened at the return roar. *What* am I doing, she asked herself.

There were three stages to the contest: damp, wet, and

40

soaked. After each wetting, the amount of applause weeded out the contestants. Each stage dragged on to maximize both the amount of beer sold and overall leer time. She survived damp and wet, a little surprised and pleased each time. Half of her slightly drunken self cringed at the exploitation, the other half applauded the daring she always felt she lacked.

At the end of wet there were only four women left. One of them was the other redhead, tall and shapely with long well-tanned legs. The other two were shorter with dramatic chests. White pails were refilled to the brim and the staff men dragged them up four stepladders.

"OK, girls, one mo' time!" the DJ bellowed into his cordless mike.

The earlier wettings had been careless sloshings out of pails swung at floor level. The final method would leave not one stitch dry in four shirts that were already revealing enough. Following the others' leads, she covered her face with her hands. The water fell on her like a wave. She shrieked and sputtered, too. Goose flesh rose and her nipples stood up. Lord, this was impossibly embarrassing . . . But it was too late to get out of it now. She had to pretend she wasn't just about naked. The DJ led them out toward the front of the stage. The two shorter women were gyrating their hips, breasts shifting under the wet cotton. The crowd howled in appreciation. She would *not* do that. Let them keep their money. She waved and turned in a circle. The other redhead blew kisses to the crowd—energetically, with the expected effect on her chest. Amanda's competitive fires were burning low. She wanted this to be over—and fast. She was cold and mortified.

The voting applause astonished her. The two shorter girls were sent offstage. Now the DJ was babbling something about two lovely redheaded finalists, a first ever at the five-years-running once-a-week contest. He led them toward the lights for the last time. The cries of "take it off!" were deafening. In the audience, women rolled their eyes and pretended embarrassment. If the National Organization for Women found this place, Amanda thought, they'd come in with flame-throwers.

41

PERSONAL

"Time to choose the winnah!" the DJ howled. A canned
fanfare blasted out, loud as the crack of doom. "Remember,
it's your applause that will make one of these sweet ladies a
hundred dollars richer."

He took the other woman's hand and raised it. "Let's hear
it for the lovely Felicity!"

Amanda's ears rang with their enthusiasm. Then it was her
turn, she, "the lovely Amanda." She couldn't tell which out-
burst was louder. Nor could the DJ. "Let's try it again!" he
bellowed. Same result. "What can we do to break this tie?"
he prompted with lecherous howls. The roar for them to take
off their shirts shook the stage.

The two women moved closer. "I am *not* taking off this
shirt!" Amanda said to Felicity. Her hair was plastered down
and her lashes pointed with moisture. Some of the water flew
off when she shook her head. "Me neither. Let's get off here,"
Felicity said. They fled the stage waving. The contest was
declared a tie, the hundred dollars divided. Amanda's friends
were waiting with jackets and towels amid male faces drooping
with disappointment. Felicity stayed with them that evening.
The next day she and Amanda nursed their hangovers. For the
rest of the week Felicity remained the group's newest member.

Because she lived in Newington, a town close to Hartford,
she and Amanda continued their friendship. Felicity was non-
traditional. She lived alone because she squabbled with her
father. She didn't hold a regular job. She was registered as a
temporary worker with a half-dozen agencies. She worked until
she had enough money. Not until it was spent did she return.
"Life is for living, not for working," she often said.

She was man crazy when Amanda first knew her. Not much
later, she was crazy for a guy named Bart. She was hazy in
describing his occupation. She advertised him as an independent businessman, speculator or promoter of some kind.
Amanda always suspected he was a drug dealer. He often took
Felicity away for three- or four-day trips during which he spent
piles of money on her. "He says I rate everything in life top
shelf!" she said. "And I say, right on!" Then came a time
when Bart was unavailable. Felicity became restless; she wasn't

42

one to defer gratification. Some months later she reported that Bart was thinking of moving out of state, and she had every intention of going with him.

It was then that Amanda lost track of her. She imagined her and Bart in the front seat of his Lamborghini speeding down the highway in the shadow of the Rockies, headed for la-la land and adventures beyond guessing. Amanda envied her freedom and the personality to exploit it. Compared to Felicity, she always felt stodgy and safe. It wasn't the first time she supposed she played her cards too close to the chest. Twice she called her friend's apartment. The first time no one answered. The second time a recording told her the number had been disconnected.

Now a memory surfaced like a bubble. During her period of loneliness, Felicity mentioned to Amanda that she had answered *Reformer* ads.

Finishing up the accounting for her shift, Amanda wondered if she should have found out just where Felicity had gone. In fact, she was certain she should have. So much so that, without giving words to the suspicion in the back of her mind, she dragged out the phone book and turned to the *F*s, where the Fosters were.

She stretched her memory. The father Felicity couldn't bear. What was his name? Edge, Ed, Ef, something like that. Short, starting with an *E*. Her eyes moved down the columns. There! An Emmett. Felicity had called him Em. She dialed. No answer. Later that evening, at home, she tried Mr. Foster again. Someone answered. "Hello, is this Mr. Emmett Foster?"

"Yeah."

"My name is Amanda Walker. I'm a friend of your daughter, Felicity."

"You can't be too good a friend."

"Why not?"

"It took you better than a year to call."

Amanda was puzzled, but hurried on: "You might have heard her mention my name."

"She and I got along like Palestinians and Israelis. She didn't tell me who she knew."

"The reason I'm calling is I'd like to reestablish my friendship, even if it's by letter. Could you tell me where she is?"

Silence. Then Mr. Foster sighed loudly. "I'd say Heaven or Hell, if I believed in either one, or in anybody's soul. She's six feet under."

"W—What happened to her?" Amanda's hand gripped the phone as though it was the only piton driven into a sheer rock face.

"They cut her into pieces like a chicken."

"Who—"

"A guy was walking his dogs by the reservoir. He found her up in the woods. She was rotted some."

"Oh, dear God—"

"The cops called it 'a kill-and-cut.' They think he used an axe for the cut part. They never found out who did it. So much for my tax dollar."

"I'm so terribly sorry." Amanda's distant, disturbing, wordless speculation was becoming prophecy. Her heart pounded and her mouth was suddenly dry. "Mr. Foster, was Felicity ever threatened? Did anybody call her with—"

"Are you some kind of reporter? You want something from me? Come right out and say it." His voice had taken on a whining tone she sensed was its normal one.

"I am—was—Felicity's friend." She spoke in a rush. "I want to find out more about what happened to her before she died."

"Why?"

"Personal reasons. Very important ones to me. But not clear enough yet to explain."

"So, like I said, what do you want, Amanda Walter?"

"Walker. I wonder . . . do you have your daughter's possessions?"

"She 'wasn't into acquisition,' she used to say."

Amanda felt increasingly desperate. "Do you have anything that used to belong to her?"

"I sold her clothes. I still got a couple pieces of her furniture. Couple of shoe boxes with her letters and stuff in them. Once

44

in a while we wrote to each other. Only way we didn't fight. That's it, though.''

"Could I come over and look in the boxes?''

"Cops been through them. Didn't find nothing.''

"Even so, I—''

"What you up to? What do you really want?''

"Please, Mr. Foster, could I just look in the boxes?''

"When?''

"In a few minutes.''

"I should say no. I shouldn't let you bother me, stir up how it was with Fel and me. I really shouldn't. But I'll say yes because . . . you know why?''

"No.''

"You sound scared.''

Justin had a Cub Scout meeting that evening. If he got home before her, he was to stay downstairs with Jilly. She would pick him up there. She drove to Emmett Foster's address, a small home on a cul-de-sac in East Harford. He was a small balding man. His red hair was shot through with gray, his high forehead a washboard of wrinkles. His living room was hot and humid. She understood why. It—as well as the dining room and part of the kitchen—was jammed with dozens of tropical fish tanks. Pumps throbbed and water gurgled through what seemed miles of plastic tubing. Huge ugly fish preened and stared at her, rising and falling before the glass as they exercised small-brained curiosity.

"I'm into cichlids,'' Em Foster said, waving at the tanks. "The chamber music of freshwater tropicals.'' He walked with a limp. "I'm on disability. On-the-job accident. I sued and won. Now I can raise my fish and don't have to deal with the world.'' He turned in the small free space in the room's center and studied her. He laughed, a tiny explosive choke, and shook his head. "Damned if you don't remind me of Fel. It's the hair and skin. Same as hers.''

An unexpected chill passed over Amanda. Someone walking on her grave . . .

"Same as mine before I got old and ugly. There should be

45

a redheaded society. Like in Sherlock Holmes: 'The Red-Headed League.' You know the Sherlock Holmes stories?''

"No, I don't. Mr. Foster, I'm in a little hurry. My son is at a meeting and—''

"Hey, be my guest." He led her to a card table stacked with plastic containers of flake fish food. Some space had been cleared off. On it stood two shoe boxes. She opened the first box and began to sift through envelopes, ticket stubs, theater and musical programs, a few Polaroid photos of Felicity with friends. She studied the blurry prints, saw no one she knew.

She was aware of Em Foster hovering behind her. She looked over her shoulder. Tears worked their wet way down his cheeks. "Not much to show for a life, is it?" he said in a thick voice.

Amanda's throat began to burn. She shook her head wordlessly.

"I wish to God we had gotten along better. Seeing you sitting there makes me imagine I'm getting a second chance . . .''

Amanda swallowed and breathed deeply.

"If you got any questions, let me know." He limped away. Amanda bent her head over the shoe box, fighting to control her emotions. From the other room she heard Em begin a long monologue. She realized each of the huge fish had a name.

A few more deep breaths of moist, organic-smelling air regained much of her self-control. For the first time she admitted to herself that she was looking for something. Possibly all the trouble she had taken to get to this table and these boxes had been an effort to find . . . well, she'd soon see.

She went through both boxes without success. That brought mixed feelings, at least one of which was relief. She replaced the papers and personal odds and ends. Before putting the tops back on, she sat back in the folding chair and looked at the fish. In the distance the murmur of Em talking man-to-fish was barely audible. She understood clearly that she never wanted to come back here. For that reason she went through the contents of both boxes again, still more thoroughly.

She shook out the emptied envelopes, tapping on the paper to loosen anything that had worked down to the corners. Halfway through the second box, a bit of paper fluttered down like a hurt moth. The tiny square of newsprint angled off to the floor. With a moistened index finger she retrieved it. The line of text was circled with pencil. A tiny date had been added.

Hairs stirred on the back of her neck. The icy wind of fear blew up her spine. She read the ad:

*Redheads wanted for coffee and conversation.*

The date Felicity had added was last February. She had answered the ad and met Floyd.

On her way out, Amanda asked Em when the police had said his daughter had been murdered. Mid-March. They weren't sure of the exact day. Five or six weeks after she had read the ad, Amanda thought. If that were so, one conclusion thrust itself forward.

Floyd Philman had killed Felicity.

Now he planned to kill her. The threats had been horribly real.

"You look worse than when you first walked in, honey," Em said. "Anything I can do?"

Amanda shook her head. "I think I know who killed Felicity."

"Who?"

Amanda shrugged. "Just a name to you."

"If you do know, then tell the cops. They couldn't figure it out on their own. You give them the word. The case is still open." He snorted. "Every once in a while I call them up and ask how they're doing—just to embarrass them. They're doing nothing."

Tossing in her bed that night, she realized finding the ad was in no way legal evidence. But it certainly raised her suspicions, caused her to reach obvious conclusions.

Floyd was making good his threats.

In the darkness her memory reconstructed his features: the bulgy Adam's apple, the gaunt jaw, and the oddly lashless eyes. His sexual innuendos now made perfect sense! The references to her body, to whores, to his mother . . . he was disturbed. She remembered his hands on her, the tugging at her sleeve. She groaned and spun between her sheets. That damned ad! Thanks to it she had become the focus of a nut's attention. Now he hovered on the near horizon of her life like a spider eyeing ensnared prey. What should she do? She tried to gather her thoughts, but with little success.

She couldn't completely believe that he was a killer, that he wanted her to be his next victim. It was all so absurd and unlikely. That Felicity had answered his ad and then died violently didn't really *prove* anything. She had to find out more. Worry and confusion kept her awake far too long. She'd better get straightened out—and fast.

In earlier times she would have confided in Pop-Up. His streak of brash practicality often originated good advice. Now the old man was dying. She wouldn't cloud his last days with what she wasn't quite certain was a real problem. When she visited him the next evening, it seemed more important that she took Justin and that he and the boy talked. She sat apart and studied her father's weary face. The set of his eyes and the march of muscles across his jaw hinted at the growing pain. The nurse would soon talk to the doctor. They would start with the heavyweight drugs. He would go into a stupor, doddering and staring. There wouldn't be many more evenings like this, with her cooking what he liked and cleaning up a bit. This peace of blood and domesticity would wind down like the reign of a grand monarch.

At two in the morning she was still awake, unable to sleep. She got up and made herself a pot of tea. Cup in hand, she walked to the telephone and sat down beside it. She studied it: Radio Shack, Taiwanese made, cheesy plastic, fallout from Ma Bell's deregulation. When she finally raised her nerve to pick it up, it was with a shaking hand. Earlier, she had found Floyd's number in the book. She punched it in. Her hand on the instrument turned clammy. She held her breath at the ringing tone, focusing her attention on her prepared speech.

After four rings his answering machine kicked in. "This is Floyd Hooper Philman, man about town. I can't come to the phone just now. Leave your message at the tone. If you're a

48

# PERSONAL

redhead, leave your age, bra size, address, phone number, and favorite sexual position. I will return all calls.''

Hearing Floyd's voice again rattled her. Was this the same voice sighing into her ear with death threats? It could be, hushed down, pitched up, masked maybe with fabric. Her words came out in a rush. "Floyd, this is the woman you met at Brothers II. I know you've been calling me. And I know what else you've done to redheads. If I hear from you again, or if you try anything, the police will get all the details. Either from me or someone I trust. I'm very serious and very able to do what I've said. Understand? I never want to hear your voice or see you again.'' She hung up with sweat beading below her hairline.

After that, she tried to put the threats out of mind. She buried herself in her routines: work, Justin, Pop-Up. Just the same, every time a phone rang, she felt a chill start up her spine. None of the callers was Floyd. Her reaction told her she'd have to do more. She couldn't stop with just threatening him, half bluffing. She'd have to be more aggressive. Even as she sought to escape him, she felt herself being drawn into the tangle of his illness and murderous personality. She swung between planning further moves and trying to ignore the situation.

Friday evening she gave Jilly the two hours of recorder lessons owed, in view of her sitting again Saturday night. She looked forward to Gordie Locker's party as much as a diphtheria shot. As with that inoculation, it seemed imprudent not to participate.

She had avoided ever visiting Gordie's house in Farmington. Turning into the carriage drive marked by stone pillars set with brass plaques reading Locker, she got a clear idea of how well franchising had treated him. She realized she hadn't known the extent of his wealth. After all, he was constantly complaining about the alimony he paid both his ex-wives. A teenager waved her onto a sweeping lawn where dozens of cars had been parked in rough rows.

The house proved to be a neo-Tudor mansion. Beyond the door lay evidence of energetic caterers, florists, and professional party-givers. Being rich meant never having to say, "I'll

49

do it,'' she thought. The affair was well underway. Champagne
in tulip glasses was being distributed by at least three waitresses
with trays resting on back-tilted palms. Glass in hand, she noted
the open bars manned by a platoon of eager young men in
evening dress, the buffet tables piled with oysters and aspics.
The ice sculpture heaps of Maxi-munchers and Muncher's
Malteds were to scale, if not to her taste. Only Gordie Locker
would evaluate job candidates under such conditions.

The possibility of becoming regional manager had never been
fully submerged by her concerns over Floyd Philman's threats.
The job promised a nice office of her own, a little travel around
the state, and a chance to finish her interrupted higher education. To some degree, she was willing to put up with Gordie's
odd way of doing things to get the position. Her agenda for
the evening: talk to him, then get out. Moving and smiling
amid the other guests, she was a bit self-conscious. She had
worn her best dress, but it was old and badly outclassed by
what the more prosperous ladies had on their backs.

She couldn't find Gordie or any familiar faces. She chatted
with strangers and kept circulating. She wandered into the
library, its shelves lined with classics of no more interest to
Gordie than hieroglyphics. She followed the eager glances of
a half-dozen men toward a head of fine blonde hair above
creamy shoulders. When the woman turned, Amanda beheld
her fashion magazine face, all its lines and planes sounding
the harmonies of beauty. She noticed her cocktail dress fit with
flattering snugness and wondered with awe what it cost. She
was so wrapped up in envy that she never noticed Hunt Grayson
standing at the blonde's side. He saw her, smiled, and beckoned
her over. He introduced her to the radiant one. "My client and
friend, Chelsea.''

Amanda felt like a charwoman presented to a queen. Her
self-image wasn't what it should be these days. Chelsea was
gracious, cool, and polite. Only after a little coaxing by Hunt
did she admit that her modeling career had broken through.
She had just scheduled a month with various New York pho-
tographers.

"Amanda's done some promotional work for me," Hunt said. "I'm trying to encourage her to do more."

Chelsea looked her over with more care. "Go for it, sweetie. After all, how long does it last? At your age."

It took Amanda a moment to realize she had been insulted. Before she could reply, Hunt had started in on an explanation of how he saw Amanda's future with his agency. She interrupted with an icy goodbye and moved away. She was upset, but not by what Chelsea had said. It had something to do with the model, being twenty-five at the most, dating Hunt, and she, ten years older, turning him down. Confusion vied with envy as she found another champagne tulip and emptied it faster than she should have. Lord, when was she going to make some right decisions in her life?

She nibbled from the buffet and tried to find Gordie, without success. She asked several guests if they had seen him. They had, but he didn't seem to be around now. She persisted. On the second floor, a couple dancing barefoot to the distant combo throb pointed toward a set of double doors. Hesitantly, she slid one aside.

"Come in, Mandy, and close the door." Gordie was at a card table with six other men. Kibitzers stood looking over their shoulders at the heaps of chips and flash of cards. Behind him was a slender woman with bleached blonde hair, brows, and lashes. She wore a conservative up-to-the-neck dress with a bow. It gave her a schoolgirl look. A second glance showed more: the cut of the hair, posture, and bust line—nearly hidden yet hinting at ample glories—invited seduction. An appeal to men to violate an illusory innocence. Her automatic disarming smile swung toward Amanda—and died as suddenly as a rodent crossing the interstate. Replacing it was a narrowed, speculative stare. The players glanced up briefly, then turned back to the action.

For an instant, her mind swung back over the years to the hundreds of nights she had stood over Ned in just such poker games, watching their fortunes ebb, flow, and ebb. How she had fretted in those days over green felt, hundred-dollar windows at the track, and the sight of bookies!

51

PERSONAL

Gordie beckoned to her. "Come on over. Bring me some luck." He playfully elbowed the bleached blonde away. "Move it, Emerald! You're about as lucky as the Pope is Jewish." She snickered, bent, and whispered in his ear—then nibbled it lightly. She made a swooping curtsey that invited Amanda to take her place. "Be my guest, best of the rest." She flashed a shrewd smile; she was no nitwit.

Amanda stepped up and whispered to Gordie. "Have you forgotten you're supposed to be interviewing people for the regional manager job?"

He picked a cigar as big around as a ball bat out of an ashtray. "Deal the friggin' cards."

"Gordon!"

"Chill out, Mandy." He shot a swift glance over his shoulder. "Bring me some luck and maybe I'll just *give* you the job."

Amanda muttered but stayed where she was. To her right stood Emerald. She winked and made a gesture urging Amanda to do her best. Amanda reasoned that at least while she was here, Gordie wasn't talking to anyone else about the manager's job. "How about a lucky touch, Mandy?"

She dug a nail into his neck. "I want to talk business!" she whispered in his ear, a smile on her face for the others.

"Ouch!"

She rested her palms lightly on his shoulders and watched the action. Ned had taught her poker, past the cards, the chips, the percentages. He had talked to her about nerve and stamina and the contempt for money that lay in the hearts of all truly successful gamblers. Who knew how many nights and days they had spent on U.S. Route You-Name-It talking about poker's magic and mystery. She watched a hundred suns come bleeding over the eastern horizon with Ned telling yet another story of fortunes lost with aces full and won with a pair of deuces. Ned knew everything about gambling. The trouble was he was born a loser.

It didn't take her very long to find out that Gordie was a poor player. He didn't know what a good hand was. He bet two pair big. They waited for him and took his money. On his

52

side was that he bet just as big when he had a good hand. In the end, though, as the evening moved on, he would end up on the short end. That would mean thousands of dollars gone, putting him in a vile mood and postponing any chance to discuss the manager's job.

She didn't really mean to help him at first. When he played a hand he should have folded she dug her fingers into his shoulder. She glimpsed his next hand, also weak, and used the same fingers. He caught on and folded. Without a word they developed a code: right hand or left, number of squeezes. Fold, call, or raise. What else was there to the game? From time to time she lowered her hands to avoid being obvious. No real problem for her. These men were amateurs; they were drinking as well. "Fish," Ned would have called them. They were playing Hold 'Em. Two cards in the hand, the other five turned up three, one, one. She had a pretty good idea how that game was played.

Ned had also taught her the subtleties of the kind of kibitzing she was doing. She didn't advertise that she was helping Gordie. She visited the bar, brought him a Southern Comfort on the rocks, went to the bathroom, meandered back just in time for a big pot.

In two hours he won back what he had lost and a little more. Then the game broke up. The other players left the room. He tried to stuff a hundred-dollar bill down the front of her dress. She shoved his hand away. "A favor. No charge."

"I don't know why I paid attention to you," he said. "Where'd you learn about cards?"

"In an earlier life."

"I knew that brain of yours was good for something besides growing hair."

"I'm delighted to see you two getting along so well." Emerald stood close by, her fetching grin in place. Amanda couldn't read her.

"Did I introduce you two?" Gordie said. "Emerald—"

"I know who she is. I hear a lot about her, don't I?" Emerald's smile was as resolute as ever. "I know you two have some business matters to talk over . . ." She leaned close to

Gordie and chucked him under the chin. Amanda couldn't help
her grin. The woman could get away with what she, Amanda,
wouldn't dare try—beard gruff Gordie in his own den.

"I hope she doesn't think I'm trying to steal you," Amanda
said. "Heaven forbid! All I want to do is talk to you about the
job as regional manager, then get out of here."

"Yeah, yeah." Gordie's face was red from poker excitement
and too many Southern Comforts. "Let's have a drink and get
something to eat. I paid for half a ton of food and I haven't
even had a slice of bologna yet."

She trailed after him while he filled his plate and played
host, both with Roman enthusiasm. He stuffed down hors
d'oeuvres by the handful, pinched behinds, slapped shoulders,
and bellowed greetings at hog-caller volume. After forty-five
minutes of this, she grabbed his sleeve. "Gordon, will you
talk to me now? I have a baby sitter. This is costing me."

He led her to an antique phone booth installed "by the faggot
who decorated this place." The booth was large, but not large
enough so far as Amanda was concerned. She wouldn't let him
close the door. In the semi-quiet he explained he had to make
a few more business decisions to open the way to creating the
regional manager position. She was too close to his sweaty
bulk. He was doing a bad job of keeping his eyes off her chest.
Yeah, the job was real. He wasn't putting her on. After tonight
she was the favorite to get it.

"Is that a promise?"

"Things got to happen with the franchises yet."

"But not 'things' between us, right, Gordon?"

He looked down at her, eyes mirroring some emotion south
of tenderness and north of lust. "If you say so, Mandy."

She spun away from him. He held her shoulder lightly. "Stay
here tonight! In the morning you got the job."

"Gordon!"

"I still remember your tit sticking out of your uniform—"

"No! No! No! Now let me go!"

He dropped her wrist and made a sad clown face. He stood
in the mansion's salon-sized entryway and blew a kiss after
her.

She hurried to her car feeling exploited and drained. She drove too fast going home. She was late. Jilly, capitalist in training, charged double after midnight, and kept accounts as scrupulously as Shylock.

The girl was at her post, but asleep on the love seat. She woke quickly. "Everything OK?" Amanda said.

"No problems." She rubbed her eyes. "There was a phone call for you. About a half an hour after you left."

"Who was it?"

"Didn't say. Weird far-away voice."

Amanda felt her fingers tighten on her purse. "Saying what?"

"He—if it was a he—didn't make much sense. He wanted to tell you when your turn was coming 'to join the other red-heads.'"

# CHAPTER
## ✥ 5 ✥

Amanda went through her Sunday routine of shopping, cleaning, and homework badly distracted. Floyd hadn't taken her warning seriously. Now the question was how seriously to take him. Had he murdered Felicity? Or was she stringing together too many coincidences? She needed to know more. The problem was how to manage that. Justin sensed her mood and asked her what was wrong. Ten was too young to share this kind of problem. "Just relationships," she said.

In the evening, her attention was further invaded by last night's disappointment: the ongoing Gordie problem and her future at Muncher's—or anywhere else. Seeing Hunt with that dishy, rude blonde was also some kind of disappointment. Only Amanda Walker could turn down dates with the man—then be skewed by seeing him with someone else.

The time had come for another of Justin's clarinet practice sessions. He was in the grade school band at her insistence. He hadn't shown her or Pop-Up's love of music. She was afraid he took after Ned, whose ear was tin and taste terrible. Nonetheless, she insisted; perhaps the seed would sprout. The band's final concert was coming up Friday. She was determined that he not be the worst clarinetist. Somewhere between her seventh and eighth "that's a *flat*, Justin," she got an idea that later sent her to bed with a good feeling about getting a handle on Floyd Philman.

Monday morning she went to the yellow pages, flipping to the psychiatrist section. There she found the address and phone of Dr. Herman Moodleman, the man she remembered Floyd saying treated him. She phoned and told the receptionist she wanted to speak with the doctor.

"Do you require Dr. Moodleman's professional services?" she asked.

"No. I just want some information. It won't take very long."

"Information about what, may I ask?"

"About one of his patients. I want to know if—"

"I'm sure you know the doctor can't break his promise of confidentiality. If this is something personal—"

"Oh, no. Nothing like that." I just want to know if one of his patients murders redheads and chops them up with an axe.

"I'll have to check with the doctor. He's out at the moment."

She called back two hours later. The doctor would see her briefly, if she could come in around noon Tuesday.

Amanda skipped Tuesday lunch and hurried over to the professional building on South Main Street. The elevator played "Hey Jude" for strings.

The receptionist, Ms. Gladby, was heavily made-up and somehow ageless. The small waiting room was decorated in don't-upset-me colors and art.

Dr. Moodleman was short and bald. His remaining hair's fringes stuck out above his ears in an unintentional punk look. Thick glasses turned his eyes into small brown marbles. He beckoned her forward into his office. He closed the door and told her to sit in "the soft chair."

She had given some thought as to how to present herself and her problem. She decided the best way was to avoid using Floyd's name at first. Speaking as concisely as she could, she told him about answering the ad, meeting "a man," receiving the phone threats, and finding out that Felicity had answered the same ad before she was murdered and mutilated. While she wasn't sure at all, it was possible she was going to be the murderer's next victim.

As she talked, Dr. Moodleman produced a briar pipe with a bowl wide as a volcano mouth. He gouged at it with a silvery tool, working above a massive ceramic ashtray advertising some kind of mind-mending drug. She looked in vain for some reaction from the man. He only sat and scraped while she described her growing anxieties. In the end that silence wore her down. She found her voice trailing down, like one of Justin's spring-powered toys. "To . . . make a long story short, he told me he was one of your patients, Doctor."

His hairy eyebrows rose.

"His name is Floyd Hooper Philman," she blurted.

"I see." The doctor found his tobacco pouch and filled the pipe bowl, jamming the load in vigorously with a spade-sized thumb. "Why have you come to me?"

"Why? Because I think Floyd Philman might be a murderer and he's going to murder me!"

"Would you like to talk further about all this, the threats, your life, your son, your job?"

Amanda sat up, startled. "No, I wouldn't. I came here to find out if you think Floyd Philman murdered——"

"Ms. Walker." The doctor shook his heavy head. "I can't discuss my patient with you." He leaned back in his chair, held his pipe high and looked up at it, as though it were an Olympic flag. "What I can say is that before me I see and hear an individual with considerable anxiety who is experiencing difficulties with life that might well be discussed."

"I didn't come here to talk about me," she said, her voice rising. "I came to talk about Floyd Philman!"

"Your suspicions about Floyd are better handled through other means, such as the police. We don't deal with right and wrong here so much as inner doings." His smile was disarming. "The *eau de vie* of human existence, we might say."

Amanda spoke slowly and distinctly, her temper smoldering. "I want to know if you think Floyd Philman is the kind of man who would murder women and chop them up."

His enigmatic smile was like a slap at her face.

"I can't believe this! Can't you say yes or no, for heaven's sake?"

He shrugged. "Not really."

"Dr. Moodleman—"

"I suggest you pause a moment and look at yourself, Ms. Walker. Rather, look *into* yourself. I sense in you some strong, counterproductive ways of thinking that might benefit—"

"Dr. Moodleman, I am normal! I just happen to be going through some tough times."

The doctor rose from his chair. "Ms. Gladby will discuss my fees and available appointments—"

"I don't need a shrink!" Amanda jumped up and hurried out before the doctor could open the door for her. She kept on going till she was out on the street. She found herself panting and shaken. Worse than all that getting her nothing, she felt intruded upon. That man with his pipe and stone face! What did he see about her that wasn't right? What narrow, dark corridors in her mind did he intuitively map? Overall, she felt a creeping disgust at the doctor, making his living poking around where he didn't belong, playing God. No one had ever done a good job at *that*.

As the afternoon went on she realized how badly Dr. Moodleman had shaken her. Stay out of my head! It's mine. I'll deal with it. She took deep breaths and closed her eyes. She knew things weren't quite right in her mind. She didn't have to go very far back to hear Hunt Grayson's suggestions that she needed to be more daring and innovative about living her life. And she agreed. The problem was she couldn't manage it right then. Bad enough all that, but she had learned nothing about Floyd Philman either.

She had to do more. She wasn't about to just sit back and wait for more phone calls—or worse.

After work she called Justin at the apartment and told him to practice his clarinet while she ran an errand. On her way to the *Reformer* offices, she told herself she should have made this visit already. It made such perfect sense. Climbing to the second floor of the remodeled frame dinosaur that housed the paper, she passed staff members leaving for the day. A lettered sign on the wall led her to Classifieds. Now she was going to get to the bottom of some things!

# PERSONAL

Another sign pointed her to a small office with a counter. Beatles and Michael Jackson posters shared wall space with calendars and production schedules. Two personal computers' lines snaked away toward some central processor. There was only one woman in the office. When she looked up, Amanda realized she knew her. It was Emerald Roscheski, the date who had slyly teased Gordie Locker at his party. At sight of Amanda the wholesome smile once again set itself into her pretty face—and remained there. She got up and came over to the counter. Today, she wore a pleated skirt and a sweater. All she needed was a letter on her chest to win the nearest cheerleading competition.

"It's a surprise to see you again, Emerald," she said. "Small world and all that. I meant to ask you the other night, but didn't get the chance: how did you meet Gordie?"

Emerald shrugged. "Rather uneventful encounter, really. I was having a burger in one of his restaurants about four months ago. I guess I appealed to him."

"It's every man's dream to debauch the girl next door," Amanda said.

The grin faded and Emerald's face took on an appraising look. Some respect in it as well. "I work hard at how I look, Amanda."

"We all do." Amanda studied the wholesome face, pondered what lay behind it. After a moment she said, "So you met Gordie . . ."

"He was making his rounds, I guess. While I was eating, he came out from behind the counter, gave me my money back, and asked me to go out. I've been more or less his steady since. I like the arrangement. I'm sure you understand." This last was pronounced with emphasis and a raised eyebrow.

Amanda lifted palms in a gesture of indifference. "Sure. Fine."

"You came here to talk about Gordon, right?" she said.

Amanda shook her head. "Wrong. I want to talk to someone about a personal ad I answered."

Emerald twisted a strand of dyed blonde hair around her finger. Her fingernails were expertly shaped, without lacquer.

"Oh, is that so?" She found her purse and pulled out a stick of Trident. Amanda declined a stick. "Mind if I ask you something?" Emerald said.

"What?"

"What's between you and Gordon?"

"As far as I'm concerned, nothing at all."

"That's hard to believe," Emerald said. "I say that because I've spent a lot of time in his company. We've been close. I'm sure you understand. We talk. He's really not as bad a conversationalist as you might think."

"You must bring out the best in him."

"I hope I do. I can't help but notice he has guts, money, cars, houses, and money to burn."

"Emerald, I didn't come here to talk about Gordie Locker and you and me. I came to talk—"

"Well, you talk to me about what I want, then I'll talk to you about what you want. Fair enough?" She worked her gum. She managed to look seventeen, though Amanda knew she had to be in her late twenties.

Gordie Locker again! Like spring pollen, he seemed to be everywhere in her life—unwanted, unbidden, and irritating. She sighed. "OK, Emerald, what about Gordie Locker?"

"What do you want from him?"

"I want a steady job and a chance to be considered for the regional manager slot he's created."

Emerald's chuckle was robust. Even her suspicious frown carried an earnest charm. "You can't be that straight, Amanda. Come on! I'm not as naive as I look. Why's Gordie always talking about you? Why's every fourth sentence between him and me have *your* name in it?"

"I didn't know it did. If it does, then that's him. I've tried not to encourage him. To be honest, he once made a scary pass at me. Every once in a while in his eyes I see—"

"He's rough, isn't he?" Emerald giggled. "I love it! I love muscle, a few love taps, hair on the chest. I can't stand a wimp."

"Emerald . . ." Amanda put both hands palms up on the counter. "Look, I'm not emotionally involved with Gordon.

We have a working business relationship: we need each other. Socially, I just want him to leave me alone. It's like walking a tightrope for me. I don't want to fall off.''

Emerald nodded, a smile curving her bow-shaped mouth. "So you're a tease. That's it!''

"Emerald, I do *not* want Gordon Locker in my love life.''

"Then why does he keep talking about you? Why does he keep comparing me with you all the time?''

Amanda swallowed. She was silent a moment, mulling over this fresh marker on the road of her boss's obsession. "I'm sorry he does. I'm sorry you allow it. Please understand, Emerald, I'm doing nothing to encourage him, and all I can to *dis*courage him.''

Emerald's eyes narrowed. "I think you're a smart one. I think you're playing for that simple little band of gold. I saw you telling him how to play his cards—''

"That wasn't what you think. It was—''

"I'm going to make a polite request. Please stay away from him. I want him.''

"Take him! Maybe then he'll leave me alone.''

"I'll try. You can bet on that.'' Emerald paced away, working on her gum. She turned and shrugged. "Well, that takes care of my agenda. What about yours, Amanda? What's this about a personal?''

She told her about answering Floyd's ad and the calls she was getting. She skipped the part about Felicity having been murdered. "He runs the same ad every week. I want to know who else besides me has answered over the weeks.''

Emerald held out her palms, as though to stop Amanda's words. "I can't do that. No way. All personals are just that— personal. It's all tied in with what's legal and what the paper's allowed to do. I can't give you—or anyone else—that kind of information. I can't give you names, addresses, phone numbers. I can't give you *anything* or I'm out of a job and the paper gets sued for heavy money.''

"Are you serious?''

"Very much so, Amanda. You have problems with this Floyd guy, go to the police. You can't find out anything here.''

PERSONAL

Amanda argued on, without success. Legal implications or not, Emerald had her own reasons not to help her. Ill-founded jealousy was one of them. She and Gordie were a perfect match. Her girl-next-door charm, his uncultured bravado. Too bad he didn't fully appreciate that reality. There weren't many women who read with pounding hearts from the *Rough-and-Ready Lovers' Manual*.

She was about to turn away, defeated, when she got an idea. "Emerald, I want to put in an ad of my own."

"Pencils and blanks on the table over there."

She sat down and in her most careful block letters wrote:

### ATTENTION REDHEADS!

*Did you answer the ad "Redheads wanted for coffee and conversation"? If so, you could be in serious physical danger. This is NOT a joke. Call 254-7647 to hear a worried woman's suspicions.*

The phone number was Pop-Up's. He was the perfect collaborator. Though largely housebound, but still in possession of his wits, he could be counted on to get callers' names and numbers right. To his questions on the phone when she told him how he could help her, she said "some creep" was bothering her and she wanted to know if he was bothering anyone else. She heard skepticism in his voice, but he agreed to help. "Nothing will happen till Thursday," she told him.

During her lunch hour on Wednesday she took both Dr. Moodleman's and Emerald's advice. She went to the law. She wandered tentatively into Hartford police headquarters. She wasn't prepared for the noise and commotion within the public area. Officers and citizens were shouting at each other over details of crimes and arrest. Attorneys were getting their verbal licks in, too. She was unintentionally shouldered aside by a large black man whose unoriginal profanity nonetheless made her ears burn. Rapid-fire Spanish from all directions failed to drown out the ringing telephones. The air smelled of sweat and disinfectant.

Bulletproof plastic guarded the two officers in front of whom lines stretched out toward the doors. She looked at her watch. She didn't have a lot of time to waste. Gordie insisted his managers keep precisely to their schedules. A female officer walked by. Amanda tried to get her attention, but the papers in her hand seemed hypnotic in their importance. She rushed on to an office door where she was buzzed through.

Amanda got in the shorter of the two lines. It moved with glacial speed. A bent man with a stick was mumbling and cursing far ahead of her. She touched the suit-jacketed shoulder of the man in front of her. "Why is it so confused here?"

He turned and looked down at her. He wore metal-rimmed glasses and had a legal look. "Drugs, of course. Where have you been?"

The commotion made more sense now. The line crept ahead. To the sides angry men were brought in wearing handcuffs and murderous expressions. One wiry Latino momentarily broke free, but was quickly subdued with precise, controlled violence. Metal rims turned back to her. "They ought to legalize it all. Let the spicks and niggers fry their goddamn brains and leave the rest of us alone."

Amanda looked back at him stonily. Her days on the road with Ned had taught her simple lessons that made racial stereotyping a dangerous, illogical practice. With only a few minutes left in her lunch hour she finally came face to face with the sergeant. She blurted out a shortened version of her story. He frowned. "Are we talking telephone threats here, ma'am?"

"Well—partly, I guess. But there could have been—"

"You take those up with the phone company." He slid a preprinted piece of paper under the Plexiglas. "Call one of these numbers." He looked over Amanda's shoulder at the next citizen to be served.

"Don't you care that he might have broken into my apartment?"

"And stole your whistle?" He couldn't smother his grin.

"He could have murdered my friend!"

"Didn't you say that case is still open?"

64

Again she recalled Mr. Foster in his despair and frustration talking sarcastically about police work. "Well, yes—"

"Something more comes up, you let us know. Maybe talk to a detective. Next!"

She reluctantly stepped aside. Slightly dazed, she made her way through the crowd and out the front door. From a door marked Records came a thin, wrenlike woman with glasses and a spot of rouge on each cheek. They fell into step momentarily going down the concrete stairs. "I'm not impressed with you people," Amanda mumbled, half to herself. The woman glanced briefly at her, looked away, then back again. "We didn't take care of you, dearie?"

Amanda held up the telephone company numbers. "Somebody's calling threatening to kill me, so I'm supposed to report it—to SNETCO. I suppose the phone repair man's supposed to stop him from breaking into my apartment again."

The small woman hesitated. "I'm going to lunch. You want to join me? Maybe we can work on your problem." She held out her hand. "I'm Flo Lomus."

"You're a police officer?"

Flo laughed. "Me? No, I'm a records clerk."

Amanda thought of her Muncher's going managerless for more than an hour. Still, she had gotten so little from the police. "If we make it quick. I'm AWOL from my job."

Flo said she didn't usually get involved with the troubles by the ton that passed through headquarters's door. But she liked Amanda's looks. She reminded her of her daughter, dead in a head-on nearly ten years ago.

Over a salad, Amanda told her story. Flo listened through to the end in silence. "It could be something. But cops work with what is—there's plenty of that—instead of what could be." She inclined her petite head back toward her building. "You saw what's happening. It's like that every day."

"Flo, where does all that leave me?"

"If your phone friend does more than talk, you come back."

"What happens if I get the same treatment?"

"You probably won't. If you do, call me. Maybe I can do something." Flo patted Amanda's hand in encouragement. She tore a page from a small notebook and wrote down a phone number. "My line. If you need help, you call."

Speeding back to work, Amanda mumbled uneasily to herself. Aside from some personal concern from an unimportant figure clerk, she hadn't done well. What had she expected? Red-carpet treatment? What were her anxieties compared to a Hartford loaded with cocaine, crack, and heroin? Because of them, people were killing each other in carload lots. Where did that leave her, an ordinary citizen? Out in the cold. There was some kind of basic inequality there, but she wasn't in the mood to analyze it. Floyd was still very much her own problem.

She spent the next days trying to avoid answering her apartment phone. Her nerves couldn't bear another conversation with Floyd's distant, sighing voice. She was being foolish. Not talking to him wouldn't in any way affect his plans to harm her—if they were real. She told Justin to answer, guilt surging at using him as a buffer. "Find out who it is before you say if I'm here or not," she told him.

He screwed up his face in puzzlement. His features were inching toward manhood. Not much longer would she dare cut his hair herself, with the bowl and nail scissors. "What's happening, Ma? Bill collectors again?"

"Wise kid!" She smiled. "Just an awkward social situation."

He agreed to field the calls that week. The first one was from Pam, checking on her social life.

"It's really booming," Amanda said. "It's turned out that Floyd is a psychopath."

"You're joking, aren't you?"

"No joking. No ha-ha here." She filled Pam in on the details.

"Sounds like you're not really sure, Mandy. I'm hoping it's all coincidence and misunderstanding."

"I dunno. I'm one very nervous lady, I'll tell you."

"I thought you'd get better from the police. You *deserve* better."

"That I know."

Pam was sympathetic. "You have to keep me up to date. If there's anything you need, let me know. Please."

"Sure." Amanda felt the need to change the subject. "How are you and Bud doing."

"Super." Pam controlled her enthusiasm. "He took me to meet his mother. She didn't have either fangs or claws that I could see. I hope she liked me. Mandy, I have to go. Look, stay in touch about this Floyd stuff."

"Yeah." Amanda hung up slowly. Get thee behind me, envy.

The second call that Justin fielded came around dinner time that Wednesday evening. It twisted his face till her heart ached for him. Before he said the word, she knew who was on the line. "Dad," he whispered.

The agreement was, of course, that Ned wasn't to call. What had been between them was in the past. She had custody. He had never showed up in court, never got an attorney to help him work out visiting rights. His luck, never good, was running bad at that time. That meant he was broke and depressed. One more of a hundred ways that being a compulsive gambler cost him deeply. Visiting rights scarcely mattered. He became a wanderer, following fickle fortune from race track to horse parlor to Vegas, L.A., Atlantic City . . .

How long she had stuck with him! She had been younger then, more inclined to listen to his version of their life together than that whispered by her intuition. Then Justin was on the way. That held them together a while longer. She believed his promises—of a regular job for him, a house, stability, and prosperity for her. But they went right on sneaking out of motels while bats flapped and darted around the lights, going to soup kitchens with the bums and hitchhiking, their few possessions in plastic bags at their feet.

When things were tougher than routine he offhandedly suggested they stay with his stepsister, a shadowy figure featured in his unhappy childhood. Younger than he, and never called by name, she was a last resort to whom Amanda knew he never truly wanted to turn. "S-sister" lived by her wits somewhere in the Northeast. She changed jobs often, but got the breaks and prospered modestly. "She always said she'd take us in any time we needed it, for as long as we wanted." To herself,

Amanda wondered how bad things would have to get before he picked up the phone and called S-sister.

Things got plenty bad.

He never called her.

Amanda stood by her man, though. She was that far out of it. Often she wondered how long she would have, if ma hadn't died and left her the money—twenty-five thousand dollars. The dear woman had accumulated it over her whole working life, stashing a buck here, two bucks there, into 5 percent passbook savings accounts. Her will said it was for Amanda; Pop-Up could make it on his own. Amanda made it clear to Ned that the money was for investment in their future—the little white-shuttered house she had convinced herself she needed, the pickup truck he wanted. It was to buy them stability. Often he suggested, after the will was probated and the money in hand, that she give him a few thousand "to see how his luck was running." She refused. If anything she would invest the money, sit on it until they got settled.

To her surprise he found an investment banker. They were living in New Orleans then, far from the bright lights in a cottage crawling with roaches. Mr. Austin McDonald wore a double-breasted suit and gold-rimmed reading glasses. The surroundings failed to dampen his enthusiasm for the power of investment. His soft southern drawl painted images of the rewards of prudent money management. He spoke of "instruments," "mutuals," "cooperative partnerships." The money should come out of her bank account "to march forward with that of the legions of wise investors." Both she and Ned were impressed by Mr. McDonald's presentation. There was no question he was the man into whose hands they should assign their financial future.

After the money changed hands, Mr. McDonald wasn't seen again. To her dismay, Ned didn't have his phone number. When she called his bank, her fears rising like the Mississippi at the levees, she was told no such man worked for them. It seemed they had fallen into the hands of a confidence man. Shortly afterward, Ned temporarily left to handle "some important business in Miami." Even then she knew that meant a siege at the jai alai frontons. She scarcely paid any mind; she was frantic over the fate of her inheritance.

Quite by chance, while sightseeing in the French quarter with Justin in his backpack, she stopped for a cup of coffee and a beignet in a modest streetfront restaurant. Mr. McDonald was waiting tables. She cornered him and wouldn't leave him alone until she heard the whole story. He confessed to being a former confidence man down on his luck and courage. He didn't have what it took to run the old flimflams on the shrewd. Conning a naive housewife and mother on the other hand . . . Of course Ned had put him up to it. He had wanted to get his hands on the twenty-five thousand. In response to her pain and despair, Austin McDonald, who had got 10 percent of the money and had already squandered it, said not to worry. Ned was going to make her fortune betting a new system at jai alai.

Two weeks later Ned came home broke. Every penny of her inheritance was gone. She confronted him with all she knew. It was the only time he ever cried in her presence and didn't write off the latest disaster as just another run of bad luck. She went to pawn her diamond engagement ring and wedding band to raise the deposit the divorce attorney demanded. The pawnbroker swung the loupe up from his eye and said, "Drug on the market, these trinkets, *ma cher*. Drug on the market." He looked her over carefully. "Keep that hair clean—and be pickier next time. Two hundred dollars, and I'm a fool."

After the divorce she had seen Ned only four times, always briefly. She thought he appeared because he wanted to check up on her circumstances, see how well she was doing financially. Maybe he wanted to steal from her. He would do it, pawn the loot, and gamble the proceeds away. She was qualified to lecture at Families of Gamblers Anonymous. With each of his calls her innards twisted, as though bound with thick rope. How could anyone just walk away from a long-term relationship? The pain still surged through her, weaker with each encounter, like a shout amid mountains echoing down to stillness. Oh, it still hurt! She picked up the receiver as though it were a spoiled mackerel. "Yes, Ned?"

"How you doing, Mandy?" His tone was optimistic.

"Struggling along." She turned and saw Justin's eyes riveted on her face. "What can I do for you?"

"I'm in Boston. Thought I'd give you a call."

"I don't have much to say to you, Ned."

"Still at the restaurant?"

"Yeah." When had he last called? A year or more? "I'm the manager there. Did I tell you that?"

"Congratulations!"

Her stomach was starting to hurt. "What do you want, Ned? I'm really tired and—"

"How's the petty cash fund?" He tried a cheery laugh.

"The 'petty cash fund' is my whole budget!" She knew he wanted money! "You have a choice, Ned. Either I hang up or you talk to your son."

"Put Justin on."

She handed the boy the receiver and went into the bathroom, ran water, and waited. She wondered, knowing Ned, how he could afford to make the call. Freeloading somehow. He was expert at it. When she emerged, Justin was grinning at the wall. "How's your father?" she said.

"Great. He's right on the edge of landing a big deal." His face betrayed not the slightest cynicism. Ned Stanton was still a Pied Piper.

She swallowed the knot in her throat. "Is he coming to visit?" She held her breath.

"Didn't say so. I hope he does!"

Thursday came, and with it the publication of the latest edition of the *Reformer*. She rushed out at noon to the CVS and grabbed a copy. There was her ad! At work in the late afternoon she got a call from Pop-Up. "What the hell are you up to, Mandy? Some woman phoned wanting to know why and how she was in danger. I believe she was scared."

"You get her name and number?"

"Yeah, I did, but—"

"I'll explain when I find out more. I'm really not sure of anything right now, Pop-Up."

By Sunday night three women had called and left their numbers. Amanda looked at the sheet with her father's handwriting now gone shaky with his advancing illness. Connie Kwan, Grace O'Shea, and Jessica Morris. She called each, held off their questions, and arranged for them all to meet Monday night at Mortensen's restaurant on the Berlin Turnpike. There they could drink coffee and no one would bother them.

Amanda went early. Connie Kwan arrived first. She was an exotic creature. Born in Hawaii of Polynesian and Irish parents, she was almond eyed and willowy. Her hair was carrot colored, thick, and straight. She didn't want to wait for the others. "Is what's happening a secret? Don't I get a preview?"

"It'll just be a few minutes, Connie. I don't want to have to tell my story three times."

Connie wasn't very patient. She sipped Cokes and bopped, fingers tapping table and haunches churning on the booth seat. She was twenty-four going on sixteen.

Grace O'Shea joined them. She was buxom, hung with costume jewelry. "Yo, redheads!" she said, sliding into the booth. "What's going down?"

Amanda made the introductions. Grace nodded. Vivid freckles spotted her face and forearms. "So we're the 'coffee and conversation' kids, huh?"

"One more to come. Or at least one more that saw my ad, and bothered to get in touch," Amanda said.

"We could also call ourselves, 'female friends of Floyd,' " Grace said with a giggle. She grabbed a menu. "Hey, I'm gonna *eat!*"

Connie looked at her plaid-faced watch. "How long do we have to wait? And how come the funny talk about Floyd?"

"Hang on."

Grace ordered double fries and offered to share. She sipped coffee to ease down the starch. She had long fingers and wore rings on seven fingers and her thumbs. Only her left-hand ring finger was naked.

Ten more minutes passed before Jessica Morris appeared. A slender, elfin girl about twenty-two, she was very pretty. Her delicate features were drawn out, pale, and poreless as porcelain. Amanda guessed she was a model or an actress.

# PERSONAL

She blinked when she saw Amanda. "You look familiar. You're . . ."

"Ms. Muncher," Amanda said with a weary grin.

Jessica was instantly excited. "I'd like to talk to you about that, how you got that job, and about—"

"Sure. Later." She swung her gaze around to the others. "I answered the ad for coffee and conversation. I met Floyd. I didn't like him. He threatened me on our first date. Then I got a call." She took a deep breath. "It was Floyd. He said he was going to murder me."

Jessica stared. Grace's ring-filled hand froze, fry halfway to her mouth. Connie laughed. "Floyd? Come on, Amanda. That's not *Floyd*."

"Oh?" Amanda's voice was icy. "I found out that a red-headed friend of mine answered one of his ads a while back. She was murdered and cut to pieces. The police never found out who did it."

Everyone began to talk at once. Amanda sorted facts out as best she could. Connie had answered Floyd's ad six weeks ago, thought he was fine and went out with him twice afterward. Grace had shared a pot of coffee five weeks ago—and said that was enough. Lovely Jessica had been badly disappointed a month ago. "I don't know what I expected," Jessica said. "It wasn't a chance to talk about my sex life, I'll tell you."

"He tried that with me, too," Amanda said. Thinking back, she noted her date with Floyd had been two weeks and three days ago.

"Hey, so what?" Connie's Oriental features gave her outrageous grin a fey look. "I talked about mine. He talked about his. What, you pretended you don't do it? You ladies are so uptight!"

"To each his own," Grace said. "I thought he was a creep. Grossarama!"

"Did he threaten any of you, in person or by phone?" Amanda asked.

The other three women looked blankly at her and shook their heads. "That's why you put the 'danger' stuff in your ad?" Jessica said.

72

"That and because my friend was killed. And he broke into my apartment, too."

Connie waved her hand. "I think you're jumping to conclusions, Amanda. All that doesn't sound like Floyd to me." She shrugged. "He hasn't bothered any of us. I think somebody else is bothering you. And I think somebody killing your friend—well, that was some kind of distant coincidence." She got up. "Me? I think I'm out of here. I got things to do."

"Wait till we trade phone numbers and addresses," Grace said. "I'm not at all sure I like what might be going down."

Jessica insisted they all touch hands. "Sisterhood in all this, all right? Let's stick together, help each other, be there if we're needed."

"Oh, boy!" Connie was the first to pull her hand out of the pack. "What is this? College stuff? I'm on my way. I got a big day coming up. Need all the sleep I can get."

After she left, Grace, Jessica, and Amanda talked for a while. They promised to communicate anything unusual that might relate to Floyd or anyone else threatening them. Grace's buxom vitality had faded during their conversation. Her fries remained half eaten. Her nervous, ringed fingers picked at her clothes and hair. "I didn't like Floyd either, guys. He scared me for some reason. I think he's dangerous. Let's all be careful."

Before Jessica would let Amanda go, she had to hear about the Ms. Muncher campaign and how she got the job. She was getting started as a model, but needed more connections. Amanda gave her both Gordie's and Hunt Grayson's address and phone number. She didn't bother with character profiles. If the lovely young woman got in touch with them, she'd notice the contrast soon enough.

That night she crawled into bed with mixed feelings. She had hoped meeting Floyd's other *Reformer* dates would uncover a consistent pattern of threats and danger. She badly wanted some certainty about what was happening. That would allow her to go back to the police with her suspicions. Instead, no one else had been threatened. And crazy Connie had gone out with Floyd a few times—with no ill effects. She tossed and turned, abusing her pillows with fists and elbows. After a long while she fell asleep.

The phone blasted her awake. Damn! Her first thought was that she didn't want Justin, a light sleeper, awakened. She rolled out of bed and hurried to the phone. Not until she reached out toward it did her sleep-sodden mind remind her that it might be . . .

"This is Amanda Walker, and it's 3:30 A.M."

"I've done a good night's work." It was the voice! Sighing, sexless, distant.

"Listen to me." Her throat was tight. "I know who you are. You're Floyd Hooper Philman, aren't you?"

Hesitation. "Yes. You're a smart lady, Amanda Walker." She sensed surprise in the sighing tones.

"I've been to the police about you. If you don't quit bothering me, I'm going to go back and—"

"I followed you tonight."

Amanda swallowed. Breath rushed through her nostrils.

"I saw who you were meeting. I know you figured out those redheads all had been my dates. Like I said: you're smart."

"I'm not going to talk to you like this!" Her heart pounded. He had followed her! He wasn't in the distance, where she had tried to keep him. He was circling closer to the heart of her life.

"I called you the other night," he said. "To tell you when your time was going to come. The time when you'll join the other redheads."

"I'm going to hang up!"

"If you want a hint, call Connie Kwan right now."

"No—"

"Do. Then you'll figure out how long you have. Because, like I said, you're a smart woman, Amanda Walker."

She slammed down the phone. Then she disconnected the jack from the instrument. She stood panting in the darkness. She walked to the window and looked down to the street. How long she stared at the shadowy scene she wasn't sure. Sometime later she turned and reconnected the phone. She went to her purse and pulled out the sheet bearing the three other redheads' addresses and phone numbers.

Understanding how feisty Connie was, she knew she'd have to endure her irritation and contempt after awakening her. Nonetheless, they had all promised to communicate threats and danger. She pushed the keys with an unsteady finger. She had to try three times before she made a clean dial. She stood by the yellow chest listening to the rhythmic ring throbbing in her still apartment. So . . . pick up the phone, Connie. She should be there, getting the sleep she said she needed.

She didn't answer.

# CHAPTER

## ❧ 6 ❧

Amanda went back to bed, but knew it was a waste of time. She wouldn't be doing any more sleeping. She remembered Connie saying she was going home to bed. Of course she could have changed her mind. Anything could have happened to change that plan. Among them might be . . .

She got up and put on her robe. In the kitchen she turned on the radio, curled the dial down to the stations where there was news on the hour and half-hour. She dragged the TV out where she could see it and turned it on, too, using her remote control to flip past test patterns, looking for a live station. There she sat like a berserk media freak changing channels and stations, looking for local news. The first broadcasts were at 5:00 A.M. She heard yesterday's news. Svelte young ladies in leotards performed impossible contortions with tireless smiles. The live media organism hadn't yet stirred and risen.

She took her shower and woke Justin. She made coffee, badly distracted. She spilled the instant over the edge of the cup, scraped it off the counter and back into the jar. She knew her imagination was out of control. She was overreacting as well. At 6:00 there was some news of local political activity, doings of the legislature and the courts. Sports, of course. A beat B. But nothing like the worst she expected. At breakfast she turned off the TV and left the radio alone. Sunshine drove off her morbidity. She made sure Justin had lunch money and readied him for the school bus. Then he was allowed to watch cartoons. She got into her uniform with enough time for another cup of coffee and a chance to stand on the stoop with her eyes closed, feeling Tuesday morning sunshine on her face.

The VW's radio worked when it pleased. It hadn't been on in three weeks. She slammed the dash at a red light. A snarl of static and the old Bosch was alive. She was nearly at the restaurant when yet another news broadcast started. She scarcely listened; she could nearly recite the ball scores from memory by now. Someone behind her blew his horn. She turned, distracted. By the time she tuned back in she heard only ". . . victim found in a vacant lot in East Hartford. Despite the mutilation, police were able to identify her. Her name was being withheld pending notification of next of kin. In other news . . ."

She pulled partway over and stared at the radio, body trembling with the thrusts of her heart. Behind her another horn blasted. She had blocked traffic. She stalled the car trying to get it going. She drove to the restaurant where she had forbidden radios. Ghetto blasters and Walkmen had appeared one morning as suddenly as Viet Cong at night. She had had no choice. She phoned the radio station and asked for the news department. All the lines were busy. That morning she scarcely paid attention to her duties. The mutilated woman who might be Connie Kwan seized her imagination and attention as completely as a horror movie ghost. She phoned police headquarters in search of information. They weren't giving out any, at least not to her.

At noon she hurried out to her car to turn on the radio. Dammit! It had stopped working again. She hurried to a dress shop down the street. She knew a woman who worked there, who let her listen to her portable. By then she had missed the noon news. Now the air was filled with teen music and strident DJ patter.

After work she bought a *Courant*, forgetting it was published in the morning. There was no news of a murder. She went home to Justin, who saw through her distraction like a CAT scan machine. She settled him down with a half truth: one of her friends might have been hurt. She paced before TV news, learned about doings everywhere from Akron to Zambia. How the hell in this media age did you get any *real* news?

The phone rang. She started. Lord, her nerves! She stared at the instrument as though it were a roach. "Want me to get it?" Justin said, remembering the scenario from earlier evenings.

"No." She snatched it up. "This is Amanda Walker speaking."

"Amanda, this is Grace!" Amanda's memory framed Grace O'Shea in the booths at Mortensen's restaurant, her plate heaped with fries. "Did you hear what happened? Connie Kwan was murdered!"

Amanda closed her eyes. Her emotions heaved like roped beasts. "Oh . . . God."

"I saw her picture on the news. It was her!"

Amanda covered the receiver. "Justin, could you go to your room for a minute? This is super confidential." She was aware her voice trembled. So was he.

"Grace, what are we going to do?"

"You know what we're going to do. You, I, and Jessica go to the police."

They made their plans: tomorrow morning. Amanda called Scotty, the second-shift manager, and asked if he'd switch with her. He said he would. Her thanks were nearly hysterical. No one answered at Jessica's number. They'd have to go without her if they couldn't get her later.

Thoughts of Floyd Philman filled her mind all through the rest of the evening. She managed to hold it together long enough to get through the end-of-day rituals with Justin that finished with him in bed. Then she settled at the kitchen table, energy sapped, fear beginning to gnaw at her. Floyd had killed Felicity and now Connie. On the phone he had said to call Connie Kwan for a hint about how long she had before "she joined the other redheads." Amanda had kept Felicity's ad clipping. She got it out and studied the date. Her tropical fish–loving father had said she had died about the middle of March. She noted the date her friend had penciled on the ad. February second. About six weeks before her death and mutilation. She turned her memory back to her evening with the other redheads. What had Connie said about the ad? Remember, Amanda . . . She wasn't sure, but she thought the woman had said six weeks ago. She'd have to remember to tell the police that. She refused to entertain the six-week period in relation to herself. Floyd would be in police custody long before her six weeks were up. She used her memory and did a little addition. She had met Floyd two weeks and four—almost five—days ago. Well, by tomorrow night he would be talking to the police.

She suffered another terrible night's sleep, six hours of tossing and two of uneasy slumber just before dawn. The mirror showed all. The lines of age—"experience," one of her friends preferred to call them—were setting in there, there, and . . . *there*. Early warning views of a fifty-year-old Amanda. Nothing like stress and insufficient sleep to bring out the worst in a woman's face.

She met Grace on the front steps of police headquarters. Grace wore sneakers and jeans. Her nine rings shined in bright sunlight that made her look a little more worn than the kinder neon at Mortensen's. She added five years to her guess of the younger woman's age. "I do *not* like this!" Grace said. "I have never before looked forward to seeing a cop."

The public areas were relatively quiet. Drug types must sleep in, Amanda thought. The black sergeant was patient and helpful. If they would have a seat, he'd try to find someone from homicide to talk to them.

While they waited, Amanda saw a familiar face, Flo Lomus, the sympathetic records clerk. With her was a slender man in trousers and rolled shirt sleeves. He carried a tape recorder and a notebook. "Flo, hi!" she said.

Flo introduced her companion. "This is Evan Dent. He's a crime reporter for the *Courant*."

Evan chuckled. "That's a bit exaggerated. I cover police headquarters now and then." He wore horn-rimmed glasses that did something neat to the shape of his nose. He looked smart. Amanda guessed he was about forty from the thinning hair; his face was young, virtually unlined.

"Nice to meet you," he said and seemed to mean it.

"I hope you're having better luck than last time, Amanda," Flo said. "Is it more of the same?"

Amanda nodded. "Trouble."

"For sure," Grace said.

"Anything that would interest the *Courant?*" Evan said.

The two younger women exchanged glances. "We better talk to the cops first," Grace said. Her gaze lingered on Evan an extra, meaningful moment. He seemed oblivious. "Well, good luck," he said.

When they were alone, Grace turned to Amanda. "Yum!" she said. No translation necessary.

An officer arrived and led them back into a warren of offices. "Detective McMahon will see you," he said. The detective had a small office with one grimy window. In it, an air conditioner coughed and throbbed. McMahon was in his late thirties, a thin, pale man whose sagging face had been dragged down by the daily drain of his duties. As they introduced themselves, his deep gray eyes hung on Amanda's face a moment while a tiny frown passed over his brow like a shadow.

"Do I know you?" Amanda said.

He shook his head curtly. He offered them seats. He held thin arms out like a pleading preacher. "Let's hear it, ladies," he said.

Words poured from Amanda in a rush. She understood now the stressed state of her nerves. Grace was equally upset, only not as vocal. She folded and unfolded her ring-laden hands. They had barely launched their narrative when McMahon used his intercom to summon a stenographer. When they finished talking about the ad, Floyd Philman, the phone calls, and the murders, he leaned back in his old heavy wooden chair and put hands behind head. "Could be something," he said.

"*Could* be?" Amanda squawked.

"Just like a cop," Grace muttered.

"Hey, ladies, there's plenty to look into. Don't get excited."

"Why don't you just arrest that creep Philman?" Grace said. "I mean, why screw around?"

McMahon dismissed the stenographer. "We'll talk to him," he said noncommittally. He pointed toward a hot plate in the corner. "Want some coffee?"

"I've got to be going," Grace said. "Mandy's better at talking than I am."

The detective nodded. "We've got your address and phone number. You get any threats or funny business starts, you call me or 911."

"Yeah." Amanda understood now how difficult it had been for Grace to make the trip. She was uncomfortable around the law. She gathered up her purse and made for the door.

Amanda poured coffee into a Styrofoam cup and sat back down. "If you don't mind me saying, you don't seem very excited about our practically solving Connie Kwan's murder— never mind Felicity Foster's that I know you've gotten nowhere with."

The detective stirred heavy sugar into his ceramic cup. Amanda read its message: Jesus Is King. "Couple reasons for that. First is I've seen a lot of murders in the City of Hartford. Second thing is that crimes aren't always what they seem." He paused and studied Amanda's face, much as when they had first met. "Nor are victims or witnesses."

"What does that mean?"

"From what you've told me I'd say you were a conservative, respectable woman being threatened by a psychopath who advertises for victims."

"And that's precisely what—"

"And I'd agree if another me hadn't been in a bar down on the Cape a couple summers ago. The Catamaran, I think they called it. It was wet T-shirt night . . ."

"Oh, no . . ." He had watched her and Felicity strutting drunk, soaked, and revealed. "That wasn't really me, Detective McMahon."

He nodded. "That wasn't really me watching you, either." He shrugged and smiled thinly. "You see, as I said, nothing is what it seems."

She didn't grasp his meaning. He questioned her in detail about what had happened. She told him everything from the moment she had answered the ad. It was clear he knew his job. If his personality wasn't to her taste, at least he seemed to want to help her. When he finished, she had no heart for small talk. Conversation faltered. She made excuses and reached for her purse. He came around the desk and put his arm over her shoulder in a fatherly way. "We'll start the ball rolling, best we can," he said. "You be careful. Hear?" She nodded. He walked her out. In the public area, Evan Dent came up to them, his reporter's instinct sensing a story. "The other redhead wouldn't tell me what's up, Tommy. Whatever it is, I want to write it."

The detective shook his head. "Not yet. We've just started on this one, Dent."

"Hey—"

"You heard the word, guy. We got nothing yet. You write something now, the right people are maybe spooked and we never find them. Later, you'll hear it all. Then you can jump on your word-processing pony. Got it?"

Evan frowned, a curious sight on his nearly lineless face. "Whatever."

The detective turned to Amanda. He smiled encouragingly. "Same goes for you as for Grace. Any funny business, let us know." He walked off with an encouraging wave.

She turned to Evan. "He's hard for me to talk to," she said.

He chuckled. "It just seems so. That's his professional game face. Don't be put off. He's a good cop." They walked together toward the main entrance. "Flo told me about him. I've only been with the paper a couple years. She's filled me in years back. She knows police headquarters inside and out." He adjusted his horn-rimmed glasses. "I'd call her a gossip, except that she seems to know precisely when to talk and when not to."

"So what did she tell you about Detective Tommy McMahon?" They walked out into the sunlight. She looked at her watch. She had time to invite him for a cup of coffee. He said he had to cover another story, but would take a few minutes . . .

Flo had told him there was a time at Hartford police headquarters when everyone was overworked. Drug troubles were just beginning to break big. Some officers and a few patrolmen were discovered to be on the drug take. There was a scandal and much publicity. Right about then Tommy McMahon burned out. His collapse took the form of not being able to make the distinction between criminals and the honest, except on the most superficial basis. To him, everyone seemed corrupt, doomed, without principles. The lines between good and evil became nonexistent in that frame of mind—one he could not shake. Tortured and depressed, he talked his feelings over with his wife and decided to quit law enforcement.

Through an accidental encounter with an evangelist he not only accepted Jesus as his personal savior, becoming a born-again Christian, but resurrected his courage to dare to distinguish the wicked from the good. It returned, Flo reported, "in better shape than when he retired it." Evan reached over and touched Amanda's hand lightly. "I mean he doesn't like sin or sinners. A good thing in a cop. So what he's not much for small talk?"

He walked her to her VW. His encouragement fell on barren soil. She couldn't help but feel that the detective saw her only as a drenched amateur exotic dancer parading lewdly for the masses. She guessed why no big push had ever been mounted to solve Felicity's murder. What was she in his eyes but another bimbo? Of all people, why did *he* have to be in the Catamaran that night? Now she understood what he meant by saying it was not really he who was there. It was he before transformation into a hard-eyed professional out to crush evildoers. All she dared hope for was that his compassion was still in place, and that his encouragement of her was real and heartfelt.

"I've told you some things, Amanda," Evan said. "Now tell me something. What's up between you and law enforcement that it wasn't time for me to hear?"

She hesitated. He had been a friend. Yet, his pen had the power to send Floyd Philman flying out of state. In which case he would forever remain a threat to her. She started several sentences, but didn't finish any.

"I don't want chapter and verse. Just a hint—strictly not for publication. What did you and Grace talk to the law about?"

"Murder," she said.

At work she tried again to reach Jessica, the third redhead she had met at Mortensen's restaurant. She recalled her sweet, elfin face. This time Jessica answered. Amanda blurted out the story of Connie's death and her visit to the police. Jessica made tiny bleating noises. Amanda imagined her delicate features paling, long slender fingers clutching the phone as hers had. "Why don't they arrest Floyd right now?" she asked Amanda.

"They're going to talk to him, Jess. And when they do they'll find out what he's up to."

"I don't like this! And this stuff about him killing women six weeks after he meets them. It's all sicko. *It scares me a lot!*" She was nearly shrieking.

"Don't worry about it. He'll be in jail before either your or my six weeks are up. I'm going to stay in close touch with Detective McMahon. I'll keep you up to date. He might want to talk to you."

She chatted on a while, trying to calm the younger woman. And to some degree restore her own nerves. There was something comforting about having the police on one's side. Jessica thanked her for having given her Hunt Grayson's name earlier. She had called him, mentioned knowing Amanda, and was able to make an appointment to talk to him about furthering her modeling career. "It is the best thing that's happened to me in a long time. If only Floyd—"

"The police will take care of him. Don't you worry."

The next day she called Detective McMahon to find out what had happened. She was disappointed to hear he hadn't yet brought Floyd in for questioning. "Got to do our homework first, Ms. Walker." His tone of voice was less enthusiastic than she remembered. "First thing we do is check on the people filing the complaint. That's you and Grace. You know Grace, also known as Foxy, Cheri Red, and Red Storm Rising?''

"I don't understand you."

"We checked on you. You manage a Muncher's franchise, have a kid in school, live at—''

"I know about myself, Detective McMahon. What about Grace?''

"She has a record. Not a long one. But she's got one."

"What did she do?'' Amanda held her breath.

"She's a part-time call girl."

Oh, no! She felt somehow betrayed. She remembered what Evan Dent had said about the detective's religious rebirth. "I— this isn't going to make any difference in how you treat this case, is it?''

"I know you're both more than wet T-shirt tootsies and whores.''

"We certainly are! Will you answer my question? Is this going to make any difference—''

"We're all professionals down here,'' he said. He chuckled with some of his old warmth. "I'll admit, Ms. Walker, you two have proved to be a bit of a surprise, shall we say. Even for this cop, who figures he's seen it all.''

She wasn't calmed by his gentle teasing. "When are you going to talk to Floyd Philman, Detective McMahon?''

"When the time comes." His voice was encouraging. "But you have to trust us to decide when that is.''

Amanda hung up and pressed palms to the sides of her head. Grace, a part-time call girl . . . McMahon at the Catamaran, beholding her clearly outlined breasts. All that didn't *seem* to be interfering with police efforts, but what terrible luck! Ned had a phrase she had heard all too often through the long downward spiral of their marriage: "We're playing against a stacked deck here.'' The deck was stacked all right—against her.

She felt the need to talk to someone about her problems. Evan was a good possibility. He was sympathetic and street-wise. Yet . . . she didn't dare. If he wrote a story about red-heads being murdered, based on an interview with her,

McMahon would be in a rage. What professional sympathy he felt for her would be destroyed. She well knew there were enough murders in the city for those concerning her to be shoved under the blotter till doomsday.

After work, she jumped into her VW and headed for Bloom-field and Insurance City Plus, Hunt Grayson's talent agency. In seeking him out she had a secret agenda, one so secret even she didn't perfectly understand it. She wanted to see him, sit beside him, and have him hear about her troubling situation. And how it seemed to be getting worse all the time. The thought that Chelsea, the dynamite blonde, might be with him made her feel faintly ill.

After waiting at Hunt's secretary's bidding, she did see a familiar face in his company. Not Chelsea, though. Leaving his office with him was Emerald Roscheski, Gordie's latest lady friend and *Reformer* staff member. The bleached blonde winked at Amanda. "Birds of a feather, Amanda? What brings you here?"

"I came in search of consolation."

"You two know each other?" Hunt's gray brows rose in surprise.

"She thinks I'm a rival for Gordie Locker's affection," Amanda said. "I can't persuade her otherwise."

Emerald nodded at Amanda. "She's a subtle one, Hunt. A real strategist when it comes to Gordie Locker, I think—"

"I've known Amanda for some time, Emerald. She tells the truth. If she says she's not interested in Gordie, she's not."

"But he's interested in her!" Her tone was one of mild despair. "She's why I'm not getting anywhere with him."

"I'm interested in having Mandy do some more modeling for me. And I'm not getting anywhere either."

Emerald threw herself into a leather and stainless steel sling chair and waved an arm at Amanda. "Our Amanda is quite incredible, Hunt, don't you think? Men are lining up begging her to join them in great projects. And the only word she knows is no!"

Hunt grinned. "Listen to her, Mandy."

Amanda stood woodenly, suddenly at a loss for words.

PERSONAL

"Gordie recommended Emerald to me," Hunt said. "She's interested in getting a start with the agency."

"You couldn't work with a nicer guy," Amanda blurted. She wasn't sure just what she was doing. Her motives seemed to be flying in a half-dozen directions.

Hunt threw his arm over Amanda's shoulder. "The nicest thing you've ever said to me, I believe."

Emerald pounced, guided by antennas flawless as satellite dishes in this area of human relations. "Don't tell me this fella wants you for a main squeeze, too, Amanda!" Her brown eyes widened and she flashed a wholesome smile of mock bewilderment. "What does this woman do—except play hard to get? That's not supposed to work in these modern times."

"It's nothing like that," Amanda said.

Hunt and Emerald finished their meeting with some final details, then she left. Amanda asked Hunt if he would come by her apartment for a chat. On the way to their cars she asked him about Emerald's potential with his agency. "She's a rare case—a woman who's already developed her professional persona."

"The girl next door."

"More than that—the sexy girl next door. We'll have to get rid of that horrid dye job, of course. Find the right opportunity for that bust-and-a-half she has. There's an excellent chance that I'll be able to market her. In short, she has potential." He smiled down at her. "But not as much as you, Mandy."

"She has something I don't: she wants to do it."

Amanda and Hunt found Justin and his friend Cooper at the apartment. Amanda handled the introductions. She studied Hunt's reaction to her son and vice versa. Not much to see there. She wondered what kind of a father Hunt would make. And again she wondered why he had never married.

The two boys played video games in the kitchen while she talked to Hunt in the living room over a pot of tea. She told him the whole Floyd story, start to finish, with a lot of emphasis on Connie Kwan's recent death. He was a good listener. She was grateful for that, and told him so. "Thanks, but never

87

mind that." His gray eyes probed her face. "It's clear you're in danger until they put Floyd Philman away."

"I guess so."

He nodded and grunted. "The police will eventually talk to him. I don't think you have to worry about this detective's opinion of your morals." He shrugged. "But you have no guarantees that Philman has any murder schedule that he sticks to. He could come through your door five minutes from now."

Amanda nodded. He was right. She was defenseless, should Floyd choose not to wait to carry out his threat. Almost without thinking, she said, "Do you want to stay for dinner, Hunt? We're not having anything great, but—"

"Delighted!"

She poured him a glass of wine from her refrigerator jug and began to hustle up dinner. She had read in a magazine years ago that if you don't have much money for food, rule number one was: learn to cook. So she had. She wasn't a genius, but she was well beyond the boiling water stage. Tonight she was making a red lentil and vegetable curry. A dollar each for the lentils and cauliflower. Onions and spices she had. Raw rice was cheaper than precooked. There would be useful leftovers . . .

As she worked, Hunt tried to persuade her to leave Hartford until Floyd was in jail. She explained she really couldn't. Justin was one of the reasons. He had put down roots in his present school, was doing well with a challenging curriculum, and had made some good, decent friends. She nodded toward his bedroom where the boys had taken their shouting and good-natured roughhousing. She went on to explain Pop-Up's rapidly failing health. She felt he was finally down to his last few weeks. She wiped her hands on a towel. "He made me swear I wouldn't leave him, Hunt. It's the only thing he's asked me through this whole cancer business. What am I going to do? Say no? There's one other thing, too: my job." She walked over and looked down at him. "Did Gordie mention to you his setting up a new position for someone: regional manager?"

Hunt nodded. "Yes. I think he was serious. He's told me

you're by far his most valuable employee. He needs you in that new job.''

Amanda was relieved. She had suspected it might be nothing more than bait for more squeeze-and-paw. ''I want the position. I won't get it if I run away from the one I have now.''

Hunt frowned. ''You aren't just going to live your life normally, are you? With some guy out there looking to cut you into pieces?''

''What do you suggest I do, Hunt? I mean, seriously.''

''If you won't leave the city, you have to be careful. You have to keep people around you. No walking alone to your car. Maybe carry a weapon.''

''I have no idea how to use a knife or a gun. I'd probably cut my finger or shoot myself.''

''You could carry mace. It's easy to use, and big trouble for anyone you use it on. Doesn't do any permanent harm. Of course it's illegal.'' He smiled thinly. ''You can think of it as a woman's weapon.''

''Wow, mace!'' Justin stood in the doorway, eyes alight as only a ten-year-old boy's could be at talk of arms and violence. ''Can I see it?''

''There isn't any, Justin. We're just talking. This is grown-up talk.'' Amanda looked at her watch. ''To run another seven minutes. Then it'll be dinner time.''

''Can Cooper eat over?''

''If he calls his parents for permission. I'll drive him home right after. You have to practice for your band concert. It's tomorrow night, even though you're trying to forget it.'' She cut his groan short with a snap of her fingers.

While putting out the plates, Hunt said, ''You seem to have him under control.''

''I could use some help.''

''What's that mean?''

She smiled. ''I'll draw you a picture.''

''Would I be in it?''

''Dinner time!'' she shouted toward the bedroom.

After dinner she walked Hunt down the stairs to his car. On

the way he said, "If there's anything I can do, Mandy, I want to hear about it."

"Thanks. Everything will be all right after the police get hold of Floyd. I'm hanging on till then."

They paused on the second-floor landing. He looked down at her with an odd intensity. "You have a great neck," he said.

"Keeps my head from falling off my shoulders."

He raised his hand slowly. She knew he was going to touch her. She closed her eyes and leaned against him. She didn't know what she was doing. She was tired of thinking. He ran his fingers lightly up her neck to her ear. He kissed her face, then found her mouth. She returned the pressure of his kiss, relaxed her jaw beneath the suggestive roll of his lips. His arms enfolded her, and it felt good.

Distantly, she heard the outside door open below. Someone had come in off the street. Reluctantly, she opened her eyes— and saw Hunt's wide open and fixed on her face. She felt somehow . . . used. "What are you looking at?"

"You're so lovely I got greedy. Eyes are my dominant sense."

She didn't believe him. She hadn't liked the distance across the gray field of his gaze. Her disappointment was doubled by his look and her own inability to ignore it. She was so paranoid! He tightened his arms around her. His mouth lowered. She hesitated, then finally turned her face up toward his.

Footsteps passed the next landing. She just couldn't be seen like this. Particularly if . . . She stepped back, her heart pounding. Coming up the stairs was Mrs. Clendenon, her man-hating neighbor. Her sour face crinkled into a smile for Amanda, then changed as quickly as New England weather into a glower directed at Hunt's distinguished profile. She ignored Amanda's introductions, put down her shopping bag on the landing. She wasn't having any man-woman stuff on *her* turf.

Mouthing polite nothings, Amanda led Hunt down the stairs and out to his Volvo. "You made a clean getaway, Hunt. Before she got out her knife and cut off your you-know-whats."

"Never mind her. When do we pick up where we left off?"
She shook her head. "Hunt, I don't know. I don't know
what that meant to me, why I did it."

"Did you like it?"

"Of course." She felt her face color. "I'm not sure if and
when to continue. Maybe we should talk sometime about us
and that look in your eyes."

"What?" He looked genuinely baffled. "What look? How
about now?"

"Justin has to practice. He has a concert tomorrow." He
opened his mouth to protest. She held up a palm and laughed.
"He won't get anywhere without my encouragement."

"Neither will I, Mandy Walker."

"Hunt . . . Thanks for letting me talk at you. We'll do it
again soon, OK?"

"Only if you want to make me happy."

For the rest of the evening she tried to make her way through
the twin tangles of her motivations and his responses. The
intrusion of Floyd Philman's morbid threats on her life had
skewed her judgment, knocked it off the foundation she had
worked so hard to build. She was trying in her own uncertain,
awkward way for some comfort and support. For now it seemed
groping on the landing with an eager, helpful man was the best
she could do.

As for Hunt Grayson . . . There was something deep down
in the man that made her uncomfortable.

The phone warbled. She swung her eyes around to the plastic
instrument on its yellow chest. She couldn't ignore it; Justin
was asleep. It was night, and *he* liked to call at night. She was
like an experimental animal reacting to stimuli: her heart
pounded, stomach tightened, and teeth clenched, as though she
was preparing for an electric shock. She crossed the room on
what seemed a stranger's legs. She snatched the receiver up,
spoke in a dry voice. "This is Amanda Walker."

"This is Hunt, Mandy. I'm sorry to bother you, but all your
news made me forget mine. I have a TV commercial I think I
can work you into."

"Hunt . . ." She sagged against the chest. "Calling me on

the phone at this hour—considering all I just told you—isn't the best thing to do.''

"Sorry."

She sensed his deflation. She really hadn't intended it that way. "My personal situation's getting really confused. My whole life is being affected." She took a deep breath. "Would this TV thing be during the day?"

"Well, yes, but—"

"I've told you I can't take a chance with your agency if it ends up costing me the only solid thing in my life."

"Remember, Mandy: you have to take some chances."

That hit too close to her self-criticism and sparked a flash of annoyance. "We'll talk about it some other time and place."

"I need an answer on this tonight."

"Then the answer's no." She hung up, but was at once sorry. He was a friend, even if she suspected something about him wasn't right.

# CHAPTER

## ❧ 7 ❧

Amanda liked visiting Justin's school. She took heart about her son's future. There she met other parents, many of them single like her. Some were single fathers, odd creations of the seventies and eighties, their exes flown to feminist fortunes and follies. She arrived early at the cafetorium, renewed friendships, and sipped the provided Folgers instant. Behind the stage curtain came titters and clatter as chorus and band members prepared to please their parents.

She had met Justin's teacher, Ms. Herald, at her parent/teacher conferences. She was on duty tonight, with a corsage and a smile. Amanda appreciated this little extra professional effort and told her so. Her horsy face angled into an appreciative smile. "Thanks. You always know the working women," she said. "The ones who know there's never enough time in the day to really allow me to be here. Naturally, my union is against it."

Amanda found a seat with the Colvins, a couple she had met at the Christmas concert. Their daughter Maude had a voice and an ear. She was in Justin's grade and soloed at every such event. Her voice was clear and pure, anchored on key like a battleship. When Amanda praised her, Don Colvin said, "Wait till she hits puberty. Then her voice—and everything else—will all go to hell!"

# PERSONAL

The program began with the junior chorus, a cluster of tykes raising tiny voices in praise of rabbits and God. Maude soloed in "Climb Every Mountain" followed by the expected enthusiastic applause. The curtains closed and the chorus crumbled to giggling kids scrambling in every direction. More scuffling and clatter followed.

Then it was band time. The curtains parted to disclose the group seated on battered folding chairs. There was Justin! She couldn't afford to waste money on a suit for him. But he passed in his dark slacks, his only tie, and almost-matching jacket. He sat with the other clarinets, instrument across his knees as he had been taught. He was whispering no louder than the others. The band director appeared in white tuxedo jacket, red carnation brilliant as a shelled tropical mollusk. He bowed deeply to applause, turned, and raised his baton.

Sure it was plunk-a-chunk-a-chunk down the simple score, but tears came to Amanda's eyes. She doubted she was alone. A stage filled with the earnestly inept was impossible to resist. When the last crescendo had been reached by most of the players at the same time, and bows taken, the curtains closed. After that came a brief period of milling in the cafetorium and halls while some parents chatted before matching themselves with their children.

While Amanda stood talking about the school's enrichment center with the Colvins, one of her school parent acquaintances came strolling in from the hall. Passing her, she said, "Trying to sell burgers here?"

Amanda frowned, shaking her head.

"Take a look in the hall, Ms. Muncher."

Amanda hurried out of the cafetorium—and stopped in her tracks. Propped against a wall was one of the life-sized cutouts of her holding Muncher's products. Its right arm had been cut off at the elbow and its left leg at the knee. The severed limbs lay on the floor. She froze, staring. The post-concert bustle faded from her attention like theme music during a voice-over commercial. She knew what it meant! That would be, in part, how Floyd would mutilate her corpse!

Faces loomed, some of them smiling. Lips moved in ques-

94

tions and comments. She could not rouse herself to action, no matter her emotions pouring like a torrent through a narrow tunnel.

Abruptly, she sprang to life. She rushed at the damaged figure and struck the side of her own ludicrously grinning face a violent, glancing blow. The cutout clattered face down to the floor. On its blank back magic marker block letters read: *Smart Amanda has three weeks left to live.*

She gasped and clenched fists to her chest.

Don Colvin stepped past her. "What the hell is this?" He turned the figure over and picked it up. "Damned kids!"

"Hi, mom. Ready to go?" Justin was at her side.

Amanda tried to heave her mind free of paralysis. It took her several moments. "Yeah, I guess." Her voice was a weak sigh.

Justin pointed at the cutout figure. "What's this doing here?"

"Some smart-aleck kids jerking around," Don said. He looked at Amanda. He could see how pale she was.

Amanda's voice was still weak. She grabbed Justin's hand. "Let's go, Scooter."

In the VW going home, she overcame her emotions long enough to say, "I loved it! You were all cute as buttons and bright-eyed as wrens."

Justin made his *Friday the 13th, Part XXX* face. "Mom, you are *gross*ing me out!"

"And don't I love to?"

When he was in the bathroom, she called police headquarters and asked for Detective McMahon. Periodic beeps told her the call was being recorded.

"He's not on duty, ma'am. Can someone else help you?"

"How can I get hold of him?"

"Can't. Like I said, he's off duty. If it's something urgent I can put you through to—"

"Who's handling the Connie Kwan murder?" she said.

"Dunno. I can check around . . ."

"Please." She waited. And waited.

Finally, the sergeant came back on the line. "Guess who? It's McMahon. If you're having some kind of trouble, you can talk to somebody else here. What's up? You in trouble, ma'am?''

"I—when will the detective be on duty again?''

"Monday morning.''

She hung up. She should have asked McMahon for his home number. She waited until Justin was asleep and called Grace O'Shea. She told her about the mutilated cutout, the three weeks to live. Her friend was dismayed. She made no effort to hide the fear in her voice. "I've been calling McMahon, too. He's a hard guy to find. I asked him if he had talked to crazy Floyd yet. He said they tried to get in touch with him.''

"And? . . .''

"He's out of state on a business trip. He says they checked with the drug wholesaler he works for. I don't think he's on any business trip. I think he's hanging around you and me and Jessica, figuring out stunts like the one you just told me about.'' The receiver rattled as Grace passed it from one ringed hand to another. "I've got a feeling McMahon isn't going to bust his stones for you either, Mandy. You got a record?''

She told her about the wet T-shirt contest that the lawman had seen before he was born again. "Oh, Lord, a Jesus freak cop!'' Grace moaned.

"I've heard people talk about him, Grace. They say he's not that bad.''

"What's that mean—for a cop?''

"I'm not exactly sure. I do know I wish you had told me about yourself, why the police . . . know about you,'' Amanda said.

Grace was silent a moment. "Oh . . . that.''

"Yeah.''

"What difference would it have made to anything?''

Amanda then called Jessica and brought her up to date. The younger woman was badly frightened. "Why hasn't he threatened me?'' she said. "Why didn't he threaten Connie before he killed her? Why just you?''

"Maybe it's because people like Floyd want to be caught. They just take more risks each time, tempt fate more and more.''

Jessica's voice thinned. "If he says he's going to kill you in three weeks, then he'll kill me before you—and Grace first!"

"There're no rules about that, Jess. Anyway, before very long the police are going to have a long talk with him. After that, I don't think he'll be a problem."

"That creepy man!"

Amanda didn't like the idea of waiting for the police. She didn't trust Detective McMahon to do his best. Nor was it appealing to hang on until Monday before contacting him. The days allotted to her by Floyd's mad agenda were leaking away. During her Saturday hours with Pop-Up he asked her several times what was bothering her. There was no fooling the man, sick as he was and in pain. She didn't want to add to his burdens by dumping her problems on him. So their time together, dwindling down as it was by the certainty of his coming death, was somehow tainted. She inwardly cursed Floyd Hooper Philman for stealing from her something nearly as precious as her own life. She overdid her farewells to her father, tears in her eyes. "Hey, Mandy, I'm still kicking," he said. That made it worse.

Somehow, her feelings for Pop-Up were catalyzed into anger directed against Floyd. That and her impatience to have him dealt with gave her an idea. Justin was going to spend the afternoon with Cooper. That gave her a few hours to do some cautious investigating. She had found Floyd's address in the phone book. She drove over to East Hartford, found his home on a crowded street of modest homes. Behind the houses was a narrow alley lined with weathered garages. She drove down several blocks, then pulled her VW tight against a thin hedge and got out. She walked back down the alley to Floyd's garage. She tried to open its doors. Their hinges sagged so badly she couldn't budge them. She peeked through a grimy window. Tools lay on a rough workbench standing against the rear wall. She saw jars and cans of auto care products. Standing against wooden supports was a bow saw.

Beside it stood a shiny double-edged axe.

Floyd's back yard featured a dying lawn and battered garbage cans. She kept an eye out for neighbors, saw none. From a distance came the cries and shouts of children at play.

PERSONAL

Two rear entrances: the kitchen door and the basement hatch.
As she walked closer to the two-story frame house, she heard
a dog barking. The sound came from the basement. Fine, she
would use the kitchen door. It was locked. She knocked and
as she expected, no one answered. She found a stone. After a
quick look around, she broke a small pane of glass in the door.
Reaching carefully through the hole, she turned the lock. She
slipped in quickly.

The barking intensified. The dog had climbed to the top of
the stairs and was throwing itself against the door which seemed
to be latched thoroughly enough. The house smelled doggy
and musty. So Floyd might well be spending time elsewhere.
She moved systematically around the kitchen. She wasn't sure
what she was looking for. Serendipity, do thy thing. The dog
was berserk, so she wouldn't be going down to the basement.
Still, there were at least four other rooms . . .

Finding nothing unusual in the kitchen, she tried the tiny
dining room. An oil painting dominated the furnishings: a nude
redhead. She was a buxom creature, doubly endowed by nature
and the artist's lusty imagination. She touched the painting's
surface. It was an original oil. She stepped back. The model's
expression was decidedly wanton. Hairs rose on the back of
Amanda's neck.

The larger-sized living room was furnished with a TV, VCR,
and hi-fi hutch, and DAK speakers, like sentinels in two corners. There were bookshelves, too. Floyd Philman was a reader
of . . . let's see. Magazines. She picked some up. *Those*
kinds of magazines, filled with photographs of men and women
having sex. She was so disgusted that she didn't notice at
first . . .

All the women were redheads.

The dog in the basement stopped barking for a moment. She
heard the noise of a truck stopping back in the alley. Floyd!
She froze for a moment. Then her wits returned. She rushed
to the small front door and unlocked it. Then she went back
to the kitchen and peered carefully out the window. Her heart
beat at her ribs. If it was *him* . . . The dog resumed its barking
with an increased frenzy and returned to throwing itself against

98

the door till the latch rattled like castanets. She saw a woman and a man moving in the next yard. She slumped against the sink, fighting the urge to run out the kitchen door. But she hadn't come this far to quit before she was satisfied. She went back to the living room.

She turned to his paperback novels, held a few in her sweaty palms. They were the same kind as the magazines. She scanned some of them, heart pounding with the tension of having penetrated Floyd's inner self.

She climbed the stairs. The bedroom held another TV and VCR. Racks of video tapes lined one wall. She pulled some out. They were all pornographic. She noticed at least one redhead illustrated on each box. She groaned softly. She was vaguely sickened, but she pressed on in her quick overview of his collection.

What stopped her was finding the kiddie porn. Red-haired little girls, scarcely more than toddlers . . .

Groaning, she covered her face with her hands for a long moment.

She spun on her heel. *He* was the one, all right! Detective McMahon was going to find out all about this!

She went into the last room, the bathroom. She found it redhead free. She leaned against the sink, aware that the dog had stopped barking. She was aware of her heavy breathing. She had better get out of the house. A sudden clatter from below jerked her upright. She gasped. Floyd had come home! Then the rapid scrapings across the hardwood floor told her he hadn't.

The dog was loose.

She heard it scrambling up the stairs, growls ahead of it like early warning signals. Oh, God! She spun toward the sink and cabinets looking for a weapon. She saw the animal bolting down the short hall. It was a Doberman, ears back, its nasty jaws gaping and toothy. Too late she realized she could have slammed the door on it. Too bad! It sprang at her. She dodged clumsily aside. It flew by, jaws snapping. She careened into spring pole–secured shelves. Down they went, cans and bottles scattering. She staggered, trying to keep her balance. The dog went for her leg. Its teeth found her flesh. A flash of pain electrified her. She screamed. Reflexes kicked her free. With despair she realized how quick the animal was. It came at her again. This time she stumbled in the narrow space. Her foot came down on a spray can and flew out from under her. She went down with a grunt. The Doberman came for her throat.

She got a hand out. She screamed again as the animal's teeth got a half grip on her wrist. With her other hand she gouged at its eyes. It whimpered and released her. She tried to scramble up, but wasn't fast enough. Red-eyed and growling, the dog again lunged for her throat. She stuck out her hand. It slid down the wiry, short-haired neck—and under the metal collar chain. She tightened her hand into a fist, the chain within. She held off the snapping jaws. The dog growled and lunged, trying to shake loose. Its warm saliva flew onto her forearm. She tried to scramble to her feet, but couldn't gain enough leverage.

The dog was strong! She couldn't hold it off for long. She was lying on her side, the white teeth so close to her nose she could smell the animal's rank breath. She imagined the powerful jaws tearing at the skin and tissue of her face. Stitches, horrid scars, ugliness . . .

Her free hand groped the floor for something with which to strike the nasty narrow head. Her other arm was tiring fast in its battle against the twisting lunges. She couldn't find . . . anything. Panic welled up, telling her to let go, cover her face, ball up, and hope. No! She would be torn apart. Her fingertips touched the edge of a spray can. It was so light! Not a weapon. But it could be!

The dog heaved at her. Her fingertips pushed the can and it rolled away. She churned her legs, trying to squirm toward it. The dog resisted, as though possessing cunning as well as strength and viciousness. Her heels found some purchase on the tiles. She heaved toward the can. She threw her arm and hand toward it. She had it! It was hairspray. The aerosol nozzle was protected by a plastic cap. She banged the can on the floor. The cap popped off.

She put the top of her forefinger on the valve and pressed. The jet squirted off to the right. She corrected her finger placement, then drew the can back to the side of her head. Her other arm was shuddering with exhaustion. The dog snapped at her face. Its nose grazed her chin. When she next pushed the valve it was less than a foot from the dog's wild eyes. The sticky cloud enveloped the animal's head.

With a howl the dog tore loose from her grip and pawed wildly at its eyes. She scrambled up and staggered away. She nearly tumbled down the stairs. Behind her the whining went on like the sound of a jammed machine.

She plunged out the kitchen door and into the June sunlight. She hurried back up the alley to her car. There she surveyed her wounds, nasty, leaking punctures near the ankle and left wrist. She got a tissue from the glove box and dabbed at them. A few Band-Aids would cover them. She had been lucky, assuming no tetanus or rabies followed. She sat back and struggled to regain her self-control. She felt drained and shaky. She wanted to start her car and get out of there. But her whole body trembled. The bruises and aches from her battle with the deadly dog were making themselves felt. She was too upset to drive. She ought to walk a bit.

Purse under her arm, she strolled down the alley and around the block, toward Floyd's house. A black woman was watering the next lawn. Amanda had an idea, despite her shaken state. Digging deep in her purse, she found her notebook. She strode up Floyd's short walk and rang the bell. From within she heard the baying of her hairy nemesis, ready to do battle again. She shuddered.

"Ain't nobody home! Mr. Floyd's away." The neighbor was waving.

Smiling to herself, Amanda retreated from the horrid house and walked toward the neighbor. "I'm Pat Patterson with the American Red Cross. Mr. Philman's on our lists as a B-negative blood donor. We have a real shortage of negative blood, all types. We're trying to talk to people personally."

The black woman shook her head. She was just short of sixty, neatly dressed, as were her small lawn and flower garden. "Might know Mr. Floyd gives blood. He does lots of favors, big and little."

"Oh?"

The woman worked the hose nozzle. The shiny arc of water died. She nodded. "Does favors for about everybody. Loaned me money once. It went for bail for my youngest when he got in trouble with the law." She waved at other houses. "He's done good all around."

"You like him?"

"He's OK. I help him out when I can. Like right now he's away. I feed and walk that dog you heard yapping. That dog is something."

"I'm sure." Amanda's pulse speeded at memory of the beast.

"All that barking, but tell you the truth, he wouldn't hurt a fly. Nicest dog ever born, that Kaiser."

Amanda stared into the wrinkled brown face.

"Like to see the man happy. We all would. You know what he needs?"

Amanda shook her head.

"He needs a good woman. Needs a wife. And you know he'd be good to the right woman." She eyed Amanda's left-hand ring finger. "You married?"

"No."

"You come around again. I'll introduce you." She looked Amanda over and winked. "Tell you true, Mr. Floyd *loves* a red-haired woman."

Driving home, Amanda shook her head. Floyd Hooper Philman, a pillar of the middle-class community, doing good works? She had hoped to hear juicy gossip about strange comings and goings and troubling personal quirks. One thing was sure about Floyd: he had the neighborhood fooled.

She picked Justin up at Cooper's and took him out for Chinese and a movie. When they returned to the apartment, the phone was ringing. She hesitated. Justin rushed ahead and snatched it up. Amanda froze, her heart pounding pain into her dog bites. He turned to her. "It's a man. For you."

She took the receiver from him, emotions rioting. She heard the cool voice of Detective McMahon. "I called into headquarters and understand you were trying to reach me, Amanda.''

"Yes! I have a lot to tell you.'' Instead of telling him about the mutilated cutout of her as Ms. Muncher, she rushed into a description of what she had found in Floyd's home and her misadventure with the Doberman.

When she finished, breathless, his voice cooled her hopes. "That was all unwise and dangerous of you,'' he said. "Not to mention the laws you broke—''

"Laws? I was nearly—''

"Breaking and entering, they call it. Trespass, certainly.''

"Detective McMahon, I'm talking about murder here.''

"Let me give you some advice. Leave the law to us. By sneaking into a suspect's house you've tainted any evidence we find. Understand?''

"You think I'd plant evidence?''

"Don't talk movie stuff, Amanda. You did a foolish thing. If that dog had torn you to pieces, you wouldn't have a leg to stand on—a legal one, I mean. We really do want to help you. But you have to cooperate.''

"I'm sorry.'' She hesitated. "I wonder if I could say a few frank words to you about myself?''

"Sure. Why not?''

"Well, I . . .'' She swallowed her suspicions that the police weren't doing all they could. "I'm a hard-working, serious woman on her own trying to make a career, be a parent, and just plain survive. I put a difficult marriage and an equally difficult lifestyle behind me. I'm on track again. And it hasn't been easy. I'm not the woman in the wet T-shirt. In short, I'm asking you to be fair-minded with me. You told me things aren't what they seem. I'm only reminding you.''

"I hear you, Amanda. And I understand. Do you have any more good words for Grace O'Shea?'' She sensed a curious teasing compassion in his voice, as well as cop toughness.

"I don't know Grace's story.'' She smoothed her voice. Nothing would be gained by chattering at him about a woman she really didn't know well. "One thing for sure. We're both just ordinary people on some nut's hit list.''

"I know you're frightened," the detective said. "I know something else. You want more action than we're staffed to give you."

"I see."

"But we *are* working on the case."

"Good." She wished she felt more relieved. "Are you going to talk to Floyd soon?"

"We understand from his employer that he'll be back in Hartford Monday morning. We'll be waiting for him."

Only after hanging up, still uneasy, did she remember she had forgotten to tell him about the mutilated cutout. And—Justin had heard everything.

She sat him down and gave him a laundered version of the situation. She was vague about the exact threats and many of the details. Nonetheless, she saw some color leave his face. "Hey, kid, not to worry. They're going to pick up this Floyd guy in the next day or so. After that, no more running scared for your mom."

He surprised her with a hug. She returned it, smelling Cooper's model airplane glue in his hair. How much she loved him! She more than returned the pressure.

It was what both of them needed.

Combing her hair out before bed, she realized she was exhausted. She threw herself down, didn't even pull up the covers, and fell sound asleep.

A noise woke her. She looked at the clock's lighted dial: 2:20 A.M. She sat up, listening intently. She heard more noise. It was coming from the kitchen, where a door led to the rear stairs. She slid silently out of bed, didn't bother with her robe. Though her eyes were accustomed to the dark, she could see little. There was no moon, and for some reason the street lights weren't on. She heard again the sound of metal against wood. Now there came a muted sound of rending nails before intrusive metal. She heard the kitchen door rattle softly open. She stood still, panic surging up like fire.

She thought of calling the police. It was too late!

Floyd wasn't keeping to any schedule.

104

He had come to murder her!

She could not bring herself to move. She was petrified as any relic. She heard movement in the kitchen dimness.

A man's shape filled the doorway.

She drew in breath and screamed. The sound was so loud she could scarcely believe it. She screamed again and again. Tension released, she turned and ran. The figure came after her. In her bedroom she screamed again.

"Mandy, for Chrissake!"

Ned's voice. Her ex-husband! Her terror evaporated before the furnace of her sudden anger. "What do you mean by breaking in here like this?"

"I wanted to see my son. I have the right."

"You gave up all your rights!" she shouted. She heard Justin sobbing in fear and rushed to his room. "Look what you've done!" she shouted to Ned over her shoulder.

Out in the hall Mrs. Clendenon was doing some screaming of her own. "I've called the police, Amanda! Hang on! They'll be here in a minute."

Amanda threw her arms around Justin. "It's just your father, kid. Showing his usual good judgment. Everything's fine. Not to worry." She shouted to Ned. "Get out in the hall and tell that nut case that everything's all right, will you? Then you can hit the road, as far as I'm concerned!"

Justin began to cry. "Don't make dad leave!" he bawled.

She went on hugging him, her tears coming too, in the wake of both terror and rage. The situation was absurd, but she was a long way from laughing.

In the end the police came, two officers, armed and wary of the ever-dangerous "domestic disturbance." Mrs. Clendenon wouldn't stay out of it. She accused Ned of breaking in and attempting to rape Amanda. Everyone was talking at once. It took all Amanda's diplomacy and patience to calm things down. She scarcely looked at Ned through it all. When she finally studied him, she saw a shaken, now balding middle-aged man, his once steely middle gone soft from bad food and hard times.

The moment came, as she knew it would, when the brisket-faced older cop put down his pad and said, "Ms. Walker, Mr. Stanton jimmied the door to your apartment. Likely motive . . ." He looked at ashen Ned. "Robbery. You want to press charges?"

"It wasn't robbery!" Ned shouted. "I just wanted to see my son. She won't let—"

"Shut up, Ned!" She looked away from her ex, saw a thatch of Justin's hair as he eavesdropped from his bedroom. My former husband, she thought, fool and loser. With whom I conspired to ruin ten of my best years. Above all, though, Justin's father. "Just get him out of here," she said, her voice a whisper. She turned a glare toward his pale face. "Before he steals my money or what's left of my nerves."

Ned got up and urged her aside. Reluctantly, she went with him to a corner of the room. "I want to spend a day with the boy," he said softly.

She looked stonily into his stubbled face. "That's not why you tried to break in here. You came to steal from me."

He looked away. " Either way, it was a bad idea. I shouldn't have."

"Don't have enough nerve to steal from strangers anymore?"

He winced. "Take it easy."

"I don't want you around! I don't want to have to look at you, Ned." She waved her lacerated wrist. "It's like pulling back one of these Band-Aids and poking the wound with a stick."

He nodded. "I understand. Just let me spend one day with the boy."

"His name is Justin."

Fire flashed in his sunken gaze. "Lay off! Say yes or no. You're not all that hard to hit, you know, Mandy."

She turned and paced away from him. So she was overreacting a bit. "You can sleep on the love seat." She trudged back to the bedroom and closed the door behind her.

In the morning she told Justin this Sunday belonged to him and his father. To see his face grin when he learned the news told her she had made a good, difficult decision. She took Ned aside, trying to distance herself from his dishevelment and frayed cuffs. "Take anything out of this apartment and I *promise* to turn you over to the police," she whispered. He nodded and forced his gaze to meet hers. "I have twenty-nine cents," he said.

She went to her purse and got her wallet. When Justin was looking elsewhere she gave Ned twenty dollars. "I just dynamited my budget for the week, in case you think I have it to throw around."

"Thanks."

Off center and emotionally drained, she floundered through the morning cleaning and shopping. Her mind gradually swung away from Ned, the losses from their marriage, back to Floyd and his threats. She had another look at her dog bites. They seemed all right. Kaiser should be taken out and bayoneted. She got out her notebook and sat down on a kitchen chair. Checking back, she realized that this week, already into the fourth since she had met Floyd, was the sixth such so far as Grace O'Shea was concerned.

She drove to Grace's address, a run-down apartment house in East Hartford. Loitering youths eyed her as she walked the graffiti-slashed walk to the building's large vestibule. She studied the mailbox tags. She found O'Shea/Ramanujan and pressed the bell stud. A black woman shouldered her way out carrying a huge bundle. "Them doorbells is deader than equality, sugar. Don't matter, 'cause the lock buzzer don't work neither. Same for the elevator."

She trudged the five flights to Grace's apartment. She recovered some of her breath walking a hall perfumed by cooking cabbage and barbeque. She knocked. A man's voice said, "Gracie?"

"No, I'm a friend of Grace's."

The door opened to disclose a subcontinental Indian male, with eyes like brown coals. She dismissed his stare as a custom of his country, if not hers. She explained she wanted to personally warn Grace about the dangerous six-week milestone ahead. No doubt Mr. Ramanujan—"call me Tani"—had heard about Floyd Philman and what he did to redheads.

"I guess you are Amanda Walker who has made Gracie very much afraid." Tani spoke rapidly in a high-pitched voice. "I have told her that I think you are a very excitable woman with too much imagination. I have told her that if this Floyd person does come here—I do not think this likely—I will handle him as a man must." From his loose blouse he pulled out the bone handle of a nasty-looking knife with a wriggly blade.

"And if you're not around?"

He sniffed and tilted his chin up abruptly. "It is so like women to be afraid. Thanks to you, Miss Amanda Walker, Gracie has not gone out from here much. This has caused some shortage of money which has interfered with my studies."

"What are you studying, Tani?"

"Astrology. In the Indian style of course."

"When will Grace be back?"

He shrugged. "She is on business."

"For how long?"

"Since last night."

Amanda knew what kind of business Grace was handling. "Shouldn't she be back by now?"

He shrugged. "Who can say?"

Amanda curbed her urge to say something vitriolic. Instead, she gave him a piece of paper with her work and home phone numbers on it. "When she gets home, whenever it is, have her call me, please."

She got out of the apartment and the neighborhood fast. She forced her mind away from dark speculations on just what sort of life seemingly jolly Grace was living. And hopefully still lived.

Her Sunday routines had been destroyed by Ned's arrival. She had time on her hands, but was too wrapped with worries about Grace to make good use of it. She saw a phone booth, pulled over, and dialed Hunt Grayson's home number. As usual, she wasn't quite sure why she wanted to talk to him, but she did. His answering machine kicked on, much to her disappointment. To her dismay, she heard his voice alternating

PERSONAL

with that of Chelsea, the blonde cover girl with the acid tongue.
They had to be living together. Their message explained that
they were out, "exploring the possibilities life offered to the
imaginative and talented." She preferred to think Chelsea had
put him up to those words. She recalled her and Hunt's brief
embraces on her apartment stairs. She wasn't the only one that
day who wasn't quite sure what she was doing.

Grace's whereabouts haunted Amanda through Sunday. By
now it was after 3:00. She hadn't been back to her apartment
all day. Maybe Grace had called. She phoned the redhead's
number. Tani said she wasn't home yet. Please not to call, as
there was no reason to be upset. She didn't dwell on his opinion
of her—and of all women, for that matter. He was from a
different culture. Even if he was a sloth and a parasite.

Her attention kept circling back to Floyd. She stopped at
CVS where phone directories were kept beside the pay phone.
She scanned only the sections for the upscale towns, Farmington, West Hartford, Simsbury, for Dr. Moodleman's address.
Shrinks didn't want for money. There it was: Mountain Incline
Road, Simsbury. Asking directions, she found the street, a
wide curving lane far from urban hassle. Dr. Moodleman's
house had half an acre of grass in front and a scenic hollow
behind. Expensive foreign cars and Lincolns lined the street
and driveway. A cookout was in progress.

The doctor's generation was one that wholesome lifestyle
messages hadn't reached. The bar was long in length and liquor.
Thick chuck steaks seared over Texas-sized cookers made from
oil drums. Adults clustered in groups on the deck, side lawn,
and patio. Children darted through sunlight and shade. She was
reminded once again of what a prosperous state Connecticut
was. It wasn't these people's fault that she had somehow missed
out.

Crashing parties wasn't her specialty. She wanted to speak
with the doctor and leave. The first problem was to find him
among what seemed like several hundred guests. Remembering
his rotund shape, she headed for the food. There he was, man-
ning one of the barbeques, a Boston Celtics Larry Bird number
33 apron curving over his ample belly. He brandished a knife

and fork with three-foot handles. Great Books–sized pieces of beef smoked and seared. Without really looking at her, he said, "Medium rare, rare, or the cow jumped over the candle?"

"Floyd Hooper Philman," she said.

He turned to her with a frown of recognition. "Amanda Walkman."

"Walker, Doctor. I know I wasn't invited. I want to talk to you for a minute. Then I'll leave."

He hesitated. Amanda wouldn't allow herself to think she was wrecking his party. It wouldn't hurt him to talk to her. His bald pate gleamed in the heat of the cooker and the June afternoon. His spiky shelves of hair resisted the humidity. "Once again, Ms. Walker, I must tell you I cannot disclose—"

"I want to tell you what Floyd's done, Dr. Moodleman. Then you can talk to your conscience and professional ethics about what you ought to do."

He put down his implements and led her through the clusters of guests to a tree-shaded boardwalk leading along the edge of the hollow. The smell of pines in the sun made Amanda think of the New Jersey shore where she had vacationed as a child. She told him about Felicity's and Connie's murders, about the further phone calls she had received, the mutilated cutout. She told him about Floyd's home filled with scabby porn. She didn't forget the sharp double-edged axe. After sketching all that in, she paused before adding, "Now maybe Grace O'Shea is in trouble, too. Bad trouble."

The doctor's frown deepened. Amanda guessed he wanted his office, his patients' "soft chair," and his crater-deep pipe, with which such talk went easier for him. He ambled more slowly, stopped and leaned against the rail. He turned to her, his tiny eyes behind their thick lenses berry bright with intelligence. "My problem, as I see it, isn't Floyd Philman. It's you, Amanda."

Her turn to frown.

"How to be responsive to you, without violating my professional ethics. I sense your own neuroses, those to be expected in a woman who bears her share of burdens. At the same time what is happening to you isn't wholly the product of your overactive imagination—"

"Dr. Moodleman, I am not—"

"Behind the screen of your psyche, behind the masks we all put up, there is some real external trouble in your life."

"Some? My 'external trouble' is Floyd Philman. For God's sake, he has a whole house filled with sick redhead porn. He's going to come after me with that axe!"

The doctor shrugged. Amanda imagined the distant shadow of Sigmund "Fraud" Freud falling across this doctor's mind. Another lockstepped clone shrugging off the right and wrong of human doings—in the name of the id, the ego, and the holy superego. "I am well aware of his pornography collection. Owning and viewing pornography is not a crime. Nor does it necessarily disclose psychological problems. It can, in fact, indicate a healthy sexuality—"

"Doctor—"

"Passing harsh judgment on it, Amanda, can be an indication of *your* denied or repressed sexuality." She opened her mouth again. Before she could utter a word, he said, "This isn't the time or the place to discuss your psychological health." He smiled thinly. "I want to enjoy my afternoon." He rested his hand lightly on her shoulder. Later she remembered that moment, with its sounds of distant crows' raking cries among the trees, the throb of conversation, children's sharp shrieks, and trendy reggae blasting through the distant house's sound system. "Listen carefully to what I'm going to say. All right?"

She nodded.

"In my professional opinion, based on three years of clinical work with Floyd, there is no way in which he is capable of murderous violence. As to his obsession with redheaded women, it's a common enough vice, and in him a harmless one."

"Dr. Moodleman, you are wrong!"

Again the shrug. "Possibly. In any case, you've got from me all you will. If you insist in persisting with these matters, I suggest you do so with the police. I don't want another unexpected visit from you."

\* \* \*

Driving home she felt a great weight of depression building within. She wondered what she had hoped the doctor would do. Maybe, after hearing all her damning facts, get in touch with Floyd and have him turn himself in. After the fact, all that now seemed an exercise by airhead Amanda at her most illogical. "I can't help it!" she said aloud. "I'm scared!"

Ned and Justin waited for her. The boy begged his father to stay for dinner. "We had a great day, mom. We went to the dog track!"

Her twenty bucks! She didn't bother embarrassing Ned by asking if he had bought his son so much as a hot dog. He sat in rapt attention with the two adults in the kitchen as Amanda worked on a quick chili. There, largely against her will, she heard the gilded epic of her ex's wanderings. To Justin it all seemed grand. She, who had been on the road with Ned, filled in the miseries and disasters in her mind, like a code expert working with a long dispatch.

"Stopped by to visit S-sister," he said. "She lives in the area now."

"Where about?"

He shrugged and grinned. "Nearby."

Amanda knew that meant he must have truly hit rock bottom not long ago. For whatever reason he never wanted to go to her. He had been forced to. Well, she hadn't done all that much for him, if anything. He still had that hunted, pained look in his eyes. The kind he used to get after a losing week of high-stakes poker or a disastrous day at the track.

She had just served canned plums for dessert when the downstairs buzzer rang. She went to the intercom. It was Hunt Grayson. She hesitated, wanting to refuse to let him in. She recalled her earlier refusals, Chelsea newly installed in his home. To her surprise she admitted him.

He carried a basket of fruit left over from one of his shootings, telling her he didn't like to see things go to waste. He knew she and Justin would enjoy it.

There was the expected awkward moment when she had to introduce Ned. The contrast between the mature agency head and her former gamblin' man was painful, but likely only to her.

Hunt wore a blazer and a yellow ascot that did well for his tanned face. He was just so damned aristocratic looking! Despite herself, she always found him attractive. Maybe nuzzling with him on the stairs had been the normal, natural thing to do. She always spent too much time thinking! "The real reason I'm here is to find out how you are," he said. "Any more threats? Any action out of the police?"

She looked pointedly at Ned, then Justin. "I'd rather not discuss it right now, Hunt. Any other time."

He understood. He also took a hint she didn't know she gave. He rose to leave.

His visit left her with a burden: having to explain to Ned about Floyd and the murdered redheads. She sent Justin out for an ice cream. As she spoke, her ex began to nod. His pale face had softened, weakened maybe, over the last years. Now he flogged it into an expression of seemingly earnest concern for her. So that when she finished, it seemed natural for him to say, "Then I think I better stay here until this Floyd character is in the slammer."

She turned back to the stack of dirty dishes. She knew from years past that he wouldn't join her there. That way he wouldn't see the uncertainty that welled up, to her great surprise. Of course she didn't want him around. But there was the matter of her very real fear that would only mount until Floyd was arrested. He could be her bodyguard. He had nothing else with which to occupy his time. No! No! He would leech from her, from her precious little hoard of emotional and physical energy. And from her scant supply of material resources. He would steal from her as he had before. There was no need to delay her refusal. It was already Sunday night. Tomorrow morning the police would collar Floyd.

She had a very hard time getting him out of the house. He dragged out his goodbye to Justin for nearly forty-five minutes, leaving behind a shower of promises that she knew he wouldn't keep. Unfortunately, Justin would learn some of the lessons she had once learned. Ned also tried to drag out his farewell to her, hoping it would turn into an invitation to spend the night. She fought the urge to say yes and watched him finally move down the stairs. She wondered how long her strength would last. How long would she so stubbornly stick to what she thought was right for herself? Denying the easy way, the quick fix. She was like an unsupervised child stubbornly finishing her piece of nutritious bread while counters heaped with sweet temptations surrounded her. Idiot! Or was she?

Justin fell instantly asleep. She was about to follow him. The day had done nothing to rest her. And a new work week was looming. She was putting the last dish in the drainer when the phone rang.

She looked over her shoulder at it. She took heart: tomorrow the police and Floyd were going to have a long talk. If it was he calling, she'd tell him that. Let *him* worry for a while.

"Good evening. This is Amanda Walker."

"This is Tani, friend of—"

"Grace is back!" she said.

"Gracie is not back. Has sent no word. Is very puzzling thing."

# CHAPTER
## ❧ 8 ❦

Early Monday morning she tuned into the news broadcasts, as she had when she suspected that Connie Kwan might be dead. She heard no mention of any women being murdered. She had dug out an old pocket radio and took it to the restaurant with her. On a corner of her small crowded desk it whispered about trouble, weather, and traffic through the first three hours of her shift. Monday was always a busy day. She had to play catch-up for the ragged weekend crews with their heavy business and careless record keeping. She used the phone frequently.

Her first personal call was to Jessica Morris, bringing her up to date and telling her that Grace might have disappeared. "Don't panic, Jess. The police are waiting for Floyd this morning. They'll find out he has everything to do with Grace being missing—and a lot more."

"I hope so. When I call the police, they don't tell me anything."

"Hang in there." Amanda hung up.

The phone rang immediately. She snatched it up. "Muncher's West Park. Amanda Walker speaking."

"This is Floyd. I have Grace."

Amanda's hands turned to ice. How she had dreaded hearing that faint, airy voice again! "The—police are looking for you. They know all about who you are and what you're doing."

"Grace has very beautiful skin. I wanted you to know that. I want you to look at your own skin tonight and see if it's more beautiful. Of course I'll be the final judge." He hung up.

Amanda snatched up her purse and dashed out of the restaurant. Over her shoulder she shouted for Ernesto to cover for her. A great way to lose my job, she thought. Worse things could happen, she mused on her way to police headquarters.

She demanded to see Detective McMahon. She was led to a chair on the second floor, puzzled, as his office was downstairs. Twenty minutes later a door opened and the detective emerged with one of his colleagues and a uniformed officer. Amanda sprang up and rushed to him. She didn't care that she wore a panicked look. "Floyd called me a half an hour ago! He said he has Grace O'Shea and—"

"Take it easy." He exchanged glances with the burly business-suited man whom he introduced as Detective Reti. He had also been assigned to the case. They led Amanda to an adjacent room. "It was the same guy who called before?" McMahon said.

"Of course it was. Floyd."

"You're sure?" Reti said.

"Absolutely! What I want to know is why haven't you done what you said—bring him down here and ask him hard questions."

"We did," Reti said. "We just took a break."

She sat silent, not sure she understood.

"He's been here since eight o'clock. His attorney showed up about nine." McMahon looked pointedly at Amanda. "We've done nothing but ask him hard questions. He was never out of my sight."

She clutched at the heavy wooden chair arms. "But . . . he *said* he was Floyd." She was aware of how foolish that sounded.

"It's too early to say anything for sure," Reti said. "But he's had answers to about all our questions."

McMahon nodded. "Lots of alibis. We'll check them all out. That'll take time."

"What about . . . Jessica and me?" Amanda's voice was tiny. "And Grace, if she's—"

"You'll have to be careful. Later we'll want to talk to you about that." McMahon looked at his watch. "Break's over." He went for coffee. Amanda peeked into the larger room. There was Floyd! Just as he had stalked like a specter over the landscape of her fears—the bulgy Adam's apple, the short-lashed eyes. I know you're the maniac! she thought. Beside him sat a gaunt man in blue pin stripe. His attorney. People like Floyd didn't deserve attorneys.

Reti took a minute to tell her nothing was certain yet, either way. Nonetheless, Floyd didn't seem as likely a suspect as he had appeared. The recent phone call to Amanda wasn't the only piece that didn't fit. He had spent the three days around Connie Kwan's murder and dismemberment peddling his pharmaceuticals in Vermont, more than two hundred miles away. He had witnesses . . . He or McMahon would be in touch with her and Jessica. ·

She wandered downstairs, as though through a dream. Floyd had to be the one. If he wasn't . . . Her mind blocked further thinking along those lines for the moment.

"Why so pale, Amanda?" Evan Dent the reporter pulled away from a group of patrolmen and fell in step with her. "Your troubles aren't over?"

"I think they're getting worse."

"Anything I can do?"

She stopped walking and looked up at his boyish face with which his horn-rimmed glasses seemed a perfect match. "Go into a phone booth and turn into Superman. Then go forth and vanquish evil."

"Yes, ma'am. What particular evil did you have in mind?"

"I don't think it's a good idea for me to say yet. Not if you're going to write about it."

"Maybe I won't. Maybe I can help you some other way."

"Thanks, Evan. I'll keep you in mind. Really."

He folded his arms. "My reporter's nose tells me there's a big murder story around you and that other redhead—Grace, is it?"

Amanda felt tears starting. What if Grace had—? She bolted off.

Back at the restaurant, she phoned Grace's number. No answer. For the rest of the workday she paid too much attention to her little pocket radio. There was no news about any murders and mutilations. Let it stay that way. Had "Floyd" really abducted Grace? Or had she wisely left town?

She was out in front of the counter trying to explain the rules of the latest Muncher Mania game to an angry lady who thought she was a winner, when Lilly called to her, "Phone."

It was Celeste, Pop-Up's day nurse. She hated to bother Amanda at work, but it seemed to her that her father had taken a turn for the worse. She had called the doctor. He recommended that she or one of her team come in for a while every day now. Every other day, even with Amanda's regular visits, no longer seemed adequate. If she agreed, there were the details of payment to work out. Amanda could borrow, if necessary, against her father's small estate. He had Medicare and a complementary health plan. She would manage somehow. Of course there would be no dollars left in the end. But his comfort came first.

She swung by his apartment on the way home and made him a pot of chicken soup. They talked over the increased nursing. She said nothing about the threats or Ned's unwelcome visit. Once again she left him with tears in her eyes.

Detective McMahon phoned her in the evening. They had released Floyd. His attorney knew what he was doing. "I don't think we have a case," he said. "We're as far from an indictment as from the North Star."

Amanda felt she was falling. She sat down quickly. "That's too bad. Remember, the guy who calls himself 'Floyd' said he grabbed Grace O'Shea."

"I remember. It doesn't make me feel good. Even if she is a semipro."

"She's much more than that! She's a human being entitled to stay alive."

"I'm well aware of that, Amanda. No need to jump down

my throat. You need the wisdom of Solomon to be in my business. As we agree, nothing's what it seems. Hey, you seem to be a hard-working professional woman all alone with a tough row. Then I look at the log this morning. What do I see? Domestic disturbance at your address. And there's a guy involved. Your supposedly ex-husband breaks in for some reason. Maybe so he can live with you again. Maybe you encourage him. Maybe you two are playing some kind of love-me-hate-me game. From my end it all sounds really confusing.''

"My ex-husband, Ned, has a way of confusing me, too. He's an expert at it. Then there's my man-hating neighbor who dials 911 as often as the weather number.''

"I'm trying to understand your situation,'' the detective said. "I apologize if it's taking me a little while.''

"I hope it doesn't take *too* long.''

"Relax, Amanda.'' She heard him fumbling at his end of the line. "You got anybody we could talk to about Ms. O'Shea?''

She gave him Tani's name. She realized he was about to hang up. "Detective McMahon, what am I supposed to do?''

"Already told you a couple times: be careful. You and Jessica both.''

She found her hand clutching the receiver in a death grip. "Aren't you going to protect us?''

"From what?''

"From being murdered!''

"That would be nice, if we could guard everybody in Hartford who's been threatened. We do guard people sometimes. But that's where politics comes into it. Who do you try to protect when you don't have the men to protect everyone?''

"You protect the 'important' people,'' Amanda said.

"I'm afraid you're right.'' The cop's voice toned toward melancholy. "I'll look into seeing if I can get a man on you and Jessica. That's all I can promise for now.''

"Thanks.''

"Have a good night, Amanda.''

She fretted for the rest of the evening, even thinking of

reporting McMahon to his superior. Instinct told her not to do it. McMahon *was* making an effort. If Floyd wasn't the killer, whoever it was had to be found—and before long. She needed the detective's help. However unrewarding his efforts up to now, should he receive a reprimand from above, she would be back-burnered for sure.

She turned on the 11:00 news. No word of any young women being murdered.

Where was Grace O'Shea?

In bed, she recalled "Floyd's" words, now repeating themselves like those on a Tibetan prayer wheel in a stiff breeze. *I want you to look at your own skin tonight and see if it's more beautiful* . . . Despite herself, she got up and dropped her nightgown in front of the full-length mirror. Her skin was still pale and creamy. Goes with the hair, she thought. When my hair grays, the wrinkles will come, top to bottom. For now, she was certainly smooth and rounded enough for the local psychopathic murderer. The scabbing dog bite punctures on wrist and leg made her think of far worse violent intrusions. He used an axe . . . She hurried back into her nightgown and under the covers.

What passed for sleep ended with Tuesday's dawn. She sat up in bed, measuring off time. It had been three weeks plus three days since she had spent her evening with Floyd. This was the morning of the fourth. How comfortable that margin of days had seemed! The six weeks apparently granted her had seemed an eternity because she imagined he'd be quickly locked up. Surprise! It was beginning to seem he wasn't guilty—an idea so chilling she still couldn't fully accept it. That meant someone else, too, was counting down her days.

Two weeks and three days left.

And the murderer could be anyone in Hartford.

When Justin was ready for the bus, she drove to the restaurant. Key ready by the rear door, she halted. Glass had been broken out to allow the escape bar to be worked. Robbery. Well, they couldn't have gotten much. The cash registers were always emptied and the walk-in freezer had a lock on it that

PERSONAL

Houdini couldn't crack. She peered in and saw no one. She walked around the building and looked in through the glass. Deserted. Just the same, she waited for the first employee, Eduardo, to arrive before she entered.

Eduardo and she looked around. Nothing seemed to be missing. She started him in on the morning routines and went to her office to call the police. She snatched her hand back from the phone. On her desk lay raw french fries. They had been placed to form letters.

**I'M SOMEONE YOU KNOW. CAN YOU GUESS WHO BEFORE I KILL YOU?**

She backed away from the desk. She fled her office, sank into one of the plastic booths. "Eduardo! Call the police for me." She was trembling.

The morning was marked with confusion and disruption. She had to deal with keeping the restaurant running, answering police questions, and controlling her shaken self. Several times she nearly burst into tears with little provocation. The officers weren't greatly concerned; nothing had been taken. Insurance would cover the glass. Knowing nothing about Amanda's personal situation, they laughed at the french fries and told her to drop them in hot fat and eat them for lunch.

She tried to reach Detective McMahon, without success. So she had to leave the horrid message where it was.

Two girls on her shift had also worked through the evening. They both swore they had been in the office to punch out. Neither had seen anything on the desk. Not until late afternoon did she hear from McMahon. He told her to dump the fries. The fingerprint unit was short-handed and overcommitted. He said he was sorry. He interrupted her protests to say he had checked on Floyd's whereabouts last evening. He had been partying in the neighborhood and had passed out on a porch. He spent the night there. And had witnesses. "It's a whole new ballgame, Amanda," he said almost cheerily.

She eased the receiver back into its cradle. She stared at the limp white letters. With a howl she swept them off onto the

121

floor, then sank down in her chair and sobbed. When she looked up, her blurred sight disclosed Madge, her senior citizen Muncher-kin, beanie askew atop her gray hair. "My arthritis is acting up, Mandy. Can I punch out early?" She focused on her boss's tear-smeared cheeks. "Don't pay any mind to that crank fry trick. Somebody on the staff did it. I haven't lived to be sixty-seven not to know an inside prank when I see it."

She phoned Tani Ramanujan and asked if Grace had shown up. "No Gracie. And no word. Is very strange."

"I told the police she's missing, Tani."

"Oh? Police? I see."

"They may come and talk to you about her. I hope you'll help them."

"To be sure, Ms. Mandy."

About four o'clock the phone rang. Ned had had some luck at the OTB. Two horses had come home. He wanted to take her and Justin out to dinner. At once, memories of their marriage flooded back. Mostly rock-hard times. Then Dame Fortune smiled and they stayed briefly at fancy Hyatts and ate room service shrimp cocktails. Her stomach started to hurt. She told him if he expected to stay around for a while, they'd have to set up a regular visiting schedule. She had a life to live. However, today she would allow him to take Justin out.

"Thanks. Hey, what about that nut that's threatened you?"

"It wasn't the nut I thought. It's some other nut."

"Who?"

"Somebody. Maybe even you." Why had she said that?

That evening, without Justin around to demand her attention, her thoughts swung back to the day's bad news. It was a whole new ballgame, a grim kind of ballgame where base hits were murders and sudden death took on a morbid new meaning. *I'm someone you know.* A red herring or the truth? Was the killer playing games with her head? If he was someone she knew, who was he? Who were the men in her life?

The door buzzer sounded. She asked who it was. Hunt Grayson. When he stood beside her he said, "I'm worried about you, Mandy. I really am."

She told him the latest and concluded, "It seems it's not Floyd after all."

Did some color leave his tanned face? "So who is it?" he said.

"I don't know."

"The reason I came sounds better all the time." He put his hand in his pocket and pulled out a silvery cylinder about five inches long. At its top was a small lever affair and a valve. "This is illegal chemical mace," he said. "Just point and press. Go for the face. Pretend it's Windex. I think you should carry it around with you—and don't hesitate to use it." He put it up on the coffee table. "Make sense?"

"I don't know what makes sense anymore." She heaved a deep sigh. She was tired of all this morbid stuff. "Want some coffee?"

"Sure."

"What's between you and the gorgeous Chelsea, Hunt?" She gave him his cup of coffee.

"I'm helping her with her career."

"By asking her to move in with you?"

"It's a temporary thing."

"Uh-huh." Amanda averted her eyes.

"She's angling toward working full time in New York."

"Whose idea was that?"

Hunt sipped his coffee. His narrowed eyes told her it was Chelsea's.

"She's too young for you," she said. "You're too smart to let her inflate your ego." Something had been wandering around in the back of her mind that emerged suddenly as words. "Or are you trying to prove something about yourself?"

Hunt put down his cup slowly. "Like?"

"Trying for the permanent relationship you've never had."

His reddening face brought out the gray at his temples. "What the hell are you talking about, Mandy?"

"I think you know—"

The buzzer rang. Ned and Justin were back. Hunt's color failed to disappear. At sight of Ned, he pointed and said, "What the hell does he represent? You allow the original bad penny in your life to keep turning up—''

"Hey, pal, stay out of what isn't your business!" Ned said.

"Take it easy," Amanda said. "I'd like both of you to leave."

When she closed the door behind them, she found Justin handling the silvery cylinder. "This is mace, isn't it? Wow! Mr. Grayson brought it, didn't he? If that weirdo comes around, you're going to zap him, right, mom?"

"Zap or be zapped," she said, faking bravado. "It'll live in my purse. We'll get him—whoever he is."

Later she stared up at her bedroom ceiling. What had she been trying to prove with Hunt, for heaven's sake? Possibly, she was jealous of Chelsea, twisting that around somehow to give voice to her strange feelings about him. Now, though, she couldn't define them. Too many of her vague concerns were intuitive, unreliable. What mixed signals she had sent him! First refusing to spend time with him, embracing him on the stairs, now attacking him for no reason that she could define.

Those concerns slid away and were replaced by the shadows skulking continually beyond the campfire of her attention: the killer and what she could do about her situation. She commanded herself: Don't curl up in a ball. Don't expect too much of the police. Think! Figure out what to do to help yourself, Jessica, and maybe even Grace. *I am someone you know.*

Two names came to her mind. Hunt Grayson and Gordie Locker. Something didn't seem right with the graying executive. And Gordie . . . well, what meanings lay at the heart of the flash in his eyes? But neither had apparently ever met Floyd Philman. Yet to murder Felicity and Connie, one of them had to know the details of his *Reformer* dates. What linked them to the newspaper? That answer came right away.

Emerald Roscheski. The bouncy cheerleader.

The dyed blonde imagined herself Gordie's steady girl. Amanda had found her with Hunt in his offices. Who could really say just how long either man had known the woman? Amanda had plenty to tell Detective McMahon—if he ever found time to take her statement.

# PERSONAL

She bought a *Courant* on the way to work, flipping through the Connecticut news at once. She dreaded finding word of Grace O'Shea's death. Her attention was seized by a headlined item: *Third Judge Shot!* She scanned the text. Someone was carrying out a vendetta against municipal judges, stalking them and shooting them in the backs of their necks with a .22 pistol. More fun in the big city. She scanned every page of every section. Not a word about Grace.

She phoned homicide after 9:00. McMahon wasn't available. She asked that he or Reti call her. She heard nothing. Early afternoon she called again, but couldn't reach either man. She felt walled in by hamburgers and responsibilities. She didn't dare leave the restaurant. The noon hour wasn't enough time to accomplish anything. Nor did she casually flaunt that one-hour limit. It was Gordie's company policy which he enforced with the help of spies and unexpected visits. She phoned the police again at 4:30. McMahon was tied up and likely not able to get back to her that day. She slammed the phone down. Delay activated her fears.

Just before she left work Jessica called. Amanda swallowed at hearing her voice. Had *she* been threatened? The younger woman was breathless. She had talked to McMahon today briefly.

"How'd you get to talk to him?" Amanda said. "I've been trying all day."

"Mandy, I have no idea." Her voice sank. "Why are you angry with me? I didn't—"

"I'm sorry, Jess. I'm nervous and worried."

"So am I. I called because McMahon told me Floyd doesn't seem to be the one, after all. Who is it, then?"

"Somebody left me a message. It said the killer was someone I knew." Amanda explained that it could be Gordie or Hunt.

"Just those two?" she said.

"Jess, I'm grabbing at straws. It could be anybody. Even my ex. When I think about it, from that strange phone voice, it could even be a woman. Just the same . . ." She went on to explain that both men weren't quite right when it came to

125

dealing with the opposite sex. Then she dropped her bombshell:
" 'Floyd' called me. He said he had grabbed Grace.''

"Mandy!" Jessica's howl was just on this side of panic.
"You think whoever it was really did—"

"I have no way of knowing."

"I want her to be safe," Jessica said in a small voice. "If
she isn't . . . I'm next. And you can bet I'm not just going
to sit around by myself and wait!"

"It all doesn't quite fit. If this six weeks business is for real,
he got to her early. Her time isn't up until day after tomorrow—
Friday."

"This is all so scary. We've got to keep in touch. Anything
you find out . . ."

"I'll call. You let me know, too." Both hung up reluctantly.


After work Amanda swung by the apartment to pick up
Justin. From there she drove to the *Reformer* building. She met
Emerald on her way out. The younger woman's face shaped
itself into its determined grin at sight of her. "It's laid-back
Amanda," she said. "Still playing hard to get?"

"All I'm playing is scared, Emerald. Could I talk to you
for a minute?"

She looked down at Justin. "About what?"

"About the classifieds. Could you come over here a second?"

She gave Emerald a special version of her problem. One that
linked the classified ads, not Emerald, with the murderer. The
girl turned reluctant. She had told Amanda before: no unau-
thorized person got information about the ads. Everything was
confidential. "Maybe this nut, whoever he is, stole Floyd's
mail, or followed him around till he met you all. Then he
followed you. He didn't have to find you through the office
here." Emerald put her hand to her dyed hair. Its brunette roots
were showing.

Amanda was getting nowhere. The direct approach then.
"Maybe you've been talking, Emerald."

"Pardon me?"

"My two suspects are Gordie Locker and Hunt Grayson. You know them both. How well?"

"Hey—"

"Maybe you're in on it with one of them. You give him the confidential stuff—and he takes it from there."

"No way! Amanda, you're way off base. I had nothing to do with what you're suggesting. Believe me!"

Did Amanda see her paling a bit? Did she have something to hide? "I don't care if you don't talk to me. I'll be telling the police all about this anyhow."

Emerald grabbed Amanda's forearm. "Don't do that, Amanda," she said. "I swear I didn't give anything away to either of those men."

"If we weren't talking about murders here, I'd probably believe you, Emerald. It's just that I can't take a chance. Understand?"

"Telling the police about me is a waste of time." Emerald relaxed and smiled. "I'll tell them just what I told you." She hurried on. "Wait till I tell Gordie and Hunt that you think one of them is a murderer!"

Now it was Amanda's turn to be hesitant. "Don't do that, please. I'm not sure of anything. I'm desperate. One of them could be the killer. But I'm only starting to think that way. And I haven't had time to tell the police. Emerald, it's too soon to say anything!"

"Is that right? Maybe I won't say anything then—"

"Thank you for that."

"And maybe I will."

"Emerald . . ."

"Somebody's playing a far-out joke on you, Amanda. Both men have designs on you, and you think one of them's going to cut you up in bite-sized pieces. I'm a little jealous of you, as you must realize. But I think somehow you're just going to . . . self-destruct." She pushed by Amanda, the customary bounce back in her step.

That evening Detective McMahon called. His voice was heavy with fatigue. Amanda began to tell him her theories that

PERSONAL

made Hunt and Gordie suspects. He cut her short. "Like I said before, sounds like you have another statement to make. I'll want to tape it. You'll have to come down here."

"When?"

"Look, Amanda, things are kind of crazy at the moment. We're getting heat from up top."

"About redheads being murdered?"

"No."

"About what, then?"

"The municipal judges' murders. We're all working like animals on those."

"But what about Jessica and me? We could be—"

"You could be. And maybe you couldn't be. We have the Kwan murder. *Maybe* it's related to Felicity Foster's dismemberment."

"But Grace—"

"We don't know anything about Grace O'Shea. She might well have left town for one reason or another."

" 'Floyd' said he had her."

"He could be lying. We can't know."

She swallowed her exasperation. "Did you talk to Tani?"

"We sent some people over. He moved out without telling anybody. No forwarding address. Maybe *he* has something to hide. Maybe business as a pimp."

"You can't . . ." Amanda shook the receiver in impotent anger. "When can I come down there and make my statement?"

"We'll have to call you. We're going nuts down here. Believe me."

"I know what's going on!" Amanda said. "The judges are more important than a couple of scared women who aren't somebodies."

"It's not that cut-and-dried, Amanda." The detective's voice was apologetic. "You have to believe me when I tell you that we're not thinking of you as unworthy of our efforts. It's just— it's circumstances, is all."

"I see."

"We'll get to you. You're not the only problem we're putting on hold. We're still doing murders down here. But sometimes the mayor tells us what order to do them in. Try to understand. And have a good evening.''

Amanda looked at the dead receiver as though it were a squashed bug. ''Have a good evening''—indeed!

Before she went into a tailspin she phoned Pop-Up to see how he was doing. They chatted about the increase in his nursing care. ''They're starting with the drugs, kid.'' He paused. ''Maybe that's not such a bad thing.'' That told her how much pain he must be in. ''Be sure you get over here tomorrow, maybe bring Justin. Before long I won't know either of you.''

She felt a wash of love that brought up tears with magic speed. She tried to lighten the conversation for both their sakes with tales of her son's recent band concert. She said nothing about Ned. Pop-Up never spoke that name without preceding or following it with ''deadbeat.''

Off the phone, she decided on a hot bath. She did some of her best thinking in porcelain. She had just poured in the Calgon bath oil beads when the phone rang. She shoved back fears and phantoms and picked up the receiver.

''This is Floyd Philman.''

She gasped despite herself. ''W—What do you want?''

''I want you to know you've caused me a lot of trouble and expense, Mandy Walker. I didn't know that one time we met that you were a nut case.''

''I . . . am a nut case?''

''I know damn well what lying stories you told the cops about me. My attorney and I have been fighting them off for two days. They're hard to convince, but we did it. No thanks to you, baby! They told me you broke into my house. I'm thinking about pressing charges.''

Oh, Lord! What next?

''I want my window fixed. And I want Kaiser's vet bills paid. What the hell did you squirt in his eyes?''

''I have marks of his affection on my arm and leg, Floyd. Your pet could have torn my face off.''

''Trespass was what you were into. The police explained

129

that." He paused. "I want money. Twenty-five for the window, seventy for the vet. Two hundred for my shyster. Say three hundred even."

Three hundred dollars! "I won't give you anything. Go ahead, press charges."

"Thanks to you I can't run my ads anymore. Cops stopped that."

"Did they tell you *why?*"

"I heard all about it and don't believe any of it. It's all your imagination. Your overreaction. I'm telling you, Mandy Walker, I want three hundred—"

She hung up and pressed her palms to her face. She was trembling. Her emotions were torn in so many different directions. She unplugged the phone jack and threw it onto the floor.

She sank with a long sigh into her bath water, added more hot. It was indeed time to do some thinking. She counted days. Tomorrow was Friday. That meant four weeks had passed since she had met Floyd.

Two weeks left.

Sometimes she doubted she should be so sure about the time. Grace had disappeared before her six weeks were up. According to Amanda's notes that anniversary wasn't until tomorrow. Of course she could have wisely left town.

*I'm someone you know.* That phrase kept circling in her mind, not to be ignored. Growing desperation focused her attention again on Gordie and Hunt, both Emerald's friends. Emerald had been filled with denials about playing a part in the dark doings. Just the same, talk of the police had made her as nervous as Grace. She wanted no part of them. Grace's reasons had sensitized Amanda to what that could mean about the dyed blonde, despite her jolly exterior. Emerald, Gordie, Hunt, two of them a team, even if one was an unwitting member. Both men practiced odd ways. Both knew Amanda's comings and goings. Gordie first. His obsession with her and the mysteries of the flash could be the tips of a murderous iceberg.

The police were otherwise engaged with the slaughter of municipal judges. She wasn't going to sit by and wait for a chance to dump her truckload of suspicions on McMahon and

Reti and hope they found time to save Grace, Jessica, and her. She had to act. The question was what to do.

By the time she slid, water shriveled, between sheets she had some good ideas.

At work the next morning she called police headquarters, the records office, and asked for Flo. The woman recognized her name immediately. She asked how her case was going. Amanda explained about the murdered judges and how short-handed the police force was. "McMahon is a good cop, Mandy. It's just that he has to take orders like all of us. How can I help you?"

She asked Flo if she could check on a woman named Emerald Roscheski and gave a description.

"That's not a lot to go on," Flo said.

"It's all I've got."

"Is she Hartford born and raised?"

"I don't know, Flo. Sorry."

"I'll do what I can, sweetie. But I'll tell you I'm short-handed myself. Computers don't do everything."

Amanda's heart sank. "Anything you can do . . ."

Amanda's next call was to Evan Dent at the Hartford *Courant*. She asked him if she could come over on her lunch hour and talk. She wanted to ask a favor . . .

Driving into downtown Hartford, she knew she had two agendas. The most important concerned Hunt Grayson. The second was making sure Evan didn't forget her. She primped in the VW rearview mirror and gave her hair a quick brush.

Evan met her in a big room jammed with CRTs, keyboards, and people talking on phones. He gave her the mini-tour with a few introductions. Reporters looked up from their screens, then their eyes swung back to work. Everything had gone to electronics and computers, he explained. Typewriters, city rooms, green eyeshades, and cigars were long gone. He showed her how the staff filed their stories, feeding the computer. At three large terminals in a corner, page composition was handled. The screens glowed with look-alike newspaper pages. She saw the type and layout familiar from her *Courant* readings.

He got a phone call and hurried off. A woman at one of the terminals looked up at her. Her black hair was shaped to fit like a helmet. Her face was strikingly exotic; American Indian blood, Amanda guessed. Her desk plaque read Zoe Deerheart, Social Editor.

"Business or personal with the *Courant*'s most eligible?" Zoe's voice was husky and vibrant.

Amanda smiled. "Personal—but not *that* kind of personal."

Zoe winked. "You should be a little sharper. He's checking you out—in his own shy way. Take advantage."

Amanda was slightly flustered. "I wasn't really—"

"He *is* shy." She waved her hand around the city room, staffed about half by women. "A lot of us have tried. No luck yet. But we're not giving up." Zoe fell abruptly silent as Evan returned.

"I'm sure you didn't come here to see how the paper's put together." He led her to a snack bar where tables and chairs clustered around a bank of vending machines. The newspaper's most eligible, she thought. Hmmm.

"What can I do for you?" Evan said.

"I wondered if you could do some research for me," she said. "I want you to find some information about a man I know."

He leaned back in his plastic molded chair and pushed his horn rims up his nose. "Does this have to do with why you were talking to the police? About—you said—murder?"

She nodded and gathered her thoughts. "I don't want you to do a story on this, Evan."

He shrugged noncommittally.

"I need the police as allies."

"Why do you need to talk to me, then, if you have McMahon on your side?" His smile was politely mocking.

She was flustered into silence.

"I'm not trying to give you a hard time. What is it? The cops not doing enough?"

She told him they were busy with the murders of municipal

judges. She wasn't yet convinced that McMahon had overcome his prejudice against her or Grace, the woman with her when she and Evan had first met.

He nodded and leaned forward. He gave her a little lecture on the power of present-day media. Sometimes a front-page story had a way of making cops and politicians change their minds. Or it changed the minds of people who gave the orders. He held out his hands, palms up. "Why don't you tell me what's going on?"

"I don't want you to put it in the paper."

"It might not be interesting enough?"

She smiled thinly. "On the contrary. I think it's the sort of thing you newspaper guys love."

"Think so, huh?" He grinned.

"I do." Somehow she managed to grin back.

"Let's do this, then. You tell me what it's all about, and I won't write a word—for now."

"What's that mean?"

"That I'll take my orders from you. If you need *Courant* dynamite to blow this thing wide open, just say the word."

Amanda sat silently. She was tempted. Suppose she didn't find out who was threatening her? Suppose the worst happened? What if her two weeks ran down to a day or two . . . A front-page story would certainly disrupt the status quo like a UFO at an air show. "All right," she said. "I'll tell you. And I have your word that—"

Evan raised a slender right hand. "Swear to God," he said.

She found enough coins for a paper cup of vending machine coffee. By the time she finished her story, they had four empty cups between them.

"Damn!" he said. "What we've got here is a serial murderer of redheaded women. You gotta let me do a story—"

"No!" Amanda was frightened. "You gave your word, Evan. I need your help, but not that way."

He sank back, curbing his enthusiasm. "So what is it you need?"

She told him she wanted him to do a little investigative

reporting on a fellow named Hunt Grayson, head of Insurance City Plus.

"You think he could be the murderer?"

She hesitated. She felt as though she were betraying someone who not only cared for her, but wanted to help and protect her. Nonetheless, she nodded. There was nothing disloyal in finding out something about a man's past. "I have another suspect that I'm going to check on myself. Someone else I know well." She didn't bother mentioning Gordie's name.

"What if the killer isn't either of these guys?"

"I think he is. If he somehow isn't, I'll cross that bridge when I come to it."

Evan winked. "You should let me interview this Emerald woman."

"No! Just do the research, please."

He nodded. "Whatever you prefer."

She touched his hand. "Thanks in advance. I really appreciate anything you can do to help me."

"Don't thank me until I do some good." He got up, his hand sliding out from under hers. "If there's anything else I can do, I want to know about it."

Driving back to work, she realized she had at least one ally among all the hostility and indifference surrounding her. A rather nice-looking ally. Zoe had said he was shy. But eligible. She'd have to see what she could do about developing their relationship after her frightening situation changed for the better.

She looked in the phone book for the number of Phyllis Locker, Gordie's first wife. "She keeps my name and takes my money," he often complained. "Why should she bother being married to me?" There was delay and faint clicking on the line. Call forwarding, Amanda guessed. The line was answered on the second ring. "West Farms Country Club. Phyllis speaking."

Amanda introduced herself, explaining that she was an employee of Phyllis's ex-husband. She had been receiving death threats, possibly from him. She wanted to talk to her about his character.

PERSONAL

"What character?" Phyllis said. "Let's get together. You
can tell me what the jerk is up to."

Amanda took Justin with her after work. The West Farms
Country Club was landscaped and manicured. Awaiting its cue
from sluggish New England spring, fairways and grounds had
finally exploded into greenery. She followed Phyllis's directions and ended up at the golf pro shop. A young man in a
Lacoste shirt with Popeye-sized forearms told her Phyllis was
on the practice tee giving a lesson. He pointed out the way.

Phyllis was kneeling before a sandy-haired woman wearing
designer culottes. The woman held a golf club, the angle of
which Phyllis was adjusting. "Nora, this is your normal align-
ment. Look, feel, and remember. You can't hit it right if you
don't line up right. That's it for today. Same time Monday.
One less day for your golf widowhood." She put her hand on
the younger woman's shoulder. Amanda caught the deer-swift
look of sadness in Nora's eyes before the soldierly grin flashed.
Marriage was hard enough without golf forming a triangle,
Amanda thought.

When Nora had wandered off with her lightweight bag of
expensive clubs, Phyllis joined Amanda and Justin. "You have
to be the woman who called. Gordie's still doing his rough-
and-ready thing, huh?" She looked at Justin. "Want to hit a
few, kid?"

"Don't know how," he said.

Phyllis laughed. She had large even teeth. Her head was
round and tanned, her body roundish but solid. She was about
five-foot-five. Amanda remembered Ned, who bet on golf too,
saying there were no great women golfers over five-eight.
"Well, you start by picking up this club and going over to that
bucket of balls there. Choke up. If you're right-handed, forget
about it and swing hard with your left hand and arm."

Phyllis led Amanda back to the pro shop. She had a tiny
office in the rear. The sign on the door read Assistant Pro.
"That's a favor somebody did me. The pay is nothing. I live
on lessons, tips, and alimony. I do the same thing in the winter
at a snazzy club in Florida." She winked. "It's a nice life.

135

And Gordie hates every minute of it.'' She narrowed her sun-creased gaze and looked Amanda over. "So now you're mixed up with him. What are you? A candidate for wife number three? Is he starting with the rough stuff?''

Amanda explained the Walker-Locker relationship as best she could. Phyllis nodded knowingly. When Amanda came to the end of that, she brought up the murders.

Phyllis's eyebrows rose. "He finally killed a woman, did he?''

# CHAPTER
## ❦ 9 ❧

Phyllis had rushed into marriage to Gordon Locker straight out of home and high school, her head stuffed with TV and film romance. She was determined to "do" for her husband. He gave her every chance. When the first franchise was launched, not only did she alter the red and white uniforms ("I used to call them Red Cross suits. Every time I saw one I didn't want to eat; I wanted to give blood."), she scrimped and did without, so that the business and Gordie could flourish.

She swam a long while in the waters of spousal duties. She endured his absences while he manned the counter when staff called in sick. She bought generic everything and he didn't complain. He wouldn't dream of eating up the restaurant's profits. To get a nickel out of him for clothes or personal needs was a difficult and depressing task. He accused her of undermining their future and his career with her spendthrift ways. She felt guilty and tried to curb her desires. The greatest of these was to be a mother. Her persisting in that vein sparked one of his most generous acts: financing a trip to the gynecologist for her to be fitted with an IUD.

It proved to be one of the wrong kinds. A uterine infection clogged her tubes worse than a heart attack victim's arteries. In sympathy for the permanent departure of the foundation of her femininity, Gordie offered her a chance to work second shift in the restaurant "to get your mind off your imaginary troubles." Shortly thereafter, she began to balk in the smallest ways: not replacing the empty toilet paper roll, failing to hand-wash his uniform pants to save money, not staying off the telephone as ordered. For this straying she was threatened and warned. But words didn't do it.

It seemed a natural course of events at that time when she dwelled in guilt that physical enforcement of his wishes would be the logical result of her intransigence. Shoves were first, along with pinches. At first they left no marks. But when she failed to "behave," her arms and back began to bloom with bruises like savage insect bites. To her surprise, she still continued to carry out her one-woman revolution. The first time he used his fist, she walked out.

He cajoled her back, telling her that the restaurant was making money and it would ultimately be for her. He would make up these rough times in spades. He sang siren songs of the Grand Tetons, Grand Canyon, Grand Cayman, grand years to come for them both. She believed him. Not at once did she realize the traditional pattern of abuse was taking hold: violence, repentance, and repetition. He put aside the effective enough tools of his hands in favor of one they both came to realize was much closer to his heart.

A knife.

It was an old hunting tool from his childhood, the classic gift of manhood from a frustrated outdoorsman father. Gordie kept it cleaned, polished, and sharpened, though he never used it. Then one day, either by accident or intent, Phyllis stayed out shopping an hour longer than she should have. When he got home, she wasn't there. He waited for her, red-eyed and raging. "When I saw the knife in his hand, I thought I was dead," Phyllis said.

She realized later that she *was* dying, bit by bit, day by day. The knife became a sadistic chum never far from her attention, like the man who wielded it. At first he had to hold her down as she struggled. She learned that struggling was dangerous. Struggle meant that the icy tip, instead of making small punctures in her buttocks, cut her. So she learned to lie still and be tortured.

At these moments of terror and submission, Gordie spoke at great length on the despicable nature of women. Phyllis shaded her clear brown eyes, as though from the light of an evil sun. "The things I heard . . . the hate. The wish to hurt. Amanda, lying there listening to this *stuff* . . . you can't imagine, but it was somehow worse than the pain." She waved her hand. "You don't want to hear all this."

"I do," Amanda said.

One day, tortured beyond bearing, desperate, and half mad with fear and worry, Phyllis found her way to a battered women's crisis center. There she poured out not the truth about Gordie's sadism and violence, but a litany of her own shortcomings that had provoked him. The professional on duty listened only up to a point, then got up and put an arm over her shoulder. "Honey, have I got some things to tell you!"

A year later she found an attorney and got what she felt was an equitable divorce settlement. Gordie, on the other hand, thought he had been robbed. He threatened violence, but she moved out of town for a while. She made a life around golf and came back with pride, wholly on her own. Their only interaction: the alimony checks sent by Gordie's bookkeeper.

Phyllis looked appraisingly at Amanda. "Most strangers stop me *long* before I finish all that," she said.

"I wanted to hear it. I think I even needed to hear it." She told the other woman about the murders and threats. "I want your opinion, Phyllis. Do you think Gordie could have murdered two women, and have three more lined up for the same?"

Phyllis leaned back and looked up at the ceiling where a genuine imitation Casablanca ceiling fan beat the conditioned air. She closed her eyes. Amanda imagined the woman's memory parading the most dismal tracts of her married days. She opened her eyes and looked directly into Amanda's. "I'd bet my life on it. In fact, I almost did."

Amanda was chilled. She had uncovered something of the

meaning of the flash in Gordie's eyes. No longer was he a possible suspect. He was moving over to the likely column.

On the way home Justin talked about how far he had hit some of the golf balls. She promised him a trip to a driving range; she had seen several on city outskirts. He was silent awhile. Then he said, "When am I gonna see dad again?"

Amanda felt an inner wrench. Her son couldn't know he was attacking an outpost in her emotional life that was scantily defended these days. "I don't keep track of your father's comings and goings. Trying to do that used to make me crazy."

"He said he's gonna try to get a job in Hartford, so he can visit me more."

"That would be nice." Please stop, Justin, she thought. I don't think I can handle any more Ned-Amanda-Justin questions. She was granted her request. And, as so often was the case, she then wished she hadn't been. He sat quietly awhile as the VW churned along, then touched her arm, something he rarely did. "Is somebody still after you?" She looked down at him, saw the moisture welling in his green eyes. He had been harboring worry like an apprentice miser. His lone question was a single coin from his hoard.

"Maybe," she said brightly. "But the police are trying to find out who he is. And so am I. That's why I wanted to talk to Ms. Locker."

"She has the same name as your boss. Are they married?"

"They were."

"What's she know, then?"

"Enough questions, kiddo. Your mom's doing fine. Don't worry about me. Maybe what you ought to do when we get home is give Pop-Up a call. He's not feeling so hot these days."

"Is he gonna die?"

Amanda's tears began tracking down her cheeks. Justin didn't notice till she sniffled. By then her face was smeared and the crystal drips were falling onto her blouse. "Get me my purse, please. I need a tissue." He groped in it for her. She blew her nose and wiped her eyes.

"Don't cry, mom." His voice told her he was about to start,

too. "Hey, wow!" His emotions changed direction. He held up the silvery cylinder of bootleg mace. "If that sicko slimeball comes up to me I'll—"

"Put the mace back, honey. Just . . . put it back in the purse."

As soon as Justin hung up from his call to his grandfather, the phone rang. He snatched up the receiver. "It's some woman," he said.

"Young man, we are going to have to work on your phone manners."

It was Jessica Morris. She wanted to talk to Amanda in person. "Come for dinner," Amanda offered.

Jessica arrived within a half-hour. She wore green shorts and a halter. White sandals and a ponytail completed the outfit. She was in the first stages of tanning. A shower of freckles somehow improved an already perfect sweep of shoulders and danced on her nose like beauty marks. She eyed the stove top's pots and pans. "You cook!" she said.

"You were expecting Weight Watchers fodder in foil?"

"The only time I eat real food is when I go home. Nobody can burn it the way my mother can."

After introductions Amanda shooed Justin into his room. She went by it later and closed the door. Jessica pulled her chair close to Amanda's. "I want to know what's happening. I called Detective McMahon. He wouldn't even talk to me!"

Amanda explained about the municipal judges' murders and where that left her and Jessica.

"What about Grace O'Shea?" Jessica's eyes were wide with concern.

"I don't know. There hasn't been any word from her. Nothing on TV or in the papers. I think her boyfriend's run out on her and her problems. Maybe she's skipped town, too. Tomorrow's the 'anniversary' of her date with Floyd Philman. If I were her, I wouldn't hang around to celebrate it either."

"But Floyd hasn't done anything."

"Seems he's the timekeeper just the same."

"Ooooh!" Jessica made small fists and beat her knees with anxiety. "What are we going to *do?*" She looked questioningly at Amanda. ''You still think the killer is Gordie Locker or Hunt Grayson?''

Amanda nodded. ''I'm getting a real strong idea Gordie deserves serious consideration. I'm going to talk to his other ex-wife before long. Then I'm going back to the police with all of it. They can take it from there. I think it's possible they'll lock the man up.''

Jessica's face whitened under its new tan. In a small voice she said, ''Hunt Grayson introduced us just today. Mr. Locker said he has something he thinks is perfect for me.''

''He does?'' Amanda was aware she frowned.

''I think you know what it is. He said it's something only a redhead can do.''

''I don't know what it is.''

''You do. It's being Ms. Muncher.''

Amanda gaped. As she sought to control her surprise, Jessica gave her the details of her lengthy meeting with Gordie. He was going to run the Ms. Muncher promotion again. He needed a good-looking redhead to be featured in it. The pay wasn't great, but it was a way for her to get a modeling foothold in Hartford. Jessica looked in genuine naivete at Amanda. ''I asked him why you weren't going to be Ms. Muncher again. He said you two had personal differences.''

''True enough.''

''I told him I didn't want to take anything away from you, that you were my friend and—''

''You don't have to say that, Jess.'' So it was to be Ms. Muncher revisited and she had been left out. Even though she didn't want the role, she thought it only fair that Gordie should talk it over with her. You never got fair treatment from him.

''He said there was going to be a contest this time, that way his restaurants can get more publicity. It's not a beauty contest, really. I mean—well, he explained it better than I can. He said he's going to talk to you about it.'' Jessica put hands to her head. ''He seemed like such a nice guy and now you tell me maybe he's the madman I'm scared to death of. Mandy, what am I going to do?''

"Stay away from him, Jess. Until we know more. It could be suicide to spend time alone with him."

"I don't know. I don't know." She got up and paced. "This is such a big chance for me. I'm all confused. Are you sure about him?"

Amanda sketched in Phyllis's torture at his hands. As she talked, the younger woman's face paled till her freckles stood out like brown spots. "I won't even talk about how he's treated me," Amanda said, "except that I've seen nasty things in that man's eyes."

After a dinner turned tasteless by trouble, Jessica said she had to leave. She took Amanda aside. "One reason I wanted to come and talk to you was to ask you if you minded that I want to be in the Ms. Muncher contest."

"The contest isn't the problem, Jess. It's Gordie."

Jessica nodded nervously. A tiny frown marred her perfect face. Once Amanda had been similarly innocent and open. Ned had started her education; it was going on to this day. She was suddenly determined that Gordie not soil Jessica. Having discovered he was an abuser, she sensed still worse lurked behind the flash. She would find out what that might be.

"Stall him. Stay away from him," Amanda said. "Don't end up alone with him." She slammed Jessica's car door behind her. "Go home and lock the door."

Later, Amanda stewed over Jessica's news. Knowing Gordie, he could have dreamed up the new Ms. Muncher campaign on the spot to seduce the lovely girl. Possibly, he intended to work it out so he got her into bed or . . . steered her to what could well be his own patented version of violent death and mutilation. Jessica, she, Gordie, work, her recent hope of a promotion, and the threat of murder. What a tangle! One thing was clear: her boss was beginning to appear to be a darker force than she had ever suspected.

On Saturday she had an even higher priority than her suspicions: what might possibly be Justin's last visit with Pop-Up. They found him subdued and glassy-eyed, a nurse bustling his bedside equipment into order. His world had shrunk to bed, bedside tables, and his chair by the window. Clearly, his energy was diminished and his will weakened. She held his hand like a schoolgirl, and made Justin do the same. Despite unwillingness in the boy's eyes, he obeyed. She was proud of him. She was ready to spend the whole day, but the nurse explained that the medication made Pop-Up rest most of the time.

Before leaving, Amanda took Justin aside. "I want you to look hard at your grandfather, and I want you to talk to him. Make sure he knows it's you. I'm not going to make you come back again until . . ."

His fallen face meant he understood that he wouldn't be seeing Pop-Up alive again. He did as he was told. In the VW he said, "Are you going to go back, mom?"

"Every day for a little while," she said. She sniffled. "Tissue, please."

After visiting Pop-Up, she had arranged with the Sargins for Justin to spend the afternoon with Cooper. She needed a few hours to visit with Darlene and four more to get to and from West Morris. The town was in the northwest corner of the state where Gordie had told her his second ex ran a "faggy" art gallery. West Morris properties, Amanda found, were being bought up by New Yorkers mad to escape the city on weekends. Rather a good place for a gallery, she thought. La Belle Hélène was the first floor of a white frame old New England home. Amanda knew only a little about contemporary art, but what hung and sat within view didn't look like knickknacks to her. The prices were kept in a book at the desk manned by a pale woman in her mid-twenties with large violet eyes. Her portholewide horn rims and hair were jet black, her pants suit white. Her name tag said she was Delphine. She pointed Darlene out to Amanda.

Darlene Cris was a big-boned woman who had allowed herself to fill out too well. She wore her auburn hair in a high bun. Under her shiftlike dress, flesh moved without the support of much underwear. She wore heavy masculine sandals which her large feet amply filled. She was talking to a prosperous-looking couple about an artist who had painted a huge canvas filled with colored blotches and thick lines in tumbled pick-up-sticks order.

When the customers departed, after leaving a deposit, Amanda introduced herself. Darlene led her straightaway to Delphine and introduced her as "my companion." To Delphine she said, "She works for Gordie. Can you imagine?" The two women exchanged healthy titters. Both made Amanda nervous.

"Am I right, Amanda? You want to talk about my marriage to Gordie? My interlude of uninterrupted bliss?"

"Yes. Because—"

"I can sum it up, the whole two years, four months, and sixteen days. Here it is: I was an idiot; he was a psychopath."

Darlene insisted Delphine sit with them as she "stirred the rubbish heap" for Amanda.

Before the marriage, she had thought herself in love, thought Gordie a macho but loving man. As sometimes happened, the wedding ceremony raised the curtain on her spouse's true nature. The pattern of Darlene's marriage to Gordie was different than that Phyllis had described. There was no period of submission. Darlene hadn't been of docile temperament. She had done weight work and was in good physical and mental condition. She resisted his abuse, greeting his blows with her own. Increasingly violent battles took the place of normal domestic doings. Then out came the knife . . .

In time the light dawned. She fled, found an attorney who knew a sympathetic woman judge. Darlene's eyes were on Delphine's face when she said, "In a way I owe Gordie. He helped me understand myself better. Did I ever tell you that in those words, lamb?"

Delphine shook her head. Her raven hair caressed a slender neck which suffused itself with delicate shades of stressed modesty. Amanda's own face began to grow red. She felt quite uncomfortable.

"Tell us about you and Gordie," Darlene prodded.

Before she could, a raft of upscale customers swept in, buying mania in their eyes. While Darlene and Delphine dealt with them, she went out into the air. She found she wanted to be away from La Belle Hélène, and was ashamed to admit it to

PERSONAL

herself. She liked to believe she was open-minded. When she found herself thinking some things were simply unnatural, it illuminated her own limitations.

When she went back into the gallery she told the two women her story of murders, threats, and Gordie as the prime suspect. It was taking longer than she wanted. La Belle Hélène closed while the owners ate their dinner. They took Amanda upstairs to rooms decorated with tasteful pieces of art and fabrics. Over a cup of vegetable soup to which she couldn't do justice, Amanda pushed her interview to its end. What did Darlene think about Gordie as a candidate for a role as a murderer and mutilator?

The large woman ladled another cup of soup from the tureen, then studied it as though answers lay there. "I never counted the times he said I deserved to die," she said, "and that he wanted to help me on my way. I don't count the number of times he put that knife to my throat or used its point somewhere else on me. Just little cuts, you know, nothing that would scar. He was crazy, of course, but he wasn't a fool."

"Do you think he had it in him to murder—if not you, other women?"

Darlene rose and put her foot on the side of Amanda's chair. She raised the hem of her shift. Her lower leg was puckered with angry white scars of disaster followed by determined surgery. Amanda drew in her breath sharply.

"He tied me up and put his knife to my throat. Then he put my leg between two chairs and broke it with a Westinghouse iron."

Amanda looked away, what little appetite she had fleeing like a frightened wren.

"He didn't do it with just one whack," Darlene stated matter-of-factly.

"What more do you need, Amanda?" Delphine said. *"What more do you need?"*

Driving back to Hartford, Amanda paid little attention to the bright late June greenery of rural Connecticut. Her mind was filling in an outline of a Gordie Locker far uglier than she had anticipated from the flash. The thin vein of sadism she had just uncovered could well lead down to a mother lode of murder and mutilation.

She had found the killer.

There were more subtle characteristics of his personality that now fell into place with cell-door authority. He showed little sense of proportion or restraint. The bold entrepreneur dared the world to punish him for risk taking. When it didn't, his twisted mind had pushed him on past mere audacity to wife abuse, forward to causing pain to strangers, then to the actual murder of women. Escaping still, he now drew her into his careening world, though passing over her would have been far safer. She would be his most dangerous victim because their lives were intertwined. He had heightened that risk with his true message: *I am someone you know.*

She had to talk to the police!

She swung by police headquarters and asked for McMahon or Reti. They both had the weekend off. Frustrated, she left a note asking them to call her. She wondered if they would. On the way to pick up Justin at the Sargins' she found the answer in a *Courant* vending box window through which a headline shrieked that another judge had been murdered. She didn't need to buy a paper for the details. The police had failed to protect the man. The pressure from city hall would increase. Public opinion would bay after the boys in blue like a hound. The problems of Grace O'Shea, Jessica Morris, and Amanda Walker? How important could they be?

She and Justin had just returned to the apartment when the door buzzer sounded. Ned announced on the intercom that he wanted to spend some time with his son. Despite her innards twisting, she released the downstairs latch. She *had* to resolve the situation with him, control his exits and entrances around the stage of her life. It was hard to concentrate on that. She had so much else on her mind . . .

She waited a few minutes for him to take Justin out. When he made no move to do so, she quickly drew a conclusion suggested by her years at his side. He was broke, needed a meal, and this was the easiest way to get one. She resented his cunning and took it very personally. But if she made a scene and threw him out, Justin would be hurt.

She waited till Ned sat talking to the boy, feet out in leisure. She bent over him from behind, hand on his shoulder. She sank her nails into his flesh. "Don't try this again, buddy!" she whispered.

She made American chop suey because she knew he hated it. Beggars couldn't be choosers, and that's what he was. Her stomach was still bothering her. She didn't like having him around! She had a scanty appetite. She left the table, wandered into her bedroom, and closed the door. She stretched out, but couldn't relax. She wanted Ned to leave.

When the door buzzer sounded, she didn't bother to get up. Justin knew who should be let in. She put her head back and closed her eyes. After some minutes she heard a voice not quite familiar, but . . . "So where is she?" Oh my God! She sat up in an instant.

It was Floyd Philman's voice!

"I know that VW is hers. Hey, kid, where's your mother, huh?"

"You said you weren't looking for trouble." Ned's tones were turning toward belligerency. She had to get out there.

She opened the door. Ned and Floyd were facing each other, Justin off to the side, a hesitant expression on his smooth face. She squirmed inwardly when Floyd's gaze fell on her. Whatever else had brought him to her apartment, the chance to ogle her played a role, too. She remembered his house jammed with redhead porn. All perfectly "normal." Thank you, Dr. Moodleman!

"I came for my three hundred bucks for my dog, my window, and my shyster," he said. "I get the money now, or I sue."

"Is that right?" Ned said. He pointed at Floyd. "You're the pervert with the house full of dirty pictures, aren't you?"

"Ned, I'll handle this," Amanda said.

"Who's this guy, Amanda? Your fancy man?"

"He happens to be my ex-husband."

"Here at the right time, it looks like," Ned said. "Mandy

PERSONAL

told me all about her visit to your house, chief. I'd say she owes you nothing. She oughta sue *you* over that pinscher you got.''

"Look, I didn't come here to listen to you, blowhard—''

"Will you two *stop* it?''

"I'll stop when I run this weirdo out of here.'' Ned wanted to play hero in front of his son. Despite the overwhelming evidence that every day of his life presented, some strange part of him imagined he was a white knight performing valiant feats to earn the love of small boys, fair maidens, and other worthies. She kn w that when so possessed, Ned could do any crazy thing. She had to stop this.

Ned jerked a thumb toward the door. "Out, you worm-necked geek!'' he said.

"Who the hell you think you are?'' Floyd's short-lashed eyes stared with rising anger. She remembered how quickly she had angered him. Mr. Hot Temper himself. What was happening? "I'll leave when I get the money I'm owed,'' Floyd said.

"The money you *think* you're owed,'' Ned said. Amanda agreed with at least that. Ned was pointing again.

Floyd stepped forward and pushed Ned's hand aside. "She pays now or pays later.''

"She pays nothin'!''

"Stay out of this, Mr. Hero. She owes me!''

"Get out of this house!'' Ned bellowed.

Amanda began: "Stop it, you two, before—''

Ned got in the first shove. After that it was too hard to keep track. Both men were shovers and punchers, rather than wrestlers. Her coffee table went over with a broken leg. Justin added his screams of encouragement to his father's clumsy battle. She tried to get between them and got a nasty, unintentional punch in the belly for her trouble. While she staggered, trying to suck back her breath from wherever it had fled, she heard another voice raised in shouting. In dismay she recognized Mrs. Clendenon beyond the wall, howling her host of questions about rape and assault. Not again! Amanda tried to find the breath to shout that everything was all right. The two men, bellowing all the while, locked themselves together in a violent embrace and bowled over her tag-sale floor lamp. Its bulb exploded. Beyond the wall Mrs. Clendenon called on the names of Jesus, Mary, and Joseph. A call to Saint 911 would be next.

Amanda had to go next door and stop her. She screamed for the two men to stop being perfect idiots. "Let them fight, mom!" Justin shouted. "Dad's winning!"

She would have handicapped them differently, considering her ex's long losing record. She tried to push past to the door. They careened into her, cursing and grunting. She went over like a candlepin. On hands and knees she scrambled ahead. She was turning the knob when Mrs. Clendenon, now out in the hall, shouted that everything was going to be all right: the police were on the way. Amanda sprawled where she knelt, dreading what was to follow.

The responding officers were the same two who had come in answer to Mrs. Clendenon's previous summons. Amanda tried to explain. Their two faces took on the placid masks of men who had heard everything before—a gross of times. They surveyed the damage and looked speculatively at her. "Trouble just wants to come your way, Red, doesn't it?" the shorter officer said.

"And you don't do nothing to make it happen, right?" said the other.

Amanda was red faced and speechless. "You ought to talk to your homicide people," she said finally. "Some guy is promising to murder me!"

"Is that right?" the shorter man asked.

"Yes!" She felt her color rising further.

"Is it one of these guys?" the older cop said.

"No, it's somebody else. And I think I know who it is. I've been trying to talk to Detective—"

"Well, hey, that's something else. What do you want us to do with these guys?"

"Get them out of here!"

Justin, whom she had forgotten, howled and ran weeping to his room. She pressed palms to her face and muttered into the

150

darkness. In time she gathered her wits. "You heard me. Get them out of here!"

Ned and Floyd began to protest. Threatened with handcuffs, they went quietly. When the door opened, she glimpsed Mrs. Clendenon hovering in the hall like a witch over her conjured kettle of trouble.

"I don't want to see either of you around here again!" Amanda shouted. "Do you hear? *Do you hear?*" Then she hurried to Justin, to offer him what comfort she could in their world, gone unbalanced, mad, and murderous.

# CHAPTER

## ❧ 10 ❧

She couldn't remember when she had greeted a Sunday as unwillingly as this one. She had a whole day in which to keep the wheels turning in her desperate private investigation. But there was no one she could reach. She wanted to talk to Flo at police headquarters to see if she had found out anything about Emerald Roscheski, but couldn't find her home number in the phone book. She wanted to find out if Grace's whereabouts had been discovered, but no one answered at her number. Tani had fled, likely permanently. Above all, she wanted to tell Detective McMahon what she had found out about Gordie Locker's criminal nature, and to propose him as the likely suspect. Out of frustration, she sat down and wrote out notes of her interviews with Phyllis and Darlene. When she did get some of McMahon's time, she would be ready to make her statement. In her mind there no longer was any question: Gordon Locker was their man. He should be arrested.

With a surge of despair, she realized that police records would show she was involved in yet another domestic disturbance. That damned Mrs. Clendenon! There was no use talking to her or to her downtrodden husband in an effort to get her to change her meddling ways. What would the detective think to find she was hobnobbing again with her ex-husband, and her *Reformer* date, of whom she had been so recently terrified?

# PERSONAL

She imagined the cop scratching his thinning scalp and mumbling about independent women who mix and match guys and can't make up their minds about how they feel about any of them. Maybe she was being too hard on him. From their first meeting on he had made it clear he wanted to help her and the other redheads.

She left Justin at home and made a quick run to Pop-Up's apartment. Pop-Up was subdued. She knew that was because of the drugs. He knew who she was. He still could walk around, sit by his window and study the neighborhood. Past that there wasn't much positive. The nurse said he was doing well enough considering the inevitable.

It was a rainy day, so she took Justin to a movie matinee. Brave men and beautiful, almost liberated women vanquished evil on three continents. Cute animals somehow played roles. After the film the two of them made their way to the VW hunched under her umbrella. Depression and anxiety warred for the biggest share of her attention.

There was one almost bright spot in the day: a call from Evan Dent. Somebody in the world cared about her. Before she could ask him if he had found out anything about Hunt Grayson, he gave her a bit of a fright. He said he had gone to the *Reformer* offices and talked to Emerald Roscheski.

"You said you wouldn't."

"I said I wouldn't write anything. I'm not going to—yet. Even if the cops don't have time for you, I do. I thought I'd see if I could find out anything from her." He laughed. "She's quite a character, isn't she?"

"She doesn't think much of me, I know that. She probably talked to you because you're a man. She likes men."

"For whatever reason, we did have a little chat."

"And?"

"However your murdering acquaintance attached you to Floyd Philman, I just can't bring myself to believe that woman had anything to do with it. I talk to a lot of people in my line of work, Mandy. I'm not a bad judge of character, or of when somebody's lying. My guess is she's telling the truth. I think she's a dead end."

153

"Then how did whoever find out about me and the other redheads?"

"I think it all starts with Floyd himself, not with his ads. Understand? Do you happen to know if either Gordie or Hunt by any chance knows the man?"

Amanda's heart thumped, as though with discovery. Why hadn't she thought of that? "I . . . don't know. But I can try to find out."

"It's not a bad idea. Anything out of the police?"

"Nothing. They're too busy with the judges' murders."

"I've done some work on those. Very ugly stuff."

"Are they anywhere near being solved?"

"There are some leads, but who knows when they'll arrest somebody? Sorry to give you that news. I'm working on Hunt Grayson. I'll let you know as soon as I have something or if I come up empty. If there's anything else you need, just let me know."

She drew a deep breath. "Run away with me to the French Riviera. You pay." She waited for his laughter.

"An excellent idea."

There wasn't a hint of joking in his tone! Well! Maybe he was interested. Zoe had called him the shy type. Such men needed encouragement. If she could just get the police to grill Gordie until he confessed that he was the killer . . . That would set her free to resume her life. Evan might even become part of it. She thought of his boyish, horn-rimmed face and wanted to hold it between her breasts and hug it till his glasses steamed.

"Before we visit the Côte d'Azur, I'm serious about my offer. If you need help, let me know."

"Yes, sir!"

"One other thing. I guess you could call this a related topic. Emerald told me she's going to take your place."

The first thing Amanda thought was that she was going to lose her job. Before she could reply, Evan hurried on. "Your job as Ms. Muncher."

"That!"

PERSONAL

"She said your suspect, Gordie, was holding some kind of competition this coming Friday and she expected to win."

The same one Jessica had mentioned—with the same optimism. Gordie was busy with his lies, considering blondes now as well as redheads, his motives tangled in Amanda's mind like a reel's backlashed line. Business, brutality, and very possibly violent murder crossed and crisscrossed her professional and private lives, binding her to her boss and to those who might be either his victims or would-be lovers. Her head spun trying to sort it all out. The best she could do was to get to the police and avoid spending a single minute alone with Gordie Locker.

Smiling grimly, she realized she was developing a list of men she didn't want to be with: Ned, Floyd, now Gordie. Who knew what Evan would find out about Hunt Grayson? Maybe he would end up on her list, too.

She couldn't concentrate solely on being stalked by a murderer and shadowing anxiety nearly as insidious as Pop-Up's cancer. The tasks and responsibilities of her days kept rolling at her, as steadily as the breakers beating Nauset Beach. There was no plea she could make to the school superintendent that would prevent the three half-days as school wound down to its late June closing. That meant she had to make some kind of arrangements for Justin's afternoons. She couldn't fail to show up at work; Gordie was a hard-liner about keeping one's hours. How ironic that the man who might well be stalking her also signed her paycheck. Since it was conceivable that she was wrong in her suspicions, she didn't dare run out on Muncher's. If Gordie wasn't the killer and she panicked, she could end up jobless and still in desperate danger. There was nothing to do but go on with her life as best she could.

She might have kept her shaky balance indefinitely . . . Then Monday Justin brought home the box.

He didn't mention it until after she had given Jilly her recorder lesson for that afternoon's sitting. In the schoolyard before the buses came, he was approached by a black boy he had never before seen carrying a shopping bag. The boy asked him if he was Justin Stanton. When he said he was, he was

155

PERSONAL

given the bag. "Man say you get this." Before Justin could
question him he ran off. Looking inside he saw a taped-up
shoe box. The magic marker letters had read *For Amanda
Walker Only.*

"Where is it?" she asked after Justin finished his story.

Justin brought it from his bedroom. The Nike shoe box was
sealed with strapping tape. She shook it. Whatever was inside
wasn't heavy. She put it on the kitchen table and got a paring
knife out of the drawer. She had no idea what it was, but her
nerves had so deteriorated that her hackles rose in the face of
another mystery, however brief and small. She ran the knife
blade around the box seams. With Justin looking on, she lifted
the lid, angling it so she would see the contents before him.

What she saw was a human hand.

She reflexively jammed the lid back down, her mind com-
pleting the processing of what she had seen. Rings. Rings on
all four fingers and thumb. She was holding Grace O'Shea's
right hand!

She jumped up, clutching the box. Her knees were held
together with chewing gum and cobwebs. She staggered.

"Hey, mom, let me see!"

"No!" Her head felt light enough to float off her shoulders.

"What is it?"

"Nothing for you, I'll tell you." She tottered toward the
bathroom, the loathsome box jammed under her arm. Her son
must *not* see . . . "Give me a minute." She closed the door
behind her. Her legs gave way and she sprawled down like a
drunk. The box fell from her grasp and hit the floor. The hand
rolled out onto the threadbare Oriental-pattern bathmat.

She turned her head away, but not before she saw that the
hand had been cleaned. Every ring had been polished to
jewelry-store gleam. Bile rose in her throat. She doubted her
legs would carry her to the toilet. She dragged herself across
the floor to the bowl. She heaved a half-dozen times, bitter
bile rising to the back of her mouth. Whimpering, she wiped
her mouth and drew in deep drafts of air through her nostrils.
She fought for control.

Grace was dead!

156

PERSONAL

Jessica Morris was next!

Then it would be her turn.

She propped herself up on the toilet, her mind racing itself into near paralysis. She didn't know how long she sat on the floor.

"Mom, hey, you OK in there?" Justin stood just outside the door.

"Sure. Be out in a little bit."

"It's the box that's bothering you, huh?"

Amanda said nothing.

"What's in it?"

"Nothing that concerns you!" Her reply was too loud and strident. "Don't ask about it again. All right?"

"I'm sorry." He was upset.

"I'll be out in a couple of minutes. I'm going to wash my face, then you and I are going for a ride."

"Where to?"

"The police station."

She went right to the sergeant on evening duty, Justin in tow. "I want to see Detective McMahon," she said.

The sergeant recognized her. "Sorry, Ms. Walker. He's tied up right now. You should've called instead of making the trip."

"Is that right? Well, I kind of had to do it. I wanted to show him *this*." She slid the box across the counter. She nodded at her son. "The boy hasn't seen what's in there. Let's keep it that way." Her knees were still shaky and her heart pounded. She resisted the urge to grab the counter for support. The sergeant put the box on the floor behind the counter. There he opened it. When he looked up again, his olive skin had paled by several shades. He picked up the phone. "Get McMahon," he said. Pause. "I don't give a damn! Get him!"

He gave Amanda directions and said he'd watch Justin. "Hope you don't mind carrying the box a little further. We're short-handed tonight."

McMahon looked beat. Too much pressure from up top, too many coffees, and no time at all to step back from anything.

157

PERSONAL

He led her to a closet-sized room, smelling of sweat and tension. "You haven't been working on my case," she said.

He pushed a hand through his thinning hair. "I don't decide my priorities. I'm sorry about that."

"You saw the report on the fight in my apartment, didn't you?"

"Even if that hadn't happened, my priorities wouldn't have changed, Amanda. Law enforcement is a tough business. Sometimes it's a dirty business." He sagged into a wooden chair. "In a vast sea of human corruption we're a tiny lifeboat that people struggle to for hope. There isn't room aboard for everybody. And because we're all human, there're holes in the planking." He looked pointedly at her. "I hope you didn't come all this way to lecture me."

She slid the box across the table. "Someone gave this to my son at school. He brought it home on the bus—like a science project."

While McMahon looked inside, Amanda turned her head. "It used to be attached to Grace O'Shea," she said.

"You sure?"

"It's the rings. Those are her rings."

He nodded and put the lid back on. "Positive?"

"Absolutely." She stared at his lined face. "She's dead. He got her, kept her, then murdered her. And I think I know who did it."

Reading from her notes, she told him and a tape recorder concisely and clearly why Gordie Locker should be questioned. He wrote down Gordie's name, address, and phone number. He went to a phone in the corner of the room. "You know Jessica Morris's number?" She gave it to him and he called. She was home. He told her he was going to send a car over for her. He told her Amanda was there. He wanted to talk to both of them.

*Now* she was getting action out of the police! She hoped with all her heart that it wasn't too little and too late.

Jessica arrived with a friend. His name was Karl. He was about six-foot-seven. Atop sloping weight lifter's shoulders his bullet head seemed pea small. His forearms were as thick as

158

cured Smithfield hams. He probably popped steroids with his morning vitamins. Beside him Jessica seemed slender as Tinker Bell.

McMahon told them about the hand. Even though no corpse had been found, it was reasonable to assume Grace had been murdered, too. Jessica jumped out of her chair, her face a colorless mask. "If she's dead, then I'm next. *I'm next!*"

"You were stupid to answer that ad," Karl said. "You had me. You shoulda been satisfied. Look at what you got yourself into."

Jessica made a small bleating noise and sat back down, emotion contorting her cover-girl face. "What am I going to do?"

"The reason I asked you to come down here is to make a big point for you both," McMahon said. "It's time to leave town."

Both women sat speechless. Time to leave town? Amanda spoke first. "I can't leave! My father's dying. If I leave, I lose my job. I don't want to leave. I want to be protected! I've told you from whom." She pointed at the detective. "Gordie Locker, my boss!"

"Gordie?" Jessica said. "That nice man? It can't be. I might end up working for him, too."

"Arrest him!" Amanda shouted.

"Don't tell me how to do my job." McMahon drew a deep breath to control his temper. The last days had left his nerves ragged. "Everything you just told me about him proves that he's a son-of-a-bitch. There're a lot of sons-of-bitches in this world, Amanda. That doesn't mean he's the one offing redheads."

The argument was on. It circled several poles. Jessica saw the upcoming chance to be the new Ms. Muncher as a breakthrough for her modeling career. She didn't want to believe it was Gordie stalking her. She wasn't going to throw away a big chance just because of Amanda's wild suspicions. She wouldn't leave town either. Both women demanded police protection. McMahon refused to give it. His admitting that municipal judges were being protected made matters worse.

"That's not fair!" Jessica shouted. He told them it would take some time to bring Gordie in for questioning. If he wouldn't cooperate, they would have to proceed carefully within the law. More time wasted there. So long as he was free . . . well, if he was their man, they could use their imaginations.

"This is all screwed up," Karl said to McMahon. "Can't you get it together?" His ham arms rose and fell in a gesture of efficiency.

"The way they do on TV and in the movies, son?" McMahon said. "All neat and tidy? This isn't the movies. This is life. Nothing is neat and tidy."

For a half-hour he attempted to persuade them to leave Hartford for as long as it took to catch the murderer. When he was unsuccessful, he returned to option two. They should move in with friends and take whatever other additional steps were necessary to see that they didn't find themselves alone.

Karl nodded. "That's it, Jess. You come stay with me. I'll protect you. Anybody tries anything, I'll kick his ass to the moon." He looked at McMahon. "I got a black belt and know kung fu. I got a different way to kill for every day of the week. I'll protect her."

The detective studied the younger man's massive frame. "Teaching you martial arts was like giving an atomic bomb to Godzilla. Watch how you throw that weight around, Karl, or you might end up on the wrong side of this desk. All you body builder/karate types are nutso." He studied Jessica's still pale face. "That arrangement suit you, love?"

"I am not your love." Jessica's voice was tiny.

McMahon sighed and waved a hand. "Not a sexist statement, please. Just a term of endearment." He covered his face with spread palms for a long moment.

"Karl's been after me to move in ever since I told him I answered an ad. This looks like the time to do it."

"How about you, Amanda?"

"I'm not sure where to go."

"Think of someplace. Today. It's for your own protection."

Her irritation burst out. "Just arrest Gordie Locker and we can all go home and sleep in our own beds!"

"Don't bet on it," the detective said.

After Jessica and Karl left, McMahon asked for a few more minutes with Amanda. Considering the message to her written in french fries, he asked her to make a list of all the men she knew.

"We want Gordie," she said.

"What if you're wrong?"

"Wrong? If I am, well . . . you know something? That makes me think it doesn't have to be a man," she said. "That weird voice could have been a woman's!"

He tossed his head while digging for a pencil and paper. "I doubt it. Men take care of the murdering for the human race." He handed her the pencil and paper. "Men's addresses as close as you know them. Phone numbers would be nice."

She did as he asked, then used the walk down the hall to explain that she was Gordie's employee, that she needed her job, which would continue for a while certainly, even if he were arrested. She didn't want him to know that she was his accuser until he was proven guilty. "He and I don't get along. All he needs is an excuse and he'll fire me. Suggesting to you that he's a killer would probably give it to him. Do you understand?"

"Yeah. I think we can manage that."

"I'm in a crazy spot, aren't I?"

"Crazy and dangerous." On the way down to Justin, he put a hand lightly on her shoulder. "I hope you'll believe I'm sorry about Grace."

Amanda nodded, her throat suddenly closed up.

"It would be nice if we find fingerprints on the box or something else. That way her dying would at least help us."

"You could have stopped it." Amanda left McMahon and headed for Justin.

She drove home feeling considerable relief: the police were really moving at last!

Just the same, the next ten days were going to be tough.

She got two phone calls later that evening. The first was from Ned, wondering when he could come by and see Justin again. She hung up on him. When Floyd called to press his demands for money, she slammed the receiver down with extra force. One thing moving away would accomplish would be getting rid of those two for a while. But where should she go?

She had an answer right away. She phoned Pam. There was a great deal to tell her. Charged by nerves, Amanda rushed through the gory stuff in more detail than necessary. Pam couldn't get a word in. "When McMahon said we should move in with somebody, I thought of your spare bedroom." Finally she drew a breath.

"Oh, Mandy . . ." Pam's voice was peculiar. "I can't."

"What's wrong? Is somebody already staying with you?"

"No. Oh, this is . . . awful." Amanda heard Pam draw a deep breath. "The reason you can't come is I won't be here. Bud and I are going to be married tomorrow. We didn't want to wait. We know it's the right thing for us. We didn't tell our friends. It's a private ceremony in front of a justice of the peace. Just our folks as witnesses. No big wedding. Then we're going on our honeymoon . . ."

Amanda lowered the receiver, even though Pam was still talking. Nothing in her power could stop its descent. She stood staring down at the shaped plastic.

Pam didn't call back.

By morning she had reached a decision. She knew where she might stay. From work she called Zoe at the *Courant,* reintroducing herself. Zoe remembered her.

"I'm looking for a character reference," Amanda said. "Want to help me out?"

"Sure. Who?"

"Evan Dent. Can I trust him?"

"Sure. Trust him to behave himself, if that's what you mean. He behaves himself too much!"

Her husky laughter brought a smile to Amanda's lips. "What I mean is . . . is he—you know, honest. No trouble in his life?"

"Oh, that kind of stuff. Sure. I should behave as decently

162

as he does. Why? Does he want to borrow money or something?"

"It's nothing like that."

"I hope whatever you're up to leads to something with our shy hero. If it does, go for it, Amanda!"

"I will. Thanks, Zoe. Appreciate it."

"*De nada*, sweetie."

She called Evan. "I'll teach you to offer to help me, guy. I have a *big* favor to ask."

"Anything you want. Just name it."

"You better wait till you hear what it is." She told him about her visit to McMahon and his advice. She was anxious and worried about where to live temporarily. Could Evan take her and Justin in for two weeks? Play bodyguard when he could? He came well recommended, she told him, so far as Zoe was concerned. She held her breath waiting for his reply. She feared for her life and needed safety and support. Beyond that she had another agenda—developing a relationship with a reasonable man who showed subtle interest in her. "Just what do you expect me to do?" he asked. She gave him her version a bit hesitantly. Coexistence after working hours, maybe shared meals. She'd be happy to do the cooking. When possible maybe he'd make sure she wasn't alone.

"I'll have to think about it," he said.

She heard hesitancy in his voice. Her heart sank. "For how long, Evan?"

"Later today."

"Fair enough."

There was another part to her new strategy. She not only had to protect herself, she had to make sure no one grabbed Justin as a step to getting to her. She explained to her son that whoever had been threatening her over the last couple weeks hadn't been caught. She was looking to protect herself and him as well, so no complaining. For these last two half-days of school she would have him get off the school bus at the Sargins'. Peggy would call a cab and send him to the restaurant. Once there, Amanda would give him a booth of his own which she could see from her office. When school finally ended, she would think of something else.

Midafternoon Evan called back. She held her breath. He was enthusiastic. She and Justin were welcome to stay with him. He didn't know how well he could do as a bodyguard. He had a job to do and traveled around the city. He wouldn't always be with her. If she didn't mind his occasional absences, she was welcome. He needed a day to get the place in shape. She would understand when she saw where he lived.

"I have to thank you, Evan. I mean big thanks, the kind all wrapped up with silver paper and a bow."

"Having you two around will be thanks enough."

Lucky lady, she thought. Once in a while you win one. She hung up saying a silent blessing for the man. Maybe she would get through all of this.

She worked with Justin getting clothes and possessions together for their migration. She gave the houseplants a good watering. Who knew when she'd dare come back to do it again? She arranged to have her mail stopped at the post office. Let *them* hold the bills for a change. One of the advantages of wearing a uniform to work was that she didn't have to drag tons of clothes to Evan's. Casual wear and her good dress were all she took. She threw her toilet articles into an old purse; she owned no luggage or traveling bags.

After work, with Justin in the passenger seat, shopping bags of clothes and possessions in the rear, she followed Evan's directions to his home in New Hartford about thirty miles from the city. He had warned her it was a small warehouse. Indeed it was as old and rambling as described. What surprised her was the quality of work he had done on those areas he had found time to remodel. He had used exposed brick, glass, and hand-worked wood to make the most of the open spaces. He broke them up with low counters, portable partitions, and art works. She gasped at the towering silvery sculptures and the paintings—slashes and bars of color that complemented the hung fabrics and throw rugs. "*Voilà!* The money pit," he said.

"Evan Dent, you have got your money's worth! This place is lovely!"

"Well, not all of it. I have a *lot* of work left." He led them out of what he called the "civilized" section into the cavernous remainder. There, hand tools lay about on workbenches. Heavier ones leaned in corners. Wooden storage cubicles were fogged with dust, their rusty padlocks unused. "Here there be spiders," he said.

"Yuk!" Amanda turned back toward the rooms' light and order.

"The sort of place only a ten year old could love, huh, Justin?" Evan's laugh echoed from the distant grimy brick.

"Yeah! Can I explore?"

"Sure. But come check out your quarters first."

Evan led the two up a flight of stairs and a five-runged ladder to a small sleeping loft. Amanda smelled new paint. "I just happened to finish this in time."

"You did it for Justin!" She gave him a hug, and smelled faint, tasteful cologne. He patted her shoulder gently.

"Hey, this is so neat!" Justin shouted. "Thanks, Mr. Dent!"

He led Amanda to her first-floor room. The wide windows looked out across a strip of lawn to a stream bubbling over an abandoned dam's tumbled stones. The last room they saw was the kitchen. "Hint!" Evan said.

Amanda explored the larder and in a short time had dinner together: quick clam spaghetti, a green salad, and Ben and Jerry's Very Berry from the freezer. Justin investigated the dusty expanses. After dinner Evan banned further explorations. "Too dark and too dangerous for you back there, son." Before the boy could complain Evan said he had something else to show him. It was the only room they hadn't seen, his small den. It was tucked into a corner made up of tall frameless windows, custom draped to provide privacy. The drapes were lined for New England winters. In an odd, angled corner stood a pinball machine, lights flashing. On its vertical score panel a Nordic-looking hero and a maiden wearing a 40D armored bra swung swords at hairy shapes. Justin went berserk. "That'll take care of him until bedtime," Amanda said on the way to the cozily lit living area.

After Justin had climbed the loft ladder in pajamas, Evan

offered to read to him. She hesitated. That had always been her personal pleasure. Evan was threatening to sweep the boy away. She smiled. A real role model. Justin needed one. She and Evan agreed they'd switch, reading on alternate nights. From the loft she heard his soft voice saying, "Have you ever heard of a book called *Kim?*"

After Justin was asleep, Evan poured fingers of Benedictine into two snifters and gave her one. He took the love seat opposite her, a small natural slate coffee table between them. The lighting was subdued but warm. For the first time in many days, she was able to lean back and begin to relax. "I have to thank you again, Evan. It's nice to be here. It's nice not to be alone."

"I'm not doing you that much of a favor, considering what's happening in your life."

"Oh, I think you are." She smiled.

He lowered a shoulder in a shadow of a shrug. "There's another favor you asked me to do. Remember?"

"Seeing what you could find out about Hunt Grayson." She had scarcely thought about the graying executive recently. "After what I've learned about Gordie, I think you can stop worrying about Hunt."

Evan's smooth brow creased. "I'm not so sure."

"You sound like Detective McMahon. He wasn't satisfied either." She filled him in on some of the surprise details of her employer's life as a spouse abuser. "He's the guy I'm hiding from."

"Maybe. Maybe not."

A chill wriggled along her spine. "What've you found out?"

"I'm *beginning* to find out some things, Mandy. I don't want to jump the gun until I have the facts."

She groaned. "I want so much to *know* who this madman is. Every time I get my mind set on someone he squirms away. First Floyd and now you're saying it might not be Gordie."

"I'm not sure, Mandy. Maybe I shouldn't have said anything till I'm positive."

She drank the last of her Benedictine. It went to her head

and gave her a bolt of brashness. "Bedtime! I sure could use a good-night kiss."

Evan rose, but shook his head. "I don't think this is the best time for personal involvement. We're into serious business here."

"One kiss?"

He grinned. "One kiss leads to another, doesn't it?"

"Doesn't have to."

"I have a feeling lovers make lousy bodyguards."

She swallowed her disappointment. Zoe had emphasized that Evan indeed had his shy side. Or maybe he was right. Her life was confusing enough right now.

Her room had its own bath, the tub fashioned from an old copper boiler. Its metal had been polished till it gleamed, fixtures fashioned into lilylike shapes. Filling it took a while, but was worth the wait. She luxuriated. At first her mind filled itself with recent, troubling events, among them the threatening phone calls that had troubled her so. How she dreaded the next one! She knew it would come when she least expected it. That was part of the torture that *he* wanted. Torture. She couldn't forget the words of Gordie's ex-wives. Torture was his specialty. Yes, Gordie was the one. Never mind what Evan imagined he was uncovering.

She thought of the attack of the vicious Doberman. She studied her slowly healing bites, poured water over the whitening wounds. It could have been her face. Just the same, that bit of good luck seemed trivial in light of the far worse act someone intended for her. Again she saw Grace's severed hand, its polished rings glinting in golden menace.

She released her mind from the downward spiral of doom and drifted off into a reverie that turned toward romance. Unburdened by threat and danger, she peopled her fantasy. Hunt Grayson had a part, and of course Evan. Her imaginative soar ended with a sensual surge that brought heat to her face. She sighed and arched her back.

She imagined that Evan was watching her through some invisible peephole like a lustful Victorian lord. Playing games with herself, she made no effort to hide her body. She knelt, then stood slowly, knees straightening, water showering down. She used the thick towels with teasing deliberation, stirring her heavy breasts, planting her foot just so on the edge of the tub and bending into a lewd view. "Like what you see?" she said to the air in a hoarse whisper.

Leaving the bathroom, she shook her head. Terminal horniness. She had been without a man far too long. "Evan? Where are you?" she called.

No answer. She climbed the ladder to Justin's loft. His sleeping head peeked from beneath the sheet. He drew in the deep drafts of heavy slumber. She adjusted the bedclothes.

Evan waited at the bottom of the ladder. She saw some color in his face and something like sincere interest in his eyes.

For an instant she was going to ask him if maybe he hadn't been peeking into her bathroom. She swallowed those words. Was she crazy? On the other hand, maybe shy Evan liked looking at her that way. She admitted that she didn't really mind it. Arousal quivered briefly over her like a hot wind, then was gone. Had he been sneaking a look? Or had her imagination and long abstinence carried her away? Time would tell.

In the morning she made breakfast for the three of them. All the subtle currents of the last evening had ebbed. They might as well have been a regular TV sitcom family bent over their orange juice and pancakes.

Justin wanted to ride with Evan as he followed Amanda to the restaurant. Then Evan took the boy on to school. For this last day of classes Amanda had arranged for Peggy Sargin to take him off the bus and bring him to the restaurant.

Justin called at eleven from a phone booth two blocks from the Sargin house. Cooper hadn't been in school and no one was at his house. Amanda realized with dismay the Sargins had had a family emergency or had made other plans that couldn't wait for the rituals of school's final day. Either way, her son had been forgotten.

"Mom, I noticed this car was sitting down the block from the Sargin house."

"Yes?"

PERSONAL

"And when I walked the couple blocks to this phone booth, it came along with me. I can see it from here."

Amanda's hands turned icy. "Is it a police car?"

"Nope. It's green. And it doesn't say 'Police.'"

"Who's driving?"

"Can't tell. Too far away."

"Listen, Justin. Do you know any of Cooper's neighbors?"

"Yeah."

"Can you go to one of them and wait for me? I'm going to come and get you right now."

"I looked at their houses on the way over here," he said. "I don't think anybody's home."

Panic bubbled up. She choked it down. "Why don't you try any house that has people in it? Stay there till I come?"

"Oh, Mom . . . I'm all right."

Fine time for him to show his independence! "Justin, please do as I say. You don't know who might be in that car. Or what they want with you."

"I can wait here. Don't worry."

She drew a deep breath. She must . . . control! "Remember what I said about somebody threatening me? Well, maybe he's in the green car. Let's not take a chance. Neither of us wants anything bad to happen to you."

"Oh." He understood.

"Listen to me, Justin. Find some people and stay with them. I'll be over in twenty minutes."

Any cop following her VW would have written out a half-dozen tickets on her journey through stop signs and red lights at high speed. Going around the last corner she skidded. Her rear tires were nearly bald. On Patterson Street she slowed. There was the phone booth. She glided slowly along. Justin was to come out when he saw her.

Her eyes probed the front doors of West Hartford prosperity. Where *was* he? If he had been snatched . . . If *he* had him, she would do anything to free him. And that would mean . . . Justin, where are you?

A door opened and a woman with a baby on her hip waved.

169

Amanda pulled over. Justin waved from behind her. Amanda got out. She looked down the street. A mid-sized green sedan was backing away two blocks down. She couldn't see who drove. She would have to be as careful with Justin from here on out as with herself.

Driving to the restaurant, she looked in the rearview mirror for the green sedan. She once thought she glimpsed it. When the traffic shifted, she saw nothing. She tousled her son's hair despite his complaint. She thought her troubles were over.

When she got back to her desk she saw they were only beginning. Gordie stood in her small office. She shooed Justin to his booth. Staff members caught her eye: the boss was pissed.

He slammed the door. His heavy face, nose, and neck were red. "What's the idea you leavin' on your shift? When I got here *there was nobody in charge!*"

"My son had an emergency. I was gone for less than an hour."

"You don't leave. Not for anything, Mandy."

"Don't—"

"Damn, you're tough to deal with. You're my best employee, but a pain in the ass, too."

"That's not all one way, is it? I do a good job for you, Gordon. And I have to put up with you, too. You don't have what I'd call the personality of Saint Francis. It hasn't been easy for me, either." She walked over to the door. She didn't want to be alone with him. Not now. Not knowing what she knew about him.

"Keep the door closed, please. You're in trouble, Mandy. The staff doesn't have to hear it."

She didn't trust him in so many ways. Behind gold-flecked brown eyes lay a nasty, dangerous man. She imagined him slamming the iron into Darlene's defenseless leg. Then dismembering Felicity, Connie, and Grace. He was her number-one suspect. Her knees began to tremble.

"You're not paid to run out of here whenever you want. I'm not really concerned about what happened to your kid—"

PERSONAL

"I am, Gordie. He's the most important person in my life."
"Is that right?" He leaned close to her. His lips were moist,
his breath surging with low-grade anger. "Then you better pick
between him and your paycheck."
"What's that supposed to mean?"
"You want to keep working here, you don't run out on
Muncher's time to help him take a leak. You don't turn this
place into a day-care center."
She was beginning to understand. Someone on the staff had
snitched to the home office. The stakes were going up. She
couldn't play just a defensive role. She took a step back from
him. She tried to gather herself before she spoke carefully,
lodged as she was between danger and doubt.
"Seeing as you raised the issue, you should know I'm in
physical danger. My life has been threatened by some nut. He's
already killed some other women I've known." She studied
his slablike face, alert as an egret wading among minnows for
the twitching tail of guilt. "I've been to the police. I've changed
where I live. I have someone playing part-time bodyguard. *I
am scared!*"
An ambiguous smile stirred his lips. Before he could speak,
she hurried on. "I could have taken police advice and left
Hartford temporarily. One of the reasons I didn't was my com-
mitment to this job. I need it. I need the money. I want the
promotion to regional manager. The only thing that can stop
me from doing my usual good work are more threats to me or
to my son. Do you understand?"
He frowned. "What the hell are you talking about? I catch
you goofing off and you make up a story."
"I'm making nothing up!" Her ragged emotions left her
with little self-control.
"Somebody's trying to kill you? Sure! So you're a wise
broad. Wise broads are a dime a dozen. It would take a nut a
lifetime to get you all."
"Gordon, that is a *nasty* thing to say." The distant, cool
part of her mind didn't doubt that if he were the killer, he
wouldn't stop torturing her verbally. She knew now the dark

171

side of his doings. Her earlier forbearance with him seemed foolish.

Was he indeed taking pleasure from these moments of her embarrassment and personal confession? Or was her imagination casting him in a role of villain that, despite his difficult personality and past, he didn't deserve? He put both hands on her shoulders. She loathed the way he found ways to touch her. She had never stood for it. Nor would she now. He spoke before she could shove him away. "You left your responsibilities and I caught you. You then make up some crazy story that I wouldn't have believed when I was nine years old." His jaw set. "I see I got no real choice." He shook his head. "I got to fire you." He looked at her coolly. "You're fired."

"No!" She stared into his face a handsbreadth from hers. At that moment of surprise and stress she imagined he wanted a close-up view of her going to pieces. Despite herself, she felt her battered emotions slide and shift like a snowfield. When the avalanche started, it wasn't in the form of tears. It was rage.

She wailed and threw herself at his bulk, fingers curved to claws. Her rage sparked his own. His eyes widened, deepened—and there was the flash!

Now she understood its dark meaning.

He held her away effortlessly. She filled her lungs and shouted, "You're the murderer! You killed my friends! And you want to kill me!" She flung the accusation like rocks. Her deep secret was disclosed—unwisely, but she was beyond caring. .

He trembled slightly with the effort of self-control. "Right now, I can see why somebody might not mind murdering you, Mandy. But not me. Not my style. I'd settle for just having you shut up." He raised his hand, as though to cover her mouth.

She thought of his abused wives, their torture, the murders. Sight of that big hand before her eyes drove the full horror of his true nature into place at this moment, like a spike into a plank.

She never planned her scream. There was nothing ladylike about it. It was torn from primal land. It shook the ceiling tiles.

"For God's sake, Mandy! What are you doing?" He looked horrified.

Someone knocked on the door, then opened it a crack. Madge. "Five seconds and I'm coming in. Lock this door and I call the police. I'm counting."

Gordon was still wide-eyed from her ringing scream. He shook his head in embarrassed bafflement. He backed away, looking narrow eyed at her. "What's with you?" he muttered. "You gone mental on me?"

Amanda realized she had badly overreacted. She staggered on someone else's knees, sat on the corner of her desk. Madge opened the door slowly. "It sounded as though your differences were getting out of hand."

A shaken Gordie jerked a thumb toward the kitchen. "Get us two cups of coffee. Leave the door open."

Madge paused, speculating. She nodded, then turned to do as she was told.

Gordie folded his arms. "Look, Mandy, I don't want this kind of trouble from you. I mean, crazy stuff. I understand some guy's running around offing redheads. It's nobody with anything to do with Muncher's. You can relax around here and around me. All right?"

"I thought you were going to try to kill me," she croaked. "See, I think you're the man who's been threatening me. I think *you* killed the other redheads. Gordie, I'm going to the police and give them your name."

"What?" He blinked, finally comprehending the breadth and basis of her fear. "You really think it's *me?*" He chuckled. "What a great idea! Forget hair and I'm thinking of my two ex-wives for starters. But there's a law against it. Besides, why would I want to kill you? I need you for the business."

Amanda glowered at him. There were laws against spouse abuse, too, but they hadn't stopped him. "I don't believe you. You're a frightening man!"

He shrugged. "You ain't so hot yourself, Mandy. You want to know where all your troubles start? You don't know your place."

"Don't lecture me! I won't be lectured by a killer."

173

PERSONAL

"I didn't kill anybody." He raised his arms in a helpless shrug. His heavy face wreathed itself in little-boy innocence. "Swear to God."

Amanda stood, her breathing gradually calming. It couldn't be! He was the one. She would go to the police about him. No question. But if somehow he wasn't . . . Who was? In any case, she had to deal with him. Unfortunately, he wasn't going to go away.

Madge returned with the coffees. She smiled sweetly. "Let's see if we can settle our differences. It makes for a better night's sleep and cuts down on staff gossip." She adjusted her beanie before leaving.

Amanda ignored her coffee. "I'm leaving," she announced. "After all, I've been fired."

"I owe you for two weeks."

"I'll take cash."

"You need the money? You can't live off your ex like mine do?"

"What do you know about him?"

"Just what my friend Hunt Grayson told me. You married a bum, smart lady." He put down his cup and walked slowly to her. He made calming gestures with palms parallel to the floor. Casually, with a finger, he tilted her chin up. "We both got excited. Let's cool it. I take back firing you."

She gently pushed his hand away. "Thank you."

"Will you take back thinking I kill people?"

She nodded. Deep down she really wasn't all that sure about it. "That's very sensible of you, Gordon. Yes, I do need the job—as much as you need me to have it." She stepped back, picked up her cup, and paced the office. She drew deep breaths, searching for still more self-control. "Could you wait here a few minutes? I want to ask you a question."

"Yeah. I got more business with you, too."

She toured the restaurant, showing her personal flag to the staff. She was still in charge.

Back with Gordon again, she asked, "Do you know a man named Floyd Philman?"

"Never heard of him. He in the restaurant business?"

174

"You sure, Gordon?" She looked piercingly at him.

"Yeah."

She couldn't imagine whether to believe him or not. She sipped her coffee. She was still a little shaken from their emotional exchange. "What other business matters do you have to discuss?"

"You looked at your contract lately?"

"No! I've had other things on my mind. I learned a while ago that I should have hired an attorney to study that document before I signed it. I didn't know then what a sleaze you are. The contract's all one way."

Gordie chuckled, ran a finger around the thick gold chain circling his neck. "Live and learn. I did, to get where I am."

Amanda tossed her head. "What do you have to say to me about my contract?"

"It says you have to do whatever I want as long as you're Ms. Muncher."

"That's all over. I hear you're going to pick somebody else."

"It's over *when* I pick somebody else. You're going to be one of the judges. And you're going to 'pass the beanie' to the new one."

"I will not!"

"It's all covered by the contract. You have to, or I'll sue you."

"Go ahead! And I'll countersue for assault. Who do you think you're dealing with, Gordie? Some airhead who thinks men are God?"

"No, that's not who I think I'm dealing with." His voice rose. "I'm dealing with a broad who doesn't know how to get what she wants by playing the high cards she has. You're supposed to know more about poker than I ever will." His thick finger pointed. "You're holding three aces and two deuces—a full house, Mandy. Since I've known you, all you do is play the deuces and sit on the aces. You lose and lose."

That hit close to home. Hadn't she characterized herself as playing her cards too close to her chest? And when she did make a play, was it indeed the right one? Both Gordie and

Hunt had been after her to go with her strengths. In her situation she didn't trust either of them. Taking their suggestions hadn't seemed right. It still didn't. But she was starting to have doubts. She took a deep breath. "What do you want from me?"

"I don't want a lawsuit. You can't afford one. If you sue, I'll hire some big-name shyster for heavy bucks. You won't get boo from it all—and you'll end up even poorer than you are now."

"Let's pass on the suit for now." She sighed deeply. "What's with the Ms. Muncher thing?"

"Day after tomorrow I'm throwing a bash outside in a tent at my place. Featured thing will be a contest—"

"A beauty contest?"

"No way. I got a half-dozen women say they're hot to replace you. They can say a little piece, walk around. We'll do some video tape, see who comes across best. Stuff like that. I'll be a judge. You'll be a judge. Hunt will be one."

"Maybe I should be a candidate instead of a judge." Amanda looked at him sourly.

"You? You've never had any use for what I wanted to give you, Mandy. Why should I piss away more of what I have on you?"

She was silent a moment. Her head spun. She was still recovering from her bolt of terror, powerful as dynamite in the small office. "What am I doing here with a dangerous man like you, talking about who's going to be the next Ms. Muncher and what I have to do? I must be crazy! I know *you're* crazy— and dangerous." She slammed her arms against her sides in frustration.

She was surprised when the tears came. Release, she supposed, the emotions saying she couldn't take any more. Gordie found her a half-dozen Muncher's napkins and shoved them at her. While she blubbered and mopped, he paced uneasily. When curious faces appeared in the door, he yelled, "Beat it!" The faces disappeared, no doubt to gossip up a storm. "Hey, get hold of yourself. I really didn't mean to fire you. I *need* you. I still have you pegged for the regional manager's job."

PERSONAL

Amanda hugged herself. She felt awash in uncertainty. She needed something to hold onto. A possible promotion could be it. "That still alive?" she said.

"Yeah."

"Don't mess with me, Gordie. Don't say one thing and then the opposite. Just one version of everything, please." She sniffled despite herself.

He scowled at her. "My place. Friday. Seven o'clock on. Only Ringling Brothers has a bigger friggin' tent." He paused in the doorway. "Hit the john. You look like hell. It's bad for business."

She let him go, then walked out of the office into the kitchen. The staff knew her well enough not to stare. But from somewhere by the fryers she heard a familiar, but still unidentified voice murmur: "He your man."

"He is not my man. Not, not, *not!*" She fled for the restroom.

177

# CHAPTER
## ❧ 11 ❧

One of Justin's friends had come into the restaurant with his family. The two boys had gone outside so they had missed the excitement. When her shift was over she climbed into the VW, still on the verge of tears. She wasn't normally so weak, but how much more could she take? As she drove, she frequently looked over at Justin and wondered how all this was affecting him. His occasional noncommunication had been inherited from his father. Ned was a great one for keeping things to himself. Her head spun with concern, responsibilities, and a steadily growing fear, driven as much by the calendar as the recent emotional circus, Gordie Locker, ringmaster. She needed a short period of tranquillity to try to sort things out. She was thinking that could happen tonight, if Evan would give her a hand.

Then she saw the green sedan in the distance behind her.

She drove on toward New Hartford hoping that the car would turn off and disappear. But it hung on a little more than a quarter-mile behind. Without signaling, she turned off the main road onto a side street. At the first corner she turned again. Then she scooted down a long alley between garages, cut across a parking lot, then onto a street paralleling the main road.

"What're you doing, mom?" Justin said.

"Playing the lose the green car game. That's one car game I never taught you when you were little."

"The same car that was hanging around me?"

"Look back and see if you see it."

He turned. "Nope."

She found a driveway sided by thick bushes, pulled in, and turned off the engine. The wheel was streaked with sweat. She knew who was trying to follow her.

The killer.

To find out where she had moved.

"Shouldn't we keep moving?" Justin said.

"I don't know what we should do." She started the VW and found her way back to the main road. Five miles from New Hartford she saw the green sedan was behind her again. Sighting it was like a blow to her stomach. All her pace and timing fled in the face of fright. He could run her off the road and murder her before anyone could stop him!

"The green car's back, Justin," she said. "I'm scared."

The boy looked behind. "He doesn't seem to want to catch up."

"Maybe he's waiting till we get to some of that woodsy, deserted road just before Evan's place." Her voice was a grating whisper.

"Try to lose him again."

She tried again, darting off the highway and cruising rural lanes lined with trees and white frame houses bearing tastefully painted signs boasting of having stood since the 1700s. Several times she thought she had eluded the sedan, but somehow it always found her, as though the VW carried a homing device. In the end she gave up. The car was too old and slow to escape anything faster than a wheelchair.

The panic that she had battled down now rushed in with a vengeance. Her self-control fractured. She turned to Justin wide-eyed, her face betraying all she felt. "What are we going to do?" she shouted.

He had never seen her like this. Seeing her temporary disintegration thrust something of the mad adult world on him. It wasn't her intention to test him. She couldn't *help* it that she

179

was temporarily abdicating. They flew along the road in a long moment of silence. Then he said, almost matter-of-factly, "Stop at a gas station and call the police."

Yes! To her muddled mind his pronouncement had parable profundity. She pulled into a convenience store parking lot. She scrambled out of the car, shepherding Justin along. The green sedan didn't pass; it had stopped somewhere behind them. In the store she asked the clerk the number of the local police. "We been stuck up so often I know it by heart," the woman said.

Amanda phoned, hearing the beep-beep of the police recorder. She gave her name and location. "I'm being followed by someone in a green sedan. Before this I've gotten murder threats and some of my friends have already died! He may be waiting to run me off the road. Right now he's a few hundred yards from here, waiting. Please help me!" Dimly, she wanted to sound better, more in control. Instead, a crazy lady had taken possession of her. The dispatcher told her to stay put. A car would be right over.

There was a mirror by the phone. She glanced in it, saw a white-faced stranger gnawing on the edge of her lip as though it was an hors d'oeuvre. Peering over the stack of cookout briquette sacks, she watched the road. Gradually, she calmed, coming to realize that this could turn out to be a long-overdue break. The killer was trailing her. If he was sitting by the side of the road waiting for her to start up again, and the police drove up to him . . . She remembered reading how many major crimes were solved with simple, routine law enforcement work. Like answering a distress call from a woman frightened out of her wits.

"Let me go out and look up the road, mom," Justin said.

"No way! Wait here. Go read the comic books."

He looked at her appraisingly. "Are you back to normal?"

She gave him a hug. "I'm better. Put it that way. I'm hoping the police will catch this guy who's causing me all this trouble."

She was standing by the front door when the cruiser carrying the New Hartford logo wheeled slowly into the parking lot.

Somebody was beside the cop. A man. She squinted against the windshield reflection. Justin pushed by her and out the door.

"Hey, it's dad!" he said.

Justin was right. It was Ned.

The cop got out with his clipboard. She had to identify herself and sign a piece of paper. He was about her age, with a five o'clock shadow and an air of professional patience. "I picked this guy up. He was sitting in a green sedan up the road. He says he's your ex-husband."

"He is." She turned toward Ned. "Why are you following me, for God's sake? Was it you following Justin the other day?"

"Yeah, it was, and so what? You're trying to keep my son away from me." Ned wore his public sullen expression. "I went to your apartment to see Justin. Your neighbor said you both left with your stuff in a hurry."

Damn Mrs. Clendenon!

"I knew you did it to get away from me, so I followed Justin's school bus—"

"Ned Stanton, what kind of memory do you have? Don't you remember there's some nut out there who's threatened to kill me? Who's already killed three women I know. I'm trying to hide from him. I don't care about you and the visiting rights you never wanted. You're not the problem. You're just an annoyance." She held out shaking palms. "Look what you've just done to me!"

"You want to sign a complaint?" the cop said.

Amanda turned away and paced. Behind her, Justin pleaded, "Mom . . ." She pressed hands to her face for a long moment, then finally turned back. "Where did you get a car, Ned?"

"Rented it. I got a part-time job."

She sensed there was some sort of connection she should be making between her larger troubles and her ex. But it didn't reveal itself. Maybe her brain was short-circuiting. She turned to the cop. "I don't want him following me to where I'm living. After that you can do whatever you want with him."

"I have a right to see my son!"

"Get an attorney, and have him call me—in about two weeks." She put a hand on Justin's shoulder. "Let's go."

She spent the rest of the trip trying to explain to the pouting boy just why his father's behavior bothered her. A look at his face told her results were mixed. When they arrived at Evan's home, her host was there. She asked him if he'd mind taking Justin for a while. She needed time to think. He turned to her son. "What do you think of miniature golf?"

"I never played."

"Until now."

Off they went. Amanda changed and went outside on the patio made from railroad ties. She took a gin and tonic with her. She stretched out on the chaise and tried to put her inner house in order. She tried sipping her drink and just emptying her mind. Only then did she begin to sort out the day, and what it meant. She stayed put for an hour, thinking.

Afterwards she went inside and called the Hartford police even though it was after the dinner hour. Detective McMahon was still there. His voice was leaden. "No luck on the judges' murders?" she asked, an edge in her voice. When he said no, she reminded him of her suspicions about Gordie. To her satisfaction, he didn't downplay them.

"We'll send an officer out to talk to him. If he's the man we want, it'll give him something to worry about. If he's not, it'll make him think twice about how he treats you."

"I told him I thought he was the murderer, right to his face. He denied killing anybody."

"You believe him?"

"I don't know what to believe." She paused, looked around the elegantly furnished living room. "Are you getting anywhere with our case?"

His turn for brief silence. "The hand got us moving."

Grace's right hand. "What have you done?"

"We're starting to check the list of men you gave us."

"I don't suppose it'll do any good to ask you to hurry up."

"Your boss is going to get a caller with a badge. That's something."

"One thing more: can I get a restraining order to keep my

182

ex-husband away from me? He's following me around because I left my apartment."

"Call your attorney on that one," McMahon said.

Back on the patio, she supposed she ought to get a "shyster," as horrid Floyd and Gordie called them. But she had no money for fees. She'd have to deal with that problem later, after the murderer was caught. Yet little was occurring to make that happen. She held out faint hopes for her two tiny inquiries: Evan looking into Hunt Grayson's background and Flo at police headquarters seeing what the computer might have tucked away on Gordie's heartthrob, Emerald Roscheski. Then there were police efforts—scanty at best.

Her attention finally turned to Gordie's gathering Friday night. She didn't want to go there. She wanted to distance herself from both him and Ms. Muncher. When she mentioned it to Evan later, he said, "Why not go? Your bodyguard will be there."

"You? Why?"

He took off his glasses and polished the lenses on a shirttail. "The *Courant* was invited. My editor needed somebody to cover it, and I volunteered. It seemed the thing to do, considering your situation. A new Ms. Muncher is news, after all. So is a big do thrown by one of Hartford's most successful franchisers." He put his glasses back on and looked at her. "I'd feel better if you were there. Your being out here alone for a good part of the night doesn't seem such a great idea."

"What about Justin?"

"Maybe we should take him."

"Yeah!"

Amanda started. Her son had been eavesdropping. "Look, Mr. Little Pitcher, everything that's said here isn't meant for your big ears. If Evan and I go out, it's a sitter for you. Don't get your hopes up."

"Sure, mom."

"Watch your tongue, fella!" She spun around and started tickling him. "I will be spoken to with respect!"

"No fair!" Justin laughed, tickling her back.

Her gaze swung suddenly to Evan. He was looking at her

PERSONAL

with an intense expression. Was it admiration? Well, wasn't she flattering herself! She looked back at Justin. When her eyes again found Evan's face she saw only what seemed a fatherly concern for her and her son.

After she finished reading and tucked Justin in, she asked him if he had enjoyed his little time with their host.

"Yeah! Evan's neat. Not bossy, like you."

She ignored his lip. "I like him, too. He's one good thing that's come out of all this trouble. Let's both be nice to him and not louse up a good thing."

Justin grinned and beckoned her closer to his pillowed head. "He asked me stuff about you," he whispered.

"Like what?"

He made a face. "Love stuff, you know. Do you have boyfriends and that."

"I see. What did you say?"

"I don't know. *Stuff*, you know. He said he was getting to like you and wished he wasn't so shy."

"He said that?"

"Yeah. What was he being shy about? You're just my *mom*."

Brushing out her hair before bed in her underwear, she found herself smiling. She had been right about Evan being shy. She wondered if she were right about him somehow watching her through some invisible chink or hole. If so, her intuition—or imagination—was telling her he was doing it at that moment.

She felt herself color. It was the uncertainty that stimulated her. The fascination of the game they—or she alone—played. She worked the brush down through the red mass. She should have it cut again, but there were too many other things to think about. The least she could do was repair the neglect of not thoroughly brushing lately.

She took off her bra, tossed it onto the bed, then gave her hair the workout it needed. She changed hands every few strokes. The motion raised and lowered each breast in turn. She shifted her weight, half turning far left then right. Between slow strokes she listened intently for some sound of Evan's observation. She heard nothing and after a while decided that the two players of the game she had so recently devised were only herself and her imagination.

Climbing into bed, she heard a single soft thump beyond a wall.

Well now . . .

At breakfast Friday morning Evan said he wouldn't be able to hang around Amanda during the day. He had to go out of town in connection with his search for information about Hunt Grayson. "It's taken me some time to home in on what might be something. Today I go for it. If I come up lucky, I'll phone you at work."

"What are you after?" she said.

"Stuff from a morgue. The newspaper kind."

She carried dishes to the dishwasher. "Evan, Justin said you were asking about my love life yesterday."

Evan blushed, unable to answer.

"I'm eligible, if that's what you want to know." She turned to him, blushing despite herself. Weren't they a matched pair! "If you like, I'd welcome a little initiative. I like you."

"Oh, sure. Sure." He nodded, put down his coffee cup, and got up quickly. "After all this stuff calms down." He nearly ran from the kitchen table.

Amanda shook her head and found herself smiling.

At work that morning Amanda got a call from Hunt. She swallowed. Was he a suspect, too? But then Gordie—oh, she was so confused! He asked her how it was going. Since she wasn't alone in her office she made some vague comments about not much better than before. After Evan's guarded statements about him, her intuitive distrust of him reared up again. She was glad that her host was running his scent to earth today. She nearly hoped he'd find something damning. What was with her? She liked Hunt. The man had been good to her. Like Gordie, he would have done even more, had she allowed it. Nonetheless, she said, "Hunt, could I ask you a question?"

"Sure. What?"

185

"Do you happen to know that guy I thought for a while was after me? Floyd Philman?" She listened intently for any hesitation or awkwardness in his response. For any clue that he was linked with the man around whom the murders seemed to revolve.

"I don't believe I do. Should I?"

"Depends on what you do for fun," she said.

"Sometimes, Mandy, you're not at all honest with me. Despite everything I try to do for you. This is one of them."

"I don't understand."

"I've been talking to Emerald Roscheski. She told me you think *I* murdered your redheaded friends and want to murder you. I can't tell you how absurd that is. Or how hurt I am that you'd even consider me—"

"I'm scared, Hunt!" Damn Emerald! "How can you blame me for including you? I got a message—the killer's somebody I know. You're a man and I know you. I'm sorry to be so human. He sent me my friend's hand in a box."

"Jesus! I didn't know—"

"I have a right to be nervous and to suspect anybody I want! By the way, Emerald is a nasty little witch for telling you that." She moved the phone from her ear and breathed deeply. "Now, what can I do for you?"

"I want to take a minute to talk about Ms. Muncher again," he said. "I've just had a chat with Gordie." He paused. "I gather you two had a bit of a disagreement yesterday."

"He said he was going to fire me. I screamed loud enough to wake the dead. Aside from that, we got on famously. After hearing all that, you won't be surprised to hear I half think he's the one who's been killing redheads, too. See? I suspect *everybody*. I guess that's the same, actually, as suspecting no one."

"Gordie? Nonsense! Not me or him. I put my money on a dark horse. Some crackpot who's done a class-A job of making you believe you know him. In fact, you don't know him from Ishmael. I suggest you live your life as though Gordon Locker were only your employer—and admirer, somebody you should make every effort to coexist with."

"Thank you for the advice," she said coolly. "What did you and Gordie have to say to each other about me?"

"It's about the choice of a new Ms. Muncher. I talked him into once again considering you as a contestant."

"I don't want to be a contestant! Do we have to go over all this again?"

"Even though there are a half-dozen women in the competition, the only real competitor will be your friend Jessica. I've put Emerald up as a favor to Gordie. She has a future in modeling, but she's not ready yet. You are."

"How many times do I have to say no?"

"During my long chat with your boss I gave him the idea he was coming across as nickeling-and-diming in all this. You know, Amanda, for all his money, he has an insecure side."

"I hadn't noticed."

"Quite so. It's his modest background and menial beginnings."

"Pass on the psychology, Hunt."

"The bottom line is the three-thousand-dollar 'appreciation fee,' as he's chosen to call it, to be given to the new Ms. Muncher."

Right then she had small regrets about her and Gordie's quarrel.

"I convinced him not to use you as a judge. Do I have your permission to continue you as a contestant?"

"I won't win. He won't let it happen."

"We'll see."

"I could use the three thousand dollars, Hunt," she said.

"You could use three thousand only about as much as a drowning man could use a breath of air. I'll see what I can do."

Hanging up, she had a thought. Both Gordie and he had made special efforts to make sure she was under the tent this evening. Did one of them have a gory agenda past those disclosed? She guessed Hunt was trying to put off her suspicions with his talk of a dark horse. Why not a "white horse"?

She phoned Jessica. "Are you coming to Gordie's this evening?"

Both Jessica and Karl were going. In the background Amanda heard him bellowing, "Anybody tries to touch her, they die!"

"I've never thought so highly of free-weight work and karate," Jessica explained. "This guy I couldn't get excited about is now looking like a cross between Rambo and Richard the Lion-Hearted." Her voice tightened. "My six weeks are up today," she whispered.

"There aren't any real rules about what our crazy man does," Amanda said. "Look what happened to Grace. He grabbed her early."

"And killed her the day the six weeks were up," Jessica pointed out.

"You're right."

"I thought about not going and just holing up here with Karl. Then we talked it over and thought it was too dangerous. We're going to spend the rest of the day in Karl's car, just driving around. Then tonight we'll be in public. Karl's going to stick to me like adhesive tape every minute. After the competition we're driving straight out of town and staying away for a while."

Amanda stopped short of telling the girl that she, the incumbent, had agreed to be a contestant. I know my price, she thought. It's three thousand dollars.

She was aware that her staff was speculating wildly on both her relationship with Gordie and the roots of her scream. She dealt with it by conducting one of her restaurant-wide walks in search of grime and slovenliness. As usual, she found it. She issued assignments and deadlines. "Any questions?" she asked into the wash of groans. Ears perked, she waited for someone to whisper about Gordie being "her man." The whispering woman wouldn't be caught out.

Before the staff adjourned to work teams, she said, "I understand from Mr. Locker that one of you called his office to complain about the way I'm handling my attendance here, and that I've had my son spend a few afternoons with us. I just want to say thanks." Her sarcasm dripped, then she let it go.

188

The lines of customers were growing. She had too much else on her mind to really pursue the traitor.

She spent her lunch hour walking with Justin. She told him how proud she was of his patience, sitting in her restaurant all morning, uncomplaining.

He looked up at her, squinting in the noonday brilliance. "How long am I going to have to keep doing this?"

She strode on in silence, then said, "It has to do with the person who's threatened me. A week, maybe longer. Less, if the police catch him."

"You never said who's doing it, mom."

"First I thought it was that Floyd man who came over and asked for money. Remember him? Turns out it wasn't. Now I don't know. All I know is whoever he is, he's crazy."

"What's this guy threatened to do?"

She felt a rush of fear like a breeze up her spine. "Bad stuff, kid."

Justin nodded, deciding his presence was necessary. "I'm running out of books, mom."

"We'll stop by the library on the way to New Hartford."

There was a call for her after lunch. She was hoping for word from Evan about Hunt. Instead it was Ned. He demanded to know where she was living. When she wouldn't tell him, he told her he had a right to see his own son. What she hadn't been able to figure since his return was why the sudden interest in their son? For a moment she wondered if maybe the interest wasn't so much toward Justin as toward her. That led her to speculate that he might have come to Hartford well before he pried his way back into her life, literally and figuratively. Maybe he hadn't returned to mend fences, but to murder not only her, but the other redheads.

She scolded herself for being so silly and put it out of mind. She had enough *real* suspects.

Just before her shift ended, Evan came into the restaurant. His normally boyish look was darkened. He beckoned her out to the deserted party room and sat down at one of its tables.

She joined him, eyes on his worried face. "What's wrong?" she asked.

"Can you get hold of Jessica?"

"She and Karl are on the road until Gordie's party. We'll talk to her there, first thing."

"We have to warn her," Evan said.

"About what?"

"Hunt Grayson."

"Hunt!"

He opened a large manila envelope. "I spent a few hours in Rhode Island in the offices of the *Providence Cryer*. I got a lead from one of my old reporter buddies and went down to check it out. Your friend Hunt has quite an interesting little history." He removed the sheets from the folder. They were xerox copies of ten-year-old newspaper articles from the *Cryer*. Evan explained their contents.

A decade ago there was a rash of disappearances of redheaded women between fifteen and thirty. Six in all, stretching back more than two years. The police had no suspects and few clues. The cases might have remained open and unsolved if it hadn't been for a domestic tragedy in which Grant Martin, owner of an employment agency, allegedly bludgeoned his redheaded wife and eight-year-old daughter to death. He was questioned intently by the police, not only about these two deaths, but on a hunch about the disappearances. Despite the pressure, he refused to confess to playing any role in them, or in the deaths of his wife and child. Certain pieces of evidence could have linked him with two of the other crimes.

When the prosecutor considered what he had on his plate, he chose to build his case on the deaths of Grant's wife and daughter, rather than on the more chancy disappearances. After a long trial filled with sensational details about Martin's sexual practices, his collection of sadistic Polaroid photographs featuring young redheaded woman, and his psychological condition, he was found guilty. Before the sentencing his attorney played a trump card. Much of the evidence used against Grant had been seized illegally. Without it, the case collapsed. The judge was forced to throw it out of court. The state's efforts to bring Grant to trial again were unsuccessful. The resulting scandal cost the prosecutor his job and led to a housecleaning in the halls of local justice.

Grant Martin held a press conference where he issued a statement for the record reiterating his innocence. Had the case gone to the jury, he promised, it would have agreed with him. This display of outrageous arrogance and egomania drove the district attorney nearly wild. He vowed to pursue Martin's connection with the missing women. Before he could, his suspect left town.

Amanda listened in silence, feeling a chill broaden and deepen within. Her attention moved far away from the restaurant and her job. She strolled a blasted landscape strewn with violence and death where all the cracked, decomposing skulls sprouted red hair. There, female flesh was meat to be hacked, torn, and tossed about. Axes, knives, and dogs' teeth ruled. The only laws were those of strength, and every man was a savage.

"Amanda!" Evan's look at her was dismayed.

She understood she had drifted off—far off. She blinked. "I'm back." Her voice shook with the force of what she dreaded was a personal prophesy. "Grant Martin . . ."

Evan sifted through his xeroxed clippings, laid one in front of her. It carried a photograph of a man's head and shoulders. Its caption read "Grant Martin."

The face was Hunt Grayson's.

"If you had to ask me, I'd say the man has gone back to doing business as usual." Evan was unsmiling.

Amanda imagined Hunt fleeing Providence, selling off what was left to him to pay attorney's fees, then struggling to fashion another identity and career in a new state. And over the many months eventually succumbing to his compulsion to kill. Her intuitive doubts about the man, no matter his openhandedness toward her, now seemed more than vindicated. If she had only paid more attention . . .

"I'd say we have our man," she said.

Evan nodded and invited Amanda to look through the clippings while he got some coffee. She did. When he returned, he said, "I want to tell you what I want out of all this."

What he wanted was an exclusive for the *Courant*. He already had pages of notes. At the same time he wanted to stay on the police's good side. Amanda's psychopath, Hunt Grayson, wouldn't be the only one in the history of Hartford. He wanted to write those additional stories, too, when they happened. He didn't want Detective McMahon to know that he was meddling in this case—and doing a better job than the police. He asked Amanda to leave him out when she went to them with what she had just found out. She was to tell them she had dug it out herself. Later, when the case broke, there would be time enough to mention he had played a small part. She promised to do as he asked, but had a condition, as well.

He shrugged. "Let's hear it."

"When we first met, before we became friends, you said if it was necessary, you'd blow the whole story wide open. Right on the front page. 'Redheads Victims of Serial Murderer!' You said you'd embarrass the police into action."

"Yeah. I said that. Still mean it."

"Evan, if somehow—I don't know how—Hunt manages to . . . do what he threatened to Jessica, and I'm the last one left—"

"You want me to blow the whistle." He rested a hand lightly on her shoulder. "My word, if it comes to that."

She managed a thin smile. "Done!" She rose and started back to her office. "I'm going to call the police right away and tell them what 'I' found out."

He looked pessimistic. "Go ahead. Give it a try." She tried for twenty minutes to get through to Detective McMahon without success. She imagined it was less runaround than the lack of resources with which he suffered. He had to be told that Hunt Grayson had taken over first place on her suspect list by a wide margin. With a sinking sense, she had to settle for asking that the detective call her first chance he got.

When she got back to the table Justin and Evan were in close conversation. It wasn't until they had picked up Jilly at her apartment house, driven to New Hartford, changed and readied themselves for Gordon Locker's command performance, that the two adults had a chance to talk again.

"I love your Ms. Muncher uniform as evening wear." Evan laughed. He was wearing a dinner jacket.

"No comment, please. Gordie demanded I wear it. There's going to be a TV crew there for a while." She groaned. "Sometimes it's just easier to do what he says." She studied her youthful-looking companion. "What do we do about Hunt? He's going to be there this evening."

"First thing we do is talk to Jessica and warn her."

"You know, in a way I always suspected Hunt. Something about him . . . Even now, knowing he has blood on his hands, I can't put it into words."

Evan grunted his assent. "Then I think we talk to Jessica and Karl about hanging close together through the rest of the evening. Maybe till morning. I'm a little confused about the time thing, but . . ."

"There's definitely something to do with six weeks. That's how much time Hunt's given all of us. Who knows why? Jessica's time is about up."

"So we keep our eyes on Hunt—all night. Some nights being a reporter's just the ticket. I go where I want, show the press card. I'll shadow our man. You hang around Jessica and Karl."

"We'll have to talk to them," Amanda said. "And get organized."

The tent, pitched on the wide acreage behind Gordie's mansion, was as large as he had promised, half turned into a theater, the rest into a bar and buffet. Mountains of food rose from long tables, as at his earlier party. On others even larger ice sculptures of Muncher's products stood in lakes of loose ice cubes, picks provided for the energetic. Muncher's promotional items were everywhere. The last cutouts of her as Ms. Muncher had been pulled from the warehouse, hung high and propped against tent ropes and poles. She saw TV crews and cameramen readying their equipment. The guests were arriving in herds. The place could hold about a thousand.

In the theater area a VIP space was roped off. The sign

said: Contestants and Officials Only. Already standing there were three private security guards. She saw some others strolling amid the crowd. She wondered if Gordie had actually paid attention to her worries about being threatened with murder. A few hours ago she thought he was responsible. Now she saw him as a quasi-ally and Hunt had taken over as villain in her suspicions because she finally had something like *evidence*. It had been lacking so much in this whole long, dreadful business.

She and Evan descended on Jessica and Karl the moment they arrived. Jessica looked cute in her Muncher's uniform. The new Ms. Muncher is born, Amanda thought with mixed feelings. Goodbye three thousand bucks! Karl wore a tux, clearly rented and too short in the legs and arms, too tight across his massive chest. Amanda started right in. "I found some evidence about who the real killer is."

When she finished, Karl was scuffing the grass like a buffalo about to charge and flexing his muscle mountain. "Let me take him! Let me do him!" He waved a flattened palm like a broadsword. "I can chop him down for good with one of these on the side of his neck."

"I think your job is to worry about Jessica," Amanda reminded. "The police will get to Hunt in good time."

"The police suck!" Karl said. "What have they done beside jerk you and Jess around? It's time for a citizen's arrest is what it is. I'm the citizen to do it!"

For a moment Amanda actually considered it. Then thought better. Hunt was Gordie's friend, a judge for the competition, an integral part of the evening's entire proceedings. All her boss's plans would be totally disrupted if Hunt were grabbed and wildly charged with murder. The whole competition would be dragged down and trampled. It wouldn't take Gordie long to find she was behind it all. She would be asked to show evidence. She had the clippings, but knew that alone they weren't yet enough. Confusion and accusations would be rampant—with her right in the middle of them. She could say goodbye to any hopes for the promised promotion. "You're not arresting anyone, Karl. Your job is to stick close to Jessica.'' She laughed nervously. "And maybe keep an eye on me, too. Plus all of us stay as far away from Hunt as we can.''

With one person chosen to be avoided, Amanda was surprised later to find another. Ned was replenishing one of the buffet tables. He wore a white dinner jacket, Maxi-muncher button in the lapel, the costume for Gordie's employees. "What are you doing here?" She realized how shrill her voice was.

"Hey, I work for the man. Just like you."

Why did her heart sink? "What do you do, Ned?"

He shrugged, touched his name tag. "Little of this, little of that. You know. Do what the man says around the house here."

"You're his servant?"

He winked. "More like a pal, you know. We sort of hang together when he can manage it.'' He had gone to Muncher central and introduced himself as Amanda's ex-husband. He and Gordie, as luck would have it, hit it off. Ned gave her a chuckle and a leer. "It's a real good match. Both of us are just a couple of high rollers.''

Amanda's dismay grew. She squirmed inside. "Does he by any chance ask you what it was like married to me?"

Ned shrugged and flashed his sliest smile. "Now and then."

"Do you tell him?"

The smile faded. "It was my life, too, Mandy. You don't have a patent on it!"

"You tell him everything, don't you?"

"Haven't yet." He chuckled. "But he keeps asking."

She couldn't keep the disgust from her face. She dug her nails into his wrist. "That's why he keeps you around, isn't it? So you can tell him about what he can't get from me!"

Ned shook his hand free. He looked over her head around the tent. "Nice place to work," he said airily. "Pay's not bad. Come winter, he said we might go down to Miami. I told him I'd show him how to handle himself at the fronton."

She whirled and strode away, her face crimson. Her ex, her

boss's flunky. Both Gordie and Ned were disgusting. Where was the recruiter from the Society to Cut Up Men? She was ready to sign up. That thought dispelled her anger in an instant. It was women being cut up, wasn't it? And always was. Part of the darker doings between the sexes.

The next familiar face she saw was a cheery one—Emerald Roscheski's. Its wattage was a little lower than normal. Amanda guessed something was bothering the woman. She had refreshed her dye job and wriggled into an ill-fitting Muncher's uniform. Her formerly concealed bosom was a secret no longer. Bust and beanie somehow didn't mesh. "This isn't going to be a good night for me," she muttered.

"Why's that?"

She darted an ambiguous glance at Amanda. "I heard you're in the contest after all."

"I, or rather the three thousand dollars, changed my mind."

"Rumor has it the smart money's not on you. It's on your fey friend."

"Jessica's a lovely girl."

"Gordie's becoming quite consumed with Ms. Tinker Bell. How's that make you feel, Amanda?" Emerald asked.

"Good riddance." Amanda looked directly into Emerald's eyes. "How's it make *you* feel?"

"Bad." She pointed across the filling tent. "That makes me feel worse."

Amanda's heart beat hard at her ribs. There was Hunt Grayson! How differently she reacted now at sight of him! The redheaded ghosts of his Providence and Hartford victims clustered around his immaculately tuxedoed frame. The police would *have* to deal with him soon. He stood talking with Gordie and Chelsea. Amanda understood what troubled Emerald. It was the rapt expression on Gordie's face, as though he was beholding a miracle at Lourdes. Possibly, he was undergoing a conversion of sorts—from an obsession with her to one for Chelsea.

"Where did she come from?" Emerald groaned.

"She's a very good friend of Hunt's."

"Until tonight. I know Gordie Locker. Sweet Jessica is already history. He'll make his move on blondie there. He *loves* blondes. That's why he made me dye my hair.'' She held out a hand and ticked her clear-lacquered nails. "I was his woman! I *was!* Look where I stand now. All of a sudden blondie is moving up to first, Jessica is second, and you're third. I'm an unbelievable fourth! To make matters worse, there's no way I can win the Ms. Muncher competition. I ought to get out of here now!''

Movement at her side. Amanda half turned. Evan whispered in her ear, "Never far from your side tonight.''

"Hello, reporter man.'' Emerald's bright smile angled somehow. Was it the tent lighting that gave her even-toothed beacon a wolfish, cunning gleam? "Still on the track of your big story?''

He was polite. "A new Ms. Muncher is news. Maybe you'll be her.''

"Not likely!'' Emerald swept off.

Amanda's eyes returned to Hunt and Gordie. She was aware that Evan was filling her in on what he'd seen making his rounds of the tent. She scarcely heard him. She understood the strength of his evidence against Hunt. But she had trouble relinquishing her recently spawned suspicion of Gordie. Possibly, he had another very good reason to push Emerald out of his life. There would be no more *Reformer* redhead ads; the police had stopped them. She had no more information to give him. He knew all he needed to about Jessica Morris.

And about Amanda.

She realized she had never believed Emerald's denials about having disclosed details of the classifieds. Though Evan had questioned her, too, and was certain she was telling the truth, Amanda's suspicions were still very much alive.

She realized how badly she needed the police.

Right then, amid the rising party noise and excitement, she was seized with a premonition of doom. No matter what she did, Gordie or Hunt or the force of capricious fate itself would find a way to strike Jessica and her down. Her arms, as though without her will, found their way half around her torso in an awkward hug that brought no comfort. The march of the last weeks' events seemed to be picking up speed now, rushing her along like a stream in flood. All her efforts to gain the shore seemed destined to fail. She would be swept onward on her fatal journey. At its end she saw herself battered by rocks, limp, white faced . . . drowned.

# CHAPTER

## ❧ 12 ❧

Gordie spoke on the PA system and temporarily closed the bars and buffets. With resentment she ill understood, Amanda saw Ned helping to shepherd the guests toward the folding chairs in the theater area. She fell into step with Karl and Jessica. A few paces ahead Evan walked, glancing now and again back at her, to see that she was safe.

The seating arrangement would face the judges with the contestants. Two professional-sized TV camcorders stood ready to capture the competition. There was much milling around as everyone sought his place within the ropes. She glimpsed four other women being herded by ubiquitous Ned. She looked away, caught Hunt's eyes on her face. A chill blowing from far beyond the hot early July night iced her nerves. He winked and pumped a clenched fist by way of encouragement. She stared back, unsmiling. She imagined she saw the blood from Grace's right hand all over his immaculate white dinner jacket.

It was awkward trying to find her way to the VIP area. Her efforts to push through the press of bodies were slow. Apologies and excuse-me's were on everyone's lips as all wandered on the edge of confusion.

Then the lights went out.

Later she tried hard to put the sequence of events in proper order. The explosion killed the lights. She was certain of that. The only illumination came from the mansion a hundred yards away. Deep gloom enveloped the muttering crowd. A few women screamed. Voices rose urging calm. She stood frozen with surprise—and fear.

She heard a loud scream nearby. A man. His howls went on and on, driving into her brain like a nail. She was aware of shapes heaving in the gloom. Women were crying out. Men shouted nervously. Nearly beside her, Gordie bellowed for calm. He shouted for his staff to find flashlights.

Scuffling nearby! "Amanda!" Hunt's voice!

"No!" She tried to lunge away. His arms enveloped her. She screamed with all her strength as he wrestled her down.

Her moment to die had come.

Other women screamed, instinctively understanding her uncontrolled fear.

She beat at him with her hands, kicked wildly like a trapped animal. "Let me go, Hunt!" she screamed. She squirmed like an eel under his weight. Terror gave her strength. She kicked on, trying to free herself from his strong grip.

"For Chrissake, be quiet! I'm not going to hurt you. Somebody else might want to."

"*Let me go!*" Her continued cries further stirred others nearby. She felt the beast of panic stir, a thousand people standing blind and nervous. The herd instinct brought forth questions, uncertainty, uneasiness. She kicked completely free of Hunt. "Leave me alone!" She lunged away into the press of anxious bodies. Hunt cursed softly in either frustration or disappointment.

A woman shrieked. "I'm stepping on someone! There are people lying on the ground!"

Amanda moved toward the voice to completely escape Hunt. "Amanda," he called behind her. "Damn it! *Amanda!*"

"Here's somebody." A man's voice. "Hey, wake up! You all right?"

Another man. "For the love of God, there's blood. There's *blood!*"

"Will you idiots hurry with the lights?" Gordie bellowed. "I'll break every one of your stones. We got hurt people here."

Lights bobbed with fireflies over the lawn leading to the house. They grew to be hand lanterns and flashlights. Gordie lunged out and grabbed the most powerful. He hurried back to the tent, the guests spreading before his rush. He followed voices to the fallen. Amanda wasn't far away. Driven by panic and fear, she shoved people aside to get to Gordie and the light.

The beam lanced the gloom, slashing by sweaty faces and bouncing off white clothing. It nosed down to disclose a massive, tuxedoed shape. The guests backed away into a tight circle. Karl lay face down. The light illuminated his squarish head. No sign of damage. "What's with this guy?" Gordie muttered. He guided the light down the wide body. "Uh-oh!"

Amanda saw the handle protruding low on Karl's back. Someone had driven an ice pick into his kidney. She gasped and tore her eyes upward. The first face that registered was Emerald's wreathed in a wild, savage grin.

A doctor identified himself and shoved into the circle. He wore thick glasses and a goatee. "Get these people away from whoever's on the ground. Use your lungs, man!" he barked at Gordie.

Gordie bellowed and the guests fell back.

The doctor knelt by Karl, placing a hand on his throat. "Call an ambulance! He's alive."

Gordie gestured at Ned, who hung back, pale and openmouthed. "Stanton, shag it to the phone!"

More lights now shined. They disclosed another man on the ground not far from Amanda's feet. Evan Dent! She shrieked and rushed to his side. He lay face up. Blood trickled down his face. She saw a cut high on his forehead and a lump, nasty even in the uncertain light. She went to her knees beside him, calling his name. She wanted to help, yet didn't dare touch him. She grabbed his sleeve with one hand and picked up the frames of his smashed glasses lying beside him. "Evan . . . Evan!"

Two women screamed behind her. She didn't look. She

touched his face. The doctor was beside her. "Move back, miss." He knelt down, knees popping. Evan groaned and stirred. "What happened to you, son?" he said.

"Somebody nailed me," Evan murmured weakly. "I didn't see a goddamned thing."

The doctor raised each eyelid quickly and nodded. Guests screamed for his attention. "He'll live," he said to Amanda. He rose in haste and turned toward horrid cries and wild weeping. She pressed anxious palms to Evan's face. She remained there kneeling, until the eye of attention found the final victim. The jostling and shuffling to allow room for the doctor gave her a glimpse among shifting calves of a fallen figure, feet toward her. A half-dozen lights shined down upon Jessica Morris and the bib of blood on the chest of her Ms. Muncher uniform.

Her throat had been cut.

That sight drove a scream up from Amanda's throat that took her rationality and good sense with it. She drew fresh breath and sent another long wail after the first. Evan sat up, looking dazed but determined. "Amanda!"

She wanted to control herself, but couldn't. Other women were crying out and a wave of panic stirred a part of the crowd. She heard shifting and the ground shook with running footsteps. Some guests were bolting. Evan rose shakily to his knees. He grabbed her forearms and squeezed. She screamed into his earnest face. He shook her, but she was beyond response. The vision of her dead friend floated before her like an apparition. He dragged her to her feet. Her knees scarcely supported her. He hugged her against his hip. "Let's get out of here!" he said.

She was distantly aware of her racing breath, hot and dry in her throat. "The police . . ." she muttered.

"We'll be hearing from them. You can bet on that."

She began a hysterical blubbering. Though despised, it wouldn't be curbed. It lasted well into the ride back to New Hartford, finally giving way to sobbing and wild tears. She momentarily gathered her wits. "He kept his word! He killed her!" she shouted.

PERSONAL

"Who?"

"Hunt. He grabbed me and—" The thought that she really wasn't sure what Hunt had done raised new doubts, impossibilities that . . . She lost control again. Despite Evan's urgings she simply couldn't get it together again.

Evan had to carry her into the house and put her on her bed. She rolled over and pressed her leaking face to the pillow. She thrashed and drew up her knees.

"I'll check the kids," he said.

He came back shortly to say that both Justin and Jilly were asleep. He tried both cold cloths and whiskey on her. She tried to control herself, but her nerves were like a fuse box with all the cables tangled and shorted. She breathed with choking grunts, her eyes staring. "I'm next," she said. "I'm next."

Evan made a vague calming noise and shook his head. Amanda tore her gaze from his nasty forehead gash and bruise. His eyes were on her face. He blinked, seeing poorly without his glasses. She clenched her fists and held them in front of her. Her sobs were wild, somehow directionless. Through smeared eyes she saw his gaze lower to her body. He reached out and put his hand on her hip. Poor, shy Evan. She covered his hand with hers, uncertain of her emotions and his intentions. If only she could stop crying . . . Her fear and the shock of Jessica's brutal death made that impossible. Evan leaned forward and kissed her breast covered by bra and uniform.

It wasn't fair, she thought distantly, that he should screw up his courage when she was so obviously distraught. She ran her fingers through the thick hair on the back of his head. She was trembling so that her fingertips tangled there and snagged the strands. She tugged a handful of hair, drew his head up. His eyes were hooded and distant with desire. "I'm a wreck," she whispered.

"Amanda." He dragged his hand down across her groin. Arousal like a distant echo reverberated in her shaken soul. She wanted to respond, but her wits were in disarray. Troll voices chorused that she was going to be the next to die.

She turned over, drew up her legs, and jammed her clenched

203

fists down between her knees. Her back was to him. "Go ahead," she whispered. "I'll try to catch up to you."

His voice was hoarse. "Look at me, Amanda."

She angled her head, saw his obvious arousal. Raising her eyes to his face she saw the tension around his jaw. Hesitantly, she raised her hand to touch the distended stretch of pants fabric. It wasn't what she wanted to do. Yet she was drawn to . . .

At the first touch of her curved fingertips he jerked away. "I'm being so *unfair*," he said.

She groaned, awash in the crosstides of fear and desire.

"I'm sorry to be the way I am," he said. "There'll be a right time. We'll find it. I promise." He hurried out and didn't return at her call. Unsure of anything except her mountainous fear, she cried herself to sleep.

In the morning, with Justin beside her, she drove Jilly back to her apartment. She was so distracted she could scarcely match the girl's enthusiasm about Evan's inspired remodeling and his pinball machine. When Amanda returned she found Evan gone and Detective McMahon waiting at the door. She sent Justin to explore in the unremodeled area.

She was still badly unraveled. Hard work with brush and make-up earlier that morning hadn't quite done the job. Color her pale and scared. Seated on the stylish living-area settee, the cop sketched in what had happened under Gordie's tent the previous evening. The electrical box had been destroyed with some kind of timed or electronically controlled plastic explosive, carefully placed to just do the job. The killer had done all his work in a few seconds, stabbing Karl and cutting Jessica's throat. The big man had survived, but she was dead at the scene. The murder knife was found, but carried no fingerprints. "The doc said he had a look at Evan Dent. Our killer worked him over, too."

"Slashed at him, then knocked him down with something," Amanda said. "I guess he was in the way."

The detective shrugged. "Where is he?"

"Out on a story. He works long hours. Anyway, he didn't see who attacked him."

He stretched out his legs. "Who's our man, Mandy? Still think it's Gordie, killing on his own turf?"

Amanda's brain wasn't working well. She grunted and rubbed her brow. She had left the clippings about Hunt Grayson at work. She told McMahon what the clippings said. He took notes. He was paying more careful attention to her now than during their initial encounter weeks ago. Keeping her word to Evan, she told McMahon she had found the articles herself. Then she explained with a frown how the graying executive had knocked her down, claiming to want to keep her out of harm's way.

"Before or after people knew someone was dead?" he said.

She hesitated. "Before? After? I don't know. I'm not sure of anything."

He kept writing.

"I heard the news this morning," she said. "The murder's gotten attention. The TV people . . ."

His face reddened slightly. "It's tough enough catching psychopaths without electronic cheerleaders and self-styled coaches."

She felt increasing sympathy for McMahon. Strain and weariness were etched permanently into his face. "How's it going with the judges?"

"Slow."

"As slow as with whoever's killed my redheaded friends?"

He didn't quite meet her gaze. "Not quite that slow."

Amanda brought them both coffee. "What happens now?" Her voice was leaden with the fear that nestled permanently deep in her innards like an evil fetus. "The killer's kept his schedule. I met Floyd six weeks ago. This is Saturday of the last week. Next Friday is . . ." To her surprise and shame her voice failed and she began to shake.

"We're working on the list of names you gave us. It's slow. For example, we didn't begin to find out what you told me about Grayson. Maybe he moves to the top of the list, huh?"

She wished her mind was working. She had vague ideas that

all her suspicions were wasted energy and misdirected as well. In her fear and weariness the killer seemed invisible, invincible, implacable as fate. All she had to offer to this man who had to deal with facts were flimsy webs of intuition that she threw wildly in all directions. Floyd, Gordie, Hunt . . . All were strange men in their ways, but which was guilty? Driven by her desperate, skittering suspicions, she wanted to add more names to her list—all the men with whom she dealt. Ned and Evan should be included. Felicity's father, too. Detective Reti. Mrs. Clendenon's serf husband. Even as she shared those wildest flings of her imagination with McMahon, she sensed she was overlooking something or someone central to her desperate situation, but was unable to make a needed significant connection.

She had struggled so hard for a chance to talk to the detective. Now that he shared the room with her, his power, and specifically his capacity to help her, seemed weak and distant. It was as though the killer was a sorcerer with the power to weaken both her resolve and his professional skills. Something like lassitude settled over her, an acceptance of the inevitability of . . .

"I'm going to put a man on you, Amanda. You won't see him—if he does his job right. He'll be looking to screen you from any unwanted 'friends.' You need help, you sing out or make some kind of flap."

Her attention was far away on the evil angel stalking her, on the six days left to her, on what so recently had become the inevitability of her death. "It won't do any good," she said distantly.

"The Lord won't let you die," the detective said.

Amanda drew herself back from the dark palace through which she walked like a doomed debutante. "Have you been in touch with Him? Did you receive His assurances?" She didn't mean to sound petty, but her words came out that way.

"Would you believe me if I told you you were in my prayers?"

"Y—Yes." Somehow she was touched by this spiritual tenderness from the worn, reborn cop. It showed itself in the welling of more tears. Oh, she was right on the raw rasp of her emotions! ''I hope whoever's watching out for me has some sense!'' Then she was carried away on a long wave of weeping. By the time it crested, McMahon was at the door. ''You'll be hearing from me,'' he promised.

She tried to rally from the prevailing morbidity hanging over her. The killer would do whatever he had to to ring down the curtain on the one-act play of her life. He had blown the electrical box with cunning and precise skill. What could stop him from tracking her, tripping her up, and . . . She groaned. Her mind's eye showed the glint of a descending axe blade—sharp as memory, merciless as revenge.

''What's going to happen to me?'' she whispered to herself.

''Mom, you all right?'' Justin stood in the doorway, his smooth brow distorted by a frown.

She hugged him. ''It's more of the same. That guy who's after me.''

''The cops don't have him yet?''

''I'm afraid not.''

Justin made a fist and swung it at the air. ''Don't worry. I'll take care of you.''

''In the meantime, *I'll* take care of *you*.'' She brushed angrily at her smeared cheeks. ''How about hot dogs and baked beans for lunch?''

''Yeah!''

After lunch they toured the nearby woods and millstream on foot, skipped rocks in the big pool downstream from the warehouse. Shoes went off and they waded, holding hands, the rocks smooth but intrusive against the balls of their feet. Water striders worked their magic, feet bending the elastic of the surface film, like kids walking on a mattress. Justin contrived to slip and plunge in. She chose to agree it was an accident. Strolling a shadowed path, he allowed her to put her arm over his shoulders. With some success she felt herself struggling against the oppressive forces she imagined arrayed against her.

That night Evan called to say he would be working late on a story. Amanda and Justin went out for fried chicken, came home, cranked up the VCR and watched a movie from Evan's impressive video collection. She deserved a little escapism.

After Justin was in bed she climbed to the highest window in the remodeled area and looked for signs of the vigilant officer she had been promised. She saw no sign of him.

She returned to the living room. She gripped the light switch and flipped it up and down rapidly, then ran to the front door to see what would happen. Nothing. She waited. Still nothing. Not a sound, not a trace of movement out there. Time passed. She was ready to go to the phone and chew out her precious born-again detective.

"You jerkin' me around, Ms. Walker?"

She cried out and whirled. A cop stood in the kitchen doorway. Behind him the door swung wide. He was about six-two, big in the chin and chest. He wore a business suit. His right hand was under his lapel, no doubt on the butt of a revolver. "I—I didn't know if—"

"Not smart, ma'am. The name's Luke. You do what you just did, you advertise to whoever that I'm your shadow. Maybe it's already too late."

Amanda felt lead in her stomach. Her only trump card. Had she already misplayed it?

"You know the story about the boy who cried wolf?" Luke said.

She nodded, swallowing with a dry throat.

"Don't test me again." He winked. "Either me, or the man who relieves me will be around. Count on it." He went as silently as he had come.

Amanda stood motionless by the door. She turned and surveyed the interior of what had become her "safe" house. She continued her inner rally, struggled out from under some of her depression. Her sense of inevitable doom faded from the consistency of thick Maine coast fog to mere scattered gray banners. Maybe, maybe she was going to make it. The cops were going to catch him—whoever he was—before next Friday.

She showered and readied herself for bed. So greatly had her mood improved—nothing like having one's own private

PERSONAL

cop—that she sat brushing her hair and wishing Evan was there.
She was certain they were moving toward more intimacy. If
he had been peeking at her . . . She tingled a bit at the thought.
She would draw him out of hiding. It would be fun. She knew
she could do it. The arts of Eve didn't have to be taught. She
tugged her hairbrush through her red waves. Stroke . . .
stroke . . . stroke. She had counted them as a child, found she
still kept a kind of cadence. Evan . . . Evan . . . Evan . . .
   The phone rang.
   The brush froze. She pulled it free and put it down. A call
for Evan, or from him, saying when he'd be home. She rose
and hurried to the kitchen. She lifted the receiver. "Hello."
   "I've found you, Amanda." The voice! So light and distant.
Could it be a woman?
   She opened her mouth to reply. Her throat shriveled like an
oyster on desert sands. A dry hiss passed her lips.
   "Friday will be your day."
   "No, it won't!"
   "And your son's, too."
   "No!" The word was a scream.
   The phone went dead.
   All Amanda's sense of calm and hope carefully manufactured
over the last hours fell to crumbled pieces. She stood frozen,
wondering how he had found her. She could have been followed
to the warehouse, as Ned had nearly done. Anyone at Gordie's
disastrous Ms. Muncher fête could have seen Evan and her
arrive together and make the connection. Too late did she
realize she hadn't been smart enough about concealing her
hiding place. She felt too weary to begin to think about moving
again.
   And worst of all, he was after Justin, too!
   Her son had to be protected, somehow.

   In bed she formed a simple and sensible idea. Sunday morning she told Evan about the call, but not about Justin also being
the killer's target. She supposed she was being a bit dishonest.
She smothered her conscience when it rebelled after he suggested they all jump in the car and head down to his favorite

Rhode Island beach. His treat. They were packing to go when she got a call from Pop-Up's nurse. He had taken a turn for the worse and was in Hartford Hospital. She sent Evan and Justin off for the day, and hurried to her father's bedside. On the drive into the city, she looked often into her rearview mirror. She didn't see officer Luke following her. Nonetheless, she was sure he was back there somewhere.

The day she had intended to use to sort out just where she stood was spent trying to chat cheerfully with a dear, dying man. Pop-Up faded out often, his glance rolling ceilingward, his stubbled jaw yawning into long silences in mid-sentence. She paced hospital halls amid gurney traffic, the clatter of meal trays, and the comings and goings of mobile pharmacies choked with a junkie joyland of pills. In good time she spoke with her father's doctor. He looked to be her age. How could he know anything? What he did know was that her father was indeed dying. "He won't be leaving here," he said. "I don't think he'll suffer long. He'll be one of the lucky ones."

Planning how to deal with this last week of being stalked by a maniac was washed away by the flow of her emotions and tears. She tried to hold herself together, but the sight of her feeble, failing father set her to wrenching her hands and gripping his sheets until her knuckles popped—as though flesh and bone could hold him back from that place from which no one returned.

She explained to the doctor that she could not avoid having to go to work. She intended to visit her father daily, in the evenings. Should the worst seem to be happening, she wanted to be called. She'd come at once.

Driving home, she thought she caught a glimpse of officer Luke in an unmarked car, but wasn't sure. She didn't see him again. He knew his business.

She phoned Jessica Morris's number. A strange woman answered, her voice raw from hours of tears. In answer to Amanda's questions she said her daughter's body was going to be shipped back to the Midwest for burial. There would be no funeral for her in "this sick, sick city." Amanda gave her sincere condolences, her voice shaky as the last oak leaf in a winter storm.

When Evan and Justin got back from the beach, she took the reporter aside. "Make you a drink?" she offered.

"Thanks. Gin and tonic." He took off his second pair of glasses and leaned back. His fair skin had been scorched by the sun. "They don't make sun screens thick enough for this thin hide."

She brought the drink and curled up at his feet. She told him about her meeting with McMahon. "This is going to be a bad week for me, Evan. Real bad. Even with a cop shadowing me. My father's dying, so there's no question of my leaving Hartford. And the killer has stuck to his schedule. I'm sure no sane person would know why."

"What's next?" he asked, sipping his drink.

"I want Justin to be safe. If I'm not with him, then I want someone with him that I can trust. That's you. I wonder if I could ask you a *great* favor. Could you take him with you to the paper on your rounds? Never leave him alone with anybody who's not one of the people you trust." She studied his face, feeling guilty for the lie of omission: that her son was on the killer's list, too. If she told Evan, he might refuse, and who else could she ask?

He held up the clear drink, ran a fingertip over the glass's mist of condensation. "I don't know if I can work it," he said. "Some of the places I go, the people I talk to . . ."

"Whatever experiences he'll have can't be as bad as—" Amanda's throat closed up. She swallowed a lump. She could not speak the word. "Please consider it, Evan. I'm desperate."

His hesitation sparked her guilt. He had already done so much for her. He could have been killed at Gordie's. The nasty bruise high on his forehead was in full blue bloom, the cut scabbing over. In exchange, he had asked for nothing, not even the obvious fleshy favors she knew deep down that he desired, and that she wanted to grant him. She had seen clear evidence of his arousal. If he were a different kind of man, he would have forced her to have already crossed that line. Earlier, she had prepared herself to serve as the seductress he clearly needed to get him going. But not *now,* with Justin, too, in danger. She had not exaggerated her desperation. "Just for this week, Evan." She knew she was begging but didn't care. "If it happens that the police don't find whoever's after me and we get into another week, I'll make other arrangements."

He lowered the chilled glass and rolled it gently across her forehead. She realized how hot she was. "Justin and I get along. I don't think he'll mind." He was smiling.

"Will you mind?"

"It'll be my pleasure." He removed the glass and touched the tip of her nose with his index finger. "But I want something in return."

"Anything," she breathed. And meant it.

"Earlier you said that if Jessica died, you wanted me to do a big article that told the world what happened to the other redheads, and what could happen to you. Remember?"

"Of course."

"I talked to my editor about it yesterday. No dice. He doesn't want that kind of trouble right now. The reasons are political. Favors are owed. The establishment has its priorities. I argued, and got nowhere. I guess what I want is to be relieved of my promise."

Amanda's heart sank. She turned and paced away to hide her face. She hesitated a long moment. "I guess I have to do it," she said.

He couldn't face her and turned aside. "I'm sorry I'm not very brave. If only I were a crusader."

"It's all right, Evan. Really. The police are very much involved at the moment. I told McMahon what was in the articles you found about Hunt. He'll figure out how Hunt managed to kill Jess before he wrestled me down. And there's that cop watching my every move. It's all going to work out in the end."

Evan still looked chagrined. "When they run Hunt to earth, my editor's given me an exclusive to write about your side of it. If you agree not to talk to any other reporter. The way I've let you down I don't really have the right to ask you."

"You do," she insisted. "You've done so much, Evan. We'll deal with all that after they arrest Hunt." She hugged him briefly, then hurried off to make dinner before he could see her tears of disappointment.

Lying in bed, she had her first calm thoughts since the caller's horrid intrusion through the thin wall of her self-control. Despite all the murders, no one but loathsome Floyd Philman had been truly eliminated as a suspect. She ran her hand down her leg, feeling the thin pad of scabs from his Doberman's teeth. She then thought of Gordie's second wife Darlene's leg smashe d with an iron. Gordie hadn't started shouting until after Jessica was killed. Why shouldn't she still think he could be the madman?

There was still the matter of her remaining doubts. Had Hunt tackled her while Evan and Karl were being attacked and Jessica murdered? Or was it afterward? Could one man have done all that, or . . . were there two unknown tormentors? She thought darkly that if she didn't survive, at least Evan would do what he could to keep her son safe.

She had read and reread the articles Evan had found about stylish Hunt Grayson in an earlier life. She had studied the photograph till her eyes ached. He was surely the man who had murdered the wife and daughter he had never admitted having, as well as very likely being responsible for the deaths of a half-dozen other redheads. He was the killer! He had to be. She had cued Detective McMahon. The police would be talking to him early this week. Maybe they would jail him and it would all be over.

Or *was* he the one? It seemed so. But she had been so sure of her tormentor's identity before and been wrong. People who had committed crimes before were always the first to be suspected when similar crimes occurred. Of course, technically, Hunt had never been found guilty. He had bounced back to rebuild his life. Surely, he knew he would be taking a mad chance to repeat a crime pattern known to the police. Unless he was compelled to do so. Again, she recalled her earlier intuitive feelings that something wasn't quite right with the

213

man. As well, he was the one who had brought her word of Gordie's three thousand dollar fee to be paid to the new Ms. Muncher. He knew her financial position; he had issued her an irresistible invitation. He had wanted her there when he killed.

She scissored her legs under the sheets, rolled over, and groaned softly. Her memory served up the night of Jessica's murder. If neither Gordie nor Hunt were guilty . . . Oh, that was unlikely, she supposed. Still, among the guests were all her recent acquaintances, including her ex-husband and one other person who had circled her life loosely like a satellite in the last weeks. The face that turned up at every party, knew all those on her short list of suspects, lay at the source of personal ad information.

Emerald Roscheski.

Who was to say the killer wasn't a woman?

At work the next day she called the police records department and asked for Flo. The kindly woman had been looking into the dyed blonde's life for the last month. Amanda had heard nothing from her. Flo wasn't at her desk. Amanda asked for a return call and hung up vexed.

Shortly afterward, she sensed a tension passing over her kitchen and counter staff. That had to mean a visit from the Master Muncher himself, Gordie Locker. She got up and walked out of her office. He was pacing the public area, serious franchiser game face in place. He ran his hands across empty tables and looked at his fingertips. He kneeled and looked up under seats and table bottoms in search of chewing gum. She wasn't worried. Hadn't she just held one of her inspections at the end of last week?

He came bulling back into the kitchen, raising a chorus of "Good morning Mr. Locker." Amanda cringed inwardly. She had never been more afraid of him. She looked over his approaching shoulder. Sitting in the booth closest to the kitchen door was officer Luke, a cup of coffee in front of him. He winked.

Gordie waved her toward the office. "Door open," she insisted.

"Sure. Who cares?"

She had expected an argument. He never wasted time before trying to put his hands on her in private. "A lot's happened since you were last in this office," she said.

"All of it wicked bad!" he said. His expression didn't soften. "That chick getting killed at my place—Jesus! You see the papers, TV? I always wanted big publicity for the restaurants. Well, I got it." He muttered softly, then looked up at her with an expression she saw all too seldom on his face. It was something like respect. "I guess you told me there was some nut running around killing redheads."

"It could be you," she said, unsmiling.

He grimaced. "The cops gave that a try, too. Some SOB called McMahon, grilled me like a Perdue fryer. He got nowhere."

"I hope he hasn't given up," she said sweetly.

He waved away her nonsense. "I should've listened to you. I maybe could have done some good for what-was-her-name."

"Her name was Jessica!" she hissed.

"And now you're next on the list, right?"

"Next and last, Gordie."

He squinted, as though to see her better. "You're pretty cool about it all."

"I'm frightened to death!"

"Hey, you need any help, you call Gordie."

"And you'll come right over, huh?"

He looked surprised. "Me? Nah. I'm real busy all of a sudden." He looked speculatively at her. "Maybe I could send somebody over to look out for you. Maybe your ex for instance."

"Gordon!"

"Hey, he still has the hots for you. He told me."

"He lies a lot. You'll learn."

He shrugged and sat on the edge of her desk. "You oughta give him another chance."

"Never! Look, did you come here to play marriage counselor or what?"

"Nah, I came to talk business." He reached into his inside coat pocket. Amanda flinched. If his hand came out with a weapon she was going to scream. It held an envelope. He tossed it on the desk. "Congratulations!"

"For what?" She frowned. She did not trust this man.

"For being reelected Ms. Muncher."

"What?"

"You're it. For another year." He nodded toward the envelope. "Go ahead. Open it."

She took out thirty hundred-dollar bills. She looked up at him with a narrowed gaze. "No strings attached?"

"Just what you have to do, the TV and radio, the personal appearances. Like before."

Amanda got up and walked across the tiny office. She folded her arms and turned to look at him. "Why the change in style, Gordon?"

He shrugged. "Like I said, all of a sudden I'm real busy. Well, you gonna do it for another year?"

She had trouble turning her thoughts toward business and away from those of being a stalked, frightened woman. She stuttered, fell silent, then said, "I'll let you know first thing next week." Her voice shook. "If I'm still alive."

"Hey, cut the crap!"

"You saw Jessica!"

"So let me send over a couple guys. They got necks so thick their heads grow right up outta their shoulders."

She shook her head. "Thanks. But I've done some things to take care of myself."

He shrugged, got up to go. "You *got* to take care of yourself, Mandy. You're a part of the business. You're going to be my first regional manager!" He held out his hand for the envelope. "I better keep the money. You haven't said yes yet. And, hell, you might not make it."

"Thanks, Mr. Sympathy!"

"Hey, I tell it like it is." He moved to leave.

Amanda tensed. He always tried to hug her—or worse— before he parted company. Today he turned on his heel and left. She wandered after him. Out in the parking lot she saw the reason for his sudden busyness and lack of interest in her. He had bought a new convertible, some kind of fancy German or Italian car with a handcrafted exterior. Her ex-husband was at the wheel, a chauffeur's billed cap somehow suiting him. In the rear seat basking in the sunshine in all her blonde glory was Chelsea.

Gordie had broken the Amanda obsession.

From behind came the unknown soft voice of her in-house oracle: "He ain't your man no more . . ."

Amanda whirled from habit, but again had no idea who had spoken. And never would.

She was too wrapped up in speculation to feel relief. Her thoughts, after circling aimlessly, focused again on none other than . . . Emerald. She had boasted of being Gordie's girl. And what about Hunt Grayson? She remembered his and Chelsea's chummy answering machine message. He and the blonde had recently been close. Her intuition told her these recent events were connected and somehow affected her and whoever wanted to murder her. But she didn't see how.

The phone rang. For her. It was Flo, who apologized and asked if she could come over to the restaurant for a short time.

"Find something out about Emerald?" Amanda asked.

"Plenty."

Flo looked just as Amanda remembered her: small, wrenlike. The rouge spots were precisely on cheeks. She launched into an apology for having delayed so long in getting back to her. She insisted Amanda hear about her workload and the difficulty of finding out about someone without a place to start. Good thing she knew what she was doing, because if she hadn't—

"What did you find out, Flo?"

"Emerald Roscheski is no stranger to the law. And that's not her real name."

"It's not? What is it then?"

"Couldn't tell, she had so many aliases."

"That sweet-looking girl has a record?"

Flo waved a thin hand. "Yes, indeed!"

"Tell me!"

"I'm a little low on energy right at the moment." Flo raised her gaze to the Muncher's menu high above the counter. "And

I think the information's worth at least a Mini-muncher and coffee. I'm on my lunch hour.''

"Sure." Amanda saw that her visitor got what she wanted. After a few bites of burger Flo was ready to talk.

Two years ago in Boston a twenty-three-year-old redheaded woman was stabbed to death in Cambridge, not far from Harvard University. Some months earlier, a girl of twelve, also a redhead, had been stabbed as well. The first victim came from a prominent Massachusetts family, so an unusual amount of pressure was put on the police to solve the crime. Even though weeks passed, the family's political connections kept on the heat. It was suggested by the newspapers and even by some of the investigators that the murders might be related. In time, the police developed small leads that might have led to larger ones. The media were waiting for the beginning of a dramatic manhunt.

Then the murderer came forward and confessed. "Can you imagine who it was?" Flo looked at Amanda shrewdly.

"No, I can't," Amanda said.

"It was Emerald Roscheski."

# CHAPTER
## ❧ 13 ❧

Instead of being tried, Emerald was given a psychiatric examination. It proved to be the first of many. Batteries of shrinks debated her mental condition, while the police tried in vain to find out who she really was. At the end of six months of probing and debate she was declared incompetent to stand trial and institutionalized. Less than a year later she escaped. Officials said it could only have happened if she had received outside help. Others felt excuses were being made for lax security. Despite determined efforts, she wasn't found. Nor, in fact, was she ever positively identified.

Amanda was stunned. That sweet-faced woman with the upbeat personality was a murderer! She could scarcely believe it. Yet she instinctively knew Flo was right.

The older woman looked at her over the last bite of her burger. "You never said why you wanted to know about the girl. I hope she's not a friend of yours. One thing's sure: she shouldn't be walking around loose."

"She's not a friend. She's my tormenting nemesis. Do you mind if I go to Detective McMahon with what you've just told me?"

"Why would he care about something that happened in another city a couple of years ago?"

It seemed Flo knew nothing about the murdered redheads. "It has to do with one of his cases."

The older woman waved a cautioning finger. "Just don't tell him where you found out. I'm not supposed to—"

"Don't worry. I'm keeping lots of secrets these days."

As soon as Flo left, Amanda called police headquarters, excitement driving the pulse in her neck. She asked for McMahon, but got his sidekick Reti. He explained his partner had been taken off the redhead murders.

Her heart sank. "Why?"

"They put him on the judges." He asked her what she wanted.

She told him she had finally stumbled on the right suspect. "I have a lot of interest in what happens from here on out. I'm next on the list. So who's going to handle the arrest?"

"Me. I have the files. McMahon's sort of kept me up to date. Which guy do you think it is?"

"None of them!" Amanda realized she was shouting. "The murderer is a woman. The name she's using is Emerald Roscheski."

"Oh, yeah? Let me bring up McMahon's records." She heard distant clicking keys. "Says here you've already fingered three guys. Floyd Philman, Gordon Locker, and Hunt Grayson."

"Yes, but—"

"Philman was clean. We can't pin anything on Locker. And this . . . stuff you reported about Grayson. We're having trouble corroborating that, too. Now you got *another* one?"

"I have *the* one. This time I'm sure. She murdered two redheads in Boston a couple years ago. You have to go after her—"

"Look, Ms. Walker, I don't have to do anything. I know more about being a cop than you do. What you're doing happens a lot to scared people. You're pointing the finger at everybody. The shotgun approach, right? You figure one of them must be right."

"No! Maybe before I did. But now I know Emerald—"

"We'll look into her."

"Aren't you going to ask me her address?"

"Sure." He showed more enthusiasm. "Give it to me."

"I know where she works."

"Where?"

She named the *Reformer*. "When are you going to pick her up?"

"I think it would be smarter if I talked to her first."

"When?"

"Maybe next week. Maybe the week after."

Amanda panicked. "You said Detective McMahon told you everything. Don't you know I got a call Sunday night from Emerald? She said she's going to kill me and my son. I know it's going to be this Friday, or sooner!"

"Yeah, I heard about it from Mac. You spent a lot of time bending his ear."

"I've been afraid for my life! What do you want me to do? Suffer in silence?"

"No, not really. You're in a tough spot. So are we with too many felons and not enough cops. Anyhow, we got a man on you. Right?"

"Yes. Just the same—"

"I'll be in touch."

Raising her hand from the dead receiver she found her skin icy. She knew who was stalking her, and the police were so slow to move. *The boy who cried wolf* . . . How could she have prevented herself from going to them earlier when she thought she knew who threatened her? Anyone would have done the same. Anyone!

Bits of clues and suspicions joined together, the whole eclipsing the parts. How could she not have seen? Emerald was a psychopath driven to kill. She had controlled herself awhile after her escape from the institution. Somehow she had found her way to the *Reformer*. Who could understand how Floyd's ad had triggered Emerald's compulsion? But it had. Four new victims, and Amanda to be the fifth unless she did something to save herself. She remembered the soft, sighing voice crawling like a viper from the phone. Not a man. A woman. A madwoman!

Yes, she should have tumbled before now. Who else but Emerald knew the details of the personal classifieds? She hadn't given them to either Gordie or Hunt. She kept them to herself, enveloping them in the arms of her mad will, coveting them. They were meals to satisfy the hunger of her deadly compulsion. It all made sense now. And maybe not too late for Amanda to save herself.

She wasn't going to stand by and wait for the police to get around to arresting Emerald. No, it wasn't the time for orderly procedures.

After work she drove directly to the *Reformer* building. Before climbing the stairs to the classifieds office, she checked her purse for her mace. The cylinder was safely in place. She entered the room, eyes sharp for Emerald. In her place behind the counter sat a heavy girl in a T-shirt carrying a Shit Happens decal. She should have been wearing a bra. She was reading a paperback sci-fi novel. "Pardon me, I'm looking for Emerald Roscheski," Amanda said.

The girl ignored her. Her mouth moved as she read. Amanda waited, studying the plodding roll of lips. She no longer had nerves that allowed her the luxury of patience. "I'm looking for Emerald Roscheski!" she repeated loudly.

The girl looked up. Color her resentful. "You're looking in the wrong place. She's not here."

"She works here."

"Huh-uh. She used to work here." She put her book down and leaned on the counter, sagging all over it. "Then yesterday she went kinda crazy, you know?"

"Crazy? How crazy?" She was far worse than merely crazy when normal.

"Crazy enough to go all to pieces. Crying, screaming, tearin' her hair. The whole bit."

"Over what?"

"An affair of the heart. Her boyfriend dumped her, I guess was what it was." The girl shook her head. "I got to tell you she came right apart. She always looked like such a sweetheart. You know? Forget that! Her whole face turned different. She pulled a big friggin' knife—a pigsticker, I want to tell you— out of her purse and said she was going to kill him. Shouting and screaming to beat hell and waving her blade like a Co- nanette. She was like a completely different person. I mean, I *had* to believe her. Dig it!''

Amanda drew a deep breath that shuddered through her shaken self. A psychopath with a knife on the prowl for whom? Gordie Locker? Herself? Any redhead she happened to run across? It was only Monday. Between now and Friday she could cut up all her supposed enemies and still have plenty of time left for her. Amanda could take only the scantiest con- solation from at long last knowing her tormentor. ''Where is she?''

The girl shrugged. ''Gone. She got her pay. She won't be back.'' She picked up her book. ''I know where she's headed, though, sure as God is a sadist.''

''Where?''

''To trouble. Catch you later.''

Trying with little success to control her anxiety, Amanda hurried to the hospital. Pop-Up was worse. She sat at his bed- side, choosing to believe he knew it was she to whom he spoke. He was babbling of steelworkers and walking down on a sum- mer night to the beer garden for a cold bucket of suds. She imagined his life dying down like a coal glowing at the end of a twig. Dimmer, dimmer, dimmer—then a last flare of bright- ness before the eternal dark.

She couldn't just sit by him until visiting hours ended. Her son needed her, too, and she was imposing on Evan quite enough this week. She rushed to New Hartford, finding every- thing under control. Evan had served soup and sandwiches and post-dinner cleanup was in progress. Her portions had been carefully put aside. Tired but beaming, Justin gushed about the day's excitement. Above his head her mouth shaped the words ''thank you!'' at Evan, who stood smiling with dish towel.

When Justin was in bed, Amanda told Evan that Emerald Roscheski was the killer. His eyes widened and he looked startled. ''That wholesome girl? I can't believe it. It seems very clear to me that Hunt Grayson's the man.''

She shook her head. "I agree something seems weird about it all. That Hunt should be killing redheads in Providence and Emerald in Boston, then here . . ." She shook her head, again getting the feeling of having missed the connections among important events. Nonetheless, she had to tell him about Flo's industry and determination among police archives. At the end of her story, he sat back, stretched out his legs. "My God, I can't believe it, a woman killing women . . ."

"And now McMahon's off the case and I can't tell how fast Reti's going to act."

"Stay away from her," Evan said. "She shows up, you go the other way."

"I can't. I'm going to try to find her. Knowing it's a woman, knowing who she is, takes a lot of the terror away. It really does."

They argued briefly about the wisdom of her going after Emerald. He said she was looking for trouble. She insisted on a confrontation. She would arrange it so there was no danger. When he saw she wasn't going to budge, he said, "Let me look for her then."

"No! You take care of Justin. He's more important than I am."

Evan took off his glasses and rubbed his tired eyes. The bruise left from Emerald's assault at the Muncher's fête now lay sickly yellow, high on his forehead. Her fatigue made her realize even more strongly how much she had put him through. At first, she had been attracted to his physical appearance: slender, good-natured and easygoing. Now the strength of his character had taken first place.

He got up and paced. "I'm not at all sure you should completely discount Hunt. The evidence against him is damning. I think there's a possibility he's somehow working with Emerald." He looked sharply at her. "I strongly suggest you stay clear of him, too."

She nodded. "That I will do."

About ready for bed, she swam in weariness. She turned down her coverlet, but she didn't crawl in. She stood wondering what she was waiting for. Then she knew.

She wanted to be hugged.

She walked to Evan's bedroom. Surprise coming, dear, she thought. She put her hand on the fancy angled latch. The door was locked. She checked her robe and nightgown, revealing but not too suggestive. She called out softly, "Evan . . ."

No answer.

She called out twice more, louder. He didn't answer. She knew he hadn't left home. He was behind the door, either sound asleep or unwilling to deal with her at this hour. She sensed this would be their last chance for any kind of intimacy. As the week raced on toward deadly Friday, Emerald stalking her in the grip of her mad scheduling, she would never be as self-possessed as she was this evening. She padded back to her bedroom, disappointed.

On Tuesday she thought of calling Gordie from the restaurant and asking to be excused from work, then thought better of it. Muncher's was still the safest place to be. Among staff and customers it was impossible for her to be alone. She had told her people to ignore the hulking plainclothesman who single-handedly filled half the booth closest to her office. This was a good place to be, even if it made finding Emerald difficult.

She called Gordie anyway, but not to ask for time off. She told him she had found out who wanted to kill her.

"Who?"

"Your old girlfriend, Emerald."

"Come on!"

"You and I finally have something in common, Gordon. She wants to kill you, too. Or so I hear." She explained how she had found out. As she did, it didn't escape her that being stabbed by a woman was something like what her boss deserved. Rough justice for a nasty abuser.

"Christ! And she's got a knife?"

"Yeah." She was almost enjoying herself. "What I want to know is where she is. I want to talk to her," Amanda said.

"I got no idea where she is. If I was you, I'd stay the hell away from her. That's what I'm going to do."

"She shows, you call me, Gordon. Promise?"

"What are you? Nuts? She wants to kill you and you want to meet her?"

"I think I can handle her." She gave him Evan's phone number.

"Yeah, yeah. Get smart, Mandy. Let the cops do it. Stay out of her way. Her kind of trouble you don't need."

Maybe if she hadn't gone to the police so often before with the names of the wrong people, Reti would be paying more immediate attention to Emerald. What had been done couldn't be helped. When hours wound down to Friday, her few allies would have to be enough to help her through to safety.

"Speaking of missing people, Mandy, where's your ex?" Gordie said. "He's supposed to be working for me. He blew yesterday and I haven't seen or heard from him since."

"You hired Mr. Responsibility, Gordon. Par for the course with Ned, I promise you that. He may never show again."

"He don't show, he's canned. You tell him that, you see him."

She hung up. The essential Ned had returned. The chatter and clatter of her kitchen staff faded as her attention turned to the connections she should be making. The ones she had dimly realized earlier needed making. For the first time she thought they might involve Ned. Connect him with what or whom? Emerald? She turned that idea this way and that, but came up with nothing.

She phoned Hunt Grayson at his agency. When his secretary put her through, his voice was cool. She recalled she hadn't spoken to him since the catastrophe under Gordie's tent. She had battled his ambiguous embrace that evening, and run from him. As well, knowing about his violent past made her uneasy. He too, it seemed, had murdered redheads and gotten away with it. Past that, Gordie Locker had stolen his woman, Chelsea. Why should he be cheery? She understood his sourness but felt no sympathy. She wished she didn't have to talk to him. No details, then. "I'm sorry to bother you, Hunt. I'm trying to find one of your new models. Emerald Roscheski."

"Don't know where she is, Mandy."

"If you have a phone number—"

"The one she gave me is no good. It's the paper she used to work for. I called there. She's quit."

"You don't have a home number?"

"She only gave me one." He clearly wanted to get rid of her.

She didn't care if she stayed on the good side of another murderer. But she *had* to confront her tormentor. "Hunt, listen, if Emerald shows up or you find out how to reach her, please let me know." She tried to keep her voice even, but knew it betrayed her. Hunt wasn't dumb.

"You sound scared, Mandy. Is Emerald mixed up in the murders of your friends? That same business that's been going on?"

"Yes!" She couldn't restrain herself. "She's not just mixed up in it. She's the murderer! Not you! I thought it was you! It's Emerald."

"Me? Why me? That's absurd!"

"I believe what I read."

"Where did you read I'm a murderer? It's a lie!"

"Never mind! Now you know why I have to find Emerald before she finds me."

"The police?"

"I talked to them. In fact, I've talked to them too much. By the time they do something, it'll be too late. If you see or hear from Emerald, let me know right away!" Hesitating, she told him where she was staying.

He rattled on with angry questions about her accusations but she hung up on him.

The rest of the day dragged by. After work she hurried to the hospital. Pop-Up was worse. He didn't know her. The doctor said it was a matter of days. They were doing what they could to kill the pain.

She left the hospital with her head down. She couldn't allow herself the luxury of sorrow. Tears were too dangerous. She had formed the habit of looking behind her every half-dozen strides. She walked away from walls and doorways, indoors or out. When she drove, every fifteen seconds she looked in

PERSONAL

the rearview mirror. Moments she spent alone were filled with anxiety.

Thank God Justin was safe with Evan. She spent her days with people and her nights with him. Maybe Emerald couldn't get to her. Maybe the woman would learn that she was suspected and the target of a police net. She might just leave Hartford and never return.

Justin was still bubbling after his second day as a "cub reporter," as Evan called him. The reporter had managed to get assigned to a story at the Mystic Seaport and found time to take the boy on a tour of the nearby submarine and battleship and made him take notes on what he saw. Justin waved his scribbles under her nose. "Read this, mom! It was great!"

Wednesday at work was a disaster. A lightning storm knocked out the transformer that fed the restaurant. She spent more than an hour on the phone to Connecticut Light and Power. Staff milled and clowned and customers got one breath of the stale, unconditioned air then split for Burger King. She organized a complete restaurant cleaning, using all the hot water to fill buckets. She ordered grills and restrooms shined spotless, forbade entrance into the big freezer, and generally weathered the outage. She shoved Emerald largely out of mind until she got a call from Gordie.

She suspected he had been drinking. "Guess who stopped by to give me hell?" he laughed. "Our buddy Emerald."

"What did she want?" Her voice turned tiny with tension.

"To kill me!" His high-pitched laughter cut down the wire like a razor. "Damned if she didn't have that knife you told me about."

"Gordon . . ."

"I took it off her and paddled her ass. Great show for Chelsea. Show her what happens to *her* if she gets out of line!" More laughter. "Then Emerald got up on her high horse—reminded me of you a little. She wanted to know what I was going to do for her for all the times she crawled into the sack with me. I have to tell you she doesn't behave like a high school girl anymore. Doesn't much look like one, either."

"What?"

228

"You'll see."

"Gordon—"

"I told her what I might do for her, but it depended on you."

"What?"

"I told her to look you up—after working hours, of course."

"I see." She had to admit, that was what she had wanted.

"You said you wanted to talk to her, didn't you? What she wants has to do with Muncher's business."

"I told you she's after me. She's already killed four women in Hartford."

"You're about forty feet off base on that. She couldn't kill time, Mandy. She's harmless!"

"I am right about her! Anyway, she doesn't know how to find me. I moved out of my apartment for a while."

"She knew where you're livin' now. Out in the woods in New Hartford."

Amanda's heart surged. "How did she—"

"Ned told her. Before he took off to Christ knows where, he followed you a couple times. Second time you didn't notice him."

Amanda's fingertips found their way between her teeth. Hold on! she told herself. Take it easy. "I still want to see her, Gordon."

"Don't worry. She'll find you, Mandy." He hung up.

Evan dropped Justin off at the restaurant. He had an assignment that would run well into the evening. She wanted to beg him to stay home that night, to tell him that Emerald had his address and was going to come after her, she was certain, with another knife in hand. She wanted to tell him that she was losing the nerve she needed to confront the madwoman. She held her tongue. She simply wouldn't impose on Evan further. He said he'd be home about eleven. She would have to go to the hospital after work. She wouldn't get to New Hartford until about 7:30. That meant only a few hours alone with officer Luke or his clone hovering for her protection. She would make it.

She left Justin in the hospital lobby. Pop-Up was hanging on. She chose to sign papers requesting no efforts be made to prolong his life through chemical or mechanical means. Let him go . . . Before the drive home, she used the ladies' room and stopped by the mirror. She gasped at the sight of her face. Lines and wrinkles had charged in like shock troops commanded by her anxiety and fatigue. Smudges darkened the hollows below her bloodshot eyes. She beheld the look of the hunted, of quarry. She felt like a doe trying to escape slaughter carrying the lead weights of her responsibilities. It wasn't fair!

After Justin was in bed, she sat facing the front door with her purse on her lap, the mace within easy grasp. I know you're coming, Emerald. Don't keep me—and officer Luke—waiting. But would she come? It was only Wednesday night. Too soon for Amanda's "scheduled" death. Not really. Emerald had abducted Grace, held her, then slaughtered her six weeks to the day after she had met Floyd Philman. And cut off her hand. Her body had never been found. Amanda squirmed and groaned. She looked at her wristwatch. Just after ten. An hour at least till Evan returned. She sat waiting, minutes passing with glacial speed.

She started. She heard a car outside. It was pulling up. She rushed to the window. Not Evan. A car she'd never seen before. Someone got out and started up the flagstone walk. Her glance darted away into the gloom. Where was the cop? She didn't see him!

Evan had installed stylish lamps along the walk. She had turned them and the powerful porch light on. In seconds she would be able to identify her uninvited visitor. Amanda gasped at who she saw.

Emerald was coming for her!

Right up to the front door! She didn't know Amanda was privy to her monstrous secrets. She was a nameless psychopath who had murdered in Boston and continued to murder in Hartford. At least two victims there and four here. The blood of six ran from her neatly manicured fingernails.

Amanda beat her to the door, making doubly sure it was locked. She stood beside it, out of view, one hand on the light switch. A few quick flips should summon officer Luke or his clone she'd never seen. She felt a measure of security. The door was thick. She stood aside from any possible line of fire. A shadow fell on the glass. The buzzer sounded.

Only a wall stood between her and certain death.

She called out loudly, "What do you want, Emerald?"

"Gordie sent me to talk to you. Open the door."

"I know he did, but I'm not going to open the door. Talk from there."

"What are you, crazy?"

"Talk from there or leave, Emerald."

The younger woman muttered something inaudible through the door. "What's with you, Amanda? What I want to talk about is your letting me be the next Ms. Muncher. That creep Gordie dumped me. He said all he could do for me is make me Ms. Muncher if you'd agree. What do you say?" Earnest pleading hung on her muffled voice.

Amanda didn't believe a word. As well, she had trouble turning her mind back to Muncher's. Fear for her life was a hard gear from which to shift. She couldn't do it. "I don't believe that's why you came here tonight, Emerald."

"Huh? Why not? What do you think? I came here to socialize with you? I need help, Amanda. I need the job and the three thousand worse than you do if you want to know the truth."

"I don't think that's the truth. I think the truth is you came here to murder me."

"*What?* What are you talking about, Amanda?" Her voice was edged with bafflement.

"I'm the last one on your list for Hartford. You've already killed four other redheads. I'm the icing on your crazy cake."

"I haven't killed anyone!"

Alert as a ferret after prey, Amanda pounced on the change in the woman's tone. She heard comprehension, understanding—guilt. "You made a mistake coming here, Emerald. There are police watching the house. I'm going to signal them to arrest you."

"Oh, God. What? You've got cops around here?" She sounded startled.

"I know all about you, Emerald. I found out from police

records about those two redheads you murdered in Boston and how you were put in an institution for it.''

Emerald's cry was low, inaudible. She stumbled somehow. Amanda peered cautiously through the glass. The younger woman was sprawled legs akimbo on the porch stairs. Her face was ashen, almost colorless. Amanda was startled. It seemed as though Emerald might have dizzied or fainted at hearing her news. Off her feet as she was, she didn't seem threatening. She scrambled up to all fours. When she rose, her eyes were wide, not with killing rage, but anxiety. Her visible dishevelment had already been hinted at by Gordie. She rushed to the door. "Please, Amanda, let me talk to you!"

"Talk!"

"Crack the door, please. I . . . I don't want to shout if there are cops around."

Amanda hesitated. Through the glass she got a good look at Emerald's face. Its customary wholesomeness had given way to a mask of desperation that she herself might have well worn. The door had a sturdy chain lock. She slipped the heavy links in place and opened the dead bolt.

Emerald lunged at the door, shoving her contorted features into the narrow opening. "Whatever you do, please don't call in the police!"

"We'll see. What is it you want to talk about?"

"A great man. A man like no one else. A man whose ideas were different from the start. A man who thought about what life meant, what responsibilities the superior have toward the less fortunate."

Amanda frowned. "I'm not sure I understand. Was he some kind of philosopher or guru? Who was he? Why do you want to talk about him now?"

"You have to listen! You have to." From behind the anxiety that gripped her expression peeked instability, like the curve of a minor sun edging past an eclipsing moon.

"Emerald, you've killed at least six women. You want to kill me, too. I'm not fooled by you. This lock is staying on, right where it is, and pretty soon I'm going to signal the police."

"No police! They'll send me back to Dungeonplace, with the bars and the nurses with needles!"

"They'll send you back because you belong there. You kill people, Emerald."

"I never killed anyone! That's the whole point. You have to understand about this special man and his profound thought; the years he took to find his destiny; the battles he fought to learn how to use his superiority to reach goals worthy of him. He had difficult times. You see he was a tortured man—far, far worse than I am.

"What he believed, he had to hide. What he wanted he couldn't share with anyone. He worked to learn how to disguise himself and mask his superior thought. He lowered himself to walk with us . . . rabble." She spoke the word slowly, baptizing both herself and Amanda into that multitude. "Understand, he had to pretend to be a person—or persons, really—that the rest of us could identify with."

Amanda shook her head. She didn't understand.

"He had his own codes of right and wrong. They were very complicated, Amanda. He tried to explain them to me, when we met from time to time." She raised her shapely fingers and waved them in puzzlement. "His ideas were just too intricate for me. They had much to do with the purpose of pain and anguish, the need for some to suffer while others escaped." Her voice picked up speed and intensity. It rushed from her mouth. "He told me he had to cause suffering. It seemed to him that we—we women—had need to suffer. I argued with him. Oh, yes, Amanda, I did! My popgun mind against his laser."

Amanda wanted to interrupt, but her fascination grew. She held her tongue.

"We didn't meet that often. And of course he had his adopted lives to lead, his roles to work through. He held a lot of jobs, ones that required intelligence and skill, ones that didn't. Sometimes he wandered. He married when it suited him. He told me he had become a parent more than once. About five years ago he got away from a wife long enough to tell me all his past had finally wired with the present to show him his 'odyssey'—that was his word. This odyssey was going to take the rest of his life. Part of it was pushing to new limits, first for himself, then for society.''

"Emerald, you're not making a whole lot of sense."

"Listen! Just listen. How can I describe how a genius thinks?"

"Why don't you just get to the point? How does this man affect you and me?"

"A little better than three years ago, we met again in Boston. He had been traveling all around the country. He didn't give me any details about where. But I think he was playing the role of husband to somebody. He was almost giddy thinking about the place he had reached in his odyssey." Emerald drove her thin arm through the narrow opening. Amanda jumped back. There was no threat in the slowly twisting wrist. Only supplication. "I was giddy, too. I realized that I loved him more than I dreamed. More than was right, considering our blood relationship." Her words tumbled out, heated by the vividness of her memories. "He told me the time had come to climb up to a new plateau where he was going to link women's suffering with a new stage of his personal growth. He told me where and how he had already helped women suffer. Oh, that took a while, I can tell you, Amanda! The new stage would go ahead still further. To murder. You probably guessed that, didn't you?

"I wasn't his equal in either imagination or nerve. So I tried to talk him out of it. I'm ashamed to say it. Because for me he was a god. I was just a mortal. He pitied me. My limitations made it impossible for me to understand him. That was such a great disappointment to him! He had had hopes for me, but I wasn't living up to them. He went off alone then. When I next saw him he told me he had killed a woman in Boston.''

"A redhead," Amanda said.

"Of course. He had special thoughts about redheads for as long as I'd known him. *Very special.*"

"Why?"

"I can't imagine."

"Who is he?"

Emerald's wholesome smile seemed sinister as a man with a cloven hoof.

Amanda drew a deep breath and blurted, "It was Hunt Grayson!"

The smile turned enigmatic. "I felt a thrill for my special person. Oh, yes! And fear, too. Fear that no one would begin to understand his profound reasons for murder. The reasons that justified it. I was ashamed of saying to him that he had made a mistake—"

"Admit it was Hunt!" Amanda hissed. "For God's sake!"

"That was the only time—the only time *ever*—that he hit me. He said that was because I had never been so stupid before. A little while later he killed another Boston redhead. Despite his true genius, he was unlucky. I guess luck doesn't care how much you have to give the world. It comes and goes as it wants. The woman's father wouldn't let his daughter's death go. He kept after it and after it. After the police. After the politicians. After the media. I guessed that before long they would find and follow the right track.

"So I went to that man who was more important than anyone else and asked him to tell me the details of what he had done to the two women. I wanted the worst details. He did as I asked. He was proud of what he had accomplished." Emerald swallowed, and for a moment her enthusiasm sagged like a sail before the dying winds of horrid memories. "I memorized all the details, down to the smallest he could remember. And then I went to the police and 'confessed.' I saw my role almost as clearly as he had seen his years before. My role was to be a sacrifice. To exchange my freedom for his." The extended fingers rolled lazily, somehow like a caress of the unknown man's body. Behind them, Emerald's dreamy, lunatic smile loomed like a lantern of long-delayed understanding. There could be no disbelieving her.

"You really *didn't* kill anyone, did you?" Amanda said.

She shook her head. "I pretended I was mad and the cops wanted a conviction. It was so easy."

Amanda understood the woman before her was certainly

235

PERSONAL

insane. But she wasn't a slaughterer of her own sex. That morbid task belonged to Hunt Grayson.

"Don't bring the cops out of the woods, Walker. I don't want to be put in Dungeonplace again. I couldn't take it. My genius wouldn't be able to spring me a second time. All I want to do now, after talking to you like this, is get out of town. Everything's turned to dust for me in Hartford. I'm gone. But, no cops!"

Amanda grabbed Emerald's arm and clutched it. "Tell me who he is. He's Hunt Grayson, isn't he?"

"Let me go!"

"You have to tell me who your magic prince is, Emerald. You have to tell me he's Hunt Grayson. If you don't I'll flip this light switch and the cops will come and—"

"No! No! I don't want to go back. Dungeonplace! Please, don't make me—"

"Tell me it's Hunt Grayson!"

She shook her head, eyes lit with wildness. "No, no. Not him." Her glance narrowed with cunning. "If I tell you, you have to let me go free. Like I said, I'm headed out of town."

Amanda had to decide: did she believe Emerald, or not? So many times she had been misled, by herself, by evidence, by lies. But this time she sensed the girl was telling the truth, yet . . . "You know I'll go to the police with what you tell me. That 'special' person you almost sacrificed yourself for will go to jail and might be sentenced to death. You don't care about that?"

Emerald shook her head violently, her dyed hair stirring with her wild energy. "I don't know what I think. I'm mixed up. I'm a psychiatric case, aren't I, Amanda? Huh?"

"Emerald . . ."

"I won't go back there! I won't go back to Dungeonplace! If I don't tell you, you'll call the cops. They'll take me back."

Amanda knew she hadn't dominated anyone since this whole dreadful business began. At this moment she saw she ruled over Emerald Roscheski, a poor, demented woman. She felt no surge of power. Instead, only a vague queasiness. She had

236

seen into the younger woman's heart, and found it a polluted place. "Yes, I will," she said.

"So I have to tell you, don't I? I don't have any choice. *He* would understand that, wouldn't he?"

"Very likely." Amanda released Emerald's arm that she had held for so long. "Tell me and you can be on your way. I won't say anything to the police for a little while."

Emerald leaned forward, teeth and chin protruding through the narrow opening between the door and frame. She lowered her voice, as though the man she both worshiped and feared stood nearby. "It's . . . my . . . stepbrother."

Amanda cried out, a single bark of revelation. She understood! The connection she had tried to make. The one that had repeatedly escaped her. Oh, how could she not have seen! This woman was "S-sister." How often had Amanda heard about her exploits! The queen bee in a hive with only one worker who returned for nourishment and solace. The woman whose bond was nearly as strong as full blood for . . .

Ned Stanton.

Her ex. The murderer.

She was so stunned that she could scarcely shape words. She spoke his name. "My ex-husband!"

With eyes startled as a deer's, Emerald nodded and fled.

# CHAPTER
## ❧ 14 ❧

She sat up until Evan came home about 11:30. "Emerald came visiting," she announced as he walked through the door.

His eyes widened. "I thought you said she—"

"I was wrong."

He moved closer. She saw the weariness from a long day's work had etched lines in his smooth face. "What did she say?"

"She said a lot."

"And?"

"I found out who the killer really is."

He looked startled, then shook his head slowly.

She realized it seemed she was teasing him by delaying. "It's Ned, my ex-husband."

"She told you that?"

Amanda nodded. "A long story goes with it. Want to hear it? It's about a crazy pair. She and her psychopath stepbrother—who deluded me completely during our entire married life!" She shuddered. Who had fathered her son. God knew what mines lay in the field of Justin's genes.

"Yes. All of it." After she finished he looked around, as though in search of reassurance from familiar surroundings. "Who sits the first watch? I hope it's you. I'm bushed."

She looked puzzled. It was hard to keep up with him. She was so drained.

"Don't you remember? Ned grabbed Grace before he had 'scheduled' her to die," Evan said. "He could do the same with you. From now on one of us stays awake." He loosened his tie. "Things are getting simple for us and the cops. One, we know who the killer is. Two, we know he *has* to get to you. Sooner or later he'll make his move. Then—wham!—we have him."

"We have him." She nodded stupidly, still numb and slow. "Do you have a gun in the house?"

He shook his head. "Got no idea how to use one. With that cop watching you, all we need to do is make some noise or signal. That'll do it."

Amanda settled into her chair, folded her arms. "I'll take the first shift."

Thursday morning Amanda woke feeling poorly rested. The day passed without event except for her endless stewing, fidgeting, and morbid contemplations. Thursday night she and Evan again sat watch.

Then it was Friday.

Despite their two-night vigil, Ned had mounted no threats. Evan again followed her to the restaurant. He hugged her, telling her to be extra careful. Then he and Justin left for an early out-of-city interview. She drew a cup of coffee and wandered into her office. She shuddered at memories of her life with Ned. She recalled Emerald's description of him doffing and donning identities like hats, practicing cunning powers of deception. For her he had played the part of second-rate husband. She groaned. She felt used, corrupted, filthy. He had polluted her body, of course, but worse was the psychological soiling. She had devoted her little life to him—all she had had at the time. He had been married to her only with his left hand. His right had been devoted to exploring and refining the torture and ultimately the murder of redheaded women. She sensed a morbid closure of his psychotic circle. As her husband he had explored his growing sadism. She had been spared less by compassion than timing. Now his madness had been nurtured

239

to reign. He had returned to Hartford to close the circle. Not only by murdering her, but his own son as well.

It all made sense. And just in time!

She called Reti at police headquarters. She told him she now truly knew who had been stalking her for weeks. "You used to come up with the suspect of the week, Ms. Walker," he said. "Now you're up to two a week." He was gently teasing her. She wasn't in the mood for it.

"But this time I *know*—"

"What happened to the girl?" Papers shuffled. "Couple days ago it was Emerald Roscheski. We started checking on her. We thought you had something. Records say she's a nut case for sure and that she's somebody else using an alias. She slipped out of a high-security psycho country club a few years ago. We passed along the word. Sooner or later somebody will come along and pick her up."

She explained they should be looking for Emerald's stepbrother, Ned Stanton. He was the actual murderer. Yes, he was her ex-husband. Reti clearly wanted to believe her, but couldn't convince himself. "I hate this domestic crap. It always boils down to husbands against wives, ex versus ex. I usually don't believe either side."

"We're not talking about a couple of drunken punches on a Saturday night!" Amanda said. "Serial murder is what it's about."

"Believe me, Ms. Walker. I do understand. I do want to help you. Where do we find this killer-drifter you once thought was Robert Redford?"

She winced. "I don't know. He used to work for my boss, Gordon Locker."

"Who's he work for now?"

"I don't know if he works."

"Address?"

"I don't know."

Reti chuckled. "That's not much to go on. We'll try to find him, but don't look for us to pick him up right away."

After hanging up, Amanda's eyes moved around the restaurant. She turned completely, 360 degrees. Somewhere beyond her view Ned was watching and waiting for the right moment. Today was the day he had promised to kill her. She realized her hands were shaking. Despite trying, she couldn't stop them. She was aware that, after all the weeks, days, and hours since she had answered the horrid ad, she was coming down to the end of her emotional strength. The well had nearly been drained. Her whole body was edging to the brink of uncontrollable tremor. She had nearly burst into tears once again just because Reti hadn't fallen all over himself to help her. She verged on hysteria.

Pop-Up's doctor called. He was at the hospital. Her father had sunk into a comalike state from which he might well not recover. There was no sense in her hurrying over. His vital signs were still strong. Just the same, she knew he was down to days, maybe just hours. She hung up sniffling. "Tissue!" she cried, as though Justin were beside her, ready to go fishing in her purse.

At noon, she took two Maxi-munchers, extra Magic Mixture, and a large coffee to officer Luke in his reserved booth. It was a ritual they had both grown to enjoy. She served him and whispered, "Did they tell you it's my ex-husband you're after?"

"They don't tell me nothing, Mandy." He rubbed his lantern jaw. "They just say watch out for you or it's my ass!" He gulped down half the Maxi.

"Who's on duty tonight? You or what's-his-name?"

"His name is Ben and he comes on at nine. You don't see him after dark. He's a black man and as big as one of those trees outside that warehouse you're camping in."

Amanda leaned over. "I think Ned's going to come after me tonight. Don't fall asleep."

Luke's eyes narrowed. There was a vein of flint along their gray faces. "I haven't slept yet. Why don't you tell me what this ex-husband of yours looks like?"

After one o'clock Evan called to see how she was doing. He put Justin on the line. "Evan wants to know if you want to go to dinner and the movies with us after work. Pizza Hut!"

Through the afternoon Amanda thought it over. Good idea,

she decided. No sense going through another routine evening at home. That would be setting herself and her son up as stationary targets for Ned. They would get home soon enough.

The hours crept by. She did little more than look up nervously every time the restaurant's doors opened. When the customer proved not to be Ned, she went back to her doodling. She covered a half-dozen pages with jagged ballpoint lightning bolts and lopsided cubes. She went through her end-of-shift routines with the indifference of a computer. In her distracted state, she wasn't sure whether she wanted the evening to arrive or not.

She met Evan and Justin at Pizza Hut. Her son was in a great mood. He tore into the deep dish extravaganza with the enthusiasm of a starving foundling. She and Evan exchanged guarded small talk and looked around frequently.

The nearby mall included a complex of eight theaters. They chose a vaguely suitable film. Evan paid their way. He insisted they sit in the last row, with their backs to the high partition. "Put me in the middle," Evan said.

"I'd like to sit beside both of you," she said. "It's good to have men on both sides, sometimes."

A short while later she had reason to regret her decision. Justin's dry voice whispered, "Mom, I don't feel so good." Without missing a beat he leaned forward and lost his dinner, some of which splashed on her calf and shoe. She got up quickly. "That's it!" she said. "We're on our way home."

With apologies to the management, they trooped out by way of the men's room. Evan, looking a bit sick himself, reported no further upchucking. Just the same she put Justin in her car for the drive to New Hartford.

Too much excitement was her guess. By the time they got to Evan's home Justin seemed completely recovered. Nonetheless, she put him to bed while Evan nosed around outside the warehouse. She looked at her watch: 8:45. A few more hours and Friday would be over. She hoped that Ned, this time at least, wouldn't be able to keep to his morbid timetable.

Evan returned. "Didn't see anybody. Didn't even see whoever's on duty this evening."

PERSONAL

"I understand Ben just isn't to be seen. But he's out there," she said. "Come on. Let's plot strategy."

In the well-lit living area she saw the last two weeks had finally extracted a toll from her host. The new lines she had seen recently on his smooth face seemed to have been etched in permanently. His movements, normally smooth and well coordinated, were jerky, uneasy. As for her, the tremors threatening to take over all day at last made inroads on her control. From time to time she simply shook.

They made a great pair.

She made a little speech about how much she and Justin appreciated what he had done for her. She hoped there was some way she could pay him back. He cut her short. "We need a battle plan," he said.

She stared at him. It was so hard to keep her wits. The tremors overwhelmed her at that moment. She stood twitching like a palsy victim. He hugged her and she sagged against him, vibrating like some fleshy tuning fork. She heard his breath coming in rapid gasps. His hand rose to her breast and squeezed it. His fingertips coned in search of her dormant nipple. She shoved gently at his wrist. "Like two people sentenced to death?" she said, "Sex just before execution?" She caressed his face. "Why not?" To her disappointment, his heavy-lidded eyes widened reluctantly. "This might be the right place, but it sure isn't the right time, Mandy." He shook himself like a dog leaving water. He went to the bar and poured a shot of Old Grand-Dad, offered it to her. She shook her head. He tossed the liquor down and wheezed. "Not as much fun, but a better way to get ready," he said.

She could well have argued the point. But she supposed he was right. Damn!

He outlined what he thought was the best strategy. They would feign going to bed, turn out the lights, then meet here in the living area. "You, me—and my hand-turned club. Did it on my lathe yesterday."

Later, in the gloom, they took their places. She sat in the chair facing the front door. Evan sat behind her with his back to the wall in the heaviest shadows, the club on his lap. Amanda looked at the luminous dial of her watch. It was 10:50. One hour and ten minutes more and it would be Saturday. She sensed that if she saw midnight, Ned's power to kill her would evaporate like an evil wizard's spell at cockcrow.

Time crept by. She and Evan had agreed not to speak. They sat in silence. Outside, the incessant *whirrr* of cicadas and the occasional purling groan of a barn owl reached their ears with the intensity that only keyed nerves could bring.

11:13.

Amanda could scarcely control her limbs. She still hovered on the verge of uncontrolled trembling. The foundation of her fear was the suspicion, now that night had come, that Ned would, after all, keep to his schedule. He hadn't failed with Connie Kwan, Grace O'Shea, or Jessica Morris. He wouldn't fail with Amanda Walker.

11:28.

She frequently turned her head toward Evan scarcely visible behind her. He brandished his club in silence. She had put her purse on the floor by her chair. The mace would be her backup. In a quiet moment she had studied the mechanism that released the stream of liquid. She and Evan were as ready as they ever would be. But Ned didn't come.

11:40.

Another twenty minutes, she thought, and the worst wouldn't happen. She knew it. Twenty minutes more would bring relief, eventual sunshine, freedom from torment as a madman's quarry. She looked at her watch repeatedly. Why didn't the time pass faster?

11:50.

She squirmed in her chair, realized she wanted to go to the bathroom. With midnight so near, she found she didn't want to move—even if she knew she was walling herself in with suppositions and self-styled rules bearing little relation to reality. A little taste of craziness that her frayed nerves wouldn't let her overcome.

11:55.
Please let it be over! Let it be Saturday—*now!*
The sound came from the unfinished area of the warehouse. Something bumped or dropped. She spun in her chair. She was startled to see Evan already on his feet, club in hand, in the middle of the room. He stood in an L of illumination from the exterior walk lamps. How fast he could move! "Did you hear—"

He cut short her whisper with an urgent gesture. He beckoned her to follow him. Finger to lips, he led her toward the single entrance to that spacious chamber of dust, rubble, and unused cubicles. She heard a distant floorboard creak. Evan positioned himself behind the door, then waved her closer. His whisper was soft and dry. "He got inside while we were out. He's been waiting till we're asleep. Stand back."

"The police—"

"Not enough time," he whispered. "Ned could have a gun and shoot both of us before the cop could get in here. I've got to take him."

As though to support his argument, something metallic was kicked just beyond the lockless door. Amanda's heart convulsed into pounding beats that she could no more still than hurry the half moon hanging high over Hartford.

She backed away, truly terrified by her former husband. So many times earlier he had entered the scenes of her days in his practiced role as compulsive gambler and general incompetent. Tonight, he had thrown off all his roles like a cape. The horror that would come through that door would be the true, merciless Ned Stanton.

Coming to take her life.

She backed further away into heavy shadows. Accustomed to the dark, her eyes penetrated the gloom well enough to see the bit of clothesline strung through the knob hole. Now it stirred! Wouldn't it have been better to have tried to keep him out than let him in? her agitated mind wondered. If Evan couldn't club him down . . . He could be killed. But it was far too late to change strategy.

The door swung wide. Behind it Evan readied himself to strike, the club raised and angled back.

A pool of light fell on the floor, sudden as an explosion. Ned had turned on a flashlight! Oh, God, he would see her! She panicked and tried to lunge away from the spot where the beam, when raised, would find her. Her pivoting foot found a wastebasket. It flew over with a woody clunk that seemed loud as a backfire.

Ned grunted with surprise. His light found her face, dazzling her. "Mandy, I want—"

Evan lunged from the side, club swinging. It struck the side of Ned's head. Only a grazing blow! He howled and stumbled off, the flashlight falling. Evan was after him, but he wasn't moving fast enough, she thought distantly. Ned had time to get an arm up to deflect the next blow. He groaned and cursed. With a wordless shout he threw himself at Evan, surprising him. The club swung once more, thudding down on her ex-husband's broad back. He tried to close with the smaller man. Evan stumbled back. A lamp table went over with a clatter.

Amanda drew breath to scream, but fright choked off her cry. Both men were in a rage, grunting and snarling like animals. They were on their feet again, each with a hand on the club. Evan was smaller and weaker. How could he win? He suddenly used his knee, driving it up into Ned's crotch, doubling him up. He tore the club free, put both hands on it and swung at Ned's head. The blow didn't strike him quite squarely. Nonetheless, he straightened up, stunned, arms out pawing the air.

That sight catalyzed Amanda into action. Her scream emerged like a siren. She flew to the light switches, her second scream slicing the gloom. She flipped the switches up and down. Evan was shouting at her not to do that, but nothing anyone said to her then could make sense.

She flew back toward the battling men. Ned's knees were buckling. Evan hit him again on the side of the neck. He staggered, stumbled, then went down. She screamed again into the tide of violence and pain. Ned fell face down on the floor, twitched, then lay motionless. Evan rushed to his side and raised the club high over his head for the *coup de grâce*.

The sight of her ex-husband sprawled and helpless, no longer a deadly threat, sparked her compassion. "No!" She flew at Evan, draped herself from his shoulders.

"Mandy, for the love of God. He's—"

"No, no! He can't hurt us now."

Still fueled by combat rage he tried to fling her off. There was hurtful violence in his efforts. He pushed her backward. "I want to kill him!" he shouted.

"No, please. He's—"

"He's a murdering—"

Behind them, the French doors flew in and open. Latch metal clattered free. Amanda whimpered and dove for the flashlight. She swept it up in both hands and angled it toward the figure towering in the opening.

A black man at least six-foot-five, 230 pounds, stared at them over the sights of the pistol he held in front of him at the end of extended arms. "That's it, citizens! The law has arrived!"

In a few moments Ned was handcuffed, still unconscious. Officer Ben took short statements. Sometime later, they'd have to say more. Probably after the weekend. He interrupted himself to look toward the kitchen. "Come out here, son," he said.

Justin emerged, white faced. Amanda rushed to him, knowing he had seen nearly everything. There was too much to explain, an avalanche of hurt and betrayal. She wondered if, given decades, she could ever deal with all of it.

"Evan, you hurt my dad," Justin said.

"I—couldn't help it. He . . ." He shrugged and squinted toward officer Ben. His glasses had been smashed in the struggle. Amanda thought vaguely that she had cost him two pairs. She would make it up to him. The man had saved her life, to crown all that he had previously done for her.

Justin bawled when the cop put his inert father over his shelflike shoulder and carted him off. She led her son into his bedroom, crawling under the covers with him. He fought her hug briefly, then submitted, sobbing steadily. When Evan appeared in the doorway she waved him away. Exhausted as she was, her mind was charged with the threats to her son's emotional stability that the last weeks had hammered into his sensibilities. She couldn't imagine how she was going to cope.

With the threats of the last weeks lifted, she was nonetheless unable to treat herself to the luxury of relief. New problems surfaced as the old sunk.

Her son finally fell into a deep slumber. She sought to join him, but couldn't. She was drained and exhausted. She was charged with energy that banished sleep. She eased out of bed and tucked Justin in. He didn't stir at her kiss.

She paused in the doorway and looked back at him. You and I have our work cut out for us, kid, she thought.

Evan was out in the living room putting things back in place. His movements were slow, almost absent-minded. She knew he, too, was preoccupied. She went up to him and touched him on the shoulder. He looked sharply at her, as though frightened. "Sorry," she said. "Didn't mean to startle you. I know this isn't a good time to talk." She looked at her watch, managing a weak smile. "One-thirty. Saturday. The first day of the rest of my life."

The problem the next morning was Justin. Up to now Evan and he had begun to develop a good, trusting relationship. The moment she saw her son come into the kitchen for breakfast his eyes told her he felt that Evan had done the unforgivable in striking his father. Evan sat sipping coffee. Normally, he would have tumbled to the boy's state of mind; his intuition was excellent. Not surprisingly, the last days—particularly last night—had taken their toll on his sensibilities. His expression was distant, made more so by his missing glasses.

"I want to have my breakfast in the other room," Justin demanded.

Amanda looked at Evan, who seemed not to have heard. "All right." She let him pour his own sugar-coated cereal— a treat—and isolate himself. Later she saw he scarcely ate any. The colored bits lay drowning while he crushed crumbs on the tablecloth with his left forefinger. She took him outside for a chat. She tried to clarify what in fact was impossible to explain—the precise nature of his father's character and history. She began bravely, but a look at his face called for a quick segue into vagueness which he interrupted.

"My dad's a good guy!" he said. "He's a little silly—like you—but he wouldn't hurt a fly."

Amanda breathed deeply. Precise explanations clearly weren't the order of the day. Or the week. The slow grind of months was more like it. She tried a different tack. It was only decent for Justin to be polite to Evan. He had been very brave in fighting with his father. He really hadn't had any choice. Both Amanda and Evan had been very frightened. It was important that Justin understand that. He should remember the times in life he had been frightened enough to fight. They wouldn't be staying with Evan more than another day. She liked to think her son would be enough of a good houseguest to be friendly with his host for the last hours of his stay, no matter his personal feelings.

She later spoke to Evan. "Please try to understand. He's been through a terrible ordeal."

Evan looked up from his reverie. "We're still good buddies. Before the day's over, I'll prove it."

She had every intention of hanging around to see that miracle take place.

They got a call from police headquarters. The Saturday staff was on duty. Ned was being held for questioning concerning the murders. It probably wouldn't start till Monday. The officer hoped everything was all right with her and Mr. Dent. "He's got quite a story to write up," he said with a laugh.

Amanda was looking forward to a day planning the continuation of her life, but it wasn't to be. The hospital called. Her father was dying. She threw on clothes and called out to Justin and Evan, telling them they'd have to get along without her. Both of them were to behave, especially Justin.

A familiar nurse intercepted her in Pop-Up's corridor. She asked if Amanda wanted a clergyman to visit with them. She was puzzled. "What did he write on the sheet when you admitted him?" she said.

"For religious preference he put a question mark," the nurse said.

"We won't bother him about that then," Amanda said.

She sat by his bed for four hours as his lean old face seemed to grow leaner still, the stubble standing out above graying flesh like white grain stalks after harvest.

She wouldn't have dreamed that after all she had just gone through she still had so many tears left in her.

Sometime after two in the afternoon his breathing quickened and deepened. His thin chest heaved under the sheet. With a convulsive burst of movement his arms flew outward. His calloused worker's hand nearly struck her. She clutched his wrist and pressed a long kiss on the knobby range of knuckles. There then came a rasping cough and he was gone.

A hospital social worker was waiting outside with fresh tissues and a sympathetic face. After introducing herself as Marge, she invited Amanda to her office. She had to lead her there with gentle elbow pressure. Amanda's world was tear smeared. Marge asked her if she wanted coffee. For some reason she did. It came in a Styrofoam cup. She curled her fingers around it. Marge encouraged her to talk about her father's illness and last days. Amanda was aware she was babbling, but didn't care. When she ran down, Marge asked about burial arrangements. She explained the available options, then invited Amanda to use her phone. Yes, here was the list of nearby undertakers, if she—or her family—had no personal preferences . . .

"There's just me and my son." Those words brought fresh tears. Her eyes burned and her checks were sticky, no matter how many tissues she snatched from the pretty colored box.

Marge left the office while Amanda called a funeral director. She arranged for her father's body to be picked up. The hospital and the funeral home would work out the details. He was professionally sympathetic. In her state she was thankful the fabric of society provided for the bereaved. She made an appointment to talk to him about final arrangements. She knew that would be cremation. If she had the money, she'd have his ashes scattered over Pittsburgh.

Marge came back to see how she was doing. Could she get home by herself all right? Amanda nodded, gathering up her purse and the hospital paperwork. Charges not covered by Pop-Up's insurance would be forwarded to her. That would use up what little he had arranged to leave to her. And she wouldn't get it until the will was probated. There would be a period of dunning notices. Head lowered, she plodded down the busy corridor toward the nurses' station and the elevator.

"Amanda!"

Amanda's head jerked up. Standing in the L by a rack of charts was Emerald Roscheski. She had a small suitcase in her hand.

"What are you doing here?"

"I'm headed out of town. Today. The cops are after me again, aren't they?"

Amanda nodded. "You knew they would be. I told you I'd tell them." She stared into the younger woman's face. The wholesome facade had crumbled. Lunacy raged there like a forest fire. How had she not seen it from that first moment by Gordie's poker table?

"The police caught your stepbrother last night. He got inside the warehouse and was coming to kill me. Then—"

Emerald shook her head. "Be still. Listen. I went to your restaurant to talk to you. You weren't there. You have weekends off. I asked your staff and found out your father was here. When I got here I found out he was dying. I figured sooner or later you'd show."

"If you wanted to talk to me, why didn't you come back out to New Hartford?"

Emerald shook her head again. Her smile was disturbing.

Through her deep grief Amanda's instincts stirred alarmingly. "Well, here I am. What do you have to say to me, Emerald?"

"I asked myself why I'm bothering. You've been just another burden in my life. All that business with Gordie . . ." She shrugged. "Neither one of us got him." She shook her head and drew a deep breath. "Deep down, though, you know what?"

"What, Emerald?"

"I wanted to be like you. To some way hold it all together, no matter what. See, I never could do it. I couldn't hold anything together. Especially my head. Gordie used to talk about you, how dumb you were, not doing things the easy way. I didn't see it that way. I couldn't stand you personally. But I knew you had the guts that I'd never have. You know how to get through the days, just you and your son against the world. You don't give up. Look, here I am, ready to run for it again. And not for the last time either, I bet."

"Emerald, my father just died. I'm a wreck. What do you have to say to me?"

She nodded. "Remember that little talk we had through the crack in the door? About the man I gave the details to about freaky Philman's dates?"

"Of course. Your superman stepbrother—my ex-husband."

"Amanda, you have to understand my position then. You wanted a name. I wanted to stay away from the police. I was ready to tell you my stepbrother's name. I really was."

Amanda blinked. "I don't understand."

"Then at the last minute *you* gave me a name. Because I'm not as brave or honest as you, I took it and got out of there. But it bothered me. I guess, after all, I didn't want to see you dead." Emerald's smile was pleasant, as though she were talking about a floral arrangement instead of . . .

"What are you saying?" Amanda shouted.

"I'm saying my stepbrother isn't your ex-husband. It's the guy you're staying with. He's calling himself 'Evan Dent' this time around." Emerald spun and fled for the Exit sign, the small suitcase bumping her knee. Amanda went after her. The woman flew down the stairs three at a time. Amanda's legs refused to work. The significance of what she had been told fell upon her like the punch line of a cosmic joke dreamed up by an incomprehensible comedian.

She sagged against the painted stair rail, clutching it with both hands. Her world whirled. She battled fainting, red roaring rising on the outskirts of her senses. Somehow she righted herself, sitting briefly on the cold metal stair plate. She put her head between her legs until she felt well enough to stagger to her feet.

She walked down to the next floor, both hands on the rail. She went to the nearest pay phone and called the Hartford police. She asked for Detective Reti, though she imagined he wouldn't be there on a Saturday. Surprisingly, he was. The moment he was on the line, she blurted out what Emerald had told her. She was living with the murderer!

"You know what, Ms. Walker?" Reti's voice was edged with bewilderment. "You and your suspicions are making me crazy." He laughed. "This guy we picked up last night on a B and E, your ex?"

"Y—Yes?"

"You told us *he* was the murderer."

"Yes, but—"

"I went in and talked to him. I was ready to put the pressure on him. Serial murder, the whole deal—"

"I don't want to talk about him! I want to talk about—"

"He said you had got a little crazy lately, because of the murders. He said the only reason he hid in Dent's place was to take your kid and be with him for a while. For my money I believed him. Ned Stanton? He couldn't kill a cockroach, never mind a human being."

"He sneaked in to take Justin?"

"He said you changed addresses without telling him. That you were deliberately keeping the boy away from him. That's why he was there. And no other reason."

"I want the police to go to Evan Dent's house. He's there with my son. *He's* the murderer!"

"Come on! You been living with him for two weeks. During any day of which he could have cooled you ten times."

"Listen to me! I want police—"

"The police need a little rest on your case, Ms. Walker. We'll do what we can later in the week. But right now I think we've burned out. Have a good day." He hung up.

"No!" Amanda shouted into the dead phone. She waved

the receiver in frustration. She dug into her billfold for more coins. She had only eleven cents in her change purse. She spun away from the phone, groping for self-control. She went to the nurses' station and asked for change for a dollar. Neither of the two women on duty had it. On the next floor down there was a change machine . . .

Armed with coins, she used a pay phone to redial police headquarters. She asked for Reti again. She was put through, but no one picked up. The sergeant came back on the line to say he wasn't available. "Listen to me, Sergeant," she shouted. "This is a matter of my and my son's life!"

"Yes, ma'am."

"I want police sent to this address in New Hartford—"

"That's outside our jurisdiction. Why don't you just call the New Hartford department? Have a good day."

She knew Reti had prompted him. The creep! She dialed information to ask for the New Hartford police number. She dialed it. The call didn't go through. She tried twice more. Same result. She was out of change.

She groaned and pressed palms to the sides of her face. Her heart was pounding and her hands shook against her temples. She had thought her dark odyssey was all over. It wasn't over at all.

In a sense, it was just beginning.

*What should she do?*

She battled with her nerves all the way to her VW. She ground it into gear, still not certain of which way to turn it— or herself. Evan was the madman! Evan of the soft voice and patience. Evan who was so shy with her and so good with Justin. "Evan Dent" wasn't even his name! Evan Dent was only one of his countless roles, this one played for her and a handful of others. In a wider sense he was truly nameless, a force that had intruded itself almost indifferently into her life. One that she could no more explain or rationalize than a state lottery winner could explain his good fortune. She caught up the mass of her red hair and tore at it. Because of *this*, Evan had killed at least six women. She and her son were to be victims, as well. Then later, probably others. All for *what reason?*

What should she do?

Then a calmer side of her, surviving somehow amid the turmoil, showed itself. So often she had been wrong in her suspicions over the last harrowing weeks. Five times, to be exact! In view of all that, it was possible that Evan wasn't the murderer either. Zoe, his colleague, had vouched for his character. She remembered all he had done for her, opened up his home at her request, squired her son around to protect him while she went her own way for a whole week. Battled Ned when they thought he was the murderer. Oh, yes, there was still great doubt.

That being so, she saw what she could do. It was quite simple, really. She had to keep her wits, that was all. She had been given a priority by that last, airy-voiced telephone call. It was to save Justin from Evan, if he was the killer. She saw, almost coincidentally, that saving him would also save herself. All she needed was a little luck and what Ned would call a stone poker face. She turned onto Route 44 for the drive to New Hartford.

If luck had turned her way, the best thing to find at the warehouse home was that Evan had gone off to cover a story or run an errand. Justin would be alone. She would whisk him into the car, and off they would go—to another state, until the reporter was investigated down to the lint between his toes.

More likely, the two were at home, hopefully not side by side. She would ask to speak to Justin. It would take only a few moments to get him out the door and into the car. She had smiled cheerily at Evan ever since she had met him that day in police headquarters. She could smile at him once or twice more to get her son—and herself—away from possible death.

She swung into the gravel drive. Her heart leaped up. Evan's car was gone! She pulled all the way into the two-car garage. She left the motor running and bolted into the house.

"Justin! Justin! Where are you, honey? Justin!"

Silence.

*"Justin!"*

She ran to his room and burst in. Empty. She called out again. No answer. She tore open the door to the unfinished warehouse. "Justin!" Not there. Oh, God, where was he? It took her a while to circle to the kitchen.

On the table was a note on Evan's letterhead.

### Gone for Ice Cream 2:10 PM

Both had signed it. Justin with his signature, Evan with a smiley face.

# CHAPTER
## ❧ 15 ❧

Amanda sank down on a kitchen chair, clutching the note until it wrinkled. She looked at her watch. It was 2:30. She had just missed them! She battled for control, bowing her head for a moment. She looked up at the nearly familiar surroundings, the refrigerator-freezer combo, the sink with its wide work areas, mugs waiting to be washed, the spice carousel, the heavy kitchen towels strung through wrought-iron drawer handles. Afternoon sun poured in like honey. Was this place a haven or a hell?

She had been here so many hours with Evan away. But she had never really *looked* for evidence that he might be the one who had committed the brutal crimes. Clues could have been all around her, but her suspicions had been dormant. She had never seriously considered that he might be . . . She rose shakily. It was certainly well past time to begin snooping. But not quite entirely too late.

She started with his room and its walk-in closets, handmade furniture, and king-size bed. She opened every drawer she could find and slid her hands along every shelf, finding nothing of interest. She covered his den like a fog, shuffling through newspapers, magazines, documents, photographs. She opened personal computer directories and checked files. She found nothing but what one would expect from an industrious reporter employed by a major newspaper.

She went on through all the remodeled rooms, most of which contained only furniture. Throughout her sojourn she kept an ear tuned for the return of his car. She prayed she wouldn't find anything suspicious; the man was with her son. She looked at her watch. Three-fifteen and the two weren't back yet. Only an hour, she told herself. She still had time for the rest of the warehouse.

She tugged at the clothesline and swung open the door to the high, dusty expanse beyond. The tools, the lumber, the empty bins, and the frame cubicles were patterned by sunlight shafts descending from the grimy skylights high overhead. She wandered about, the dust swirling up like mist in bright golden columns. Only the workbenches and tools had seen recent work. Several heaps of splintered lathing lay on the dusty concrete. The acrid scent of dry, ruptured plaster hovered like an arid perfume. On she wandered, one eye on her watch, ears primed for the sound of Evan's car. When it didn't return, she circled back again to the three frame cubicles, the last remaining uninvestigated area. Each had a hasp and tongue latch closed by a heavy padlock. Two of the locks carried ten years of grit and dust.

The third was shiny.

Someone had used that cubicle.

Heart churning, she hurried over to the workbenches, digging amid the tools till she found the black metal question mark of a pry bar. She hurried back to the cubicle, the bar in raised hands. She worked its forged tip behind the hasp's flange and heaved. The bar slipped from her awkward grip. It clattered on the cement floor, barely missing her toes. She heaved it up and tried again.

The tip caught between metal and wood. She hung on the bar, annoyed with the weakness of her hands and forearms. The metal groaned. Six screws held the flange to the wood. She could see they were coming free. She reset the bar, raised her foot, and set it against the wooden wall. The flange shifted and the bar slid out. Only one screw was still set in wood. She raised the bar above her head, drove it down. With a clatter the hasp swung free of the tongue. She threw down the bar and pulled the tongue. Hinges spoke as she pulled the door open. The cubicle was about ten feet square, and dim. She stepped in and groped the walls in search of a light switch. She found it. The single overhead bulb lit the bookcase and floor-model freezer humming gently in the quiet. On the bookshelves she saw more tools. She went over to them. She found two axes and a half dozen long knives. All had been dutifully cared for. They had recently been oiled and sharpened. Their blades carried gleaming edges that twinkled as she turned them, like sinister stars. Alone they proved nothing.

The old freezer top opened with a chrome handle. In its mechanism was a hole for a padlock. None was in place. All she had to do was work the handle and heave up the lid. A frown of puzzlement working her brow, she bent her back and pushed up the lid.

The light fell on the frosted plastic bag lying within. It half filled the interior. She squinted and bent over to see through the dusting of frost crystals. What was inside there? July's moist air condensed in the chill to clouds that obscured her vision. She puffed out her cheeks and blew down at the plastic. The cloud swirled away momentarily allowing her to see . . .

As though through clear ice she glimpsed a white face, its brow patched with stiffened red hair. Across naked breasts arms were folded.

The right arm had no hand!

She had found Grace O'Shea's body.

Her scream rose like a siren, echoing in the small cubicle. She slammed down the lid and whirled away from the frozen horror. She screamed again as she ran across the dusty concrete. The sound echoed from the distant walls and ceiling. She burst through the door into the living area. In her wild haste to reach the phone she slipped as a throw rug went out from under her driving feet. She landed hard. On hands and knees she crawled for the phone. She remembered the New Hartford police number. She snatched up the receiver, palm greased with sweat.

There was no dial tone.

Something was wrong with the phone. She slammed at the cradle buttons with the bottoms of flattened fingers. The phone was dead.

She hurried to the closest door that faced the driveway. She threw it open, ready to spring into her still idling car for the dash to the nearest neighbor's house a quarter-mile down the road.

Justin was walking toward her.

Behind him Evan's car sat on the edge of the driveway.

Her son held his hand up in front of him. In it was an ice cream cone. Rivulets were beginning to make their way down over the cone's covering paper napkin. "I had a banana split! And I ate the whole thing," he said. "Evan said it better not affect me like the Pizza Hut pizza." He thrust the ice cream at her, frowning. "Was that you yelling a little bit ago?"

She took the cone in a numb hand. "Where's . . . Evan?" she said.

"He went out back of the warehouse for something. He sure wants to be friends again, mom."

Somehow the cone disintegrated in her hand, crushed by the spasm of her grip. "Oh!" The ice cream *spluuded* to the gravel. She didn't look down at it.

"Mom!" Justin squinted up at her face.

"I want you to get in my car. Right now. We're going . . . to run an errand."

"I'm tired of cars. I want—"

She dug her fingers into his forearm. "Get in the car!" she said in a low voice.

"Owww! Hey!"

She looked around through the sun-splashed garden and lawn, back toward the house. She didn't see Evan. He was still busy in back. They could get away. "Let's go!" She took the flagstone steps two at a time. She glimpsed her VW still idling safely in her garage bay. She shooed Justin ahead of her, tore open the car door.

"Hey, mom. The tires!"

She grunted and leaned out from the driver's seat. The two

left tires were flat. She scrambled out and walked around the VW. All four tires were flat. How?

She bent over and looked at the concrete. Large-headed black tacks were scattered all across her bay.

Scattered before she had returned from the hospital.

Scattered by Evan Dent.

Because he didn't want her to leave. Ever.

And the phone had gone dead.

She choked back a wordless cry. She grabbed Justin's wrist and ran out of the garage, jerking him along. "We're leaving! One way or the other," she said.

"What's with you, mom? Who put all those tacks on the garage floor?"

This time she couldn't control her outcry. Evan stood in the driveway, arms folded. He looked untroubled. The lines that had etched his face so recently had disappeared, leaving him youthful, ageless. He wore no glasses. Absently, she realized they had been a plain-glass part of his reporter costume. He smiled warmly. "It's time, Amanda," he said.

She battled back terror that would lead to panic. She had to save Justin!

Evan moved toward them. His arms unfolded—to disclose a knife as long as a monster's tooth.

Somehow amid the rubble of her mind she found a strategy. She shoved Justin away from her. "Run! That way! Go get help!"

"Huh?" The boy stood looking at her, then at Evan. "I don't get it."

Evan was several steps closer, his pace almost casual. He could have been approaching to talk about nothing more than Japanese beetle grubs in the lawn—if it weren't for the knife in his hand.

"Justin, run! *Get help!*"

Still the boy stood baffled. Evan strode closer.

"Justin, he wants to kill us. He's the one! *He's the one!*"

He understood. "But—what about you?"

Evan was within a lunge of the boy.

"Run!" she screamed with all her strength.

At last he ran. He burst across the driveway and between two blue spruces. Headed in the direction of the neighbor's home. At ten he was fast on his feet. He'd have a chance, especially with her going the other way. She bolted for the house. Fear gave strength to her legs. She tore open the side door, slammed it behind her, locking it. She knew she couldn't keep him out. All she needed was a few seconds to get to her purse.

There it was on the kitchen table. She snatched it up. Her hand dove down into it, searching for the mace, the cylinder Evan didn't realize she owned.

"Amanda . . ." Evan was calling to her from outside.

He had chosen to follow her. Thank God! If Justin could just get help in time . . . Where was . . . ?

The cylinder was gone! In the bottom of her purse her desperate fingers found . . . a stone. To replace the missing weight.

Evan had removed the mace!

She raised her head and looked back through the living area. The French doors hadn't been repaired. They swung wide from a push from Evan's raised foot. Their eyes met across the rooms. "Neighbor Rubin's away on vacation, Amanda. The closest other house is four miles away." He chuckled. "Thinking of the cop assigned to you? When they called to ask if we wanted him for a few more days, I said no thank you. Now we have plenty of time. It's going to happen at last."

"What is?" Her voice shook.

"I've done the looking. The looking is important. Now—"

"Looking at *me*. You *were* looking at me in the bathroom and—"

He nodded. "One-way panels I put in. All your friends but Jessica were here—for a short while. Oh, yes! Looking first. And then the love-cutting."

Dear God! She backed away, though he was still twenty yards away. Where could she go?

"You were the greatest temptation. Your beautiful body and hair blended with your exquisite capacity for fear . . ." He crossed the rug. "No woman I've needed to love-kill has aroused me more. Earlier, I had to touch you, even though it wasn't *time*. Running the risk that you would guess . . .''

She remembered his hands on her, twice. How she had misunderstood! She had been completely fogged, dreaming of romance. When the reality was a horror of a man. Revulsion heaved up at memory of his dry kisses and fingers coned on her breast.

"I wasn't sure I could continue to control myself. So earlier in the week I had to lock my door. Do you *remember?* The night you came knock-knock-knocking . . . But it was too *soon*. The details of death and cutting have to take place in order and on schedule. That's so important.''

Amanda sidled away, the small of her back sliding along the kitchen counter. She wanted to run. But to where?

"Amanda?''

"What?''

"I'd like it very much if you screamed again.''

"No!'' She spun and ran back into the building's rear. She flew into her bedroom, turned and slammed the door. She flipped the lock lever. If Justin hurried back with help, she'd have a chance. The door was solid wood.

He knocked, but she said nothing.

"Third time's the charm, Amanda. Come out.''

She understood she should keep him talking. Justin needed time. "Third time?'' she said.

"Twice I tried. That night we went to the movies I took three guests. Not just you and your son. Did you know that? My third guest was an ice pick. I took it from the Muncher's ice sculptures. I was going to put my hand over your mouth and shove the pick into your temple where the skull is soft. After you, the boy. Then an easy escape from your police bodyguard . . .''

Amanda's knees sagged. She stumbled to the bed, sat on its edge. If Justin hadn't vomited . . . Oh, Lord, she had been seconds from death!

"Then I decided to take pleasure from your fear and anxiety until the last possible minute of magic Friday. I allowed us to sit together in the dark, waiting for the 'killer.' Oh, that was a delight because I could see and smell your fear! I was so excited . . ." He exercised what she had until now thought of as his pleasant, boyish laugh. "Then, when magic Friday had nearly ended, I got up quietly, club ready in my hand. I was going to crush your skull with one blow."

She understood that he hadn't moved *after* Ned began to make noise. But well *before*. Her blundering, oafish ex-husband had saved her life that night, even as she was recoiling from him in terror. She had been lucky and never understood. Every recent event had been the opposite of what it seemed!

"I needed to kill Ned," Evan said. "Then I would have had the whole night to look and cut while the stupid cop sat in night dew. Before dawn I would have been gone. But you had to flash the lights, then show your compassionate side by throwing yourself at me, like Pocahontas."

Beyond the door Evan's voice grew agitated as he recalled his frustration. "I had never failed to keep to my schedules. Never! Over all these years, redheaded women have died *on schedule*. The control is so important, Amanda. You have to understand that. *So* important.

"But then all along you were more *difficult* than the multitude back over the years. You kept struggling against your fate, against your certain death. You spent so much *energy* against me! I had to take more steps, plot more strategy than ever before. It was as though your being more desirable allowed you to be more of a challenge. I rose to it, though, beginning with my first telephone call and then stealing your nasty little whistle. On and on it went. The 'note' written in french fries was inspired. It was a delight and a risk at the same time. I was 'someone you know.' Would you guess me among all the others?"

"I didn't," Amanda admitted heavily.

"And what an amateur detective you were. Homing in on my stepsister! I had to visit to warn her about you. And you were so worried I'd write about her in the paper. Writing an exposé was the last thing I wanted to do. I had to seem gutless and pretend to let you down. Even so, you continued with your correct suspicion that she was the source of information about weird Floyd Philman's dates. I was forced to get your mind off her.''

"The articles about Hunt Grayson, Evan?''

"You were getting too close without realizing it. You were chasing red herrings faster than I anticipated, eliminating them. I had to provide another. I used the desktop publishing equipment in my office to make the originals. The photo was from a publicity file. Then I ran them through the copy machine to hide their freshness. Of course I couldn't have you telling the police that I had provided the bogus articles. So I asked you not to give them my name. I was going to so much trouble, taking so many risks to have you die on schedule . . . It was all novel, and very exciting.''

"Why the cutout at my son's concert, Evan?''

His answer was a long laugh, chilling as an ice cube down her back. She looked at her wristwatch. Only about seven minutes had passed since Justin ran off for help. And he had four miles to go! Never mind needing time to return with help. How long could she keep Evan at bay with conversation? She fought her dismay.

"I found the role of being your confidant and morale-booster more stimulating than I could have imagined, had I planned it to happen. Do you remember my call after I love-cut sweet Grace?'' His voice transformed itself to the faint, airy telephone tones: '' 'I want you to look at your own skin, Amanda.' That was followed by my sympathy when we met at police headquarters the next day.'' He chuckled and a shudder rolled across her like a wave. "Also, I enjoyed listening to you much later by the *Courant* vending machines. It excited me to pretend to hear what I already knew. You gave me the idea that straight Hunt Grayson might be the bad man. I was very much aroused by being so close to you physically—and emotionally—and from that spun off my 'search' for evidence against him. Then . . . when you asked to move in!''

How could she have been so *dumb?* "You hesitated.''

"I was growing still more aroused. I had to ask myself if I could control myself. Could I keep to the schedule with your hair and body under this same roof? It was like having a dream coming true—and yet being tested at the same time.''

*Craaak!* He drove the handle of his knife against the door. ''Unlock, my love!''

Amanda steadied herself against the night table. She could scarcely stand. The hands of her watch seemed frozen. She raised her glance to the window. She got up, shaking like an old car burning cheap gas. She was at ground level. If she could slide the railed sash aside, she could step out and . . . She turned the lock easily. She put the fingertips of both hands on the broad metal latch, and heaved.

The sash didn't budge.

She heaved again. Beyond the door Evan was raving on about his knife and how he would love her with it. She swallowed her whimpers and bent her back. Her fingers slid off, two nails bending double. She shook her stinging hands, then pressed them to her face. She had to control herself! Her only chance was to keep away from him long enough for Justin to—

''Are you trying the windows, my love? While you were away, I fixed all the first-floor ones, along with the phones and your car. They won't open.''

Amanda sank back from her effort, smothering her whimper. She was trapped! And no mercy once mad Evan got through the door. She drew a breath so deep that it shook her. ''If you kill me, too, they'll know. The police will know. They'll put you away forever.''

The light laugh again, more terrifying than a movie madman's careening howl. ''I'll be away from here, on my way to another city. I have safe deposit boxes holding identities in a dozen banks across this country and others.''

''Who are you, really? What's your real name?''

Again the laugh. No more revealing than her echoed voice tossed back from an arctic valley. A chill walked up her spine on icy feet.

''Why do you kill . . . redheads?''

''I see you're trying to get me to talk, to delay me until your son brings help. You have to excuse me, but I don't think the lad has quite what it takes. He doesn't have the right stuff. Nonetheless . . . no more talking.''

He fell silent.

She stood motionless for long moments, warring with panic. She couldn't lose control! She rushed to the window, gauged the area of the pane. She could fit through! Snatching up the bedside lamp, she tore off the shade. She unscrewed the bulb and gripped the empty socket. She swung the brass base at the glass. It shattered. She swung repeatedly, knocking the nasty Vs of shards from the frame. She threw down the lamp and stuck her head and right shoulder out.

He was waiting outside the window for her!

Reflex or intuition started her retreat an instant before he shouted "Surprise!" His knife swung in a lethal arc. The blade grazed her neck like a thin string of fire. She fell back inside.

She had been cut!

Her hand flew up, came away smeared red. For a moment she froze with terror and panic. Then she realized she wasn't badly hurt, just a superficial nick. She turned back to the window. Evan was beginning to climb in!

She dove to her hands and feet, groping under the bed for the lamp. Her desperate fingers brushed the cool metal. Then she swatted it out and gripped it in both hands. Evan held the window frame, ready to heave himself in. She brought the heavy brass down on his fingers. She missed, then wildly struck again. She felt the metal hit flesh and bone. He groaned and let go. She had hurt him. His face was white. The smile he flashed was more stunning than a savage curse. "I still love you, Amanda. Love you to death.''

She backed away, the lamp still in both hands. Evan disappeared at a run, angling behind heavy bushes past which she couldn't see. Where was he going? She waited for his return. He didn't show up immediately. She toyed with slipping out the window, running for it.

That was what he wanted.

So . . . She hesitated. She had to get out of the room! Sooner or later he would get in, and she would have no chance. She saw again the arc of the knife slicing the sunlit air, imagined it sinking into her abdomen, convulsing organs, rupturing arteries, grating against pink, hidden bone. Her innards would burn. Death would stalk forth, cape spread for a permanent embrace. She couldn't just *stand there*.

Which should be her exit? Door or window? Assuming he was waiting by one or the other, it was guess—and bet your life, she thought. She had to decide. A decoy, then. She swung the lamp again and smashed the other window pane. She hurried to the door, silently released the lock. Hand on the L of the latch, she pushed it softly down. She edged the door open a hair, just enough to see . . .

He wasn't within sight, along that angle. But he could be waiting, back to the wall, ahead and to the left. She drew a deep breath and edged the door wider. She set her knee against it. If he lunged she might be able to lever it shut before he got in. She swung the door further, ready to put her head out and look along the wall.

Glass tinkled behind her!

Was he crawling in? She whirled, scream bubbling to her lips. No one. One of the shards had fallen out of the frame of the pane she had just smashed.

She turned back, put her head through the doorway, looking left. She was ready to spring back. Evan wasn't there. She hesitated. It was time to make a break for it. She wondered if her legs were up to it. She took two strides into the hall.

"Amanda!" Evan burst through the door to the unfinished warehouse. He ran toward her across the living area.

In his hands he held an axe.

She spun and fled back to the bedroom. She slammed the door. Her frantic fingers flicked at the lock lever. She failed to move it. Second try. Evan's bulk crashed against the wood. The latch lever dipped, rose, and rattled. "So quick for a woman, Amanda!" he called through the door, no anger in his soft voice. "So elusive. So worthy of my attentions and efforts. You're the best of all I've led to death. Special. Oh, special!"

The axe bit into the door or frame near the lock. Amanda cried out, despite herself, a weak little yelp of fear. She told herself to move—get to the window. Her legs failed to obey.

Fear draped itself over her like a wet sack. The axe fell again, escorting death with its metallic bite.

The window! Get out! She moved, then, but like a sleep-walker. She crossed the room. The axe worked the door with increasing haste. She put her head and shoulders through the frame. She felt so weak . . .

Behind her, wood splintered. She wriggled forward. Almost out! Just fall down to the ground. She kicked her feet wildly and heaved with her hands. Fear shot through her like current.

When Evan grabbed her ankle she couldn't hold back her screams. She shrieked wildly as he pulled her back through the window, grip not weakened by his swollen fingers. She sprawled into the room, squirming and kicking. She ended up on the floor, half propped against the wall. He stood over her, his axe raised high. Distantly, she was aware of a keening shriek that was her long scream.

The moment of her death.

Her senses sped her a tableau looming with his dominance: the axe high, white arms quivering, weight back, eyes heavy lidded, mouth gaping, tongue slightly forward, and, high on his right thigh, masked by cloth, his unmistakable arousal. When she had been merely his guest he had twice reacted to her the same way. Inflamed not by her femininity, she under-stood far too late, but by her fear and emotional turmoil. His aphrodisiacs. And she, dim-witted and vain, had charged his response to affection's account. How could she have been so naive? Now she was going to die for her poor judgment.

He flung down the axe, grabbed her hair with his left hand, and smashed a fist into the side of her head. Blackness closed in and took her senses with it.

In time she was being moved, carried. Her senses slid away again, then returned. They dragged her fear back with them, along with her one faint hope. Her son. Through slitted eyes she saw her watch. Oh, no! All that had happened had taken less than a half an hour. Four miles Justin had to go. Maybe he would stop a passing car. She hoped he had thought of that. Even now help could be coming . . .

Her head ached horribly when she was lifted up. Evan was fooling with her hands. What? She made her eyes open. He was sliding loops of plastic rope over her wrists. Her senses washed away again. She was aware of being hauled up by her arms. Then there was bright glare. Her feet groped for the floor. Her shoulder sockets were strained. Behind her he manipulated the ropes until she was barely able to stand on the balls of her feet. Her shoes were gone. She raised her eyes and saw he had set up a small table. On it were all the knives from the shelves by the freezer that held Grace's corpse. And the axe. Their blades gleamed beneath the pole-mounted spotlights she had seen standing in a corner during her investigative tour an impossibly long hour ago.

He saw her head move. "Still hoping for miracles from your son?" he said.

"You don't have time for . . . this."

"I think he's probably crying under a tree a few hundred yards from here. Trying to figure out just what's going on." He walked around in front of her. "I worked hard to get him to like me, you know. You made it so much easier when you asked me to 'protect' him after his school was out." He chuckled. "Count on Amanda Walker to make the wrong decisions. Do you remember how I shyly asked him about your love life? Your love life! *I* am your love life. Your last, most worshipful lover. I deceived you both all the more. He did come to trust me. That's why I wanted to watch his eyes when I killed him. Talk about surprise! I won't have that pleasure, I guess. Anyhow, I'm sure he's quite bewildered."

Amanda knew she was going to die. But at least Justin had got safely away. Realizing that brought back some of her nerve and control. She stared stonily at him. "Well, hurry up and kill me. You've waited too long already. You missed your 'schedule,' Mr. Superman."

"Yes, yes!" He nodded vigorously. "After the police carted off your ex, I was well aware I had failed for the first time to keep my schedule. I was displeased, even . . . shaken. When you went in to comfort Justin, I picked up my club and started into the bedroom. But I saw just in time that there was no time to prepare an alibi, no way the law would believe a 'dark intruder' story. I wandered the rooms, still confused. I finally saw I had to wait . . . until now.''

He moved closer till their bodies nearly touched. "You have been worth the disruption, Amanda. Your vitality, your resistance have raised me to new heights.'' He had a knife in his hand. Its blade was long and thin. She tried to back away from him, but once on tiptoes there was nowhere to go. Her shoulder sockets ached. The ropes rasped her wrists. "At one time I would have never considered taking the chances I did to kill sweet Jessica. That was a great departure for me, you know.'' He grabbed the top button of her blouse, pulled the fabric out into a little tent. "To murder, then not to handle the soft flesh with my hands and knives . . . That was daring. I proved to myself that I wasn't *compelled* to cut the flesh. What a leap of discipline, even after such a long, successful career! You have to appreciate that after killing Jessica I deliberately struck my head against the corner of a table, and cut my own skin to mislead everyone.'' He touched the healing wounds. "Pretty soon all better.''

He waved at the ropes. "Grace O'Shea hung there, you know, not so high as I've hung you. She wondered what I was doing polishing the rings on her sturdy white hand.''

"Oh, God . . .''

"She was alive when I cut it off. And stayed alive long enough for me to do wonderful other things with my blades. I enjoyed cleaning up the flood of blood from where you're standing.''

Amanda screamed.

He grabbed the button again, and drew back his knife. It flashed and she whimpered. He had cut off the button. He dropped it on the floor. He cut off a second, dropped it. He pulled the blouse back, completely baring her neck. "Yes, you're wounded . . .'' He stepped to her side and grabbed her hair. He pulled it around before her eyes. Inches from her lids the knife sawed—so easily!—and loosened a thick handful of her mane. He pressed it against his face, covered his nose and

271

inhaled. Then he dragged it down to his mouth, thrust some of it inside, sucked it, tongue squirming in the wet red nest.

Amanda's eyes shuttered with loathing. He was only beginning. Hair and clothes first, then he would start cutting her. Just a little first, here and there. And then . . . Her little spark of calm winked out. The first tears angled down her cheeks. She was too terrified to sob.

She blinked away the wetness. He had removed her hair from his mouth, except for strands clinging to the moisture inside his lips and hanging down beyond his chin. He reached down her blouse, pulled out the front of her bra. He shoved the hair down, stepped back. It itched. *"Why? Why redheads?"* she shouted.

"There's no reason." He smiled. "And that's the reason. Just like life itself, Amanda."

"You're insane!"

"Yes, yes. Of course." He smacked his lips. "Your hair is sweet in my mouth. I'll taste your other hair too, you know."

She looked away, revolted. He stepped to her side again and ran his hand along her neck. The faint stinging told her his fingertips were tracing the cut. He leaned closer. She tried to twist away, repulsed. He grabbed her hair and held her head. His tongue cruised the wound, licking away her clotting blood. She tried to shake her head. His grip on her hair was hard as iron. He nibbled her ear. Her face contorted with loathing. "Stop it. Stop it! Ouch!" He had used the tip of his knife on her lobe.

"A few drops shed in tribute to the stupidity of your resistance, Amanda." He tongued them away. She tried to wriggle away, but the ropes pained her wrists and her calves hurt when she moved off center.

He walked around in front of her. His expression had changed from the youthful openness that had deceived her so to a mask of florid, heavy-lidded arousal. Paralyzed with anticipation of what was going to happen to her, she watched unresisting as his knife finished with her blouse buttons, and the seams of her bra, slacks, and briefs. So systematic and thorough was he that when he finished, she was naked under loose panels of cloth—fabric transformed by his insane wizardry from protective articles to burlesque show enticements.

After that she kept her eyes up. She didn't want to see what he was doing to her, or to himself. Now and then she felt the cool flat of the blade nosing over her body, exposing it, then sliding away to another spot. "Such skin!" he hissed. "I *knew*. Oh, I knew it would be as poreless as porcelain. Lovelier even than the sweet sweep of Grace's back. Only a glance at your hand and neck and I knew! And how the blood will look on it . . . strawberry lilies floating on a lake of cream."

She began to shake convulsively. To the silent tears she now added sobbing, despising it for fully disclosing her psychological helplessness. "Evan, please. Please don't torture me. Just—kill me. Quick!"

"Do you think that's the first time I've heard that?" He snickered. "I'm the authority on how redheads should die. The world's most experienced in that matter. I don't need advice from any of you." He ran the edge of his knife sideways across her left nipple. The slightest change of the angle of his wrist and . . .

"Please! Oh, dear God! *Please!*"

He ignored her, went about his investigations. She knew it would be only moments before he began to cut her. Being utterly helpless, she closed her eyes and tried to turn her mind elsewhere. She chose Justin, who would survive after her, grow to manhood and have a family of his own. She knew it was naive to assume she could keep her attention on him when the knives began to bite into her flesh.

She screamed. He had jabbed the knife tip into the outside of her thigh. She was wide-eyed with pain.

"You don't leave the festival, Amanda. Oh, no! I want you with me until . . . you truly can't be with me anymore." He slashed away the fabric and sucked the small wound, his mouth wet and toothy, like a leech's. His tense, frantic movements told her he was growing more excited. He knelt before her and began to cut away at the clothes hanging at her groin. She tried to move backward, on tiptoes. Her calves ached. It was impossible! She closed her eyes again as the knife cleared the way to . . .

He was using his teeth to tear her hair out.

When she opened her eyes again, she cried out.

Justin stood behind Evan.

He had stepped out from the shadows. At first her heart soared. He had brought help! She was going to be saved!

When he began to walk forward on silent, sneakered feet, she understood.

He had never gone for help.

His smooth face was streaked with recent tears. As Evan had promised, he had gone out under a tree and cried with bewilderment. Now here he was, confused and wondering what kind of game the two adults were playing. She knew with the certainty of the depth of her despair that the boy was going to ask them!

She and her son were going to die!

That knowledge boiled out of her in a mad scream that went on and on until her lungs were empty. It raised Evan's now sloed eyes. Below, his mouth gaped like an idiot's with his deranged lust. From smeared lips protruded straight and curly strands of her hair. She drew breath to scream again. Before her lungs filled, Justin spoke.

"Mr. Dent?"

Still on his knees, Evan spun and raised his knife. His eyes were at the boy's chest level. When the cylinder of mace whipped from behind Justin's back, the stream of liquid shot right into those eyes, splattering in all directions. Evan sprang up, the knife flying out of his hand. He managed a muffled choke and a feeble claw at his face. Then he went down and tried to crawl across the floor.

Some of the chemical fumes found their way to Amanda's face. Her eyes began to smart. Her nose burned. So much worse than ammonia! "Justin! Cut me down!"

"In a minute." The fumes had brought fresh tears to the boy's eyes. Despite them, he aimed a fresh stream at Evan's head. The mace soaked his hair and shirt. This time he toppled over from hands and knees and didn't move. Justin snatched

up the knife and cut the rope somewhere behind Amanda. He
was coughing and choking from the fumes. Her aching shoulders were relieved. She struggled with the loops around her
wrists. Her eyes were fastened on Evan's motionless body.

"Are you mad I took the mace out of your purse this morning?" the boy asked.

"I am *not* mad." She raised her aching arms and hugged
him hard. "What I want to know is why you did it?"

"Evan was trying to hurt dad bad. Dad is a good guy! Then
he told me he so much wanted to be friends with me. I knew
he was trying something. So I thought I oughta protect us."
He looked at the sprawled figure. "He was the sicko after all,
huh?"

She burst into tears and sank down on her knees. She pulled
the boy to her and hung on like a limpet. What a man he was
going to turn out to be! He patted her clumsily on the shoulder.
She sobbed, shook, and blubbered, the worst of the fear and
dread washing away with the salty drops blackening the dusty
concrete floor. They hung together, ignoring the wisps of stinging, choking fumes.

After a long while, Justin said, "I think we have to do
something with him."

Together they dragged Evan to the cubicle and flopped him
down by the freezer. Amanda checked to make sure all the
tools were out of the area. She found four thick spikes that fit
through the screw holes of the flange she had pried off. Swinging the hammer clumsily with both hands, she drove the spikes
through the tough pine. She picked up the cylinder of mace,
preparing to squirt Evan again. "Better let me do it," Justin
said. "I just practiced outside against a tree."

He explained that he had hidden the mace in his room. He
had had to wait until Evan wasn't around to go in and get it.
He had waited outside, scared, as the two adults battled. No
matter what, he told himself, he'd have no chance without it.
It hadn't been easy to see his mother so frightened and in such
danger. He had cried a lot, but kept his wits.

Amanda hugged him over and over, and brushed the tears
of relief out of both their eyes.

Together they hurried into the living area. She pulled a sweat-suit on over her tattered clothing. They tumbled into Evan's car and set off in search of help. They hadn't gone a quarter-mile down the road when a familiar Volvo approached them. Amanda blew the horn and waved wildly. Hunt Grayson was at the wheel, a sour expression on his tanned face. "You two aren't easy to find. I had to ask Gordie where the hell you're hiding. I came all the way out here to get some straight answers about where and what you read about me being a serial murderer."

# CHAPTER

## ❧ 16 ❧

For a short while Amanda and Justin were the objects of media attention. Long articles about her ordeal were written for the local newspapers, none of them of course by Evan. He was undergoing psychiatric observation. As well, she heard from Detective McMahon that the law was "trying to find out who the hell he was." He had personally questioned Evan and found him not the amiable scribe he thought he knew. The real Evan was spooky and disturbing. "There's a guy who is miles *past* being just crazy."

In her dreams, Evan still walked free, knife in hand, chasing her to groaning wakefulness, scores of redheaded ghouls sleep-walking in his wake. As time passed, his dream face lost its distinctive features. It took on those of other problem people in her increasingly busy life. This face one day, another the next. The faces blurred still further into the vaguest visage of capricious fate whose vicious slashes one tried in vain to dodge.

Thank goodness Justin was willing to talk about what had happened—the betrayals, the danger, his fears, her abuse at a madman's hands. They often ended their mutual therapy sessions bawling in each other's arms. Her son showed the enviable resiliency of youth. She kept fingers crossed that his scars would be only on the surface. Deep down she was beginning to suspect her son had been granted the good luck his father never had.

Hunt Grayson was generous enough to accept her apologies for her suspicions. But not so much as to resume their personal relationship. She had lost him. Now it was business only between them. With his help she found herself on a half-dozen local TV panels on Sunday mornings. There she took her turn talking about rape, abuse, parenting, and other women's issues. A local cable company, working on a small budget, asked her if she'd like to fill in as a summer hostess on their local daytime talk show. As well, Hunt found her a half-dozen modeling jobs, a few of them well paying. "You're a *made* personality now, Mandy. You stand for courage and reliability. A no-nonsense woman. A professional. And marketable. You won't want for bookings."

Just the same, at first she kept her Muncher's job. That made her so busy she needed to be cloned to get everything done. Opportunities didn't wait. Even with a new car, videotaping, and jamming the weekends with new business, she couldn't keep all the balls in the air. Reflex kept her going, no matter what the mirror—and a critical Justin—told her.

One day Gordie came into her restaurant, Chelsea in tow. She moved like a dream in a thousand-dollar fall outfit.

"The man an' his woman," muttered someone. "She *dressin'* and he *stressin'*."

"Whoooeee!" another voice chimed in.

Advancing toward her office, Gordie wore his expansive, open-handed smile.

"What can I do for you, Gordon?" she said.

"Do for me? Hey, I'm here to issue you a personal invitation."

"To another of your parties? If so, the answer's—"

"To our wedding." He turned and put a hand behind Chelsea's wasp-thin waist.

The model smiled and waved her left hand to show off a diamond big enough to feed a Third World country for a year. "We're being married at Mount Carmel in a month. It's going to be a rather . . . large wedding."

The staff was still, ears cocked like coyotes listening for rabbits.

"What do you think?" Gordie bellowed.

From behind, the anonymous staff member's patented mutter was heard. "You gonna be a three-time loser!"

Gordie spun but, like Amanda, failed to identify the mutterer. "Shut up!" he said.

"How nice for you both," Amanda said. She turned away, hiding a smile. "If you'll excuse me, I have some work to do."

"There's one other thing," Gordie said. "A promise you made me."

Amanda turned back toward him. "I don't remember making you any promise." Her wariness around the man returned in full measure.

"You're still number one with me. You're still first and best choice. You're the *all-time* Ms. Muncher." He pulled a familiar envelope from his inside coat pocket. "Right here. The three grand you said you'd take to do the job."

"Did I say that?" Amanda smiled ingenuously.

"Yeah. You did."

"I don't remember."

Gordie stepped forward into her personal space. "Well, *I* do."

"Is it written down anywhere? Somewhere you could show me?"

"No. But you said."

Amanda retreated and sat on the edge of her desk. "I might still consider it. As you might know I've been doing a bit of professional work outside of my job here. I'm getting a reputation as a professional model and broadcaster. I'm also getting a better idea of how much I'm really worth—as a model and a human being." Her smile widened. It was sincere. She was enjoying herself! "I'll be Ms. Muncher for you. The fee is fifteen thousand dollars."

Gordie barked out a cold laugh. "I wouldn't pay you fifteen Gs if you did the job naked riding a polka-dot unicycle."

"That's absurd, Amanda dear," Chelsea said. "Even *I* couldn't get that much."

"That's what it'll cost you, Gordon," Amanda said. "Take it or leave it."

He shook his head, finger pointing. "No, no! You forget you work for me? You're drawing pay. You have a contract. I'm calling the shots here."

"Are you working up to a threat? Be Ms. Muncher or else?"

"Do it! For three Gs."

Amanda stood up and shook her head. "No!"

He strode closer, the flash in his eyes. Amanda put hands on hips. "You touch me and I'll sue you up one side and down the other. I'll end up owning your mansion and having you work for me!" His face reddened. How she had once been intimidated by his smoldering rages! No more.

Chelsea put her hands on his bulging shoulder. "Gordie, you can't just—deck her. My God . . ."

"Yeah, all right. If I can't do that I'll fire her."

"Wait a minute!" Amanda walked up to him. She loosened the bobby pins holding her beanie in place. "You can't fire me. Because I just quit!" She wound up and fired the red and white missile full into his face. Then she grabbed her purse and headed for the door.

Her staff gave her a full round of applause.

"Take me with you!" Eddie Green called plaintively.

She blew them all a kiss.

Three months later she took over as full-time hostess for "Ladies Unlimited," a popular TV show featuring interviews with women in the news. Ratings went up. There was talk of limited syndication. A professional associate was putting one of his small houses in upscale Simsbury on the market. For her he named a fair—though not low—price. Single parent or not, she had no trouble getting a mortgage. The bank people had seen her on the tube. They thought she was a celebrity. Maybe she was. Even if not a rich one. Yet it seemed that, too, might one day change.

The growing cable company was talking about tearing up her contract and writing a new one. Then there was the modeling. Hunt ran interference on that. She only did the more lucrative assignments. Now and then she went to New York for shoots and of course to make an occasional commercial. Her last, the final one in a "recognition" series for a big low-cal fruit drink, brought her nearly twenty thousand dollars, even minus Hunt's 10 percent. Quite good for not many hours of work.

She bought Justin a new bike. The media had painted him as a hero, rather than a desperate, frightened boy who had inherited something of his mother's spunk. Like her, he carried the reputation well, and was becoming one of the class leaders in his new public school.

She went to a recommended divorce attorney. He drew up a document clearly laying out a fair agreement about custody, visitation rights, and finances. At least *she* thought it was fair. Ned balked. He wanted to leave the he-she-Justin interactions unstructured. He went off and found an attorney of his own. He went back to work for Gordie, so he had a few dollars. Possibly now they would stay in his pocket awhile. His step-sister had persuaded him to join Gamblers Anonymous. After the attorneys went *mano a mano*, everything was down in black and white. She would see that the agreement was followed— to the letter.

After the final signatures, she and Ned went off for a cup of coffee and at least a show of the fair-mindedness they both would need to give Justin the kind of joint attention he deserved. He told her married life had made his boss a new man.

"Gordie? I can't believe that," she said.

He assured her it was so. But it hadn't come about through tenderness and submission to Cupid's assault. After six weeks of marriage, he had taken a swing at Chelsea. She left the mansion at once, saying she was going back to her family. When she returned, she brought some of the family with her— two brothers with no necks, and shoulders like dray horses. They made short work of Karl, the late Jessica's boyfriend hired as Gordie's bodyguard, then put the franchiser in the hospital. Since hobbling back to everyday life, Gordie had been the most adoring and generous of spouses. And likely to remain so.

Floyd Philman did file a suit against Amanda. Her attorney prepared a countersuit. Before legal fees mounted, Floyd lost interest. He had found the redhead of his dreams.

As for Amanda's romantic life—men had materialized like mushrooms after heavy rain. This new lot wore Rolex Oysters, drove big cars paid for with bigger bank accounts. They owned companies that made things. They wheeled and dealed in condos, software, and walk-in medical centers. Some of them even had education, manners, and good taste. They liked the stardust of a redheaded media personality on their arm. All seemed to enjoy buying her champagne. She played the field like the best in the American League.

She saw the police more frequently than she had expected. She gave McMahon, Reti, and state psychiatrists testimony about her mysterious assailant whom the cops at least described as a "card-carrying psycho." They hated to bother her, but the problem was they had been unable to find out anything about "Evan"—or his stepsister "Emerald," who had also disappeared from the face of the earth. Where they had been before coming to New England was a vast, impenetrable cipher. During what officials guaranteed was the last of their meetings, they admitted that Evan had somehow escaped from his maximum-security mental hospital. He had just disappeared, the guards said.

For several weeks after that the police provided Amanda and Justin with protection. She wasn't greatly alarmed. For some reason she thought it was unlikely Evan would ever torment her again. In time, the police received reports that he had been seen in St. Louis, then Dallas. He seemed to be heading for the West Coast. He was spotted in Vancouver and L.A. Two years later when she met Superintendent McMahon while chatting with Phyllis Locker at a police-celebrity charity golf tournament, he told her that Interpol had reported a verified identification of the man in Vienna. She doubted it was he—in Austria or anywhere else he had been "seen." He had many faces and more roles than found in all of Shakespeare. He was never what he appeared to be.

Given any choice, she would have fought with all her strength against his entering her life. In the end, though, her siege of fear and terror had boosted her to a higher personal plateau that alone she had failed utterly to reach. Repeatedly, she had misunderstood all the events during his short reign over her. She had wandered through the maze of those six weeks with no idea what course of action was wisest or best. Or who was who. Or whom to love. Having survived, she now grasped the profundity sealed in the simplest event. Reason was forever inadequate to unravel the intricate fabric of available choices. No one was wise enough to penetrate the screens of mysteries thrown up before even the blandest commonplaces.

Evan Dent? He was everywhere.

*D*